MY IMMORTAL, 'M CARA
by Victoria Perkins

My Immortal, 'm Cara

Victoria Perkins

Acknowledgements:
As always, thanks to my family for their support,
my editor Becca
and the others who waded through
my nonsense to find the story.

This book is dedicated to my person Inklings: WIT. Without your help, humor and amazing talent and potential, Tex and Zev never would have made it out of my head. I'll be forever grateful to each and every one of you: Christa and Jen, with whom I share a brain (and you know… yeah… exactly), Becca who kept me honest, Stacy who loved Tex and Zev from the start, my silent students as well as some I wished were a bit more silent. Each of you holds a piece of my heart. Carry on, focus, and I love you guys!

Prologue: All I Need is the Promise of a Lifetime

TEX

Romeo and Juliet were idiots. I'd always despised their story. The whole 'rather die than be without you' thing proved how little they knew about love and life. And by the time I was seventeen, I felt that way about most love stories. All the sap and rhetoric spouted by the poets and playwrights just made me angry. When you loved someone, you opened your heart, then had it ripped out and torn to pieces. The pain was inevitable; at least, it was for me. I was quite happy in my cynical little bubble. After all, I had everything I needed. In my mind, love wasn't worth the heartache. Then, one morning, I realized how wrong I was. All because I met him: my Immortal.

ZEV

I've never understood the attraction to Romeo Montague. Was it the flowery speeches? A bit *kvenkyn* in my opinion. The moonlit proposal just hours after meeting Juliet for the first time? Most people forget that he'd actually gone to the party to see another girl. Literary critics and hopeless romantics alike, I assumed, were enraptured with the idea of someone willing to give up everything – family, friends, home – for love. I doubted that anyone had ever been that completely, utterly and hopelessly in love, *ad vitam aeternam*. A willingness to sacrifice everything for one person? I couldn't see myself being so much in love that another person's life and happiness would ever mean more than my own. That was, until I met her: *'m cara*.

Chapter One: Cruel Summer so Wake Me Up When September Ends

TEX

"Killeen!"

My mother's voice broke through the fog of my dreams and I groaned. Mom was the only one who ever used my first name; everyone else just called me Tex. Killeen Texas Novak, that's me. And, yes, I'm aware that my name's a bit odd, but it's not like I chose it. I was named after the town where I was conceived. Mom considered herself droll, but I wasn't sure where I stood on that opinion. I was just glad she hadn't met Dad in Toad Suck Park, Arkansas. Don't get me wrong, Killeen's a great name for a town, and I've heard it's beautiful, but it's not such a great name for a girl. As a small child, having 'kill' as the first part of your name opened up a wide venue for teasing, especially when kids decided to mispronounce your name as 'killin' instead of similar to 'Colleen.' Granted, 'Tex' has its share of nicknames, but by the time I was old enough to understand the rhyming implications, it was too late to change.

"Killeen!"

"I'm awake, Mom!" I called out before I actually opened my eyes.

"Just wanted to let you know I'll be at a shoot all day." Once a model, Mom now managed rising talent in our hometown of Fort Prince and the surrounding areas. "Enjoy your last day of summer vacation." The door slammed before I registered what she'd said.

Last day.

School tomorrow.

Crap.

I'm a senior.

I tried not to think about the upcoming year as I rolled off my bed and headed for the bathroom. Besides the impending doom that was high school, I really didn't want to consider what else tomorrow was. I climbed in the shower, cranking up the hot water until billows of steam poured into the room. My summer-tanned skin glowed red by the time I stepped back into my bedroom. I scowled into my mirror as I passed by and my pale eyes flared back.

It wasn't until I caught a glimpse between the curtains that I realized just how early my mom had woken me. I sighed and checked my clock. Sure enough, the gray outside wasn't an overcast day, but an early morning sky. Granted, I hadn't been planning to sleep in very much since church started at nine-thirty, but this was ridiculous, particularly for what should've been my last day of freedom.

"Can't do anything about it now." I muttered as I resigned myself to being a victim of my mom's absentmindedness. Okay, I may have been acting the slightest bit overly dramatic, but since it was five-thirty in the morning, I felt justified.

I dug some comfortable clothing out of my dresser and pulled the towel from my head. The lack of weight still surprised me. I shook my head, cropped curls sending a fine spray of water into the air. I'd cut ten inches yesterday, donating my thick black hair to a place that made wigs for cancer patients. It wasn't my first donation, but the new style was the shortest I'd ever had. Contemplating the wisdom of my decision, I pulled a black NHCS hoodie over my light blue v-neck and ran a brush through my hair. With more than enough time before church, I decided to tidy my room. I paused momentarily. Had I just used the word 'tidy'? That was definitely a 'Grandma Bug' word, not a 'me' word. I must have been more tired than I'd thought if I was reverting to childhood speech patterns. By the time I finished putting away the laundry I'd done last night and making my bed, gray had turned to rose and then to gold behind my powder blue curtains. I slid my cell phone into my pocket, grabbed my black tennis shoes, and headed downstairs to the kitchen.

Our house wasn't big compared to the others on our street, but it was big enough to warrant a cleaning lady twice a week. Since we weren't expecting Clare until Tuesday, I ignored the dishes in the sink, but picked up the half-empty can of some weight-loss milkshake that had been sitting on the expensive white marble counter for who knew how long. I tossed it in the recycling bin on my way to the cupboard. Mom's newest food fad had meant a lot of extra trips to the recycling center. At least it was better than her last diet. I shuddered as I recalled the day Mom had drained a carton of orange juice while eating an entire plate of brownies. Just the memory was enough to make me lose my appetite. Well, almost. I bit into my apple as I waited for my toast. Mom always said my metabolism came from her mother, the aforementioned Grandma Bug. Though barely five feet tall, I easily out-ate my five-feet, ten-inch, size-zero mother. I gave credit to all of my physical activities: soccer, gymnastics, karate, walking to and from church, and waitressing. I'd never been one to stay still for long, unless I was reading. Case in point, by seven o'clock, I was heading out the door to take a stroll around our significantly wealthy, and slightly snotty, neighborhood before heading down to the poorer – by comparison anyway – section of Fort Prince to New Hope Free Methodist Church.

I waved at the Gundersons as I passed their palatial estate. They returned the greeting from their veranda where they were eating their usual breakfast of imported pastries and coffee. Early sixty-something-or-others, they were the average resident of Whit Lane. Filled with one-time music executives and big-shot businessmen, most of the people on my street were at least two decades older than my mother. Needless to say, we didn't associate with our neighbors very much. I didn't mind, but my social-butterfly of a mother was always on the lookout for new friends. I kept my pace slow, admiring the houses as I passed. A few were vacation homes, used in the summer or for skiing in winter. Now, with September around the corner, they stood empty.

As I turned onto Ava Circle, I noticed cars in the driveway of the old Ross place. Even I, with my limited knowledge of automobiles, took a moment to appreciate the beauty parked behind the dark blue Blazer. A muscle car for sure, and not owned by anyone going through a mid-life crisis. This one said 'young man' through and through. Part of it was the lack of a personal license plate declaring "#1 Stud" or some other desperate cry. The other part was disappearing into the garage. Dark shirt. Well-worn jeans. Very well-worn. Nice view.

Wait. What? Where had that come from? I shook my head and hurried past the driveway before the young man could catch me ogling. As I began my descent into the valley that served as downtown Fort Prince, I turned my interest from my new semi-neighbor to the beauty surrounding my beloved town. Nestled in the foothills of the Colorado Rockies, the glittering snowcaps and deep green pines had been the backdrop of my childhood. I'd learned to walk on the winding paths of my suburban-ish backyard. Sightings of coyotes and moose were as common to me as a rabbits or deer. The clean, fresh scent of crisp mountain air brought a thousand memories, and the clear blue sky was as familiar to me as the rich wooden paneling of my bedroom. But even as I drank in the wonders around me, I felt a strange restlessness. A desire to see an overcast Midwestern sky, a flat Kansas cornfield, the ocean crashing against Maine rocks; to bask in the heat of the Louisiana bayou and recline on the sandy beaches of California. I frowned, unsure if I wanted to pursue this train of thought to its source. Suddenly afraid of what I might find, I set my mind towards unpleasant things to distract me. Namely, Gretchen Knowles and Susan Snow, my two former best friends.

I let my feet carry me down familiar paths as my brain traveled back to the main reason I was dreading my last year of high school. While I was taking a fairly heavy academic load, I actually only needed Bible and American History to graduate. I'd done most of my required classes the previous three years, and had even taken a correspondence course for twelfth grade English during my junior year when I'd been considering finishing school over the summer. When I'd decided to stay at NHCS for another year, I'd chosen to audit senior English.

Mrs. Davidson was a great teacher and it was one of the few classes about which I was still feeling optimistic. Fact was, up until the Fourth of July, I'd been eagerly anticipating my last year of high school. Now I was wishing I'd graduated early with my friends from last year and gone away to college as I'd originally planned. Maybe to Wycliffe University with Elle Monroe. Elle's dad, stepmother and two stepsisters lived there, so her tuition was low. Elle's older sister, Andie, was working on her Masters in journalism and ran the school newspaper. Elle and I had meant to visit in June, but I hadn't been able to get the time off work. Instead, I'd listened when Elle had come back with stories about a lovely college town and beautiful campus. Even if I hadn't gone away to Ohio for school, I could've signed up for Colorado State University like my other friends, Jennifer Newell and Christa Stewart. Instead, I'd let Gretchen and Susan talk me into staying with them at New Hope Christian School. It had seemed like a good idea at the time. I'd never dreamed they'd abandon me because of a guy.

Erik Robertson: class president, captain of the soccer and basketball teams, all-around Big Man on Campus. Tall, muscular, blond hair, sparkling hazel eyes, dimples... well, you get the picture. Now I could add 'Source of Serious Problems' to his list of accolades. I'd known Erik since kindergarten and was, therefore, immune to his numerous charms. Seemed that once you'd observed a guy getting a pencil eraser stuck up his nose, you didn't tend to view him in a romantic light. Unfortunately, Gretchen wasn't so lucky. She'd been pining after Erik since seventh grade. It hadn't been a problem until July 4th when Erik did the unthinkable. He chose me. To my astonishment, Gretchen had been angrier than Erik when I'd refused. She and I hadn't spoken since.

Now I was facing months of seeing people I no longer talked to, a group I wasn't a part of. The realization bugged me more than I cared to admit. I'd been at NHCS my whole life and had never wanted to go anywhere else. And now, beginning what should've been the best year of my life, I wanted nothing more than to run as far as possible. The summer had been cruel, and September wasn't looking much better.

ZEV

The phone next to me sounded and I ignored it... again. I knew that the next ringtone I would hear would be my father's, and I knew what he'd say without needing to take the call. He'd ask why I wasn't talking to them, and then pass the phone to my mother. My hands contracted on the steering wheel, and I had to focus to relax my grip. I glanced in my rearview mirror, startled by the anger I saw reflected back in my dark eyes. I was usually much better at concealing my emotions. When the next round of calls began, I cranked up the radio and turned my attention back to the midnight blue Blazer a few yards ahead. Judging by the faint glow above the mountains, it was almost dawn and we were getting close to our destination. A few minutes later, I sped past the sign.

Welcome to Fort Prince, Colorado.

With no one else in the car to hear me, I let out a string of expletives that would've earned me a slap upside the head from one, if not both, of my parents. Even though they treated me like the adult I was, they had no difficulty knocking some sense into me when I needed it. And, as much as I hated to admit it, there were still times that I needed the attitude adjustment. This time, however, my petulance was justified, even if a bit immature.

Before I'd exhausted my knowledge of curse words – the gift of rhetoric in over sixty languages tended to give one plenty to choose from – I pulled into the driveway of a beautiful black and tan, three story, colonial-style house. With a reluctant grimace, I had to acknowledge that it was a lovely house, and I'd resided in a few places considered to be quite magnificent. Still didn't mean I had to like being yanked halfway across the country for my senior year of high school.

I let the song play out as my parents climbed out of the Blazer. Dad didn't even look my way before heading towards the front door, keys winking back the rising sun. Mom, on the other hand, turned in my direction, pointed at me, and raised an eyebrow. I mimicked the expression, but Mom's eyes showed no amusement. *Kamangha-mangha*, Zev. I swore again. I was in serious trouble with no means of escape. *Potes curreve sed te occulere non potes*. I hadn't been this cornered since being treed by a puma while hunting in Canada. As I prepared to face my mother, I looked back fondly on my encounter with the hungry feline.

The lecture lasted only as long as it took for us to take the first load of boxes inside. Mom was nothing if not concise. She managed to fit what should have been an hour's worth of words into ten minutes. Part of it was how fast she talked, but a larger part of it was her expansive vocabulary. Fortunately, all of this meant that she could get an entire chastisement out of the way and not ruin the whole day. It was too bad that my day had been ruined before it had begun.

Once she'd finished, I switched over to autopilot while Mom and Dad fell into their usual banter. Long years of marriage had given them the ability to communicate in half-sentences, even in the most mundane of conversations. It could be a little annoying, so I usually tuned them out. Unpacking seemed like as easy a job as any to do without much thought. I didn't process much beyond foot placement until my last trip outside. As I turned towards the garage, my arms full of boxes, I caught movement out of the corner of my eye. Trained to be conscious of my surroundings, I half-turned my head for a better view.

Oh. It was a girl. A tiny little thing who didn't look old enough to be walking anywhere by herself. I wasn't sure why the petite figure held my attention, but she did for several seconds. Then, before she could get close enough to see me, I shook my head and went on my way. Lots of unpacking to do and, of course, school to look forward to tomorrow. I could almost imagine sarcasm dripping from my thoughts, acid burning holes into the pavement beneath my feet. Cursing September and the entire rest of the school year, I trudged up the stairs to my new room.

TEX

I slapped at the alarm clock after just two rings and rolled out of bed. My head was still foggy from a strange dream, and I almost tripped as I headed for the bathroom. As I showered, I tried to recall my dream, wanting to understand the unsettled feeling I'd woken with, but the details eluded me. All I knew for sure was that it had to do with the restlessness I'd felt while out walking the previous day, the desire to leave Colorado. As I climbed out of the shower and headed back to my room, I shook my head. I had enough other things on my mind that worrying about some silly dream was pointless. I tossed clothes from my dresser as I searched for my favorite pair of jeans. They were just the things to help ward off the beginning-of-school blues.

"Killeen, I put your new school clothes at the foot of your bed." The stairs creaked as Mom went back down to the kitchen. "I've got breakfast ready."

I glanced at the garments and sighed. "I saw them, Mom. Thanks." I pulled a tank top from my closet and threw it onto my jeans. I'd get to the new stuff eventually, if only to avoid hurting my mother's feelings, just not today. Today, I needed the support of familiarity, not the attention-attracting sparkle of a glitter-encrusted top and matching mini-skirt. I wasn't even sure if the skirt would pass the New Hope one-inch-above-the-knee rule and today didn't seem to be the day to find out. My gaze fell on the tall black boots and I winced. Despite my aforementioned dislike of disappointing my mom, I didn't think I'd be trying on the five-inch-heel hooker boots any time soon.

It didn't take me long to get dressed, and though I wouldn't meet with Mom's high fashion standards, I thought I looked fine. Comfortably faded blue jeans. Red tank top under a short-sleeved black cotton shirt. I fixed the last couple buttons and then faced the dilemma that was my hair. I had no idea what to do with it. Yesterday, by the time I'd gotten to church, my curls had gone their own haphazard ways. With a resolved sigh, I decided that an attempt to style was futile. I ran my brush through the mess and glanced at the clock. I was early for once and the thought depressed me. Then I remembered that Mom was downstairs waiting for me and my spirits fell even more. For about three seconds, I debated sneaking out of the front door and bypassing the kitchen all together. Before I could totally make up my mind, my stomach growled, and I gave up trying to avoid my mother in favor of breakfast. I trudged downstairs.

"Killeen, you're really wearing that for the first day of your senior year?"

I suppressed my grin. I knew Mom wouldn't like my choice of clothes, but I didn't take offense. She couldn't help it. As a young woman in her twenties, she'd modeled for several clothing chains in the south, which was, of course, how she'd met my talent-scout father. I never knew him, but I'd heard the story a few times growing up, usually in relation to ways that I reminded her of him. While I'd inherited my mother's jet-black hair, she constantly reminded me that I hadn't gotten my fashion sense from her. Or any of my other physical characteristics for that matter. I couldn't help but be reminded of this fact every time I saw my tall, willowy mother. Every feature was symmetrical perfection. I had no doubt that my unexpected appearance was the only thing that had put a stop to her rising fame. One of the things I loved her for was the fact that she never blamed me for her career change. While not exactly cut out for motherhood, she always tried and often succeeded.

"Honestly, I don't know about you sometimes." Mom shook her head and handed me a plate of chocolate-chip pancakes. "Anyway, happ..."

"Don't say it!" I cut her off before she could finish. I wanted no reminder that I was seventeen today. I didn't exactly have the best luck when it came to birthdays.

"Okay, okay." She threw up her hands and went back to her cooking. A stream of early morning sunlight came through the window, lighting up my mother's translucent skin, skin that hadn't spent a moment increasing its melanin though it had seen its fair share of fake-bake products over the years.

I sat down, said a quick prayer, applied liberal amounts of butter to my pancakes, and started to eat, savoring the flavor of my favorite breakfast. Any day that started with Mom making breakfast was a special one. Since we valued our lovely but overpriced kitchen, Mom usually avoided it, leaving the cooking to me. An incident involving my sixth birthday cake and a thousand dollars in smoke damage had cured her of the desire to pretend to be domestic. However, pancakes were the one thing she could make without setting our house on fire. The day had a promising start, though I doubted it would end on such a high note.

***

I sat in my car as long as I dared, watching other students mill around outside, wander through the doors, greet old friends. My friends weren't there. Three of them had graduated and were away at college. Two others were no longer speaking to me. A couple of more familiar faces walked by, but I felt no desire to join them. I knew everyone – well, the returning students anyway – so it wasn't like I was going to be completely alone. One of the advantages of being in the same tiny, private school K-12. Also one of the disadvantages if two of the popular kids had labeled you a pariah.

And speaking of... without even a glance in my direction, Gretchen and Susan strolled by. And, of course, at their heels were the faithful groupies, including a few that I didn't recognize. For a brief moment, I wondered if all underclassmen were equipped with a sixth sense regarding pack leaders. I watched as Gretchen and Susan approached the source of all our problems: the aforementioned Erik. I hadn't talked to him since July either, but that was mostly because he'd been on vacation from the first week of July to the third week of August. I wasn't sure if he was still upset about me turning him down, but I wasn't itching to find out. Instead, I waited until the last possible minute before grabbing my book bag and dashing towards the main entrance. That's why I didn't see the other student reaching for the same door until after I'd yanked it open, and hit him square in the face.

ZEV

No one else was awake as I made my way downstairs. I opened the refrigerator door, reached for some orange juice, and then changed my mind. I really didn't feel like eating this morning. I hated the first day at a new school. I hadn't wanted to move just a week before school started, but my only alternative had been to stay in Ohio and start at a new school there thanks to the *het casgen, 'n ddiwerth adwr* of a superintendent who'd taken over my previous school. Neither prospect had been appealing, so I'd decided to stay with my family. And family, of course, was the reason for the relocation. I snickered to myself, a spiteful sound, I knew. Ellis, *'n wenwynig anifail*, my brother. He'd been out of the country for a while, but decided to move back this summer. Of course, once he'd settled here, Mom and Dad insisted that we join him. It wasn't that I didn't love Ellis. After all, he was my brother. We just didn't always see eye to eye. And I had a suspicious feeling that there was more to this move than the reasons my parents had given. I had no real facts to support this feeling, but it wouldn't go away.

I grabbed my car keys off of the hook next to the door. My other hand grasped the knob, but didn't turn it. A piece of paper hung on the door. I read it quickly, eyes skimming over the words I assumed would be present. I wasn't wrong.

Zev, we're going to go out for a special dinner this evening. Please be here. I miss having my kids all together. I winced at the pang those words caused me. A pang accompanied by the faded memory of eyes the same color as mine. *We'll see you after school. Have a good day. Love, Mom.*

I stuffed the note into my pocket before hurrying out to my car. I was running late and fought the urge to speed, pulling into the parking lot with bare minutes to spare. As I rushed up the sidewalk, I felt my cell phone vibrate and I scowled. I'd completely forgotten about it. I looked down as I walked, trying to juggle my keys while getting my phone free from my pants pocket. I didn't notice that someone else was heading for the doors too. I reached out with my key-filled hand, raising the phone with the other.

Something hard hit me. I heard my nose crunch before I registered the pain. *Besmislica*! Blood gushed and my hands went to my face, dropping what they'd been holding. I swore out loud, in English this time.

"I'm so sorry!" A clear female voice made me realize that someone else was here. I was gentleman enough to regret swearing. "I'll get the nurse."

I shook my head, ignoring the stabbing pain as I snapped my nose back into place. I held it for a moment, eyes closed. I spoke through gritted teeth. "I'm fine."

"You're bleeding." The girl didn't sound panicked, just mildly annoyed with my disclaimer, or maybe with the choice words I'd uttered upon impact.

"I bleed easy." It took great self-control not to laugh. The blood had already slowed to a trickle. I opened my eyes. *Buais mo yn disgwyl a.* She was awfully small to inflict so much damage, barely five feet tall, if I guessed correctly. Something about her size tugged at my memory, but I couldn't quite figure out why.

"I wasn't paying attention and now your nose is bleeding." Her clear eyes were sincere. She glanced away when my eyes met hers, biting her bottom lip and crossing her arms. "Are you sure you don't want the nurse?"

"Positive." I smiled, trying to set her at ease. "I'm fine." I glanced down at my shirt and wondered if 'blood-soaked' could be an actual shade of fabric. "Just need a new shirt." She opened her mouth again to apologize and I held up a hand. "I've got one in my car." I scooped up my keys and jogged back to my car. Sure enough, I'd left one of my bags... the memory clicked. *Stebinantis.* The person who had been out walking yesterday morning was the same one who'd just assaulted me with a door. I cleaned my face with a hand wipe I'd found in the console, hoping nothing had dried yet. I wasn't sure how to take this turn of events. I remembered how the figure had come down the sidewalk, oddly enthralling. Then, I'd been sure that she was just a kid, and had shoved the moment from my mind. Now, as I stripped off my t-shirt and pulled on a white polo shirt – part of the uniform from my last school – I felt an unfamiliar rush of adrenaline associated with this girl. I glanced in the side mirror for a quick check, forcing my breathing to stay even. No blood, just a slight bruised look under my eyes that would clear in a few minutes. I ran a hand through my dark brown hair, and then turned, sure she'd be gone.

The girl was still there, watching me. As I took a step in her direction, she opened the door and held it for me. I gave her a sideways glance as I stepped through the doorway, getting a whiff of some floral scent as I confirmed my previous impression. Yes, it was the same girl and the coincidence of it annoyed me for a reason I couldn't quite understand.

"You're new." She held out a hand as she let the door shut behind her.

"That obvious?" I muttered, sticking my hands in my

pockets.

My response seemed to throw her for a moment, but she pressed on. “I’m Tex Novak.”

That got my attention. “Your name’s Tex?”

I was sure she flushed under her tan and found myself wondering if that was a normal reaction for her. “It’s a nickname. Anyway, I’ll show you to your homeroom. You’re a senior, right?”

I nodded, and grudgingly gave up my name. “Zev Avatos.”

“What?”

“My name. It’s Zev.” I wished I hadn’t spoken and couldn’t keep my tone from turning sullen. I stared straight ahead, willing myself not too look at her. It didn’t work.

“Neat name.” She was grinning as she led me down a second hallway. Then, her smile vanished. “Crap.”

Now it was my turn to ask. “What?”

“We’re late.” Tex’s gaze locked on someone standing at the end of the hall.

TEX

I stared for almost thirty seconds. I didn’t even blink when he swore. Usually, I would’ve given my own sharp-tongued retort, but I had a bit more sympathy for the stranger whose nose I’d bloodied. It might’ve even been broken. I could’ve sworn I’d heard it snap. That thought got through to me and I began apologizing. “I’m so sorry. I’ll get the nurse.” I’d already taken a step towards the door when the young man spoke.

"I'm fine." He insisted, voice more annoyed than agonized.

Annoyed? I'd offered to help. My own temper flared. Well, two could play it that way. "You're bleeding." When I heard my tone, guilt struck and my anger ebbed. I shouldn't be mad at him. It wasn't his fault that today sucked. I missed what he said as he finally looked down at me.

"I wasn't paying attention and now your nose is bleeding." I tried to explain myself, but was unable to hold his gaze. I'd never seen eyes quite that color before, and I found the fact that I couldn't read them disconcerting. I didn't know what to do with my hands, so I settled for crossing my arms. "Are you sure you don't want the nurse?"

"Positive." Then, he did the craziest thing: he smiled. Blood covering the lower half of his face, crimson splattered on his shirt, and he smiled! I wasn't sure if I wanted to laugh or call for a straightjacket. I opened my mouth to question his sanity, but he held up a hand. "I've got one in my car." He grabbed something from the ground and jogged away.

One? One what? Had I missed something he said? I watched him go, finally getting a good look at who I'd battered. A new student, definitely. Most likely a senior. I'd never seen him before... wait a minute, maybe I had. Something about the way he walked gnawed at the corner of my memory. I couldn't figure out why until he reached his car: a very familiar looking vehicle that I'd seen parked in a driveway yesterday morning. He was the good-looking guy I'd seen carrying boxes into the old Ross place. Wait, had I just called him good-looking? I so had not! Okay, his eyes were killer, the longest lashes I'd ever seen on a guy and irises a shade of blue that was almost purple. Indigo, I decided, like light... but not in a hot way, of course. His hair was dark brown, and had that careless look that I'd always despised. Couldn't a guy comb his hair? But it fit nicely over a face almost too pretty for a boy. Had I just called him pretty? Hold on! What was he doing?! He's taking off his shirt! Why?! Oh, he had another one. *That's* what he meant before. Hm, nice abs. What was I saying?

Frantic for something, anything, that would get my mind off the very unlike-me jumble of thoughts, I opened the door, holding it for him as he passed by. Before following him, something on the ground caught my eye. His phone. He must've dropped it. I snatched it up and darted inside, slipping the cell into my pocket without any conscious thought. I wanted to make amends before returning it.

"You're new." I held out my hand even as the stupidity of my action and comment occurred to me.

"That obvious?" He stuck his hand in his pockets, tone snarky enough to impress even me.

I tipped my head back. He was tall, probably six-four, six-five. "I'm Tex Novak." That earned a glance in my direction. My name usually did.

"Your name's Tex?"

I flushed when his gaze fell on me, and I took a second to wonder why I'd had that unusual reaction. I pushed away the thought and continued. "It's a nickname. Anyway, I'll show you to your homeroom. You're a senior, right?" He nodded and said something that sounded like a foreign snack food.

"What?"

"My name. It's Zev."

Idiot. I'd embarrassed him. Way to go, Tex. Still, I couldn't help but grin. "Neat name." Finally, someone who had a stranger name than mine. While you might not think of 'Tex' as an odd name in a world where we have children whose names come from fruit or letters thrown into a word blender, in my school of feminine names like Adalayde, Emily and Rosey, my choice of nickname made me the square peg of the student body. Zev and I turned down the second hallway. "Crap." I recognized the figure at the far end of the otherwise empty corridor. Vice Principal Snyder.

"What?"

"We're late." Lovely. I was going to be in trouble before school had even begun.

"Miss Novak, I trust that you and your friend have an outstanding reason for being late on your first day of school."

Have I mentioned how absolutely sucky today was? I tried to smile politely. "Sorry, Mr. Snyder. I kinda hit the new kid with the door."

Vice Principal Snyder turned his glare from me to Zev. "He looks fine to me."

"It wasn't that bad." Zev gave a smile much more effective than mine. "Then Tex offered to show me to my homeroom."

"First name basis already, how sweet." Snyder sneered. I felt my cheeks flame, but wasn't sure if it was anger or embarrassment. "And convenient since her homeroom is the same as yours." Snyder's eyes scrutinized Zev, a grudging approval in his dark gaze. The collared polo was definitely more formal than what the rest of us wore, even with jeans. Designer jeans that... okay, stay focused.

"You're a senior?" Zev's voice cut through my thoughts.

I sighed. Due to my height, or lack thereof, and what my mother referred to as my 'baby face,' most people assumed I was a freshman. Once, last year, someone actually thought I was in seventh grade. I quit wearing pigtails after that. I'd hoped the new haircut would help. Apparently, not so much.

Snyder continued as if Zev hadn't said a word. "Zev Avatos."

"You know my name?" Indigo eyes shifted and I had a momentary wish that they'd turn back to me.

"You're the only new senior." Snyder folded his arms across his chest. "Last minute transfer from Ohio. Top of your class."

"You do realize that we're going to be even later if you continue with my academic history?" Zev interrupted with a smoothness and confidence I envied.

"Pardon me?" Snyder's entire face turned a funny shade of magenta and, for a crazy second, I racked my brains, trying to recall the CPR I'd learned last summer.

"Of course we will." Zev turned to me. "Which room?"

I pointed. Causing a jolt that shot through my entire nervous system, Zev grabbed my hand, pulled me around the still sputtering Mr. Snyder, and down the hall. I didn't have time to analyze my reaction to his touch because he dropped my hand as soon as we reached the classroom door. Taking a steadying breath, I went first even though every cell in my body screamed for me to run away. The door creaked loudly enough that by the time I'd stepped into the classroom, all eyes turned my way. Fortunately, for me anyway, the attention lasted only as long as it took for Zev to enter the room. Twelve pairs of eyes switched from me to him, and I felt a surge of relief. I headed for one of the empty seats behind Emily Daniels, a quiet girl I'd known since fourth grade. We'd never been close, but cordiality was preferable to the waves of outright hostility coming from the other side of the room.

"You're late, Tex." Mrs. Peterson glanced up from her attendance sheet.

"Yes, ma'am. Sorry about that."

Mrs. Peterson was in her late sixties, but appeared older with her snow-white hair and pleasantly wrinkled face. Her demeanor, however, made her seem much more like a student than a widowed grandmother of seven. All three of her kids were in Kansas, so Mrs. Peterson made every NHCS student feel like family. While I had only two classes with her this year, she was one of my favorite teachers.

"Zev Avatos, right?" Mrs. Peterson was still looking in my direction and, with a start, I realized that Zev had slid into the seat behind mine. He must have nodded because Mrs. Peterson continued without waiting for any other answer. "Welcome to New Hope Christian School. We're just assigning lockers."

ZEV

I knew instantly that I didn't like this *'n anhyddysg llyffant*. The first sentence out of his mouth told me everything

I needed to know. "Miss Novak, I trust that you and your friend have an outstanding reason for being late on your first day of school."

"Sorry, Mr. Snyder. I kinda hit the new kid with the door."

His eyes turned to me. "He looks fine to me."

I bristled at his tone. *Hrokafullur stykki af skitur*! It was only through ages of practice that I was able to give a smile and deflect his question. "It wasn't that bad. Then Tex offered to show me to my homeroom."

He kept going. "First name basis already, how sweet. And convenient since her homeroom is the same as yours."

It took half a second for his statement to register. The words popped out of my mouth before I could stop them. "You're a senior?" I hadn't seen that coming. Even seeing her in school hadn't made me think her more than fourteen or fifteen. This girl had surprised me more in the past ten minutes than anyone had in a long time. At least, I reassured myself, I didn't have to worry about the fact that I'd been checking out a girl so much younger than me. I almost laughed at the absurdity of that train of thought, but it held a weight I didn't want to acknowledge. Before I could dwell on anything, the man – Snyder, she'd called him – said my name and I reluctantly turned my gaze to him.

"You know my name?" Even as I responded, I felt a desire to look back at Tex. Her appearance, unique name, and somewhat offbeat personality drew me to her again. *Iontach.* I didn't know if I liked this or not. Snyder droned on and my annoyance flared.

"You're the only new senior. Last minute transfer from

Ohio. Top of your class."

"You do realize that we're going to be even later if you continue with my academic history?" Funny. I'd never seen that particular shade of red on a person before.

"Pardon me?" Snyder almost choked on the words, and a part of me wished that the *berlendir musang* would.

"Of course we will." I glanced at Tex. "Which room?" She pointed and, without a thought, I grabbed her hand, intending to pull her after me with a bit more speed than was wise. Problem was, as soon as my fingers closed around hers, I felt a bolt of electricity shoot straight through my fingers to my now galloping heart. *Thirrje admirimi!* I didn't even realize we'd moved until I saw the door in front of me. I released her hand, ignoring my body's protests. I'd never wanted anything as much as I wanted to take her hand once more, to know if I'd been imagining what I'd just experienced. Tex's slight hesitation offered a welcome distraction. She'd obviously been attending the school for a while. Why wasn't she hurrying inside? Surely her friends, probably a boyfriend (I felt a twinge of something else that I didn't want to examine), were waiting for her. Had her dash to the building not been because she'd been running late? Had something else been keeping her outside? My questions remained unanswered as I followed her into the small classroom.

I didn't acknowledge the stares of the eleven other students and gave only the most basic, but cordial, of greetings to the teacher. I followed Tex, and sat at the desk behind her. I'd done the 'new student' thing often enough that I'd memorized the patter. Nothing much more than the numbers and names changed. Even the types of kids stayed the same. I'd already spotted 'he-who-will-be-prom-king' as well as his flock of admirers. The blond boy appeared nice enough, even if a bit simple. Everyone turned to him for answers, but it was the *beteken-soek* brunette who wanted to run things. She'd been eyeing me since I'd entered, and I had a bad feeling that her affections for Blond Boy might divert to me. I ignored her and then stood again. The teacher wanted us to put our things into our lockers. I didn't have anything other than my lock, but I followed Tex anyway. After all, I was supposed to blend in, right? Wasn't conformity the desire of all humans? It wasn't a strange interest in this *nzuri, ya kushangaza* creature who'd literally broken my carefully detached mask. *Kamwe*! I wasn't secretly hoping for the opportunity to touch her skin again just to find out if I'd imagined the spark.

Nope. Not at all.

Pleh. I was so screwed.

TEX

Why was he following me? Okay, so our lockers were near each other's, but I could feel his eyes – those beautiful... what was I saying? I'd met this guy (okay, maybe 'met' wasn't the right word) less than twenty minutes ago and I already sounded like one of those girls mooning over Erik. I scowled and tossed my bag into my locker. I was not some flighty flirt who swooned. In fact, boys never turned my head. With my usual stubbornness, I refused to acknowledge my reaction yesterday morning. Besides, I never turned theirs. At least, not since Teddy... but I refused to let my mind go down that path again. Instead, I focused on not thinking about the new boy. I had a bad feeling that particular task would take all of my willpower.

***

Why was I sitting in physics class? Oh, right, because I'm an idiot. After realizing that this year I'd be less social than a depressed hermit, I'd changed my schedule to something more demanding to keep my mind off of my pathetic troubles. Physics was on the top of my list of challenges. Now I would be starting each day with the only NHCS teacher who outright despised me. And that wasn't the worst part. You see, to me, physics was like being immersed in a world where I didn't recognize anyone, and everything was blue, or maybe chartreuse.

"Well, well, Miss Novak. How nice of you to take one of my classes again. I missed you last year." Dolores Conner paced at the front of her classroom while I tried to ignore her comments. She'd never forgiven me for taking chemistry online when I couldn't fit it into my schedule the previous year. I'd had other classes I'd wanted to take. Any class, in fact, that she wasn't teaching. Now I remembered why.

"My pleasure, Mrs. Conner." I muttered, doodling nonsense in the margin of my notebook. Nonsense that looked strangely like the first and last letters of the alphabet. Crap. Just as I was sure that those cold, dark eyes were going to move by, a strange noise echoed in the classroom. Wait, not noise. A song. A ringtone. Who'd be dumb enough to... I scrambled to pull the phone from my pocket, but it was too late. Mrs. Conner was in front of me, hand outstretched, two seconds after the first note hit the air.

"A cell phone in school, Killeen?"

"Tex." I spoke from between gritted teeth, hoping my voice was more respectful than it sounded in my head. The ringing stopped.

"You know those aren't allowed."

I didn't respond, knowing I couldn't trust myself to maintain the proper tone.

"Tsk, tsk. Detention before the first day's half over."

"That's not her phone." The voice behind me brought a coil of squirming warmth in the pit of my stomach. I blamed my digesting breakfast.

"And you are?"

"Zev Avatos."

"Ah, the new boy." Mrs. Conner pursed her scarlet lips. She was known for humiliating students, most often new ones, during the first week. Since the only other new student in the class was a quiet-looking redhead, Zev's comment drew her to him like a moth to a flame. A crazy black-haired moth to a really hot flame. Oh crap. I really needed to think about this new and disturbing cognitive process I'd acquired. But, Mrs. Conner was trying to bait Zev, and I was way too curious about the outcome to reflect on my own issues. "Mr. Avatos, I hear that you were at the top in your previous school. Did you take a pre-physics course there or just chemistry? I find that transfer students often overestimate themselves in my classes."

I thought I could hear Zev's smirk. "I didn't bother with

sciences at my last high school."

"How unfortunate."

Zev interrupted. "I found it rather repetitive since I'd been taking my father's courses at home for several years."

"Your father?" Mrs. Conner's pale cheeks had gained two spots of color on each overly-powdered cheekbone. "And, what, exactly, are his qualifications?"

Now I was certain of Zev's amusement and fought my own urge to smile.

"Well, Dr. Enos Avatos has PhD's in biology, physics and physiology from Cambridge, Oxford and Yale, respectively. He's taught at all three and guest lectured at Harvard. Qualified enough?"

One of the other seniors, David Catori, half-turned in his desk, green eyes wide. "Why are you even in this class?"

"I needed another credit to graduate."

I jumped. Zev's voice was closer than it had been just a moment before. A hand appeared over my shoulder.

"May I have my phone back?"

"Well," Mrs. Conner huffed, "None of that excuses a violation of our rules."

"I knocked the phone out of his hand." I tried to interject as I handed over the phone. Mrs. Conner was so intent on the conversation that she didn't seem to notice when Zev pocketed his phone.

"That's enough, Killeen."

"I believe she prefers Tex."

Now I had to chew on my bottom lip to keep from laughing. That wouldn't have been beneficial for either Zev or

I.

"Excuse me?" Mrs. Conner was aghast.

"Her name. Tex. Not Killeen."

"And I suppose you prefer Zev instead of some normal name." She reached for her class list, ready to reveal some horrific moniker like Archibald or Eustace. Her mouth opened but nothing came out.

"It's just Zev."

"Well then, just Zev." Mrs. Conner pulled two bright pink papers from her desk.

That wasn't going to be good.

Mrs. Conner continued. "You can join *Tex*," she stressed my name in a way that almost made me cringe, "in detention."

Oh yeah, I was off to a great start.

***

"Tex, can I see you for a moment?" Linda Douglas, NHCS principal, stood in the library doorway just moments after the bell rang.

I sighed and went to her. Mrs. Douglas was nice enough. I just had a sinking feeling that I knew why she'd called me over. I wasn't wrong.

"Mrs. Conner tells me that she had to write you up for having a cell phone."

"That's my fault, Mrs. Douglas."

How did he do that? Zev stood no more than a few inches away and I hadn't heard him move. Zev carefully edited our meeting. "Tex picked up my phone, and I hadn't had the chance to turn it off."

From the corner of my eye, I saw Zev smile and my heart jumped. Really? One smile had my pulse racing like... every thought flew out of my head as a trio of very familiar faces appeared directly behind Mrs. Douglas. All three glared at me and I almost missed what the principal was saying. "I'll let it go this once. In the future, Mr. Avatos, remember to turn the phone off *before* you get to school. And, Tex, since you two know each other, why don't you make sure Zev gets to his classes on time."

Oh, that was going to be fun since I couldn't seem to keep my thoughts from wandering whenever he was around. I hoped I didn't have a lot of classes with him; otherwise, I could kiss my good grades good-bye. Oh. Kiss. That brought up a whole other set of images, and I felt my face burn. Then Gretchen, Susan and one of their sophomore friends pushed past me, and I snapped out of it. I turned in time to see all three girls leering at Zev in a lascivious, wolfish fashion. The unexpected wave of jealousy confounded me. *All right, Lord*, I prayed silently, *we're going to talk about this as soon as I get a chance. A crush is the last thing I need right now.*

"Any of us would be happy to show you around." Jackie Xavier flipped her strawberry blond curls over her shoulder and batted her eyes.

I wanted to slap that coy simper right off her face. To my consternation, the majority of my desire had to do with the way she was mentally undressing and devouring Zev right in front of me.

"I'm happy with Tex doing that." Zev didn't even glance

my direction, but his comment made me feel a bit better about not being able to smack Jackie. "Besides, we've got the same schedule."

Well, there goes my GPA. Wait, how did he know what my schedule was?

"And, if you'll excuse us, I'd like Tex to tell me a bit more about my classes."

My skin burned as his hand closed on my elbow, and he steered me past the very annoyed trio. As we walked by the table where our physics books sat, he grabbed them with his free hand. We didn't stop until we reached the farthest back table, almost in the stacks themselves. He pulled out a chair and released my arm. I could still feel his fingers as I sank into the seat. He sat next to me, and I could feel him staring. Finally, I raised my head. He smiled and leaned forward. "So, what should we talk about?"

ZEV

Why was I sitting in physics class? Oh, right, because *io sono uno stupido idiota*. I hadn't paid enough attention to the number of credits I'd needed to graduate and, coming here, found myself one science short. To make matters worse, the teacher was arrogant, and more than likely knew less about the subject than I did. A fact I could pretty much guarantee. And, she obviously didn't like her students, including the one currently being ridiculed. I bit my tongue against the words that wanted to escape, to lash out against the *crnomanjast kurva* attacking Tex. Probably not the best move a new student could make.

Tex was muttering something, but I was more interested in what she was drawing. Any insight into this girl's mind... a noise interrupted my train of thought. A very familiar noise.

"A cell phone in school, Killeen?"

I said something in Egyptian that I was glad no one else could understand. I'd completely forgotten about my phone. Tex must've picked it up, and now she was getting into trouble. Another part of my brain tucked away her first name, writing a mental post-it to ask where the nickname came from.

"You know those aren't allowed." The woman wore an expression more odious than any I'd seen in a long time. "Tsk, tsk. Detention before the first day's half over."

Even if I hadn't been more interested in Tex than I should have been, I wouldn't have let someone else take the blame for something that was mine. "That's not her phone."

Mrs. Connor's gaze turned to me. Her tone sounded sweet, but I could hear the vindictive undercurrent. "And you are?" This *meiga* was not making herself any easier to like.

I managed to keep my voice civil. "Zev Avatos."

"Mr. Avatos, I hear that you were at the top in your previous school. Did you take a pre-physics course there or just chemistry? I find that transfer students often overestimate themselves in my classes."

My insides boiled. *Mal de brujas*! I answered her question without malevolence, however, sensing that a better opportunity was coming. "I didn't bother with sciences at my last high school." Mankind, including this egotistical woman, was nothing if not predictable. I knew the corners of my mouth were twitching in anticipation, but doubted she was observant enough to catch the almost-smile.

"How unfortunate." Mrs. Conner didn't disappoint.

I interrupted before she could get going. "I found it rather repetitive since I'd been taking my father's courses for several years."

"Your father? And, what, exactly, are his qualifications?"

A rush of anger tainted my amusement. How narcissistic could one person be? *Feitur svin*! I decided to list a few more qualifications than necessary. "Well, Dr. Enos Avatos has PhD's in biology, physics and physiology from Cambridge, Oxford and Yale, respectively. He's taught at all three and guest lectured at Harvard. Qualified enough?" At least I'd only mentioned my father's recent degrees – and none of my own. I suspected that the *tudatlan varangy* might suffer from spontaneous combustion if I'd done that. For a moment, I was tempted to speak up again, if only to test my theory.

***

"Any of us would be happy to show you around."

Was someone talking to me? I was trying very hard to be aware of Tex without actually looking at her, and it took more of my attention than I'd thought possible. My reply, then, was cursory, and probably not what the girl wanted to hear. "I'm happy with Tex doing that. Besides, we've got the same schedule." I'd stolen a look when she'd transferred it from one notebook to another and been a little too exulted to discover that it matched mine. "And, if you'll excuse us, I'd like Tex to tell me a bit more about my classes."

Without considering the consequences, I grabbed Tex's elbow, and almost gasped out loud. The sensation wasn't one of pain, but it was the most powerful thing I'd felt in more years than I cared to think of. I don't know how I walked back to the table with my body on fire, but once I reached it, I had to force myself to let go. With a start, I realized that I'd picked up our books. Apparently, me on autopilot was still pretty smart. While still silently congratulating myself on my superior intellect, I sat down next to Tex, sure that I'd dazzled her.

She wasn't even looking at me.

I stared. Hadn't she felt it too? This couldn't be just me... could it? My heart plummeted into my stomach. Of course it was just me. No way was a girl like that going to be interested in the *udskud af jordens*. She'd probably been mortified by my behavior and was trying to think of a polite way to tell me to leave her alone. The only girls I attracted were ones like the trio who'd accosted me moments ago. Usually, I was happy enough with their attentions, but that was before I'd met the *nevjerojatno*, captivating young woman currently sitting next to me.

Then she stared at me with clear gray eyes, so guileless, so free of any negative emotion, and I felt something I hadn't felt since my family had come to America. It had been so long that I almost didn't recognize it. Hope. I leaned forward, smiling, and asked, "So, what should we talk about?"

Tex ducked her head and muttered something I didn't catch. I moved my chair closer and my heart skipped a beat. Seriously? I was reacting to this girl like some lovesick *hajvan*!

I tried harder to maintain some sense of decorum, of cool detachment. "What was that?" Somehow, I doubted my efforts were successful.

"I said," Tex glanced behind me, towards the front of the room. "Keep your voice down. The librarian is really strict."

"Oh." Nice, Zev, that's intelligent. Genius, in fact! Impressive. Real witty. Wait, she'd said something else and I'd missed it. Chagrined, I asked her, yet again, to repeat herself.

"Hard of hearing? Need me to sign to you?" Tex sounded amused, and I didn't mind that it was at my expense. She scooted her chair so that we were almost touching. I ignored my heart's enthusiastic percussion, hoping that she couldn't hear the thudding in my chest, as she continued. "If you want to talk, we'll have to be quiet."

"Oh." *Zagnjurivanje stakla krtica.* I chastised myself. I could have at least thought of a different one-syllable response. "Sure." Yeah, that was so much better.

"Unless, you didn't want to talk to me." Something flashed across Tex's eyes and then disappeared behind a mask almost as good as the one I wore. It didn't take much for me to figure out the problem. She thought my monosyllabic replies were because I didn't like her. How could I explain that I was a moron who couldn't seem to speak around her? *Ik voel je om me heen.* Unable to endure hurting this near-complete stranger, I reached towards her. My fingertips barely grazed her arm, but the result was instantaneous for both of us. Our eyes locked and I knew she'd felt it too. Something much bigger than the two of us was at work here. I refused to say some*one*. I'd given up that path. I was a different person now. But the tingling sensation emanating from where my skin touched hers made me wonder just the slightest bit if maybe I'd been wrong. Then Tex was talking, and I didn't care about anything else.

Chapter Two: Listen to Your Heart Cuz We're Accidentally in Love

TEX

We talked in hushed voices, knees millimeters apart under the table, and forty minutes disappeared in seconds. We covered the basics: he'd moved from Ohio and now lived with both parents in one of the wealthier sections of town (a fact I already knew) and he had one older brother. For a moment, I imagined a shadow passing over his face when I asked about siblings, but he continued to the next topic and I didn't push. We discovered that he was exactly a year older than me and didn't seem to mind when I blew off his well wishes for today, offering my own perfunctory ones before pressing forward with the conversation. We moved on to trivialities as we headed for our fourth period class which, unfortunately, was Bible. Unfortunate because twelfth grade Bible dealt with marriage and family. Both were topics I felt more comfortable ignoring. Today, to my relief, was just introductions and basic first day stuff. By the time we reached lunch, we'd shared our preferences for music – classic rock (me) and alternative / punk (him) – books – supernatural fiction (me) and mysteries (him) – and a weakness for chocolate-covered pretzels (both of us).

As we entered the cafeteria, I finally turned away from Zev long enough to purchase a bottle of flavored water. It wasn't until then that I realized people were staring. I flushed and grabbed my beverage, heading towards the exit. Anything to get away from the gazes. Some had been just ones of mild amazement, but a few held more malice. I didn't notice that

Zev had followed me until I stopped at a picnic table at the edge of the grounds. Ordinarily used for outdoor classes on nice days, it was currently abandoned as students re-assimilated to the norms of lunchroom behavior. Over the next few weeks, as boundaries were set and territories staked, most of these tables would be occupied. I sat down.

"What's wrong?"

I jumped. Zev had slid into a space just inches from me and I hadn't heard him. "Nothing." I muttered. He raised an eyebrow and I turned my gaze to the bottle in my hands. "It's a long story."

Zev chuckled, though I couldn't see why. My comment wasn't funny. "I've got plenty of time." He produced a lunch and handed me a pear. He pulled a second one from the bag and took a bite, eyes never leaving my face.

My heart thumped erratically, and I twisted the stem off my pear. How could just a few hours with this boy make me feel like this? Like I'd trust him with every secret, every hidden desire and fear – with my life. And I really wanted to tell him everything. Not just the crap with Erik and Gretchen, but all of it. My issues with celebrating my birthday. My inexplicable and sudden desire to leave Fort Prince. My nagging feelings of discontent and general disquietness. Was that even a word?

As these thoughts flashed through my head, I heard a gentle voice. *This one, beloved.*

I held my breath, sure I'd misunderstood. Or I was going crazy. I didn't do that whole 'love-at-first-sight' thing. Not since...

Again, a little more firmly. *This one, beloved.*

I sighed. Arguing with God never worked. Not for me anyway. I wasn't Abraham. Besides, deep inside, I knew that I didn't want to argue this away. For once my spirit and my heart were in agreement. I decided to listen to my heart.

***

Students were coming out of the cafeteria by the time I'd finished my story. Every time I thought about stopping, I'd hear the annoying, nagging voice telling me to keep going. I'd never spoken this freely before, least of all to someone I'd only known for a half a day. I refused to look towards Zev, half-hoping that he'd be gone when I was done, tired of my monologuing. As I'd expected, silence greeted the end of my story. I stood, ready to go back inside and face the rest of my senior year as I'd thought I would. Alone.

"American History next, right?"

He needed to stop doing that! Yodel! Collar with bell! Anything!

Zev stood at my side, face blank, eyes blazing with an emotion I couldn't quite read, but one that still managed to turn my insides to mush. He glanced down at me and the mush ignited. "We all have stories, Tex."

We fell in step as I asked, "When do I get to hear your story?"

Zev scowled with alarming viciousness, and I almost didn't move around the door quick enough. As it was, I barely missed a collision. "That would've been ironic." I mumbled, more worried about whatever I'd said that annoyed this very strange young man.

"Sorry." Zev followed me into the classroom. "My story just takes a bit longer to tell. Some other time."

I nodded and found a seat in the back of the room. Something told me that Zev wasn't being entirely truthful. Not that it was any of my business. I mean, what were the chances he was hearing a Voice telling him to confide in a virtual stranger?

The bell rang and Mrs. Talbot, our forty-something teacher, began her traditional first-day lecture in a voice so dry it made the Sahara look like the Amazon. I let the words flow over me. I'd taken two other classes with Mrs. Talbot over the last few years, and could quote the speech verbatim. She meant well, but hadn't mastered the art of inflection.

A small square of paper landed on my desk, bouncing against my folded hands. I unfolded it and saw an unfamiliar scrawl. *Please excuse the juvenile method of communication, but I didn't want to wait to tell you this. I've never met anyone like you before. I don't talk to people. I never let them close. But there's something different about you. And I think there's something here between us. Isn't there? If I'm wrong, tell me. But I don't think I am. Do you feel it too?*

I turned my head enough to see Zev out of the corner of my eye. I could feel the blood pool in my cheeks as I smiled and nodded my head. I slipped the note into my pocket and returned to pretending to pay attention. It took all of my energy to stay in my seat, silent.

Again, I heard that Voice. *Are you ready for this, Tex?*

Everything will change if you follow My path.

I took a half-second to weigh the question. My answer was unquestioningly affirmative.

I didn't get much out of the first class. Mrs. Talbot launched into her traditional objective historian rant, but I didn't hear a word she said. Zev's presence behind me was way too distracting. I was careful to keep my gaze on the lecturing woman at the front of the room. If I saw Zev, I knew I'd lose what little focus I was maintaining. As it was, I was hyperaware of his hands, resting on his desk, just inches from my back. And I knew that those eyes were drilling a hole in the back of my head.

Despite the tension between us, Zev and I kept the conversation light as we moved from history to psychology – one of the few classes I was looking forward to – then to English and, lastly, to computers. My elation at reaching the final class of the day fled as soon as Zev and I stepped back into Mrs. Peterson's room. The class was large by NHCS standards and included not only Gretchen and Susan, but their entire entourage. The same one I'd been helping to lead less than three months ago. An out-of-season snowball took up residence in my stomach.

"Relax. Breathe." Zev's fingers brushed my elbow as he whispered to me. No other voice, saying those same things, would have soothed me. But, with just two words and the briefest of touches, Zev had sent my pulse skittering for reasons totally unrelated to the Queens of Mean. The cold inside melted away as the heat from Zev spread through me.

I ignored the dirty / envious looks from almost every

female in the class and headed for the back of the room. As I dropped into my seat, I realized that I had only forty-two minutes left with Zev. I was suddenly anxious to cram in as much as possible. Tomorrow, he'd realize that he'd gravitated towards the wrong girl and rectify the situation. The ice threatened to return.

Relax. Breathe. That Voice calmed me as well. I thawed. *Trust Me*.

"I think you left off at the part with the fireflies." Zev was talking to me.

"What?"

He smiled and I grinned back, feeling like an idiot. "Your story. You were telling me about how you used to think that leprechauns were Irish midgets, and fireflies were their flashlights."

"Right." I remembered, but felt even more foolish. Why had I been telling that story? I'd been a little kid! Then, I saw Zev's expectant face, and found that I couldn't refuse him anything, even a mortifying story. In just one school day, I'd found someone I would do anything for.

What was wrong with me?

ZEV

I couldn't look at her after her story was done, afraid she would see the depth of what I was feeling. Rage at those who'd caused her grief. A protectiveness more ferocious than any I'd felt before. And something else I didn't want to name. If these emotions were strong enough to frighten me, I knew that they would send her running. *Ja sam utapanje u vama.* She stood and I rose to my feet, astonished to find that I could stand steady on legs that felt like rubber.

"American History next, right?"

I felt more than saw Tex stiffen. Had I startled her? Surely she hadn't thought I'd leave? But I knew that's exactly what she'd thought. My voice was soft. "We all have stories, Tex." We walked towards the doors together.

"When do I get to hear your story?"

I yanked the door open with more force than I'd planned, just missing Tex. I took a split second to consider the irony and barely managed to keep the expletives inside my head. She must've seen me scowl because she turned away, muttering something under her breath. I apologized and then tried to explain myself with a half-truth. "Sorry. My story just takes a bit longer to tell. Some other time." I knew, though, that Tex couldn't fully understand the total veracity of that particular statement.

I sat behind her, stealing a piece of paper from a nearby student who wasn't looking my direction. I couldn't wait. I needed to know if she felt something for me or if it was a case of over-inflated ego. On more than one occasion, I'd been told that I suffered from that particular affliction. Once I quieted the voice that told me I was behaving like a child, the words came quickly and I jotted them down: *Please excuse the juvenile method of communication, but I didn't want to wait to tell you this. I've never met anyone like you before. I don't talk to people. I never let them close. But there's something different about you. And I think there's something here between us. Isn't there? If I'm wrong, tell me. But I don't think I am. Do you feel it too?*

I folded the paper and tossed it over Tex's shoulder before I could change my mind. I clasped my hands together so tightly that my joints popped, feeling, for all the world, like some goofy adolescent with a crush. I didn't hear the teacher's incessant drone as I waited for Tex's answer. She turned her head so that I could see the hint of her profile and her blush-stained cheeks. My heart leaped. She nodded her head just the smallest bit, and I soared.

I spent the rest of the lecture studying Tex and picking apart her story from lunch, mentally filing the questions as they arose. Questions like: what had caused the series of scars across Tex's hands and forearms? Why had she turned down Erik? And, how in the world had she become friends with Gretchen and Susan? After half a day at NHCS, I'd already identified their type, and Tex just didn't fit in. A wave of sympathy washed over me as I recalled her explanation about why she hated her birthday. How long had it been since I'd felt sympathy for anyone? But, as Tex had related her list of bad birthdays – starting with her father's abandonment, moving on to her grandfather's death while on his way to her third birthday party, and ending with last year's unintended and catastrophic 'celebration' that had resulted in DUI's for several partygoers and six hundred dollars worth of damage to her house – I'd found myself caring more and more.

Then, without me realizing it, the day was done and I was following Tex to her car. In my whole life, I'd never spent six and a half hours that felt more like twenty minutes. I barely felt the sun beating down on me as I fixated on how the light reflected off her hair, giving it the blue tinge one usually found on bird feathers. *Ya kupendeza.* Tex stopped just in front of me, completely engulfed in my shadow. She was so small. I felt another surge of protectiveness.

"Will I see you tomorrow?" I mentally smacked myself. In a school this size, the question was absurd. My intent, however, I hoped was clear. I didn't just want to see her in passing; I wanted to spend every moment at her side, watching her, listening to her. *Uau*! Stalker much?

Tex's smile was soft, something new in her eyes. "I'd like that." She paused, eyes darting to her watch. Then she peered up at me and time stood still. "I have to go."

"Oh." My world fell. "But you'll be here tomorrow?" *Eu estarei esperando*, I wanted to add. I'd never sounded like that before, but I didn't care. I just wanted her answer.

Tex nodded, eyes still locked with mine. Before I could stop myself, I lifted a hand. My fingertips ghosted over her cheek and I could almost see the sparks. *Se segueix el meu cor.* What was I doing? My hand dropped to my side. I could see the start of a blush creeping up Tex's neck, and I decided to save her additional embarrassment. I muttered a farewell and dashed to my car, moving a bit faster than an ordinary person, but my head was spinning too much to be careful. Besides, it wasn't like I was supernaturally faster like some *ddisglair* fictional character.

I settled into the silence of my classic automobile, a 1967 Chevy Impala that had once been my sole pleasure in life. At this moment, however, I didn't take any joy in the sleek black exterior or soft, tan leather interior. I took a deep breath and rested my forehead on the steering wheel. With a shock, I realized that my hands were trembling. Even with my eyes closed, I could see her face. The scent of gardenias clung to me, and the sound of her laughter rang in my ears. I swore and slammed my hand against the dashboard, pulling back just in time to save myself from an expensive replacement. Not that I couldn't afford it. And I actually enjoyed the manual labor. In fact, due to a recent and very bad week in which I'd hit two deer, a possum and an unfortunate Yorkie named Elmo, I'd had to do quite a bit of work on my car. I just didn't want to have to explain new damage to my parents.

I swore again, more loudly and vilely than before. *Yn gostwng pen gwydr dwrch daear*! I hadn't once thought about what I was going to say to them. And I was even less sure of what they were going to do. The thought of deceit crossed my mind and I shook it away. I didn't want to treat my burgeoning feelings for Tex like something that needed to be kept a secret. Besides, I doubted that I could keep this hidden for long. Besides, it wasn't like I'd done this on purpose. Falling for Tex was a total accident… wasn't it?

Then, I heard a voice in my head, a memory floating forward in time. "Don't bother getting close to anyone, Zev. There's no point. You're not selfless enough to put someone else before yourself and, until you do that, you'll never truly be in love." The voice echoed as I started my car and headed home. By the time I pulled into my driveway, I'd come to a decision. For Tex, I would try. For her, I would change.

TEX

I almost walked into my car. I really couldn't think with those eyes boring into me, his steps in sync with mine. I stopped and raised my head, not meeting his gaze. I wasn't sure I could take that. I settled my gaze on a point just to one side of his face.

"Will I see you tomorrow?"

I smiled, hoping I wasn't misinterpreting his tone. He sounded so vulnerable that I felt a deep need to protect him. "I'd like that." I glanced down at my watch. I'd almost forgotten that I had to work tonight. When I looked back up, my eyes locked with his. Yeah, not a smart move. "I have to go."

"Oh."

How could such a small word break my heart? He sounded so sad that I was sure I hadn't imagined any of today's connection.

"But you'll be here tomorrow?"

I nodded, unable to look away. From the corner of my eye, I saw him lift his hand. What was he... oh.

Electricity.

Fire.

Lightning.

I couldn't explain the sensations that exploded through every cell. I'd never felt anything like this. Not with anyone. Nothing could compare to the brush of his skin against mine. Then it was gone and I couldn't believe how much I felt its loss. I could feel the heat rising to where Zev's fingers had been. Before I could fully process what had happened, Zev muttered something that sounded like "good-bye" and dashed towards his car. Again, my brain registered that something was odd about how he moved, but I didn't have time to ponder the numerous quirks of the hot new boy in town. I didn't even try to justify my adjectives as I climbed into my car. My hands shook with such force that I had to try twice to get my key in the ignition. I devoted all of my attention to driving, pulling my thoughts away from where they wanted to be, drowning in a sea of purplish-blue. I was so intent on driving as fast as legally possible that I was in Didyme's parking lot before the thought hit me.

"Lord, no." I couldn't stop the cry from escaping. "You promised." My whisper was an accusation. "You said it was him." But I kept returning to our first meeting and the vulgarity he'd uttered. I shook my head. Everyone slipped and if he was a new Christian... other flashes popped up. Things I hadn't noticed before, hadn't let myself notice. A darkening in his eyes every time God was mentioned. A careful avoidance of any spiritual discussion. Had I, in just a few hours time, turned into one of those girls who forgot about God when she saw a handsome face? I felt tears gather at the corners of my eyes, and swiped the back of my hand across my eyes. Anger strengthened my voice. "Why did You tell me, that he was the one? Was it some cruel joke?" Even as I said the words, guilt washed over me. "Sorry, Lord. I know You're not like that. I just don't understand."

You accepted this path. A gentle voice reminded me. *I said it would be hard.*

"But what do I do?" I already felt a peace spreading

through me.

Stay strong. Stay true. Wait.

I closed my eyes. Could I do it? Did I want to? Zev's face appeared in my mind, the pain in his eyes clear.

This one, beloved.

I opened my eyes. Yes, I could. For Zev, I could be strong. I could stand firm. It wouldn't be easy, but I knew, in the end, that it would be worth any pain. I was sure that more than my heart was at risk; Zev's very soul was at stake.

***

"Tex, you've got a full table." The manager passed by on her way to the kitchen. "Family of four."

"Thanks, Sylvie." I sighed and took another mouthful from my apple. I tossed the core into the trash, and washed my hands before leaving the break room. My feet were already sore, and I had three hours left on my shift. Sylvie had forgotten that I was back in school, and had scheduled me late. I didn't mind though. It helped me keep my mind off a certain someone.

I stepped out into the dining room, took five steps, and then stopped dead in my tracks. I knew that I resembled some sort of dying fish as I stood with my mouth hanging open, but I couldn't seem to stop my gaping. I closed my eyes and then opened them again, convinced I was seeing things. My jaws snapped shut, and I smoothed down my black-and-white uniform, suddenly grateful that Sylvie hadn't gotten her requested dark orange and brown color scheme. God appeared to have a great sense of humor where I was concerned, but it fortunately didn't seem to extend to the point of humiliation. I reached for my order pad and pen with shaking hands, almost fumbling them onto the floor. I took a deep breath and crossed to the four dark-haired customers, one of which glanced up when I was just two feet away. His beautiful eyes widened and the other three heads swiveled my way, responding to his reaction.

"Good evening." I couldn't believe how normal I sounded. "My name is Tex and I'll be your server tonight."

ZEV

I saw his car as soon as I pulled into the driveway, that hideous monstrosity Ellis had purchased back before his trip overseas. It was the ugliest car I'd ever seen, and I winced as I parked my *fermoso* baby next to the mustard-yellow 1970 Gremlin my brother drove. I closed my eyes, mentally preparing myself to see Ellis. Instead, a different face swam in front of my closed lids. Delicate features topped with haphazard black curls. Pale gray eyes that could see into my soul. I'd yet to decide my feelings on that matter.

As soon as I entered the house, I tossed my keys on to the counter and headed for my room, fully intending to wait there until dinner. I had some serious thinking to do.

"*Frater.*"

I stopped but didn't turn. "*Frater, ave atque vale.*"

"Out having fun while I do all the work? Nice to know that at least a few things haven't changed."

Well, that hadn't taken as long as I'd thought. "High

school, Ellis. Perhaps you've heard of it. After all, we do have a cover to maintain."

Ellis snorted – his version of laughter. "Some of us think that there are more important things we should be doing, Zev."

I turned, taking the extra few seconds to curb my temper enough to refrain from breaking Ellis's jaw. I couldn't, however, stop my tongue. "*Purra minua*, Ellis. Did you have this discussion with our parents? As I recall, this has to do with them as well."

"*Git kendini vida*!" Ellis raised his fist and stepped towards me, but I didn't move. It wouldn't have been the first time my brother had hit me, and I doubted it would be the last. In fact, when he'd been twenty and I'd been fifteen, he'd inflicted the wound that had left the scar on my bottom lip. If I'd still had the ability to scar, I'm sure most of them would have been at the hand of my older brother.

"Ellis!" Only my mother's voice could've stayed my brother's hand. "I will not have you behaving like this in my house."

Ellis and I turned in the same direction. Our mother's face was calm, but her eyes flashed. Dark eyes so much like Ellis's, but with a warmth that had abandoned my brother years ago. For him, life was a pursuit, a never-ending hunt fueled by hate and vengeance. For me, I saw no meaning behind pointless revenge and had chosen my own way of rebelling. Ellis had never forgiven me for abandoning the quest. Our family had tried to stay together in the aftermath, but things had grown more and more tense with each passing year until Ellis had gone off on his own. Now, it seemed we were picking up where we'd left off.

"You two get cleaned up. We have reservations at Didyme's in one hour and I want my family to look their best."

I heard Ellis mutter an insult in my direction. "*Ninyi ni kama miaka mitano tarehe ufa.*" Swahili was one of the few languages neither of our parents knew very well.

I scowled, but didn't rise to the bait. I knew better. Instead, I went upstairs to change my clothes. As I entered my room, I considered my little accident that morning, and decided to take a shower in case any dried blood lingered. Normal people wouldn't see it, but my family was far from normal. Besides, the hot water might ease some of my tension. Well, maybe enough for me to get through a meal without trying to kill my brother. Mom and Dad wouldn't be too happy if I added attempted murder to tonight's itinerary, and I really didn't want a lecture on dinner etiquette.

Forty minutes later, the four of us were in the Blazer. Our parents talked to us and we replied to them, but we didn't speak to each other. That was the usual way things went in my family. The restaurant was nice enough for such a small city, and Dad's fifty-dollar tip got us a quiet table at the back. The hostess, smiling at Ellis the same way all females did, assured us that our waitress would be with us shortly. A few minutes later – though it felt like an hour based on our banal small talk – I heard the approaching steps. Tennis shoes on carpet. Small, light... a whiff of gardenias and my heart skipped a beat, doing acrobatics I hadn't believed possible. My head snapped up, knowing who I was going to see even before my impeccable vision confirmed it. My parents and Ellis took in my change of demeanor and turned toward the source before she spoke.

"Good evening." Her voice was more beautiful than I remembered. *Uimitor*. Even in my head, I sounded like a moron. "My name is Tex and I'll be your server tonight." She smiled, looking everywhere but at me. Looking at my parents. Looking at Ellis. As I recalled all of the women who had fallen for my brother over the years, I felt sick. I dropped my gaze to my hands as Tex rounded to my side of the table. I barely heard my family giving their drink orders. I was too busy listening to the scratch of Tex's pencil against the paper. Her even breathing and racing pulse contradictions to each other. Wait a minute. Racing pulse? Why was her heart beating like that? I heard my brother's smooth voice. Oh. That was it. Of course.

"Zev." The tone of my mother's voice meant she'd said my name more than once.

I really wanted some alcohol. Nothing too strong, just enough to take the edge off what I was feeling. "Just ice water. Thanks." I didn't look up. I heard her take two steps then stop. Curiosity won out. I raised my head in time to see her turn back towards the table. Her eyes flashed white fire and I felt my heart react. *Diamlah hatiku*.

"I'm sorry." She smiled at my parents. "I'm not sure why your son's being so rude, but since he is, I guess I'll take the initiative." She held out a hand. A small, delicate hand with carefully trimmed, neat nails. I wanted to take it in mine, feel her soft skin. *Jama. Mul oli muutunud lalisemine loll*. She continued. "I'm Killeen Texas Novak." That explained the nickname. "Tex, please. I go to school with Zev."

Three pairs of eyes moved in my direction. Tex's gaze didn't waver from my mother's face. She continued as if she didn't notice the shift in atmosphere. "We had a rather abrupt meeting this morning when I hit him in the face with a door."

That got a response. Ellis did his impression of a dying flamingo – the only description of his laugh fit for polite company – causing Tex's eyes to shift to him. I flexed my fingers, wanting nothing more than to close them around Ellis's throat. Not anything serious, just enough to stop that braying noise coming from his mouth.

"I didn't find it quite as amusing when Zev was covered with blood." The acidity in Tex's voice shut Ellis up in an instant. I felt a fleeting hope that maybe Tex wasn't enamored with my brother. I squelched it. I'd been down this road before. Given the choice, girls went for Ellis. I could list all of them: Adah, Jael, Betta, Sandi, sixteen different Ann's, those Norse twins… preoccupied with my sulking, I must've missed the introductions, because the next thing I knew, Tex was walking away with a promise to return with our drinks.

"Explain please." My father, as always, kept his voice calm and even.

"I think it's obvious." Ellis had no such control. "While I am spending my time tracking and hunting, Zev has been fraternizing with some *ielasmeita*."

I slammed my hand down on the table so hard that I felt the wood crack beneath my palm. Shock registered on all three faces as I spoke in a tone I'd never used before. "If you ever speak about her that way again, brother of mine or no, you will regret it. *Jdu pro tebe.*"

"What are you going to do?" Ellis snarled. "Kill me?"

"That's enough." My father's voice cut through the air between Ellis and me. "Zev, you will explain."

I stood, fighting back my temper. I'd spent years reining it in, but I felt it rising just the same. "I need a minute."

"You will..."

My mother put a hand on my father's arm and shook her head.

Dad nodded once, understanding her unspoken plea. He tried a different tactic. "Take some air."

"*Merci*." I spoke through clenched teeth. Even as I turned to go, I saw Mom's eyes darting towards where Tex was returning with a tray of full glasses. I hurried past her without a word, unable to trust myself enough to speak even though I wanted it more than anything else. I stepped through a set of double doors and found myself in a quiet courtyard. A gated stone fence and well-kept plants gave the illusion of an elegant country garden, perhaps an estate in Europe. I crossed to a bench and sat down, cradling my throbbing head in my hands. Years of carefully controlled emotions were emerging, and I didn't know if I could survive the onslaught.

I heard her steps, recognized them in a way I was certain I always would. Less than forty-eight hours since I'd first laid eyes on Tex Novak, and I knew I'd be aware of her for the rest of my existence. I was so caught up in my moment of self-pitying realization that her words startled me.

"Care to explain your very odd behavior?" Her tone held no accusation, defusing the anger I'd felt towards my family for similar questioning.

I blurted out half of my thoughts without thinking, knowing the other half were too crazy to try to explain. "I knew you'd be attracted to Ellis and I couldn't handle that." I waited, unsure what to expect.

Okay, hadn't predicted that reaction. Laughter. Tex was standing directly in front of me; I could see every detail of her shoes. Then a hand cupped my chin and I almost jumped out of my skin. She forced me to raise my head. How could I resist with that delicious hum flowing through me, radiating from the places her cells connected with mine? Molten fire pooled in my stomach and, as I gazed into her eyes, I knew any attempts to run away would be pointless. I was beyond smitten. Without knowing how it had happened, I had fallen, head-over-heels, waves-crashing-into-the-shore, *da mihi basilia mille*, soaring-through-the-stars, *nunc scio quid sitamor*, hopelessly, utterly, and unintentionally in love. *Ti si moja usoda. Za vedno.*

Tex's voice dropped to a whisper. "Not even close." She smiled, and my heart tried to break through my ribs. "Besides, he's too old for me."

The words hit me like a blow, and I chuckled darkly. Confusion passed over Tex's face, and I forced a smile. I closed my fingers around her wrist, and the sensation was so intense it was almost painful. It didn't matter what I felt. It could never be, even if she did feel a fraction of what I did. She didn't know my secret. She couldn't know the truth. *Aldrei.*

TEX

When I was twelve, my mom's then love-interest took us

mountain climbing. Being my usual rebel self, I couldn't be content with the easy way up the almost-sheer wall. Instead, I followed Austin (or Jason or Chad or something like that), and was doing fine until I was about twenty-five feet from the top. Then I wasn't twenty-five feet from the top. I broke my right leg in two places, cracked my collarbone and left wrist, and cut my arms, legs and back so badly that only plastic surgery could have eliminated my scars. The worst was a jagged line from my right shoulder blade to my left hip, requiring more stitches than I cared to remember.

That pain faded to a distant second when Zev refused to look at me. I maintained my 'professional' face as I jotted down his order and then turned to go. As soon as I'd taken two steps, I realized that I wasn't just hurt. I was mad. I turned around, letting my anger burn away everything else I was feeling. I caught a glimpse of Zev's face as I turned and my heart flipped. Okay, maybe not *everything* else. I held out a hand and properly introduced myself to his family. I didn't look away from Zev's mother even when everyone turned to Zev. I continued, the levity in my voice becoming more natural. "We had a rather abrupt meeting this morning when I hit him in the face with a door." A sound from my left caught my attention. I scowled when I realized that Zev's brother was laughing. "I didn't find it quite as amusing when Zev was covered in blood." I felt a thrill of satisfaction when Ellis's jaw snapped shut with an audible click. I was tempted to help him keep silent by shoving my order pad down his throat, but I was pretty sure that my employer would frown on that. Besides, it wasn't the right impression to make on the family of the guy

I... I wasn't going to finish that thought.

"It's nice to meet you, Tex." Mrs. Avatos's voice drew my eyes back to her.

Chocolate warmth embraced me and I couldn't help but respond. Zev had his mother's smile.

"I am Dinah Avatos. This is my husband Enos and my eldest son, Ellis." Mrs. Avatos had a lovely voice, low-pitched and soothing, with just a hint of some exotic accent that I couldn't quite place.

"It's nice to meet you." I hoped my words seemed genuine. "I'll be back with your drinks." This time, I did walk away. I walked all the way to the kitchen before my calm cracked. I took a deep, shuddering breath and reached for a cup. My shaking fingers scrabbled against the glass, and I paused again. This time, when I extended my arm, my hand was steady.

As I returned, I could hear raised voices and my steps faltered.

"What are you going to do? Kill me?"

"That's enough." A calmer voice cut off the other – Ellis and Enos perhaps? It continued. "Zev, you will explain."

Explain? Confusion beat hesitation and I moved forward as Zev spoke. "I need a minute." I felt a pang as I realized that I could already recognize his voice with just a few syllables. *Lord, are you sure?* I was lost in my own thoughts as I stepped into the table's line of sight, so I didn't hear what Zev's mom had just finished saying.

"*Merci*." Zev turned as his mother saw me. I couldn't read her dark eyes, but then Zev was walking my way and I lost track of everything else. He pushed by without a word and my earlier wounds throbbed. I set my jaw and kept going. I'd made a decision and I wasn't going to back down now. I refused to become one of those weepy, angst-ridden drama queens who needed a two-by-four to the head.

"Iced tea with lemon." I set the frosted glass in front of Dinah Avatos, very much aware of her scrutiny. "Raspberry lemonade." Enos Avatos. "Mango margarita." Alyce Klinger, a twenty-two year-old waitress, set the brightly colored alcoholic drink in front of Ellis. She'd missed the fireworks and so moved on without a question or comment.

"Aren't you going to ask me for my ID?" Ellis leered at me.

Was he flirting with me? Seriously? I repressed the urge to punch him in the nose, and answered in a sugar-and-cyanide-laced voice. "I'm sure you're old enough, sir." I set Zev's ice water in front of his empty seat, catching the flash of temper that crossed Ellis's face. "Are you ready to order or do you want to wait for Zev?"

"We'll wait a few minutes." Dinah lightly touched my arm. Even with my tan, her dusky skin made my complexion look pale. Zev favored his father's coloring – about halfway between Dinah's and mine. Ellis was a bit darker than his mother. My eyes met Dinah's and she spoke the next words deliberately, a clear message in her gaze. "He just stepped outside for some air."

"I'll be back in a bit then." I nodded my head once to indicate that I'd understood. Keeping my pace unhurried, I went back the way I'd come. Once out of sight, I ducked out of the nearest exit and entered the courtyard.

I saw him almost instantly, drawn towards him like a magnet. I knew the thought was cliché, but I didn't care. I just wanted to reach him. His head was in his hands, fingers digging into his dark hair. He didn't look up as I walked towards him, but the tightening of his shoulders indicated that he'd heard me coming. I tried to keep my tone gentle without giving away how much I was invested in him. "Care to explain your very odd behavior?"

Nothing could've prepared me for what came next.

"I knew you'd be attracted to Ellis and I couldn't handle that."

The laugh just burst out of me. The idea was so absurd that, for a moment, I thought he was joking. Then, my brain registered the total vulnerability in his voice, and my heart broke, effectively putting a halt to my shocked mirth. I reacted instinctively, reaching towards him. I caught his chin in my hand, relishing the jolt as our skin touched. As his head rose, his eyes met mine, his gaze so naked and open that I caught my breath. Every romantic, sappy cliché I'd ever heard or read fled my mind as too trite. Every bit of flowery prose sounded too crass and brusque. Every gesture, scripted or otherwise, hid in shame as inelegant and unworthy. Everything I thought I understood turned upside-down and inside-out. I saw Zev as the Creator of Love wanted me to see him, and he was so much more than I'd ever dreamed.

This one, beloved.

I blinked. My epiphany had taken the smallest fraction of a second, and I struggled to remember what Zev had said last.

Oh, right. He thought I'd been attracted to Ellis. My soul cringed at the thought, and I whispered, "Not even close." Then I smiled, reliving my retort to Ellis just a minute before. "Besides, he's too old for me."

Something about my statement must've amused Zev because he gave a funny little chortle, but it didn't sound right. His countenance was too dismal and bleak. Then he smiled and the sun broke through the clouds. Okay, maybe all the clichés hadn't left. His hand grasped my wrist, and I found that I didn't care about phrasing anymore. All I wanted to do was stay here, his fingers around my wrist, staring into his beautiful face and those incredible eyes. I sounded like a moron. A love-struck moron. But, despite my romantic notions and desires, common sense won out. "We both should get back." I couldn't get my voice above a whisper.

Zev rose so suddenly that I caught my breath. He was beyond graceful, particularly for someone as tall as he was. He took a step closer and I could smell the soap he'd used before coming. Something crisp and clean, like sheets hung outside on a sunny day. I liked it. And I could see that his hair hadn't quite dried. In an almost offhanded way, I wondered just how thick it had to be if it was still damp. I almost reached up to run my hand through his locks. *Locks*? Okay, no more chick flicks for a while.

The hand that wasn't already touching me moved towards my face. Long, slender fingers caught a curl fluttering at the edge of my vision. He swept it back into place and let his hand linger. His action was so close to what I'd considered doing just seconds before that I almost thought I'd imagined it. Then his fingertips stroked the skin under my ear and traced down my jaw and I heard the stutter when I exhaled. I needed to move – NOW.

Something must've shown on my face because Zev's features softened, almost saddened. He dropped both of his hands and my skin burned where his had been. He gave me a funny half-smile and swept his arm out to indicate that I should go first. Before I turned, I knew I had to speak or I'd lose my nerve. I couldn't make myself look at him though; that was too much. "We're not done. I'm not letting this go. I want to know."

"Know what?" His voice was low, dangerous.

"Everything."

***

I stepped back into the break room and shut the door, leaning back against it. I closed my eyes and drew in a deep breath of air. I'd never had to try so hard to seem normal, and I wasn't sure I'd fooled Zev's family. After returning from the courtyard, I'd gone back into 'job' mode and been the model waitress, giving just enough attention and offering the right amount of small talk. I'd avoided looking at Zev as much as possible since I lost the ability to perform even the simplest of tasks when around him. I'd felt his gaze on me more than once, and had almost dropped Ellis's rare filet mignon at one point. I'd noticed the older brother's intrigue as well, and did my best to present subzero interest, hoping he'd get frostbite. Once or twice – okay, seven times that I'd counted – I'd been unable to stop myself and I'd stared at Zev. Five times he caught me, and each time, my pulse fluttered. I was pretty sure his mother noticed at least twice. As for Enos and Ellis, I didn't know what either one of them saw. They seemed too self-absorbed to care beyond how this affected them, but lack of interest didn't mean lack of observation. Then, just before they'd left, Zev's hand nudged mine, pressing something against my palm.

Now alone, I opened my hand. The note had been scribbled on a piece of paper from my order pad. How had he managed that? I pushed the question aside and read the message.

If you're certain you want answers, I'll give them. You won't like what I have to say and I'll probably end up hurting you. I don't want to stay away from you, but I will if you decide that this is too strange or difficult. I'll understand and won't hold it against you. I'll respect whatever choice you make.

I read the words a second time before crumpling the paper into a ball and throwing it into the wastebasket. Idiot. Did he really think I was going to walk away? Not a chance.

I maintained my resolve through the rest of my shift as well as the drive home. It wasn't until I was curled up in bed, comforter tucked under my chin, that the doubts came flooding in. What was so awful that Zev thought I'd want him to leave me alone? Some dark secret in his past? Maybe the reason his family had to move? Were things moving too fast? For him? For me? Or, was it as I'd feared? That Zev wasn't a Christian and didn't want to be involved with me because I was one.

I tried to pray, to hold on to the promise God had given me, to trust that He'd foreseen these circumstances. Unfortunately, action wasn't always as easy as intention. It was almost three-thirty before I fell into a restless sleep, full of vague and shadowy dreams that left me with a sense of agitation and unease. All in all, my nerves were frayed more than they had been the day before.

Yesterday.

Zev.

Note.

Crap.

My stomach clenched and I knew that breakfast was going to be impossible. I heard Mom's car start and breathed a sigh of relief. At least I didn't need to worry about a Q&A about my first day of school or my current flustered state. I knew that even my generally unobservant mother wouldn't miss my lack of appetite.

In direct contrast to my approach the previous day, I pulled into the nearly empty parking lot, scanning the vehicles with equal parts anticipation and dread. I spotted it – and him – almost immediately. Again, I felt a pull in his direction. I slid into the empty space next to his Impala, my 1989 Sunbird looking pretty shabby despite my conscientious care. Zev stood at the front of his car, leaning on the hood, head inclining just the slightest bit with my arrival. I had a sudden mental image of my favorite fictional character and gave a nervous giggle. Zev's clothes didn't diminish my entertaining vision. He'd dressed more casually today: faded denim with rips at his knees, scuffed black running shoes and a plain t-shirt. A black, formfitting t-shirt that showed off the muscles I'd caught a glimpse of yesterday morning. My stomach and heart decided to switch places while doing cartwheels. I was suddenly thankful that I hadn't eaten breakfast.

Ask him about Me.

That was unexpected.

It's time to ask him.

I had a sinking feeling that God's instructions were not going to mesh well with Zev explaining his note, and I had a sudden desire to ignore the command. It didn't last long as an earlier memory resurfaced. Zev's soul was more important than my heart. I sighed and stepped out of the car, dragging my practically empty bag with me. I slung the strap across my shoulder, taking an extra moment to adjust its fit against my hip. Then I walked around the front of my car and joined Zev. As I stopped by his side, I felt, with a strange certainty, that we were at some sort of intersection and what happened here could – would – change everything.

ZEV

Tex didn't even notice when I stole the paper from her order pad, but I wasn't surprised. I was an excellent pickpocket. I had a more difficult time keeping my family from seeing what I was doing. But, I am talented and I not only got the note written, but managed to pass it off to Tex as we were leaving. I smiled when my fingers caressed her palm, pulling back before it became too much. Oh, *dashuria e minave*, if you only knew.

As soon as we got into the car, Ellis started. "What was

that all about?"

I didn't reply, knowing that he'd find my silence more aggravating than any lie I could make up. I caught a glimpse of Mom's disapproving glare and swallowed my grin.

"I saw you touch her hand."

Okay, maybe I wasn't as talented as I thought.

"Who is this girl?" My dad's question silenced Ellis. "Explanation time, son."

I took a deep breath, and almost choked on Ellis's cologne. After my coughing fit passed, I spoke. "You're not going to like it."

***

I didn't sleep that night. Part of it was the fight about Tex. Ellis had shouted until both Mom and Dad stopped him, and even then he'd glowered at me until I finally went to my room. I'd heard his car roar down the road an hour later. The other reason for my insomnia was probably well into dreamland. I spent some time wistfully thinking about a starring role in those dreams, but other thoughts kept interfering with my more pleasant ones.

I'd promised to tell Tex everything, and as I lay in my new queen-sized bed, staring up at an unfamiliar ceiling, I began to wonder if I was making the right choice. Ellis was the mastermind, the planner. I thought with my heart, or what was left of it. My entire life had been based on impulsive hunches, acted upon with very little thought or consideration. But, for quite a while, those decisions had been muted, emotionless. I'd been surviving, going through the motions, but all of that changed when I met her. Now I was living in Technicolor, surround-sound, high-definition. And I was feeling my gut instincts once more. This time, my gut told me to tell Tex everything. I began muttering curse words in a random Chinese dialect as I started to think of all the things I was going to have to share. Before I'd fully finished either thing, I fell into a light sleep.

A couple hours later, the front door slammed, startling me so much that I had my six-inch Buck knife in hand before I was actually awake. As soon as I realized what I held, I dropped it. I'd only kept the weapon around as a precaution, and had forgotten that I'd put it back under my pillow when we'd moved. It was habit, ingrained from the earliest shadows of my childhood. It was this indoctrination that made me pick up the knife and return it to its usual place before looking out of the window. I hadn't put my curtains up yet, and I could see beginnings of a gray-gold sunrise. I shrugged. It was pointless trying to get back to sleep now, even if I could. I headed for the bathroom, trying very hard not to think about what was coming. But the memory of gray eyes wouldn't give me peace.

I had those eyes on my mind as I dressed and headed in to the school. I was there before the teachers and got more than a few funny looks thrown my way as they arrived. I barely noticed. All I could see was gray. *I bukur*, clear, pale gray.

I sat in the car for a while, my favorite CD providing background noise, a perfect score to the chaotic film that was my thoughts. As the sun crested over the mountains, rising enough to flood the interior of my vehicle with warm

September light, I climbed out and rounded to the front. I leaned back against the hood, more weight on my feet than the average person at rest. Then again, I never claimed to be average. That thought brought back my doubts and questions, and I reacted like any other man in my situation would have. I brooded.

My forlorn reflection didn't last long, however. Before I could fully immerse myself in angst, I heard a car. My heart pounded as I glimpsed a Pontiac approaching. I'd never realized the beauty of this particular car. What was I saying? *Ara naqra*, I must have been in love if I was waxing romantic about a Sunbird. My only consolation was that Tex didn't drive one of those creepy cars that seemed to be smiling.

And, just like that, Tex was out of her car and reaching for her faded, battered bag. For a brief second, I wondered how old it was. Then she bent her head to adjust the straps and I caught my breath. *Inima mea.* The sun's rays struck her at an angle that made her glow with an almost ethereal light. This morning, she was wearing something new. A deep violet-blue shirt and jeans. I only noticed because they flattered her figure. Then a light breeze tossed her curls, and she raised her head. I wasn't fully facing her, my pride and fear of rejection making me attempt some air of indifference. But, even with my limited view, I was mesmerized. As she joined me, I turned, captivated by her smooth skin, luminous eyes and wind-tossed hair. I couldn't seem to eliminate the sentimentality from my vocabulary. A rush of emotion blasted through me. *Dashuria ime, arsyeja e mia, zemra ime.* I almost blurted out one of the worst four letter words one could say to a lady. Not that one.

Something much worse. Love. I almost told Tex how I felt. Then I remembered my promise, and almost did say another word.

"Good morning." Tex's tone was light, but I could hear an undercurrent trying to say more.

"Beautiful morning." I could feel a stupid grin forming, but found myself helpless to stop it. I finally understood the language of the poets, the drivel I'd blamed Shakespeare for making popular. *Il mio angelo, il mio tutto.* My hands were almost shaking with anticipation. "I'm sure you have a lot of questions and I promised answers..."

Tex cut me off in a voice tremulous with something I couldn't identify. "Before you tell me anything else, there's something I need to know."

"Anything." I promised brashly.

"God."

"What?" I hoped I wasn't understanding.

"What's your relationship with God?"

She was asking the one thing I didn't want to talk about. Familiar fire burned in the pit of my stomach. Fire that had been fanned to flame at the exact moment another blaze had ignited. I found that I could look away, could turn away. In fact, I didn't want to see Tex just then. When I spoke, I kept my volume down, but didn't try to curb the malice. My words left an acrid aftertaste in my mouth. "Have you ever heard someone burn alive?" I heard the sharp intake of air, but pressed forward, clipping off each painful syllable. "I don't mean the screaming or crying because many of them died singing praises to their God. I mean the sound of flesh boiling, charring, while crowds cheer? You can close your eyes, but even if you try to stop the noise, it echoes in your mind forever. And, believe me, I know what forever feels like."

"I don't understand."

I spun towards her, every muscle tensed and ready for a fight. Wanting somewhere to vent my anger. "Of course not! You can't! You didn't see her burn! You didn't listen to the people chanting for her death!" The words came out with a vehemence I savored. "Her name was Elizabeth. I loved her and your God killed her."

TEX

I held my breath after asking the question. I could tell from his face before he turned that his answer was not going to be good. Even so, I wasn't prepared for what he said next.

"Have you ever heard someone burn alive?"

I couldn't stop myself. I gasped. He must've heard me, but continued anyway. The words seared my heart and soul, burning as deeply as the flames to which he referred.

"I don't mean the screaming or crying because many of them died singing praises to their God. I mean the sound of flesh boiling, charring, while crowds cheer? You can close your eyes, but even if you try to stop the noise, it echoes in your mind forever. And, believe me, I know what forever feels like."

"I don't understand." Maybe I did, but I didn't want to.

He moved so quickly that I recoiled. His hands were clenched into fists and, for one frightening second, I believed that he was going to hit me.

"Of course not! You can't! You didn't see her burn! You didn't listen to the people chanting for her death!"

I didn't want to hear any more.

"Her name was Elizabeth. I loved her and your God killed her."

My mind reeled as confusion and emotion warred. I wasn't sure which fact I wanted to fix on first: that Zev had been in love, that the girl he loved had been burned alive, or that he blamed God for her death. The first caused me a pang, but it wasn't like I hadn't expected it. Zev was a very good-looking eighteen year-old. The likelihood that I had been the first person he'd been attracted to had been practically nonexistent to begin with. Now I knew for sure and would consider the implications later. The second fact brought up more questions, and I immediately shoved it aside. The third fact gave an answer to my question. Zev's relationship with God did exist, and it was an incendiary one.

By the time I processed my thoughts, Zev was halfway across the parking lot, heading for MacClay Park. For a moment, I considered going after him, but the thought was fleeting and then all I really wanted to do was hide. By the time I pulled my car door shut behind me, my hands were shaking, but I wasn't sure if it was anger or anguish. Okay, maybe it was a little of both. I turned the key and let my CD play, the familiar lyrics slowly soothing my chaotic thoughts. I rested my forehead against my steering wheel and began to pray. It was the only thing I could do.

"Lord, what do I say to him? He's so angry."

I told you that this would be hard.

"But you didn't tell me any of this other stuff. About this girl."

No one is told someone else's story. You know that.

"Yeah, I know, but some warning would've been nice."

Are you going to turn your back on him now?

"Is that even an option?" I felt my heart, my soul, ache even as I said the words.

You always have a choice.

"But this is what you want of me?"

Yes.

I paused, weighing my choices, deliberating more than I had previously. I'd answered too hastily before, expecting God to safely guide my heart through the turbulent waters of romance – I really needed to lay off the clichés – even though He'd promised it would be difficult. I realized now that I'd fooled myself, believed that nothing could be as hard as what I'd suffered before, especially since I was going into this current experience with my eyes wide open. Or at least, I'd thought my eyes were open because I knew more than I had before. Apparently, I was wrong. Without a conscious desire on my part, my thoughts traveled back. Back to one of the birthdays I hadn't told Zev about. Back to Teddy.

Chapter Three: Lightning Crashes and the Thunder Rolls

ZEV

I closed my eyes and let the wind blow through my hair. The tang of sea air brought back a rush of memories: childhood hours spent playing along the shores of Galilee. Occasionally I gave myself permission to reminisce, to long, for those more innocent times. Ellis discouraged my sentimentality, of course, claiming it distracted me from the hunt. I let the influence of my brother's negativity melt away as the sun warmed my face. How could I be angry on such a beautiful day as this? *Sorprendente*. The coast of England in June was truly one of *El Hannora*'s most glorious creations. The only thing I admired more were the majestic peaks of the western New World. Though recent explorations hadn't taken Europeans that far into the new continent, my family had seen those mountains more than once.

"Mother and Father want you to join them below deck."

Ellis's voice broke through my morning accounting of blessings, a habit I'd had all my life and one that he'd been interrupting for almost as long. He didn't understand my desire to continue conversing with *El Olam*. Ellis had forgotten Who we served long before we'd reached these shores for the first time. I felt a burst of pity as I turned toward my older brother.

He continued. "They want us armed before we dock."

I nodded, deferring to him for this aspect of our journey. I relied too much on instinct. Our parents had taken their cues from Ellis since the beginning. They could fight, but didn't relish the kill as he did. While I didn't share his enthusiasm, the challenge of the hunt excited me and my skills were proficient, though not quite up to par with his. Nevertheless, we made a good team, the best of our kind. At eighteen and twenty-three, we were in the prime of our fighting years – and had been since the curse.

Ten minutes later, my parents and I joined Ellis at the rails, watching as our ship came in to port. Our servants were below, gathering our things. We didn't usually flaunt our wealth, but a bit of show always helped when going into a new country. Not that we hadn't been to the island before; it had just been a while. Back then, we'd been passing as merchants. Currently, we were Lord and Lady Avatos and their two sons, a family of Greek nobles come to purchase land on the beautiful British Isle. Our latest quarry moved in high social circles, and we needed to do the same.

It didn't take us long to disembark and find a buggy. Enough money could buy almost anything, as long as you were a good Catholic like Her Majesty, of course. Our relationship with *El Olam* predated any formal religion, so we had no qualms about embracing the old Church or the new Reformed faith if the situation called for it.

Mother and Father had sent a representative ahead a month ago and we'd hoped he'd have lodgings waiting for us. We weren't disappointed. As soon as we told the driver our name, he knew where to take us. The house was just outside the city walls, not that it could rightly be called a house. It was actually a castle, a fortress that had once belonged to an English lord, executed for some reason or other during one of the many monarch changes over the last few decades. As we climbed out of the buggy and headed for the heavy oak doors,

I fell in step with my mother, letting Ellis and my father pull ahead.

"A castle?" I pitched my voice as low as I could. I didn't want Ellis to hear. Any questions on my part, no matter how innocent, had the tendency to promote lengthy speeches about the importance of our ability to blend in with our present surroundings, and were often laced with disparaging comments regarding my intelligence and sense of loyalty. To my recollection, the last nice thing Ellis had said to me was in regards to a stick figure drawing of a cat that I had done when I was four, and even then he followed it with the advisement that I could probably do better. "How long do you believe we will be here?"

"It could be some time." Mother looked up as we entered the castle. The high vaulted ceilings were beautiful, as were the elaborate furnishings. It appeared that we'd spared no expense for this place. For us to have gone to such lengths, the target must have been larger than others we'd hunted. Our lives were generally nomadic. Mother confirmed my suspicions as she answered. "Ellis believes that there may be an entire congregation here."

"Royalty?" It wouldn't be the first time those with royal blood sought Divine power. That usually meant a longer commitment from my family, which explained the lavish lodgings. If we were to spend much time here, Ellis and my parents would want to live in comfort. Not that I was going to complain. Staying in one place was a novelty that the castle made all the more appealing.

"Perhaps." My mother stepped away from me and crossed

to my father's side. She laid a hand on his arm and they moved off to claim their room. Ellis and I went our separate ways to find our own spaces. Our pattern had been established in a more-than-distant past, changing very little as we journeyed. Though we adapted to each new environment, much of who we were stayed the same. Predictability wasn't always a bad thing.

As I entered the quarters I'd claimed as my own, I spoke to the empty air. "*Domus dulcis domus.*" Home it was. For now. I walked to the window and looked outside. Lightning forked through the sky as a storm rolled in, bringing with it a strange foreboding. I shook my head, trying to rid myself of the disquieting feeling, but it refused to leave. Change was coming.

***

Two weeks. Two weeks of summer in England. Two weeks of absolute boredom. Ellis was doing his thing, scouting, planning, all that. Mom and Dad were providing cover, going to parties, establishing our right to be a part of this world. My preparation role in all of this was to be a personal infiltration contact if need arose, but until I had someone to manipulate, my only options were going to parties with my parents or waiting.

I hated waiting, but I hated parties more.

Of all of us, I was the best with people, which was why I had my particular job. I tended to set people at ease. That didn't mean, however, that I liked people. I'd been around long enough to have grown tired of all the games that the human race played, and I preferred the lonely hillsides to the royal court. Fortunately, it didn't take me much time for me to establish a relationship with people, which meant my attendance at festivities wasn't often required. So, until I was needed in public, I spent my days hating current fashion trends, and enjoying the scenery. I was strolling along early one morning when a flash of color caught my eye. I tensed, but checked myself before I did anything out of character. Good thing, too.

It was a girl.

She appeared to be about sixteen or so. Her hair was flaming red, a mass of *vacker* curls piled impossibly haphazard on a slender neck, her fair skin smattered with freckles. It was the hair I'd seen. Her clothes were plain, blending in with the landscape.

"Yer the Avatos lad. The younger, aye?" Her voice was pleasant, with the rolling lilt I'd been expecting. "The missus said ya were a handsome one." Her bright green eyes sparkled.

"And?" Something about this girl intrigued me, but I was careful. I kept my accent to the class and ethnicity of my cover. My mission was more important than my curiosity. Fortunately, the arrogance in my tone fit with both. "What is your opinion on this?"

"I'll be letting ya know." She grinned and I found myself smiling back. "I'm Elizabeth."

***

The following two months far surpassed most of the previous years of my life. Elizabeth was a joy to be with. Her laugh, her love of life, her passion for *El Olam* – all these things drew me to her in a way I'd never known before. I'd had a crush or two before, but never felt such a link with another person. My only concern was when I found out that, unlike the rest of her very large family, Elizabeth followed the teachings of recently deceased rabble-rouser, Martin Luther. I promised myself that when our time came to depart, Elizabeth would come with us. I just wasn't going to clear it with my family first. I already knew what Ellis would say.

"Zev!" Ellis must have been calling my name for a few minutes to have already attained that perturbed tone.

I grinned, feeling sheepish. I'd been daydreaming about red hair and freckles. "What is it, *fratello*?"

"I found our target." Ellis settled into one of the heavy oak chairs. "Actually, there are twelve targets. The largest group I've seen in one place since the congregation in Rome two centuries ago."

"Taking out that many Perpetuum could be a problem with the noble affliation." I switched over to hunter mode. "Will we need to send for re-enforcements? Jael or Jobey?"

"No. We can handle it. All of us will need to do our part though." Ellis leaned forward, hands clasped, brow furrowed. "I have the schedule for two days from now, and that's when it must be done. We will need to spend all of today and tomorrow planning."

"*As vitam paramus. Adversus solem ne loquitor*." I muttered in Latin. As usual, Ellis ignored me when I changed languages. He knew it was my way of processing information and he didn't acknowledge it, even if it annoyed him.

"Four targets for you, five for me and the last three for Mother and Father." Ellis didn't raise his eyes from the table, his mind probably seeing the plan unfold before him. "I have a way in for my targets. You will need to charm your way into the convent for yours."

I felt dismay and revulsion write their way across my face. Ellis knew me well enough to answer before I'd asked the question. "I checked them both thoroughly. One novice and three clerics. They hide under the protection of the Church and hold their true services in the dark of night."

"Are you sure?" I was disgusted by the thought of killing the pious.

"Let me say it this way." Malicious humor flashed across Ellis's visage. "They definitely had the wrong Bible. And I do not mean the one the Queen despises." When I didn't reply, he continued. "We could exchange targets. Mine have just become old enough to take the oath."

I turned away. No matter how long I'd been doing this, I despised assassinating the young. Ellis had no such qualms, citing Sodom and Gomorrah as well as dozens of others as justification. He'd been happy when the messengers hadn't found enough righteous to save the condemned cities, and he'd rejoiced as the fire fell from heaven. Vengeance and Ellis were well-acquainted.

"I thought not." Ellis's voice was low. "Send one of the servants to find Mother and Father."

"I need to tell Elizabeth..."

"Send a message." Ellis cut me off. "The mission is more important than your trifling affections."

I knew that arguing with Ellis was pointless, specifically when a kill was this close. Obsession wasn't a strong enough word. I would make it up to Elizabeth later. I'd have to send her a message anyway, to tell her when and where to meet my family so that we could leave. With a target this size, chances of a clean getaway were slim. I called two of our most trusted servants and sent them back out on their respective errands. Christophe and Phoebe had been with us since their childhoods and were as trustworthy as their ancestors had been in the generations before.

We refined our plan through the night and into the next day, eating as we worked. Phoebe and Christophe began packing and making the arrangements necessary for us to disappear. Per Mother's instructions, the all of the servants we'd acquired for this cover had been sent on their way with enough money to have a pleasant life. Only the single family remained and they finished packing the necessities before the sun had reached its zenith. I stood at my window for a moment, sword in hand, watching the bustle below as they prepared to leave for the rendezvous. It was then, as Phoebe helped her daughter into the cart, that I realized that I'd heard nothing back from Elizabeth. Phoebe had never neglected to complete any task I'd given her, but there was one whose orders she obeyed above mine. With a flash of insight, I realized what must have happened.

The door rebounded off the wall with enough force to shut it again. If it had been made of anything less than English oak, it would have splintered. Ellis didn't turn from his place at the eastern window even as the sound reverberated off of the stone walls. His sword was sheathed, resting against his hip, and as I strode forward, he put his hand on the hilt. "Keep your mind on your assignment, *lillebror*."

"You told Phoebe not to give me Elizabeth's message, didn't you?"

"There was nothing to give, Zev." Ellis turned from the window so that the early rays cast his profile in a harsh light. Even so, he was a handsome figure. His eyes darted to the sword in my clenched fist and then back to me, unconcerned that I was armed.

"I do not understand." Confusion overran anger.

Ellis returned to his previous position at the window and took a sip of wine from his goblet. "Do you recollect the last time we were here?"

"What?" I wasn't following his train of thought and fought my desire to stab him in his back... no metaphor intended.

"Richard invited us to the tournament. There were so many amazing matches, yet you spent the entire time talking to that writer. What was his name?"

"Geoffrey?" I'd placed the memory. Over a century and a half had passed, but I still remembered the tales he'd told.

"That's the one."

"What's are you talking about, Ellis?" As I often did when my emotions took over, I lapsed back into our native tongue. "Why didn't Elizabeth send me a message? What don't you want me to know?"

"Don't fool yourself into thinking you love this girl. You know better. We all do." Ellis's tone sharpened. "Don't bother getting close to anyone, Zev. There's no point. You're not selfless enough to put someone else before yourself and, until you do that, you'll never truly be in love." He faced me. "Besides, we have no time for love. You know what needs to be done and if you interfere, we'll lose our chance at taking out twelve of our enemies."

"Interfere with what?" My voice held a dangerous edge. "Where's Elizabeth?"

"Do you know what the queen uses Smithfield for now?" My brother's expression softened with pity. "It isn't tournaments."

All the air rushed from my lungs as I realized what Ellis meant. Elizabeth's conversion had been discovered. The treatment of noble English Protestants was horrific enough; I didn't want to know what they would do to a poor Irish girl. All I could see was green as I spun around and ran. I heard Ellis yelling after me, but I knew he couldn't catch me. As I raced for Smithfield, my thoughts screamed. *She'll deny it. That's all she has to do. She can deny the Reformers and stay with me. I can keep her safe and she can worship however she wants. El Olam, You cannot take her from me. Dieu, aide-moi.*

My extra-sharp senses picked out the image even through the throng, and I pushed my way towards it. As I fell to my knees in front of the stake, I could hear the rumble of the crowd behind me. They watched me, crumpled under the broken figure bound to the stake. Even under her rough homespun dress, I could see the outline of the misshapen mess that had been her legs. Her face was a cacophony of color, of crimson, black, purple. One eye swollen shut, the other brilliant green peering from ruined flesh. Three days. Three days since I'd last seen her. The world spun around me. How could this happen so fast?

"Zev." My name fell from bloodied lips.

"Just recant, Elizabeth." I heard myself whisper. She flinched and I felt an eruption of some strange emotion. "Recant and they'll let you go. You can come with me and be safe."

"I cannot deny my God." The sorrow in her voice brought more of my yet-unnamed feeling.

"What about me?" The words cracked.

"Do not make me choose between you and God, my love." Elizabeth didn't waver as the men came forward with torches.

I recognized what filled me. Loathing. But not for those who'd done this. I despised Elizabeth in that moment. And I hated *El Olam*. I stood. "God is going to kill you." The ice in my statement wasn't thawed by the approaching fire.

"And I die with His name on my lips." She smiled then and the crowd roared. Red and orange flames shot up from the dry wood and caught the hem of her dress. Even over the noise, I could hear her asking her God for strength.

I felt a scream building in my chest as Elizabeth's skin blackened and charred, but I didn't release it. The crackling of flesh echoed in my ears louder than the crowd crying out for her blood. *Ewyllysia erioed faddau 'ch.* I wasn't sure if I was directing my malevolent thoughts at *El Olam* or Elizabeth. A hand on my shoulder turned me away from the nightmare I'd once loved. I felt no fear, even as I recognized one of the Queen's interrogators.

"Are you one of them?" He'd caught part of my conversation. "Do you follow her God?"

I shook my head, forcing the words past numb lips. I refused to be caught up in a war about a God I no longer wanted to serve. "The God of the Reformers is no God of mine."

Something on my face or in my words must have shown the truth of my statement, because the hand fell away. The people were still cheering as I walked away. Before I'd gotten too far, Ellis found me. He kept out of reach, but didn't refrain from voicing his opinion. No power on earth could keep Ellis from speaking his mind.

"We must act, Zev, if we are to stay on schedule. You have only an hour to reach your destination if our plan is to work."

I stopped walking and faced my brother. My tone was flat, dead, as if something important and vital was now missing. I supposed, in a way, it was. "*Rwy'n gadael.*"

"What do you mean?"

"I am done, Ellis. Finished. I am through with this quest. I will not obey Someone who lets this happen." My eyes burned, but I refused to allow myself the luxury. "And do not waste my time with pleas. It is not as if you are doing this for His sake. I care not for vengeance against those who defy *El Olam*. Not anymore. I quit."

"You cannot do that."

"*Laissez-moi tranquille.*" I turned and began walking. One

foot in front of the other would take me far away. Where I'd go, what I'd do, I didn't know. It didn't matter anyway. All I knew for sure was that I was through letting Him run my life.

TEX

"Killeen, your friends are going to be here in an hour. Shouldn't you be getting ready?" My mom stood on the other side of my door, but I didn't move from where I was sitting, cross-legged, on my dove-gray bedspread.

"I'll be ready on time." I answered her, but kept my eyes fixed on the papers in front of me. When I didn't hear anything else, I assumed she'd returned to the lower level of the house to finish putting the last minute touches up for our guests. I honestly believed that she was more excited about my birthday party than I was. Not that I didn't appreciate the gesture, but, unlike my mother, I didn't really enjoy being the center of attention. And I wouldn't have agreed to a big party this year if it hadn't been for him.

I picked up one of the e-mails I'd printed out and began to read.

I'll never forget the day I walked in to Elle Monroe's cabin. I'd thought I'd be spending the summer bored out of my mind and then I saw this tiny girl with long black hair. Elle had told me that she'd invited one of her friends to spend the summer with her up at the lake, but I never dreamed that her friend would be someone like you. I don't know if you remember, but I couldn't take my eyes off of you that day.

I smiled. I did remember, and I'd felt the same way. Teddy Sanders had the most impossibly beautiful chocolate brown eyes and the softest curly blond hair. I'd noticed him the second he'd crossed the threshold, and when Elle had introduced us, neither of us had been able to look away. Fortunately, Elle had a crush on Teddy's cousin, a dark-haired guy named Elmer Johnson, so she had no problem with us spending all of our time with the boys. Even so, I'd only told her about some of the time I'd spent with him. I loved Elle, but her whole 'God' thing made it difficult to share certain things. Then there was the distance issue. Teddy's family was from Maryland, and he only spent summers with the Johnsons. At the end of our magical summer together, we'd exchanged numbers and vowed to write as well. To my amazement, I'd received e-mails almost every week. Each word he wrote was flowery, romantic and full of promise.

I can't believe it's been two whole weeks since we last saw each other. Every time I close my eyes, I see your face. I can still feel your hand in mine. Feel your lips against mine. Every love song on the radio reminds me of you. I'm counting down the days until I can be with you again. I love you.

I smiled and sighed. I'd been talking about Teddy since I'd returned from vacation last summer, and all of my friends were eager to meet him. I'd been devastated this year when I'd learned that the Johnsons had sold their cabin at Kristalline Lake, but Teddy had promised that he'd be coming to Colorado so that we could celebrate my fifteenth birthday together. I picked up the last e-mail, dated three weeks ago.

Babe, I miss you so much. Sorry I haven't been writing as often, but things are crazy around here. I'm trying to get as much done as possible so I can head out to see you. The only thing I want is to be with you again. Remember the night we walked on the beach and got caught in that rainstorm? Each time it rains, I think of that night, and just want to be at your side, touching you, holding you. Love you.

I read the last few sentences again, and felt my face growing hot as I recalled the night he'd mentioned. Independence Day. When I'd seen fireworks this year, I'd immediately flashed back to those few hours Teddy and I had spent together. Those memories sustained me through hours of needling by friends who didn't completely believe that I had a boyfriend. Today, however, my friends and my mom would be meeting Teddy for the first time and I couldn't wait. My cell phone buzzed and I grabbed for it, a thrill of anticipation running through me. Maybe it was Teddy!

I tried not to let the disappointment take away from my original excitement. It was a text from Gretchen asking what I would be wearing. I sighed and replied in as little detail as I could manage. My friends and my mother were cut from the same cloth: fashion-obsessed, anti-comfortable cloth. If Mom was home when Gretchen and Susan came over, they spent more time talking clothes with her than they did hanging out with me. I didn't bother to psychoanalyze myself. I knew my relationship with the two most well-known girls in school didn't make much sense. Besides, it wasn't like they were the only friends I had. While I wasn't wildly popular, I had a few close friends and even more acquaintances, enough to make for a fair-sized a party. The only disappointment was that Elle had gotten sick and couldn't make it. Before tossing my phone back onto my bed, I checked my incoming messages to make sure I hadn't missed anything, or anyone, important.

Nothing.

I carefully folded my letters, returned them to my desk drawer and then headed for the closet to find something to wear. As I pulled the door open, a flash of red caught my eye and I stood, rooted the spot for almost a full minute. I suppose I shouldn't have been surprised. There was no way Mom was going to let me be a fashion victim at my own party. Personally, I thought the dress was a bit much, but I knew it would bruise Mom's feelings if I didn't wear it. While she didn't quite understand me, Mom honored my individuality and rarely asked me to dress up. As I reached for the silky material, a small part of my brain considered the look on Teddy's face when he saw me in this dress. I smiled. Maybe Mom knew what she was doing after all.

Twenty minutes later, I descended the stairs as slowly as possible. Most of the time, I had no trouble staying on my feet, but I usually wore much more comfortable, and practical, shoes. The sparkling gold heels Mom had bought to go with the dress weren't exactly conducive to walking. Or standing. Or doing much of anything except sparkling. Once I reached the bottom of the staircase, I tugged at my dress, trying to decide on which section I preferred the most coverage: the low-cut bodice or the hemline that stopped a good four inches above my knees. I shook back my hair, the loose curls tickling my bare shoulders and arms. They were heavy and hot on my back, hanging to my waist and, for once, sleek and smooth.

"You're beautiful." Mom's smile made her seem more like my older sister than my mother; she could still attract every male in a room. For a moment, I wondered about some of my male friends and their reasons for hanging out with me. Then Mom took my hand, and I pushed the thought away, determined to have a good birthday for once.

"Thanks." I tried not to stumble as she pulled me into the lavishly decorated living room, prattling on about the elaborate table settings and how excited she was to meet Teddy. I fastened onto his name and smiled through her chatter.

The muscles in my face already ached by the time my guests arrived, but I forced myself to keep smiling even as I peered past each gift-bearing friend, searching for that familiar face, those dark eyes. It was almost eight o'clock before I realized that I hadn't heard the doorbell ring for over thirty minutes. I counted heads. Everyone on the guest list had arrived. Everyone except the person I wanted to see most.

"So, Tex, where's this boyfriend of yours?" Gretchen sidled up beside me, voicing the silent question I'd been asking myself.

I shrugged – not an easy task in a strapless dress – and tried to keep my countenance serene. "Probably caught in traffic. You know how it is around the airport."

"Of course."

I bristled at her patronizing tone, but didn't say anything. Too many people were watching, and I didn't want to make a scene. Before Gretchen could say anything else, my phone rang. I glanced down at it, and shot a smug glance in Gretchen's direction. "It's him." I answered the call as I walked to the back porch for a quieter spot to talk.

"Hi, Teddy."

"Hey Babe." Even punctuated by static, his voice made me shiver with remembered caresses. "What's up?"

My stomach clenched. "Funny, Teddy. Where are you?"

"Home, silly. Where do you think I am?"

I choked back the tears that wanted to surface, refusing to let Teddy hear anything in my voice. "I thought you were coming here. It's my birthday. Remember?"

"Right. Your birthday." A high-pitched giggle in the background hit me like cold water. And a ton of bricks. A very cold ton of bricks. "Listen, Babe, we need to talk."

No, not today. I was finally going to have a good birthday. He couldn't do this to me today. I kept my back to the house, not wanting anyone inside to suspect that something was wrong. "What about?"

"Look, this just isn't working."

How did Teddy manage to stay so calm and unruffled when my world was shattering into a million pieces? "What do you mean?"

"Come on, Babe, you know it's true. We live on opposite ends of the country. We never get to see each other."

"But we write all the time and talk." I hated the way my voice sounded, but had no way to change it.

"That may work for a kid like you, but I need more than that." Another fit of feminine laughter from the background. Then Teddy's muffled voice as he spoke away from the phone. "Samara, doll, not right now. Wait until I'm off the phone." He started talking to me again, but I barely heard the words: excuses and platitudes meant to keep me from behaving like the child he apparently thought I was. For a moment, I felt like reminding him that he was only a year older than I was, but I found that my voice had vanished. He continued. “Look, if I’m ever in the area, I totally plan on looking you up. Maybe we can hook up. You know, like we did at the lake. But I think it’d be best for both of us to just move on. You understand, right?”

He wanted to see me if he was in Colorado? Then the rest of his words registered. Like at the lake. Bile rose in my throat, and I was suddenly sure that I was going to throw up all over the porch, my beautiful dress, and my sparkling shoes. Then I remembered that everyone inside was probably peering through the French double doors behind me and I pushed back the nausea. As I did, I heard Teddy add one more thing.

“Besides, it wasn’t like we really meant it when we said we loved each other. Right?”

Before I thought through what I was doing, I pulled my arm back and threw my phone out into the blackness that was beyond our yard lights. I heard it strike something, but found that I didn’t care. I needed a new phone anyway. Now all I had to do was go back into my party, and pretend that everything was still okay. And come up with some reason as to why I’d just turned my cell into bits and pieces of junk. I felt a tear roll down my cheek as, in the distance, I heard the rumble of thunder. A perfect ending to yet another perfect birthday.

ZEV

I barely glanced at the sign as I entered the park. In fact, I didn’t really see much of anything. My encounter with Tex and the memories her question had brought back were the only things on my mind. I couldn't differentiate between the two. They spun and tangled together, merging into my hatred towards the One who'd caused me so much pain. My feet chose their own way as I wandered aimlessly into the playground area. So engrossed was I in my thoughts that I didn't realize I'd walked into the slide until I felt metal against bone.

I grabbed my shin, swearing in several languages as pain radiated up my leg. Clarity flooded my mind, and with it came a pain sharper than the one I'd experienced from my memory of Elizabeth. *El Olam* was taking another person I loved. First Zila, then Elizabeth, now Tex. I sat on the bottom of the slide and buried my head in my hands. Part of me wanted to pace, to scream at the sky, at *El Hashamayim* who I no longer wanted to acknowledge. But a greater part of me was spiraling downwards, my soul heading for the black pit I knew was waiting for me. Dante had expressed it well: *Lasciate ogni speranza voi che entrate.* I had no hope left within me. I couldn't find the strength to stand, to move, and I lacked the desire to even try. What was the point? I let the darkness close over me and drowned in despair.

"Zev?"

I didn't move. Acknowledging the voices in your head was a sure sign of insanity.

"Zev, come on. The bell's going to ring and you don't want to be late two days in a row."

Why did the voice in my head say that? I couldn't help myself. I looked up and sucked in a lungful of cool mountain air. Tex stood at the edge of the path, something in her normally translucent eyes that made them cloudy and unreadable. She motioned for me to follow her, but didn't come any closer. Something inside me balked at her standoffishness and I found that it gave me the strength to stand. I walked towards her, waiting for the rush of questions I knew would be forthcoming. Before I reached her, however, she turned and started to walk away. Annoyance and anguish warred. Without waiting to see which one would win, I followed.

We walked up the path in silence, me biting back the retorts and pleas that wanted to burst out. How I managed to keep myself from making myself sound like a lovesick fool, or an insensitive cad, I didn't know. I followed her past our cars and into the building, dimly aware of jealous and curious eyes as I moved up to her side once through the doors. She didn't look my way, but I couldn't stop myself from stealing glances out of the corners of my eyes. Her lips were pressed together, an unnatural expression on her youthful face, one I couldn't understand and wanted to ask about. Dread uncoiled in my stomach as I thought of all the implications her possible answer could have.

We slid into our seats as the second bell rang, leaving us no time to speak, even if we'd wanted to. I wasn't sure if I did or not. Wouldn't it be safer just to let things go? To not open myself to being tormented more than I already was? Then I caught a glimpse of Tex, of smooth skin and dark curls, of pale eyes unguarded and vulnerable. *Nebudu ztratit.* I knew I couldn't give her up without a fight. Even if it was myself I would be fighting.

***

Determined to set the standard for the year, Mrs. Conner worked us from start to finish, with barely a pause between her final word and the high-pitched tone that signaled the end of class. The hallways were hardly an ideal place for the type of conversation that Tex and I needed to have, but I supposed that our second period study hall would be perfect. I could find out how far away I'd driven her, and what I needed to do to bring her back. She'd assure me that my lack of belief didn't matter and we could move on. No one based a romantic relationship on shared faith anyway. I was so caught up in my thoughts, that it wasn't until I reached the library door that I noticed Tex's absence. I turned, ignoring the glares of the students who had been walking behind me, and saw Tex disappearing around the corner.

Study hall was miserable. I sat at the back table in the library, and stared at the wall. Several of the girls approached the empty seat at my side, but quickly gave up trying to gain my attention when I refused to even look their way. All efforts to avoid despondency and desolation vanished without Tex's presence. I let gloom settle over me and I wallowed in it, drowning in the self-pity I'd perfected over the years. *Inutile.* I called myself insults in dozens of languages. *Frikacak.* It didn't help. *Gunoi de pe pamant.*

Even seeing Tex again in the hallway didn't change my mood. Until she smiled at me.

Her eyes were red, as if she'd been crying, but as the

corners of her mouth lifted and dimples deepened in her cheeks, a ray of light pierced through the dark clouds around me. *Moja zvezda.* I felt my lips curve upwards in response as she crossed to my side.

She broke the silence first. "I know there are some things we need to talk about, but this isn't really the best place. If we could put off the heavy stuff until after school, I'd appreciate it. Let's just stick with the mundane things, small talk."

She peered up at me and I found that I couldn't deny her anything. *Ero perdutamente innamorato.* I almost cringed at the desperation in my voice. Almost. "After school? We can talk after school?" My desire for silence had fled along with my despair. I felt a tenuous hope that she wasn't going to drive me away. *Fan liom.* Apparently, I hadn't abandoned hope completely.

Tex nodded, looking down at her hands. She appeared to be gathering her courage to say something. After a moment, her head lifted. *Dwi yn boddi ynoch*! The depths of strength and conviction in her gaze awed me. Her lips trembled and I felt the urge to comfort her, to still her lips with mine. Then she was speaking, and I focused on her words. "After school, we'll talk. And then you can decide if you still want to be with me." She turned her eyes away. "I'm not letting you go unless you ask me to."

I stared after her as she hurried into our next class. She was giving *me* the choice? Didn't she realize that I was the one who should be begging her to keep me? What could she have possibly done in her short life that would merit such a statement as the one she made? A nudge from behind propelled me through the doorway and I followed Tex to her seat, still in a daze.

TEX

Even before my reverie had faded from my mind, I knew what my answer was going to be. My relationship with Teddy had been a turning point for me, the last in a string of poor decisions that had shown me what I was missing in my life. Or, I should say, Who I was missing. I knew how much I owed God for all He'd forgiven me, and I couldn't let my fear of being hurt get in the way of what I needed to do.

"Will he break my heart?" I whispered the words.

Silence.

"You want me to choose without knowing the outcome." It was a statement, not a question, but I received an answer nonetheless.

Isn't that the very essence of faith?

I scowled, but it didn't last long.

Tell him everything.

My stomach tightened. "Is this what you want of me?"

You know it is. I have told you My desire. The choice now lies with you.

Sometimes I really hated free will.

My eyes were shut already and now a face swam in front of my closed lids. A face I could draw from memory. If I could draw. Strong jaw line with just a hint of stubble, like he'd been too distracted for a close shave. Messy dark brown hair that I longed to run my fingers through. A nose that appeared too straight for having been hit with a door the day before.

Eyebrows that might have been a bit too thick but suited him. Cheekbones that any model, including my mother, would envy. Full lips that – okay, I was going to be completely honest with myself – I'd dreamed of kissing, wondering what they'd feel like pressed against my own. And his eyes. A color I'd never seen before. Breathtakingly beautiful, but so sad, full of anguish. My arms ached to hold him, to tell him that he didn't need to hurt, that God could take that pain... all right, all right. I had my answer and I breathed it out in a barely audible statement.

"Your will be done."

I stayed in my car a bit longer, letting my favorite music soothe me as I prayed for Zev. I was so caught up in my intercession that I didn't hear the first dozen cars pull into the parking lot. It wasn't until an exiting vehicle blared their horn at the absent-minded seventh grader cutting in front of them that I glanced at my watch. Gritting my teeth, I grabbed my bag and stepped out of my car. I was almost past Zev's car when I thought to look inside it, to see if he'd returned for his book bag. The expensive-looking tote still lay on his passenger's seat. I didn't need God's nudging to turn and head for the park, but I sent up a small prayer that He'd keep any of the teachers from spotting me. Once on school grounds, we technically weren't supposed to leave again without permission. I figured that this was one case where necessity superseded the rules.

I hadn't gone far when I spotted Zev. I stopped at the edge of the path and watched him for a moment. He was sitting on the bottom of the slide, his head in his hands, eyes closed. His shoulders were pulled forward as he hunched over his knees, trying to disappear into himself. Every fiber, every muscle, every atom of my being wanted to cross the dew-damp grass and take him in my arms, ease his pain.

I didn't move. If I went now, I'd never be able to tell him everything, to give him the opportunity to make an informed decision. More importantly, I knew I wouldn't have the strength to keep God in first place in my heart. If I touched Zev, I couldn't be sure of what would happen next.

"Zev?"

Nothing.

Maybe I wasn't talking loud enough. "Zev, come on. The bell's going to ring and you don't want to be late two days in a row."

When he looked up, my resolve wavered. All right, it more than wavered. It took all of my willpower to keep my feet where they were. I latched on to the memory of God's voice reminding me that this wasn't going to be easy, but it was His will. Easier said than done. I indicated that Zev should follow me. After a moment, he stood and I again marveled at how graceful he was for someone so tall. As he started to walk towards me, I realized that I wouldn't be able to keep hold of my faltering control if he got close enough. I acted upon the example of one of my favorite Bible characters and, like Joseph, I fled. Well, I didn't run. I walked, but I went ahead of Zev so I couldn't see him.

I wanted to speak to him, but was afraid that if I opened my mouth, everything I was thinking and feeling would spill out, and this wasn't a good time for my guts to pour out of my mouth. That disturbing image snapped my attention back into place. On occasion, my strange imagination surprised even me, but at least, this time, it was useful. As we passed by our cars, I heard the door of his car open and then slam shut, but I didn't stop, merely adjusted my pace until I was sure he was a step behind me once more. I didn't want to dwell on the fact that I was so aware of his presence that I knew how close he was to me without actually seeing him. We wove our way through the hallway, and made it into homeroom just as the second bell rang. I barely heard the announcements as I tried to keep my eyes away from Zev. This day was going to be impossible. I needed support. If I could just get through first period, I could get out of study hall and go see Shaun Grant, the youth pastor here at New Hope Free Methodist Church, and the person who, along with Elle, had been there to led me to God after that disastrous summer. They'd both been constant sources of encouragement over the past two years, but since Elle was halfway across the country, Pastor Grant was my remaining source of Godly advice. I clung to that escape hatch as the minutes dragged out into eternity.

***

"I'll keep you in my prayers, Tex." Shaun patted my shoulder as we walked to the door.

I sniffled and thanked him. I knew my eyes were red, but the feeling of peace inside transcended any concern over my appearance. I hadn't gotten more than a few steps towards the library when the bell rang and students flooded the hall. It didn't take me long to spot Zev towering over the others and I altered my course to meet him. His entire bearing spoke of pure misery and I felt my heart go out to him, my own feelings intermingled with the God-given sympathy I'd gained. I smiled up at him, unable to stop myself. By the time I reached him, his scowl was shifting into a grin, a sliver of sunshine on a rainy day. Wow, that was sappy.

I spoke in a rush, needing to get everything out before I lost my nerve. "I know there are some things we need to talk about, but this isn't really the best place. If we could put off the heavy stuff until after school, I'd appreciate it. Let's just stick with the mundane things, small talk."

"After school? We can talk after school?"

Was that a tremor in his voice or my own overactive imagination? I wasn't sure. I studied my hands, gathering the strength I needed to speak again. After a moment, I raised my head, certainty flooding me. "After school, we'll talk. And then you can decide if you still want to be with me." I found that I couldn't look at him while making my final statement. "I'm not letting you go unless you ask me to."

Before I could hear Zev's reply, I spun on my heel and headed for Calculus. I went straight to the back of the room and slid into a seat. Out of the corner of my eye, I saw Zev come through the doorway and walk my way. I couldn't help it. I watched as he approached, completely oblivious to anything else until I felt a hand on my arm.

"Tex."

I started and turned towards the voice. My heart sank as I realized who'd been in the seat next to me.

"I haven't seen you since July." Erik leaned closer and smiled, his hand still warm on my arm. "And we didn't get to talk yesterday."

"Uh, yeah," I stammered. "I know." I could feel the heat rising in my face and prayed that it wasn't visible.

"You hung around that new guy all day."

I could hear the subtle accusation in Erik's words and opened my mouth to say something distancing but polite. Before I could, I saw Zev sink into the chair in front of me, and the glimpse I got of his face made my temper flare. I yanked my arm away from Erik and snapped, "I don't think that's really any of your business." I felt a small pang of guilt at the startled expression on Erik's face but cared more about what Zev was thinking.

The shrill tone we called a bell sounded as I leaned forward. Out of the corner of my eye, I could see Mr. Brendan opening his book and I knew I had only a few seconds to clear up what Zev had just seen. Thinking fast, I whispered, "Save me a seat in Bible, please. I don't want to sit next to Erik again." Then, unable to stop myself, I ran my fingers across the top of one broad shoulder, feeling the tingle travel up my arm as I returned my hand to my desk. I doubted he'd noticed the touch, but it would be enough to get me through the remainder of the day, a reminder of what I was fighting for.

Mr. Brendan cleared his throat and I valiantly tried to concentrate on what he was saying. By the end of the period, I honestly felt sorry for the guy. Out of the six students in the room, only three were listening, and one of them was his daughter Lily. Though I couldn't see Zev's face, I could see the fingers of his left hand restlessly tapping on his notebook. Long, slender fingers. Clean nails. Several small scars on the backs of his knuckles. All right, maybe I was a bit too riveted by his hand, but I never said *I* heard a word Mr. Brendan said. The other member of the class who didn't have Calculus on his mind was Erik. I knew this because I caught him alternating glares between Zev and myself. At one point, I had to bite my tongue to keep myself from yelling at him, interrupting a speech about... well, I'm not entirely sure what the speech was about because it was around that time that I noticed the way the muscles in Zev's back rippled under his shirt when he moved. Needless to say, thoughts of Erik were eradicated by the memory of Zev in the parking lot the previous morning, removing his bloodstained shirt...

My GPA was so screwed.

I was engrossed enough in my own thoughts that I almost didn't hear the bell ring. I stood, ready to walk to Bible with Zev. Instead, I caught sight of him as he vanished through the door connecting Mr. Brendan's room to Mrs. Peterson's. My heart sank. Either he hadn't understood what had happened with Erik or, I shrank back from the thought, he'd decided that I wasn't worth the trouble.

As I stepped into Mrs. Peterson's classroom, my doubts fled. Zev was sitting in the back of the room, smiling at me in a way that made me forget everything else existed. Almost shyly, he lifted a hand and motioned to the desk on his right. His book bag sat in the chair, saving it for me. I returned his smile, feeling like I was going to explode and trying desperately to keep myself from doing so. Besides the fact that such a reaction was bound to be messy, we still had a lot to get through before I'd be able to accept that he'd made a fully informed decision, and I didn't want to build my hopes too high. As I slid into the seat, the tips of his fingers rested against mine for the briefest of moments, and I knew that I had no chance. I couldn't stop this, not myself anyway. Only Zev could put an end to what was happening. And if he did, I feared that I would crash and burn.

Chapter Four: Crash and Burn a Long, Long Way From Home

ZEV

I entered the classroom feeling like things might turn out okay after all, but my stomach plummeted to my feet as I saw the handsome blond lean towards Tex, his hand settling on her arm as if it belonged there. I had a sudden urge to kill Erik Robertson, and my previously dispelled mood returned with a vengeance. I dropped into the chair directly in front of Tex. Even as disconsolate as I was, I couldn't bear to be any further from her, even if the proximity increased my misery.

"You hung around that new guy all day."

I gripped my hands together so tightly that they hurt. A bit of pain was better than me jumping out of my seat and strangling the *otrovnim zvijer* behind me. Or, at least, that's what I kept telling myself. I braced myself for Tex's reply, most likely an excuse about how she'd taken pity on the strange new student.

"I don't think that's really any of your business."

Without realizing what I was doing, I held my breath. Could the annoyance in her tone mean that she wasn't interested in the *limane nirk*? Maybe I hadn't misread her earlier. I couldn't be sure though. Tex didn't seem to have the normal 'girl' way of thinking. At least, not any girl I'd met before. My mental photo album flipped through people of the female variety, most of whom were little more than myriad hair styles and colors, and a few other differing attributes I didn't really want to dwell on at the moment. What I really wanted was to know what was going on inside that incredibly complex brain Tex had. I relegated the memories of previous romantic triumphs to a back corner of my brain. My every muscle was tense, every sense attuned to the figure behind me. I didn't even acknowledge the bell signaling the start of class.

Then, Tex was as close as her desk could allow her to be. *Eu podia sentir-lhe tudo ao meu redor.* It wasn't close enough. She whispered, "Save me a seat in Bible, please. I don't want to sit next to Erik again."

I was starting to relax when her fingers ghosted over my shoulder, the heat just discernible to my extra-sensitive senses. Flames shot across my nerves and I almost jumped out of my seat. As it was, I couldn't stop my fingers from curling into my palms, imagining that they were closing around Tex's hands. I let my mind drift as Mr. Brendan began a lesson I'd had memorized since the third time I'd been through this particular textbook. My brain kept replaying the shock of Tex's touch and didn't seem to want to hear any of my arguments against turning around, pulling Tex from her seat and holding her against me. Running my hands through her hair, over her soft skin. Cupping her cheek as I bent toward her. Her lips soft against mine. *Moj razlog, moja ljubav.* I shifted in my seat and heard the slightest change in Tex's breathing. I grinned. Apparently, I wasn't the only one not listening to Mr. Brendan's lecture. It was good thing I could do calculus in my sleep; otherwise, I'd never pass the class.

Forty-two minutes never felt so long. As soon as I heard the bell, I was on my feet and dashed into Mrs. Peterson's room, getting to the back desks before the room had finished emptying out. I tossed my bag into one seat and slid into the adjacent desk. I was beaming as Tex walked through the door, the crestfallen expression on her face making my chest tighten. *Co jsem myslela?* Maybe she hadn't meant the message for me. Maybe she'd been talking to someone else. I motioned to where my bag sat, and the clouds in her eyes disappeared, taking with them most of my self-doubt. When she handed my bag to me, I couldn't help myself. I 'accidentally' allowed my fingers to graze hers. The smallest vestige of contact was enough to make my skin hum and my mind flood with fantasies of kissing her, touching her. I had never wanted anyone more than I wanted her. I tried not to let her question about *El Hakkadosh* infringe on my very unholy daydreams.

Bible class would've been a blur similar to calculus if Mrs. Peterson had been as unobservant as Mr. Brendan. Unfortunately for me, this particular teacher had a gift for spotting inattentive students.

"Zev, if you'd care to join your classmates in taking out a blank sheet of paper, I'd appreciate it." Mrs. Peterson tone was one of patient amusement that kept me from being too annoyed with her for interrupting my current musings.

"Sorry, Mrs. P." I offered my most charming smile, the one I used to when I needed information out of a female, or the occasional male.

Mrs. Peterson smiled back, but didn't seem to swoon like other women did. Was I losing my touch, or was she one of those few who were immune to my natural allure? I didn't take the time to wonder, finding that I cared less about this development than I would have two days ago. Now I only had one person whose perception of me mattered. All previous conquests had faded away, as insubstantial as air and as unimportant to me as faith.

“All right class, as I mentioned yesterday, senior Bible is about preparing you for the future. Getting you to set goals, to understand which ones are realistic and what you will need in order to accomplish these goals.” Mrs. Peterson addressed the class. “What I want you to do is write them down. I want at least two each for the following times: one year from now, two years, five years and ten years.”

I scowled down at my paper. I hated these types of things. It didn’t matter what I wrote, I knew nothing would come of it. I didn’t have personal goals aside from enjoying my time on earth as much as I could. My eternal fate was sealed. Had been sealed for a very long time, and nothing I could do would change that. I sighed and scribbled down some nonsense that I knew would appease the teacher. A fair amount of study into human behavior gave some insight into what types of answers authority figures wanted when asking such open-ended questions. While it made essay questions a breeze and my grades outstanding, it led to a rather boring academic existence.

Once finished, I wanted to turn and read Tex’s list, curious to see where she pictured herself in the years to come. Like most people, she most likely viewed these goals as in the distant future, even one year being far away. No one I’d met ever had a true grasp on the concept of time, but Tex had proven me wrong in other instances, and I was sure that she’d astound me again. Before I could act on my impulse, Mrs. Peterson called for our attention once more.

“Now we’re going to take a look at what steps you will

need to take in order to achieve your goals. Is college right for you? If so, what type of college? What type of degree do you need? Is your dream job realistic? What are your back-up plans? How are you going to pay for college? What about marriage? Family?" Mrs. Peterson's questions faded into background noise as images crept to the front of my mind.

A beautiful sunset. Me down on one knee, fading rays glinting off of the gem in my hand. Sliding the band onto a slim, tan finger. A passionate kiss as twilight settled over us.

A charming little church nestled in a mountain wood. Flowers, preferably gardenias to match the perfume of the bride. A figure in an elegant white dress coming towards me. *Fermoso!* A solemn, heartfelt promise.

A simple, quiet home. A child held in the arms of his mother. Dark brown hair like mine. Pale gray eyes.

"Zev?"

I started as a hand came to rest on my shoulder. A familiar floral scent followed.

"It's time for lunch." Tex smiled down at me, letting her hand remain where it was for a lifetime of moments. "You kind-of drifted off there."

"Just thinking." I mumbled, feeling my neck grow hot. I was blushing! I hadn't done that since I was a child!

"About what?" Tex stepped back as I rose to my feet.

I hadn't thought it was possible for me to be more rattled, but the heat in my cheeks told me otherwise. I opened my mouth to downplay what I'd been fantasizing about, but found that I couldn't think of a single lie. *Je suis noyade en vous.* When I looked down at Tex, I realized that I didn't want to lie to her. So I offered a simple, one-word answer. "You."

"Oh." Tex's eyebrows disappeared under her unruly curls, and her eyes widened.

I could see a hint of red in her cheeks and grinned, bringing more color in under her tan. Okay, maybe I wasn't losing my touch. She definitely appeared affected by me. This realization pleased me more than I knew it should. I glanced around at the now-empty room and weighed my options. I wanted to be alone with her, wanted to get the answers to my questions and reveal my own secrets. I wanted to know if she could care for me when she found out what I was. But, more than that, for the first time in my existence, I wanted more time.

My resolve weakened, and I motioned with one hand while reaching for my bag with the other. "Same table for lunch?" As we headed outside, I felt the sting of guilt. I was pulling her deeper into my secret, and I knew it would hurt all the more when she turned away. But, if I only had until the end of the day, then I would enjoy as much of her company as I could.

As I'd discovered yesterday, time sped up when I was with Tex. Before I'd realized it, Tex and I were sitting in English, listening to Mrs. Davidson assign a reading from *MacBeth*. I didn't write the information down, seeing as I'd read the play more times than I could count and seen at least a dozen performances, including opening night in the Globe Theatre. No matter which way my conversation with Tex went, I didn't think I was going to be in the mood for 'toil and trouble' tonight. *Drwg Rhywbeth hon y ffordd hon.*

When the bell rang after computer class, I turned to Tex, not caring if my eagerness showed on my face. "Where do you want to go to talk?"

"I know a place. It's not far from here. If we cut across the corner of the park, it's only a ten minute walk." Tex gathered her books and headed for her locker.

We didn't speak as we dropped our things off in our respective cars and set off towards MacClay Park. The silence continued until we reached a high metal gate, the only entrance through the walls surrounding Willow Grove Cemetery. When Tex reached for the gate, I couldn't help myself.

"Here?"

Tex glanced up at me, nodded once and pulled. The rusted hinges moaned in protest, but gave way, opening just enough for Tex and me to slip through. I followed her up a slope, the path so overgrown with grass and dying wildflowers that I could barely see it. On the top of the hill was a small grove of trees shading a park bench and it was there that Tex stopped. She sat on the bench and looked up at me. Taking the hint, I sat next to her and waited for her to begin. Tex studied her hands for a moment, took a deep breath and then started to talk.

TEX

"I know a place. It's not far from here. If we cut across the corner of the park, it's only a ten minute walk." I retrieved my books from my desk, hoping my voice wouldn't betray my nerves. Zev was right behind me as I walked to my locker, but I didn't say anything. Instead, I led him across the parking lot, through the park, and up to Willow Grove Cemetery.

The cemetery was one of my favorite places to go and think. The most recent plots were from almost three decades before, the oldest dating back to the 1800's. Carson's Cemetery across town had opened when town officials deemed Willow Grove to have reached capacity. Very few people bothered to come to Willow Grove, so the maintenance crew let the grounds, notably the older sites, go wild. The top of the hill was one such place. The bench was old, the wood cracked and darkened from years of exposure. The trees, tall and ancient, loomed above calf-deep grass and the tangles of wild plants. It was peaceful and quiet, exactly what I needed. When I reached the bench, I sat at one end and raised my head to look up at Zev. After a moment, he took the seat next to me.

I found that I couldn't look at Zev and think at the same time, so I turned my gaze to my hands. I muttered, "Lord, give me the words to say."

Start at the beginning.

I inhaled, then exhaled, trying to calm my heart and nerves. It didn't work, but I knew I had to go forward. "A couple of months before I turned fourteen, I went with my friend, Elle Monroe, to her family's summer cabin. Our first week there, I met a boy named Teddy Sanders." I kept my voice as even as possible, darting glances at Zev throughout my speech, waiting to see the change to disgust and revulsion, but he remained impassive. Then, I reached the worst part of my story. The part I was most ashamed of. The part I desperately didn't want to tell anyone, least of all Zev. "On the Fourth of July, Teddy and I went for a walk along one of the quieter beaches and it started to rain. The nearest shelter was an old boathouse, so we went there to wait out the storm."

My resolve faltered and I stopped.

Tell him everything.

"Tex," Zev took my hand in his and warmth flowed over my skin. "It's okay." I looked down at his hand. His strong fingers curled over mine, and I summoned up the last of my courage.

I talked for almost an hour, my eyes tracing patterns of scars, pale against dusk. He didn't remove his hand, but twice his fingers twitched against my palm. Once when I spoke about the events of that rainy night. The second time when I mentioned Teddy's final statement to me. At that point, I thought I heard him speak, but I pressed on, afraid I wouldn't be able to finish if I paused.

"I told you this for two reasons. First, because I want you to know about my past. And, second, because I need you to understand why God is so important to me." I felt his grip tighten and certainty blasted shards of ice through my entire body. I was going to lose him. "God loved me when I thought no one could. He forgave everything I did. I owe Him more than I can repay."

"*Noli me tangere*!" Though I didn't understand the words or why he'd chosen them, his behavior gave me no reason to misunderstand their meaning. He yanked his hand away as tears spilled down my cheeks. I knew what was coming, but I'd made my choice and I intended to see it through. Anger settled on his face and I winced at the pain in his eyes. Agony tore through me as I realized my words would cause him more suffering. Inwardly, I pled with God for a reprieve.

You must give him the choice.

I clenched my hands into fists, nails digging into my palms deep enough to leave indentations. I ignored the physical pain, too caught up in the emotional anguish. “I care about you more than I thought I could ever care about another person, but I can’t be with an unbeliever.”

“So you’re choosing God over me?”

The tone was forbidding enough to make me cringe, but not enough to stop me from saying what was necessary. “I’m choosing your soul over my feelings.” I stood on legs that almost didn’t hold me and, for once, had to look down to see Zev’s face.

“Don’t bother.” Zev’s eyes blazed with such intensity that I took a step backward. “I’ve had a spot in hell reserved for longer than you can imagine.”

I sucked in a breath, torn by his words. I knew I couldn’t stay or I’d recant my decision just to ease his pain. I reached out and stroked Zev’s cheek, wanting to remember the sensations flowing from the tips of my fingers to every inch of my being. I whispered one last thing. “Come back to Him, and then come back to me.”

I turned and hurried down the hill, not looking back. I couldn’t see past the moisture in my eyes, but didn’t pause to wipe it away even as I stumbled through the park. I needed to get to the safety of my room before I gave myself over to the torment of a breaking heart. I didn’t really pay attention on the drive home, realizing only that I arrived safely and dashed up the stairs without a word to Clare. Fortunately for me, Mom was working late and I didn't need to think up an excuse to ignore her. If I didn't leave my room, Mom would assume I'd gone out with friends, and not be concerned when she didn't see me for dinner. I hadn't told her much about my issues with Gretchen and Susan. Now I was grateful for my decision to keep those problems to myself. Isolation appealed to me and I sank into it.

Had I said before that I would crash and burn? Understatement of the century. If that were the case, I'd at least have bones and ashes left. Try crash and disintegrate. All the king's horses and all the king's men couldn't put me together again. I curled into a ball on my bed, drawing my knees up to my chest. I wrapped my arms around my legs, holding them to me, as if the physical hugging would repair the damage to my heart.

Well done, My child.

"That doesn't really help." The words cracked.

Peace.

"Peace?" As often happened when I was upset, my temper flared and I had to fight to keep from shouting into the empty room. "How am I supposed to find peace after what I did? I already lost all of my friends and now You've taken the one person who could've made this year not just bearable, but enjoyable. The person I'm falling in love with. The one I thought You wanted me to fall in love with. And You want me to have peace about hurting him?"

Peace isn't dependent on circumstances, Tex.

My voice fell to a whisper. "He's never going to forgive me."

If I've forgiven you, does it matter if he does?

I shook my head as new streams squeezed out from under my tightly shut lids. "He hates me."

Shh, trust Me. Trust Me.

"But..."

Trust Me.

Slowly, my muscles unlocked and I was able to move again. I reached for my Bible. It felt heavy in my hands, and I didn't really want to open it. I didn't want to read words meant to comfort. I knew that once I did, I'd have to acknowledge that I'd done the right thing by being obedient, and that meant giving up my anger. And, at the moment, my anger was the only thing keeping me from turning into one of those deranged damsels who dissolved into despair. I loathed those types of people.

The only thing?

I closed my eyes, the gentle chiding enough of a reminder to bring things into focus. "How can causing that much pain be right?" I whispered, resting my forehead on the soft leather cover. The scent brought back memories from the past two years, of other times I'd sought solace in those pages. "I wanted to protect him. Take care of him. And now I've lost him."

But I haven't. Everything is in My care. Including Zev.

I nodded, unable to speak past the lump in my throat. I knew He was right. He always was. And always would be. I'd done all that was asked of me and now the choice belonged to Zev. All that was left for me was to wait and pray. So that's what I did. Through the neighborhood sounds of the Petersons' groundskeeper mowing the lawn and their toy poodle, Princess Fifi, yapping. Through sunset and dinner. Through Mom's enthusiastic exercise video. Through her nighttime routine of locking up the house. And through the night. I waited and I prayed.

Then came morning.

ZEV

I could hear the minute change in Tex's voice, and knew that we'd reached the heart of the problem. "On the Fourth of July, Teddy and I went for a walk along one of the quieter beaches and it started to rain. The nearest shelter was an old boathouse, so we went there to wait out the storm."

She paused, a blush rising in her cheeks. Without any hesitation, I reached for her hand, tempted to tell her what I felt every time we touched. *Ek aanbid jy*. Instead, I reassured her. "Tex, it's okay." No matter how bad she thought her transgressions had been, I knew that mine were much worse. Besides, she'd already made a claim of faith. That eliminated most of the negative possibilities right there.

Tex didn't take her eyes from our entwined hands. "I'd never had a boyfriend before. Never had a guy notice me before."

Somehow, I found that impossible to believe, but I didn't interrupt.

"So when Teddy kissed me, told me that he loved me, I believed him." The color in her face was draining away, leaving her pale under her otherwise golden skin. "Believed him so much that I didn't say no."

Ei koskaan! My outward appearance didn't change, but inside, a part of me was vehemently denying her words. She couldn't have meant what I thought she meant! Good Christian girls didn't do that. I pushed away the images of all of the '*goeie Christelike meisies*' I'd seduced over the years. Tex was different.

"Teddy knew exactly what to say."

I didn't need to hear her say his words. I already knew them. Had used them in dozens of languages. They echoed now in my mind. '*Je veux que vous*.' 'Let me show you how much I love you.' '*Amicule, deliciae, num is sum qui mentiar tibi?*' And, of course: 'we'll be together forever.' I felt my fingers twitch and regained my control. She wasn't done.

Tex continued. "Part of me knew that he was just saying those things to get what he wanted, but part of me didn't care. I wanted to be loved. Wanted him to love me. I let him convince me to have sex with him."

For a moment, I felt a flare of anger towards Tex. Then a dozen faces flooded forward, more crowding behind them, more than I wanted to think about. My emotions cooled. I couldn't play the virtue card, and had no right to be angry with Tex for what she'd done. I pushed aside the chaos swirling in my head and listened to Tex relate what had happened in the year following that summer. When she reached the end of her story and repeated Teddy's final words to her, I couldn't stop an oath from escaping past my lips. As it was, it took most of my concentration to not rip my hand off of hers. Not because I didn't want to be holding her hand, but because I wanted to kill that *salach francach*. Slowly and painfully, if possible. I mentally ran through the list of tortures I'd witnessed over the years. The Inquisition had been particularly inventive.

Then, Tex was speaking again, and all thoughts of retribution melted away. "I told you this for two reasons. First, because I want you to know about my past. And, second, because I need you to understand why God is so important to me."

My fingers tensed convulsively and I almost didn't stop them from crushing the bones they were currently cradling. Why did it always have to come back to Him?

"God loved me when I thought no one could. He forgave everything I did. I owe Him more than I can repay."

My voice came out in little more than a hiss. "*Noli me tangere*!" I yanked my hand away, knowing it was shaking with the effort it took me to rein in my temper. I bit my lips to contain the yell building inside because I wasn't sure if I wanted to scream at her, at *El Echad*, or at myself for being such a *zadek-klobouk*. It was happening again!

Her face was white, and there were tear tracks down her cheeks. "I care about you more than I thought I could ever care about another person, but I can't be with an unbeliever."

In my mind, I heard the crackle of flames. Heard the echo of another voice. 'Do not make me choose between you and God, my love.'

I spit my words at Tex, over four centuries of venom in one sentence. "So you're choosing God over me?"

Tex stood, but I stayed where I was. When she gave her answer, I was glad I had. I wasn't sure what would have happened if I'd been on my feet. "I'm choosing your soul over my feelings."

My soul? She was going to put this on me? "Don't bother." I heard my voice, rough with anger, speaking words meant to cut, to wound. Tex stepped backward, the shock on her face fueling my anger rather than pacifying it. "I've had a spot in hell reserved for longer than you can imagine."

I heard her quick inhalation and felt a burst of satisfaction that I'd managed to upset her. I almost regretted my pettiness. Then, she moved towards me and lifted her hand. What was she doing? Her fingers rested against my cheek for the briefest of moments. "Come back to Him, and then come back to me." She turned and fled, leaving me with her statement resounding in my head, the feel of her hand on my cheek. I stared after her until she disappeared through the gate, and then I was alone.

I couldn't think, couldn't breathe. I'd ignored my soul for so long that I hadn't realized it could still cause me pain, but I knew that what I felt was beyond a broken heart. A piece of me had disappeared with Tex. How was that possible? I barely knew her. I couldn't miss someone I hardly knew. Could I?

It's not just her you're missing, Zev.

I knew that voice. And I didn't want to hear it. "I don't miss You." I whispered fiercely.

Come back to me. The gentle and loving words fractured my defenses more effectively than an onslaught of accusation could have.

"Why should I?" I knew I sounded like a self-indulgent child, but I didn't care. "What did You ever do for me?"

Silence.

Memories came forward. Though not my oldest

recollections, I'd relegated these to the furthest reaches of my subconscious. A dark sky lit with the hosts of heaven. A fleeing family. The dead brought to life. Three crosses on a hill. A curtain torn in two. The empty grave.

Shame flooded me, igniting my temper. I jumped to my feet, turning my face towards the sky. Rage churned inside me, taking away any coherent claims I'd considered making. I screamed in inarticulate fury to *El Hashamayim*, to the God of the Heavens, the noise tearing from the depths of my neglected soul. As the sound faded into the late afternoon air, my anger receded, taking my strength with it, and leaving me with a gaping hole inside. I fell to my knees and dropped my head. My throat burned as I gave voice to my despair. "How can You do this to me again?" *Abbas.*

Come back to me. You have been gone so long. Come home.

"Why? Why would you even want me? I turned away from You. Did so many awful things..."

I love you. I never stopped loving you.

"I know, but I don't want you to."

It doesn't matter. I do and I always will. Selama-lamany. Selalu.

New pain, fresh and different, radiated through my being and I cried out. *El Hanne'eman*! *El Shaddai*! *El Roi*! My hands covered my head and the tears came. *Dduw, chyfnertha 'm*! Sunset came and, with it, the cooling of the air. The stars appeared, brilliant against black velvet. *El Hannora, El Haggadol, El Chaiyai, El-Channun.* I didn't move from where I knelt, drowning, dying, destroyed beyond repair. *El malei*

Rachamin. *El Yeshuati*. The hours passed.

Then came the morning.

Chapter Five: Time Stands Still, My Immortal

TEX

I woke with a start, making myself dizzy as I sat up too fast. I pressed a hand to my head and closed my eyes until the spinning stopped. My stomach growled, and I realized the other reason I was lightheaded. I hadn't eaten since my meager lunch the day before. I opened my eyes and swung my legs over the edge of my bed, not realizing until that moment that I was still wearing my school clothes. The events of yesterday flooded back to me, but the fear and grief had gone. In their place was a calm I knew to be nothing short of supernatural.

This cloud of tranquility stayed around me as I showered and dressed. Mom's door was still closed, so I did my best not to make any noise as I descended the stairs. I ate as I prepared my lunch, moving in the slow, sleepy movements of one whose mind isn't really on the task at hand. I pulled into my usual parking space, noticing that Zev's car was still there. Judging by the dew still glistening on the jet-black paint, it had been there all night. Zev was nowhere to be seen.

"Lord?" Panic punched through the serenity surrounding me.

Trust Me.

Peace settled in once more and I grabbed my bag. I smiled at a few people as I walked through the halls, but made no effort to engage in conversation. I slid into a seat at the back of the room, praying silently as I waited for class to begin. Just as the first bell rang, Zev came through the door. My heart did a strange flip, some double-tuck handspring thing that would've won Olympic gold if age limits were enforced. He seemed tired, but as soon as his eyes found mine, he smiled, and I forgot how to breathe. I don't mean I forgot *to* breathe. I mean, I forgot *how*. Time stood still. If I'd thought him handsome before, it was nothing compared to how he looked at that moment. He sat in the desk in front of me, and then turned to face me.

"Thank you."

I blinked. All right, hadn't expected that.

Zev continued, his shining eyes never leaving mine. "I wouldn't have found my faith again if it wasn't for you."

My smile stretched so wide that it hurt. It had all been worth it! Then I processed the full array of emotions on Zev's face. Something was still wrong.

"Are you free after school today?"

I nodded. I honestly couldn't recall if I was supposed to work or not, but I didn't care. If I needed to, I'd call off. I hadn't taken a sick day since I started that job.

"Good." Zev softened. "You told me your story, and now it's my turn. Afterwards, you can decide if you still want to be with me."

My own words echoed back at me and I opened my mouth to tell him that I wouldn't change my mind, no matter what he told me. Especially not now that the spiritual distance between us had closed. However, the bell interrupted what was sure to have been a wonderful and touching speech.

Peace, My child. Be patient and let him tell his story.

Part of me wanted to argue with that voice. To tell God that I'd done as He'd asked. Now that Zev had recommitted his life, we could be together. But even as my mind formed the words, I knew that I couldn't do it. I'd promised God that I'd see this thing through, and now I knew that it meant hearing Zev's story before pursuing a relationship with him. I sighed. Well, I'd waited this long to find the person I was supposed to be with, a few more hours wouldn't hurt.

***

Zev and I headed for the parking lot after the final bell, seeing, but not caring, about the curious glances thrown our way. I supposed it had been like that all day, but I hadn't paid attention to anything except the joy radiating from Zev. Between study hall and lunch, he was able to fill me in on everything that had happened after I left Willow Grove the day before. I almost cried as he recounted his conversation with God and the resulting revelations. I was ecstatic, but attempted to temper my enthusiasm. Part of me was still wary, remembering God's earlier caution, but a greater part was impatient, wanting only to finish out the day and leave with Zev.

"Tex."

A familiar voice called from behind me and I sighed. Another conversation with Erik was not what I wanted right now, but I knew if I ignored him, it would just make things worse. I grabbed Zev's wrist as I stopped, feeling that already-familiar tingle as our skin met. He glanced down at me, a mixture of puzzlement and sadness in his eyes. Oh. He thought I was backing out. I gave him a soft smile and motioned back towards Erik. "He wants to talk to me."

“I’ll wait by my car.” Zev tucked a stray curl behind my ear, the pad of his thumb grazing the pulse point in my neck as he retracted his hand.

My heart did another impressive routine and stuck the landing. A perfect ten. “I’ll be there in a minute.”

He nodded once, glancing towards Erik as he muttered something that sounded like “*Froncer en haut, bucko. Il ne travaillera pas*.” I made a mental note to ask its meaning at a later date. Judging by the smirk, it had most likely been a disparaging comment directed at Erik. I was so mesmerized by the grace of Zev’s gait as he walked to his car that I didn’t notice Erik until he was at my side. I again reminded myself to lay off the chick flicks before I turned into some empty-headed, cookie-cutter girly-girl. Maybe I needed a break from adjectives for a while as well.

“I don’t get it. What’s so great about the new guy?”

I turned towards Erik, annoyance already bubbling inside me. I pushed away the impulse to give a rude retort. “What do you want, Erik?”

Erik shifted his weight from one foot to the other, eyes downcast. “I was kinda wondering if you’d changed your mind.”

“About what?” Confusion drew my thoughts from Zev.

“Um, about going out with me some time.” Erik’s cheeks flushed.

He couldn’t be serious! One look at his face, however, told me that he was. I sighed. “I told you before that the answer was no. Why don’t you ask Gretchen?”

“Gretchen?”

I would've laughed at the tone of his voice if I hadn't been so annoyed by his persistence regarding me. I'd thought only fictional boys were this dense. "Erik, she's been crazy about you for years."

"That explains a lot."

My respect for Erik went up a notch as I heard the exasperation in his voice. Maybe I'd misinterpreted his jealousy before. Still, I was more eager to get going rather than I was trying to discern Erik's true motives. "I'll see you tomorrow, all right? And, Erik, why don't you ask Emily out? She's a really sweet girl." I turned to go.

"Tex?"

I stopped and waited, repressing the impulse to blow off the rest of the conversation and run to Zev.

"What's going on between you and Zev?"

I debated giving Erik a sarcastic comeback, or maybe just a reminder that my social life didn't concern him. But his tone was friendly concern tinged with resignation, so I gave him the truth even as I started towards Zev. "I don't know."

The ride to the Fort Prince University library was a quiet one, Zev and I each consumed by our own thoughts. I didn't even realize where we were going until he parked the car and I saw the familiar building. Once a church modeled after an old English cathedral, the massive stone building now housed the largest collection of books in the area. I'd always loved this library, with its arched, stained-glass windows and Gothic architecture. As always, I smiled as I gazed up at the impressive structure. Students passed us by without a second glance, absorbed in collegiate conversations or busy studying syllabi. Visiting high school students wasn't unusual in a town the size of Fort Prince.

We walked up the steps and my curiosity got the best of me. "What are we doing here?"

Zev smiled at me. It was the same smile he'd worn earlier that day, a mixture of grief and joy. "Come with me."

He started towards a corridor I'd been down once before when I'd gotten lost during a fifth grade field trip. Mrs. Bliss had lectured me for five minutes about paying attention to my surroundings, but stopped when she realized we'd wandered into a professor's lecture on the counter-productivity of banning literature. "That's a dead end."

Zev just kept walking, and, of course, I kept following. At the end of the hallway, I stopped, ready to say something witty, possibly quotable. Then, Zev raised a hand and reached for one of the ornate brass candleholders attached to the wall. Before I could ask what he was doing, he pulled down and, to our right, a section of the floor moved. All right, hadn't seen that coming. I knew my mouth was hanging open, but I just stared, unable to do anything else. This awkward position was developing into a very bad habit. In the back of my mind, I heard the childhood warning that if I kept it up, my face would freeze 'that way.'

"This library used to be a church."

"I know." I found my voice and interrupted. "I've lived in Fort Prince my whole life, Zev." My eyes moved from the dimly lit staircase to Zev's face.

One corner of Zev's mouth twitched up. He stepped up to the edge of the opening. "Humor me?"

I nodded, shivering as Zev held out his hand. My goosebumps had little to do with the chill wafting up from the darkness below. I moved forward and placed my hand into his much larger one. His face broke out into a full smile as his fingers came to rest on my wrist. I flushed when I realized that he could feel my heart fluttering like the wings of some crazed bird. A raven or crow most likely; nothing as delicate or beautiful as a hummingbird. I had a sudden image of my heart actually exploding if he kissed me. I really needed to work on calming down around him or we would have serious problems if – *when*, the aforementioned muscle insisted – our relationship progressed. My brain decided that it didn't want to argue the semantics.

"This building was modeled after a church in England." Zev began down the steps.

"Um, light?" I stood on the second step and peered down at the stone disappearing into blackness.

"Oh, right." Zev seemed to be thinking for a moment. "There's a lantern at the bottom, but for the steps, you'll have to trust me."

I gave Zev a half-smile, suddenly shy for an unknown reason. "I trust you."

Hm. Another unexpected jolt to my nervous system. Zev's hand was out of mine, his arm circling my waist before I could respond to either motion. In that moment, I found that I didn't care about the dark. Or the possibly treacherous stairs. Or the fact that the Fort Prince University library had a hidden staircase underneath one of its dead-end corridors. Actually, I didn't care about anything except the arm wrapped around me, the heat of his skin radiating through layers of clothes.

Zev continued the history lesson as we made our way down the stairs. Only my fascination with his voice kept my attention on what he was saying rather than wholly on his touch. "The original church had a series of secret rooms where the clergy would hide various political targets. When the founders of Fort Prince decided to construct an identical church here, the builders included the underground passages but didn't make it public knowledge. Over the years, as the architects died, that bit of information has been lost."

"But you know about it?"

We'd reached the bottom and Zev bent to retrieve something from the floor. He removed his arm from my waist and I had to bite my tongue to keep from asking him to return it. Quite literally. My tongue throbbed when it was released. Then a flicker of light cut through the dark and I realized what he'd been doing. The old lantern cast a golden glow over us both, and I realized that no light came from the entrance. I glanced back the way we'd come.

"There's a trigger on the steps, about halfway down. It shuts the door so no one has to remain behind to do it." Zev must've guessed why I'd been looking up the stairs. He took my hand again, threading his fingers through mine. "This way."

We walked the next hundred yards or so in silence, hands linked. I was surprised by how much I liked the cool, dark tunnel. Well, maybe it was the company. I was more aware of Zev's hand in mine, our wrists pressed together, his pulse pounding against mine, than I was of the rough gray rocks that made up the floor and low ceiling. Even with the dim lantern light, I could see the top only an inch or so above Zev's head. Then, we passed through an archway and, even in the pitch black, I had the impression of great size. There was a brief flash of light and then a flicker as a torch on the wall caught flame. Without any prompting on Zev's part, the first torch ignited a second, then a third, and so on around the room. To my amazement, the spacious cavern was filled, floor to ceiling, with bookshelves packed with archaic tomes, rolled parchments yellowed with age, and a few hundred volumes that appeared to have been published in the last fifty years.

I turned towards Zev, impressed but confused. "I don't understand."

Zev motioned towards an old-fashioned couch in the center of the room. "You might want to sit down for this."

"Okay." I spoke the word slowly, uncertainty creeping over me. A thousand thoughts flew through my head, none of them making sense. I sat.

Zev paced in front of me, fingers pressed together, index tips against his mouth, drawing my attention. He didn't speak for several minutes, and I stared, unsure if I wanted to break the silence. Tension thickened the air.

"I'm not sure where to start." Zev turned towards me, honest bewilderment in his voice. "I've never had to tell my story to anyone before."

I tried to help. "Start at the beginning."

Zev stared at me, as if something I'd said had caught him off guard. For me, it was common sense, but, apparently, there was something coming that I couldn't have foreseen.

Something I never would have expected.

ZEV

I ran home as the first hint of sunrise appeared over the mountains, giving in to the joy coursing through me, allowing myself to run at full speed. *Lavdi Zotit!* The scenery sped by while my heart sang with praises I'd believed long forgotten. *El Hakkavod, El Chaiyai!* I slowed up a bit when I reached my backyard. Did I want to talk to my parents before school or after?

Tell Tex the truth.

I stopped so suddenly that only my quick reflexes kept me from falling. Horror washed over me. "What?" I whispered.

Tell Tex the truth.

"*El malei Rachamin*, she'll never understand."

It's your turn to trust Me.

I sighed. "This is what You did to her yesterday, isn't it?"

Silence.

"I know, *El Shaddai*, You won't tell me someone else's story." I glanced at my watch and made a decision. "After school, I'll tell her."

Take her to the library.

Oh. That. *El Roi* wasn't going to let me get away with a neat little summary.

No, I'm not.

I scowled, but felt no real anger. "Okay. I'll do it." I scaled the trellis at the back of the house and climbed in through my bedroom window. "But I'm not telling Mom and Dad until after I get back. If Ellis overhears me, he'll kill her."

Silence.

In this instance, it seemed, that *El De'ot* agreed with me. I'd meant the statement figuratively, but fear chilled me as I realized that there might have been more truth to it than I'd originally intended. *El Sali*, protect us both.

***

"Start at the beginning."

I felt an absurd cackle rising in my throat. I hadn't known where to start my tale, but Tex's suggestion caught me off guard. It was more the ironic accuracy of her statement than anything else that amused me. I muttered, "*In exordium, Deus partum polus quod orbis terrarum.*" I didn't say it loud enough for Tex to hear though. Though it was possible she'd recognize the first verse of Genesis, even in Latin, she wouldn't understand the joke.

Start at the beginning.

I started to swear, but managed to catch the words before they slipped out. Not that it would have mattered to Tex since the expletives would have been in Romanian, but I would've known, and now it mattered to me. I didn't think I could look at Tex while telling my tale. I turned towards a bookshelf and ran a finger along the aged spines, trying to gather my thoughts.

All right. The beginning. "Do you know the Bible story about the Tower of Babel?"

"Of course."

"Then you know how the people scattered once they

realized that they didn't speak the same language anymore." I didn't need to see Tex to know that she was nodding in agreement. Anyone who'd spent their childhood in a Christian school would know the basics. "But there's a story that not many know. Well, not unless they're like me." I paused, expecting questions. Tex merely waited for me to continue. "After the Tower, two brothers, Aitan and Enos, led a tribe of fifty or so to the eastern sea. After seven years, Aitan revealed that he and half of the tribe had found a new obsession. The Perpetuum, as they soon called themselves, sought to become immortal. They believed that immortality would make them equals with *El Elyon* Himself. Some of Enos's group left, while the rest remained with the brothers, not participating in the Perpetuum's practices, but not stopping them either. As time moved on, the practices grew darker, more wicked. The trail of blood and death they left behind..." I shook my head, unable, even with my immense vocabulary, to put the horror into words. The slaughter of innocents. The atrocities committed in their quest. "They are the truth behind the myths of vampires, werewolves, the monsters hidden in the shadows."

I paused for a moment, weighing the truth of the statement. "Three years passed and *Elohim* sent a messenger to Enos, ordering him to kill the Perpetuum." I turned, giving Tex a smile that I was sure didn't look entirely natural. "Enos refused. The messenger then addressed those of the tribe who were not part of the Perpetuum, giving them all the command. This time he warned the people that rejection would result in dire consequences. None accepted the responsibility, too self-involved to take the risk." I perched on the arm of a nearby chair, needing to see Tex's reaction to what I was going to say next. The ancient wood creaked under my weight, but I knew the oak would hold. I'd made the chair myself. "For their disobedience, *El Olam* cursed them with the one thing the Perpetuum wanted. Immortality. And it is a curse. Many desire immortality, not just the Perpetuum, believing it a blessing to be able to live forever. To cheat death. But it's not. Watching everyone else die. Never able to achieve the reward of Heaven yourself. A soul trapped in a body on a sinful and dying planet, nothing to look forward to except the promise of an eternity in Hell after Christ's return. It's the worst form of torture."

Tex's eyes reflected her puzzlement. "I don't understand. What does this story have to do with you?"

I took a deep breath and closed my eyes, inwardly begging *El Emet* to let me off the hook.

Tell her.

No such luck.

I obeyed, opening my eyes and meeting Tex's gaze. "I was eight years-old when the Tower fell."

Countless emotions flickered across clear gray pools while I waited for the backlash.

Without taking her eyes from mine, Tex opened her mouth and said the one thing I couldn't have predicted. "Uh-huh."

Didn't she understand what I was saying? "Tex, I was born a little over a hundred and fifty years after the Great Flood." Maybe this would get through to her. "I can't die."

"Yeah, um, could you expound on that a bit?"

She wasn't accusing me of lying? Of being insane? I

couldn't wrap my mind around the possibility that this might actually turn out all right. *Certum est, quia impossibile.*

Tell her the rest.

Okay, here it goes. I looked down at my hands, picking at a splinter of wood that was older than Tex. Older than her great-grandparents even, but still far, far younger than me. "When *El Olam* cursed us, all those who were of age – those who could be held responsible for their decision – stopped aging. Our cells regenerate at a phenomenal rate, far beyond anything science could hope to achieve." I pulled the collar of my shirt aside to show her the mark just under my collarbone. "This appeared on all of the cursed and it's the last physical mark any of us received. Any scars we have are from before the curse. Anything else vanishes. Basically, we get sick, we get injured, but we heal almost instantly. The worse the wound, the longer the healing process, but it happens. We literally cannot be killed."

"Your nose."

I lifted my eyes to look at Tex again. *Erinomainen.* She was beginning to understand. I nodded. "It broke, but I snapped it back into place. It had finished healing by the time I went to change my shirt."

"I thought God wouldn't let anyone live forever." Tex had moved to the edge of the couch, elbows on her knees, hands together. She leaned forward, a look of extreme concentration on her young face.

"Technically, everyone does. Well, their souls do anyway." I couldn't watch as I said the next part. "For us Immortals, when Christ returns, we'll be judged along with the rest of mankind. And for our disobedience, our souls will be sent to hell."

I heard Tex's gasp, but didn't know what it meant, didn't possess the strength to raise my head to see her. I pressed my lips together, unable to speak around the lump in my throat. Since Elizabeth had burned, I hadn't cared where my soul would end up. Now, the full reality of the choice I'd made settled on my shoulders. Eternal separation from *El Chaiyai*, the God of my life. Gentle pressure on my wrist startled me and my head snapped up. I'd been so wrapped up in my thoughts that I hadn't heard Tex cross to my side. The torchlight glinted off of her tear-filled eyes. *Ang aking puso-aari sa iyo, magpakailanman, aking anghel.* How had I been so blessed to have someone like Tex in my life?

"Oh, Zev." She lifted her hand from my wrist and rested it against my cheek.

Well, that completely derailed my thought process. The train flew off the track. Choo choo. Wait, she was talking. Better pay attention. Come on, Zev, *svarbu*!

"Your soul isn't going to Hell." She gave me a watery smile. "God promises that if you ask for His forgiveness, He'll give it to you."

What? The simple statement of faith distracted me from Tex for a moment. Was it... could it... was I forgiven? For everything?

You are.

Ylistys Jumalalle! *Jumalan kiitos!* I felt a torrent of joy that almost sent me to my feet. It would have if I hadn't been so completely captivated by the idea of eternity in Heaven that my brain didn't have the remaining capacity to make my legs work. Eternity in the presence of *El Echad.* Familiar names flooded my mind. *El Hashamayim.* The God of the Heavens. *El Erekh Apayim avi ha-tanchumim.* Every part of me shook as my body tried to contain my elation. *El Hakkavat.* I wanted to shout. *Alabado sea Dios!* I was forgiven! *El Yeshuati! El Hannora!*

TEX

Pain filled those beautiful, dark eyes. "I was eight years-old when the Tower fell."

All right. Wait, what? Tower? He wasn't talking about the Tower of Babel, was he? He couldn't be. It wasn't possible. Was it?

All things are possible with Me.

A thousand thoughts and feelings raced through me. Disbelief. Wonder. Confusion. Awe. Love.

Right. There was that.

Hear him out, beloved.

I was having enough difficulty forming words, and then Zev looked up at me, and I lost the capacity for speech altogether. He was the one God had chosen for me, and I knew that he was what I wanted. The only one I'd ever want. I would listen. I would believe. And I would follow God's directions. That's pretty much all I could do anyway.

I opened my mouth to tell Zev all of this, but all that came out was, "Uh-huh."

I almost chuckled at the complete astonishment on Zev's face, but his next words took the laughter out of me. "Tex, I was born a little over a hundred and fifty years after the Great Flood. I can't die."

That answered one question. And brought up about a million more. I stuck with the easiest option. "Yeah, um, could you expound on that a bit?"

Zev devoted himself to picking at a splinter of wood sticking out of the arm of the chair. With a start, I realized that the chair, this building, this country, was younger than the man sitting across from me. I clasped my hands together in front of me to stop their trembling. I really hadn't had a clue as to what I was getting into when I'd agreed to God's request.

Do you regret it?

I studied the bent head in front of me, felt the usual erratic palpitations my heart had whenever Zev was around. Another perfect ten. No, I didn't regret it.

"When *El Olam* cursed us, all those who were of age – those who could be held responsible for their decision – stopped aging. Our cells regenerate at a phenomenal rate, far beyond anything science could hope to achieve." Zev tugged on his collar, revealing thin black lines marring the otherwise unblemished skin on his left side. "This appeared on all of the cursed and it's the last physical mark any of us received. Any scars we have are from before the Tower. Anything else vanishes. Basically, we get sick, we get injured, but we heal almost instantly. The worse the wound, the longer the healing process, but it happens. We literally cannot be killed."

The words popped out as soon as I tied the two ideas together. "Your nose."

Zev raised his eyes and I knew, with absolute, one

hundred percent, however cliché, certainty that I would never regret my decision, no matter what the consequences.

He gave further explanation. "It broke, but I snapped it back into place. It had finished healing by the time I went to change my shirt."

Right. Changing the shirt. The memory of that moment came to mind in cheesy, romance movie slow-motion, and I grabbed for a diversion. "I thought God wouldn't let anyone live forever." I shifted on the couch, placing my elbows on my knees as I leaned forward, hands still together.

"Technically, everyone does. Well, their souls do anyway." Zev bowed his head, hiding his face from me. "For us Immortals, when Christ returns, we'll be judged along with the rest of mankind. And, for our disobedience, our souls will be sent to hell."

"Oh." I gasped, tears flooding my eyes when his words registered. Agony ripped through me as I realized the torment Zev had suffered for thousands of years. I couldn't quite comprehend the vast number of centuries, but didn't really need to. I was on my feet and moving even as God asked it of me.

Reassure him. Remind him of My promises.

I touched his wrist. "Oh, Zev." When he raised his head, I placed my hand on his cheek, his skin hot against the chill of my palm, smoldering embers to cool silk, ready to catch fire with the slightest hint of oxygen. "Your soul isn't going to Hell." I smiled, feeling warm liquid spill down my cheeks. "God promises that if you ask for His forgiveness, He'll give it to you."

I could see the truth seeping into Zev's mind. His eyes lit up, changing them to a shade that made my knees weak. And that wasn't a cliché. I really wasn't sure if my legs could hold me much longer. I shifted, hoping to get better footing. Then Zev smiled and my heart did a series of pirouettes that a prima ballerina would've been jealous of. Apparently, gymnastics had progressed to ballet. He turned his face towards my hand and pressed his lips against my palm.

My head spun and then there was pain in my knees. Zev bent over me... wait, why was Zev bending over me? Oh. I was on the ground. That explained a lot.

"Tex, are you okay?" Zev knelt in front of me.

I nodded, moving from my knees to a more comfortable sitting position.

"Guess I have quite the effect on you." Zev's grin was annoying and attractive at the same time; I wasn't sure if I wanted to smack him or kiss him. Hmm, interesting choice.

Okay, off that track.

"It wasn't you." I tore my eyes away from Zev and turned them towards the ground where my feet had been, searching for something. Ah, there! A few loose sheets of paper poked out from under the chair Zev had been sitting on. I grabbed them and held them up. "I slipped on these."

"Oh."

Crap. Now he was sad.

I added, "But you didn't help my sense of balance any."

The smile returned, just as bright though not as smug.

I had to look away before I made a complete fool of myself. All right, more of a fool than I'd already made. I skimmed the writing on the papers I held. What I found managed to take my mind off of the feeling of Zev's lips against my palm. Warm, soft, full lips... all right, maybe not entirely off of the incident. I forced myself to focus on the words. Words make sentences.

Yeah, articulation was turning out to be an issue around Zev.

"What's this all about?"

Zev held out a hand, and I passed the papers over. He straightened, then held out his free hand to help me to my feet. I didn't hesitate, sliding my hand into his. With disconcerting boldness, I didn't release him once I'd returned to an upright position. Instead, I turned back to the royal blue couch I'd been seated on less than ten minutes before, pulling Zev with me. He didn't offer any resistance, settling himself at my side and resting our linked hands on his knee. He wasn't smiling anymore, but, when he turned his gaze towards me, his eyes were clear, untroubled for the first time since I'd met him.

"There's a bit more of my story that you need to hear." Zev paused, appearing to need a minute to gather his thoughts before he started again. I let him do so without interruption. "We, the Immortals, were given a chance for redemption. We were to fulfill our original task: eliminate the Perpetuum. *El Olam* promised us that once the last descendant of the Perpetuum died, the Immortals would regain their mortality. By this time, the Perpetuum had scattered." His thumb traced a circular pattern on the back of my hand, making it difficult for me to concentrate, but I put forth a valiant effort. "And that's when our quest began. First, we traveled as a group, but it didn't take us long to realize that we would need to split up. The Immortals chose Enos's wife, Dinah, to be the history keeper. Each time a member of the Perpetuum surfaced or was eliminated, she would take note. This room holds the history of the Immortals, our triumphs and disasters. The name of each person we've killed, every act of violence committed by our enemies, and by us."

Something registered in my mind and I interrupted whatever Zev had planned to say next. "After all these years, the Perpetuum," the word felt strange on my tongue, "are still around?"

Zev looked up from where his eyes had been following the motions of his thumb. He nodded. "Aitan was quite skilled at recruitment and many of his followers have the same gift. By the end of the century, his numbers far surpassed our own. And *El Olam* told us not to distinguish between those who had been born into the Perpetuum and those who had converted. The penalty was to be distributed evenly. Tracking became more difficult. As one century turned into two, into three, into millennium, the Immortals began to lose hope. Many tried suicide, discovering that even self-inflicted death was no longer an option. Without a way out, despair set in and the bond between the Immortals faded. Most abandoned the mission, choosing exclusion from society or pursuit of pleasure, wanting to get as much out of this world before the torment of the next. A few still hunt."

"What about you?" I asked.

"I hunted alongside my brother until the mid-1500s."

I was following the story a bit better now, connecting

things as my brain started to accept what Zev was telling me. The year. What I knew about history. Zev's previous comment about the girl he'd loved. "When Elizabeth died." A muscle in Zev's cheek jumped and I knew I was on the right track. "She was martyred, wasn't she? For being a Christian."

Zev's voice held a note of nostalgia and sorrow, but none of the bitterness or extreme grief I'd heard before. "Elizabeth was a Protestant in England during the reign of Queen Mary."

"Oh." I didn't need him to say any more. I had the whole picture now, and a part of me wished I didn't. I squeezed his hand, hoping to say with the pressure everything I couldn't put into words.

He continued. "For a while, I helped Ellis on bigger tasks, with larger groups, but for the past five or six decades, I've stuck with helping my mom."

His mom? My thoughts flew back to meeting Zev's family. My eyes widened, but this time I managed to keep my mouth shut. Yay for me. My brain reeled through the names I'd linked. Dinah, the historian. Enos, the leader of the Immortals. Aitan, the leader of the Perpetuum. Zev's mother, father and uncle.

"Yes." Zev saw my face and must have realized what I was thinking. "My family. They're the ones who started this whole thing."

ZEV

"What about you?" Tex asked.

My thumb rubbed against the smooth skin of Tex's hand as I answered. "I hunted alongside my brother until the mid-

1500s." Her hand was so small in mine.

"When Elizabeth died."

My entire body twitched. I hadn't expected her to put things together that quickly.

"She was martyred, wasn't she? For being a Christian."

I felt a wave of bittersweet sadness, though nothing like the agony I'd felt just the day before. In my return to *El Echad*, I'd come to terms with Elizabeth's death, discovering peace at last. I found that saying the words didn't bring pain. "Elizabeth was a Protestant in England during the reign of Queen Mary."

"Oh." Tex's fingers tightened around mine, and warmth flooded me.

I wanted to tell her more. "For a while, I helped Ellis on bigger tasks, with larger groups, but for the past five or six decades, I've stuck with helping my mom." Tex's expression was almost comical. I could see her putting everything together and helped her along. "Yes. My family. They're the ones who started this whole thing."

Tex pointed towards the papers in my hand. "And those are part of your mom's records?" She'd accepted my revelation with hardly a pause. Clearly, she was far stronger than I'd originally thought. It still didn't change my desire to protect her. To wrap my arms around her... "Zev?"

"Hm?" Tex watched me expectantly, waiting for an answer to her question. I felt my face grow hot. "Sorry. Got distracted."

Tex grinned, as if she knew what I'd been thinking. *Hala kalbim ol.* My heart constricted at the sight, and her grin widened. She lifted our hands, and I realized that she'd felt my pulse spike. Abashed, I opened my mouth to say something that probably wouldn't have made much sense. Then Tex's lips were against the inside of my wrist and I forgot every language I knew.

And my name.

Tex chuckled, her mouth moving against my skin, making my heart do very strange things. Maybe a new dance step. Set to some very upbeat music. I shut my mouth, my teeth coming together with an audible click. I still couldn't think of a single word to say, so I contented myself with staring.

"Nice to know I have that effect on you, too." Tex was still smiling as she returned our hands to my knee.

"Um," I stammered, trying to think of an intelligent reply. Something witty, romantic, anything but random noises that made me sound like a *chipiron en un chaco*. Okay, that didn't make much sense either. *Ich bin kein Eimerkapf.* Not any better. "Uh. Hm." Oh, yeah, mission accomplished. Wait a minute. I replayed her sentence in my head. She'd said "too."

Tex turned her head away and I realized that my lack of a response had sent the wrong message. I dropped the papers onto the couch and reached for her. I hooked my finger under her chin and brought her face around so that I could meet her gaze. *Cintaku.* I found words. "You definitely do."

An eternity passed around us. All right, it wasn't an eternity, since I had an idea of what that really felt like, but I would have been content with just those few minutes instead of all the thousands of years I'd already lived. Then Tex moved her head just enough to break contact and time moved on. She cleared her throat, eyes darting around until they came to rest on the papers at my side. I reached for them, reluctant, but ready to continue our conversation.

***

I watched Tex pace, charmed by the way she walked. *Eleganti*. I was fascinated. *Agraciado*. Absently, I wondered if she was a dancer and made a mental note to ask her. Tex was talking, her words clipped, precise even, with their rapid-fire delivery. Despite my preoccupation with Tex's progression back and forth across a small section of the room, I was able to follow her monologue.

"Let me see if I understand. You, your parents, and your brother, are something like over four thousand years-old because, about a decade after the Tower of Babel, your psycho uncle, in his pursuit of immortality, did enough awful things to warrant God's intervention, and, when you and all of your people refused to do what God told you to do, God made it so that none of you could die until the last of your uncle's group is wiped out." Tex glanced at me and I nodded to indicate that I'd followed the run-on sentence. She continued. "This room contains all of the records of the Immortals' pursuit of the Perpetuum." She lifted her hand, gesturing with the papers she now held. "Like these ones that give a detailed account of the deaths of two railroad tycoons in the late 1800s."

I wanted to defend myself, my family, but I held my tongue. Tex had to come to grips with my past if we were going to be together. And now, more than ever, I wanted that to be possible. *Amor est vitae essentia.*

Tex stopped walking and turned towards me. "Was this you?"

I shook my head. Before I could stop myself, I blurted out, "The name of the Immortal at the bottom of the last page is the..." The sentence faded away.

Tex finished it for me. "The killer." I nodded. After a moment, she added, "But you have. Killed. Your name is on some of these records."

I didn't look away or allow myself the shield of a wordless answer. "Yes."

Tex held my gaze for a moment, then shifted her attention to the papers, flipping through until she reached the last one. Her eyes widened slightly as she read the names written there. "Ellis. And Jael." A small smile appeared.

"What?" Curiosity overrode everything else. Why was she smiling at my brother's name? My stomach clenched, and not in a good way.

"My favorite Bible story." Tex's smile widened. "Jael and Sisera."

My anxiety faded and I snickered, partially in relief, partially in remembrance of the incident Tex had mentioned.

"What?" It was her turn to be puzzled.

I explained, unable to keep the amusement out of my voice. "Yeah, that's one of the few that people know, even if they don't realize it. Jael'd fallen in love and gotten married to this..." Once again, my sentence trailed off. Tex was staring at me, incredulous.

"That's not funny."

She sounded annoyed. No. Wait. I changed my mind. She

sounded like she was going to cry and I felt a surge of panic. “What’s wrong?”

“All of this is so unbelievable, but I’m trying really hard and you’re making jokes.” Tex’s voice was stiff.

I’d reached her side before I’d fully made the decision to go. I put my hands on her shoulders so she couldn’t turn away, struggling with the urge to pull her closer. “I’m not joking, Tex. I’m laughing about the irony of that being your favorite story. Sisera was a Perpetuum and Jael is an Immortal.” Tex finally raised her face so that I could see her. I gave a crooked smile. “In fact, I used to have a crush on her when I was a kid. She’s older than me and always had a thing for Ellis. For a time, anyway.”

Something flashed across Tex’s eyes and then was gone. One side of her mouth twitched upwards again. “Silly girl.”

I grinned, warmth engulfing me from head to toe. I’d long since gotten over my infatuation with Jael, but she’d started a precedent regarding girls and my brother. *Jeg vil elske deg for alltid.* Tex’s two words banished those feelings. “I’ll be sure to pass that along the next time I see her.”

Tex couldn’t quite cover up her shock and I decided that I rather liked the way it looked on her. I slid my right hand from Tex’s shoulder, up her neck, resting my palm on her cheek, my last two fingers on her jaw. My thumb brushed against her lower lip and, suddenly, none of this was funny. “I won’t be angry if you want to walk away, now that you know what I am.” I could feel the pain inside of me, claws ripping away at just the thought of her leaving. But, I knew that I had to be fair.

"Why would I walk away?"

I studied her face, wanting to commit it more to memory than I already had. As if that were possible. No matter how many years passed before Christ's return, I knew I'd never be able to forget what she looked like at this moment. Nor would I want to. She knew what I was, but I felt the need to repeat it, not wanting to give in to the hope I felt welling up inside of me. I knew only too well how hope and love could crush and destroy. "Tex, I'm an Immortal."

Tex shook her head. She lifted her hand to her face, covering mine as well as she could. "No, you're not." Even though her voice was low, her words were firm. "You're *my* Immortal."

Chapter Six: Catch Me, I'm Falling Harder Than the First Time

TEX

I didn't really remember the drive home. Part of my brain was still processing the whole 'thousands of years-old assassin for God' thing. A not-so-small portion of my mind was recounting every touch, every word, gauging action and reaction. But louder than all of that was the part of me that still couldn't believe what I'd said. I'd actually called him, "*my* Immortal." Like I had some claim on him. Then, there were his whispered words, so soft I'd begun to believe I'd imagined them.

"Yes, *'m cara,* I am."

The mere possibility that they'd been real was enough to make me shiver. And then, recalling the way his eyes had darkened just before he'd spoken... my heart rate doubled just thinking about the depth of emotion in those almost-purple irises.

I tossed my book bag onto the kitchen counter and headed for the fridge. I really needed something to drink. When I emerged with a bottle of water in my hand, my mom was standing in the center of the room. I took one look at her wild hair and make-up free face, and all thoughts of Zev flew away as concern replaced them. To be honest, he wasn't far away, but he was at least out of the general vicinity.

"What's wrong?"

Mom glared at me and I suddenly wondered what time it was. I glanced at my watch. Oops. Midnight. And on a school night. While I hadn't had a curfew since – well, ever – I usually made it into bed by eleven thirty on school nights, and I always phoned or texted to tell her if I'd be late. Not that it had happened much, especially in the last few months. No wonder Mom was so freaked. I started to apologize, but Mom cut me off.

"Sylvie called."

Crap. I did have to work tonight. I'd have to call Sylvie tomorrow and apologize.

"She said you didn't show up for work." Mom's words were curt, unusual for my easy-going parent. "I called Gretchen and Susan."

This was just getting worse.

Mom took a step towards me. "They said you were probably out with some guy."

And we were at worst.

"Tex, what's going on? This isn't like you."

I sighed. "Let's sit down." I waited until Mom and I were both settled at the kitchen table, then sent up a quick prayer for wisdom. I felt a rush of relief as the words came. "First, I need to tell you about what happened with Gretchen and Susan this summer. Then, I'll explain where I was and who I was with." Mom nodded, unusually quiet. "Do you remember the picnic I went to on the Fourth of July?"

I spoke for ten solid minutes, summarizing everything that had happened over the previous two months. Once I finished, I paused, waiting for the barrage of questions I knew was bubbling inside my loquacious mother. She was silent for a few seconds and I studied her face, trying to find some hint at what she was thinking. The soft glow of the energy bulbs created a halo of golden light around her head and shadowed her features. My fingernail clicked against the dark walnut finish as my patience waned and nervousness increased.

"I never really understood why you hung out with those two." Mom reached for my bottle of water and took a sip. "Especially after your whole Christian thing two years ago."

I wasn't sure which part I wanted to respond to: Mom's easy acceptance of what had happened or her casual reference to my faith. Mom didn't understand my change, chalking it up to normal teenage spiritual dabbling. She herself had been through almost as many religions as boyfriends. I didn't have to wonder where to go next, though, because Mom went there on her own.

"Tex," Mom put a hand on my arm. "I am sorry about your friends, but I'm a bit more concerned about this guy."

"Zev." His name was silk on my tongue. Crap! Focus, Tex. "His name's Zev Avatos. He's new, just moved here from Ohio with his parents. They bought the old Ross place and moved in this past weekend." I edited my first sight of Zev and skipped ahead to the stuff Mom would want to know. "He's eighteen and a senior at New Hope. After school today, we went to the university library. I guess I just lost track of time."

"It's midnight, Tex. Am I supposed to believe that the library's still open?" Mom leaned closer and dropped her voice a notch. "You don't have to lie to me, you know. I just want to make sure you're being safe."

"Mom!" Heat poured into my face as I realized what she meant.

Unfortunately, my mother misinterpreted the reason for

my embarrassment and sat back, both hands in the air as if she was surrendering. "It's all right. You don't have to tell me anything. Dr. Miller can write you a prescription for birth control..."

"Mom," I held up a hand. "I don't need..."

Mom continued as if I hadn't said anything. "Until then, the condoms are in the purple tissue box next to my bed."

I tried to scream, but barely managed to make a strangled noise that sounded like a cross between a dying guinea pig and an angry goat. Don't ask how I know what either of those sound like, I just do.

"But don't look in the blue box. You don't want to know what's in there."

I wondered if the coroner would mark *mortification* as my cause of death. It would be very likely; unless, of course, *brain implosion* was an option.

"Mom! Please stop!" I considered getting down on my knees to beg, deciding at the last second that perhaps I had a small shred of dignity to which I could still cling. "It's not like that."

Mom gave me that annoying look that all parents have. The one that says 'sure, of course it's not' in a tone more sarcastic than any human vocal cords are able to produce. She pushed her chair back from the table and stood. "It's late, so I'm going to head for bed. Please, if you're going to be off with this new boyfriend of yours, call or leave a note next time so I don't worry."

I'd recovered enough to apologize. "Sorry about tonight, Mom. I'll remember next time." I felt a twinge of guilt at

Mom's words. I knew she loved me, but I'd never realized that she worried about me. Then again, I'd never really given her a reason to before. I'd always been responsible, sometimes more so than my mother herself. Well, my sixteenth birthday party had been a bit of a disaster, but that had been thanks to Gretchen, Susan and some out-of-town friends they'd invited. I didn't really count that.

It wasn't until Mom disappeared upstairs that I processed the word she'd used. 'Boyfriend.' Was that really what Zev was? We'd talked a lot about history and the Immortals, but not about who we were to each other. It hadn't seemed important at the time. I trudged up the stairs, mulling the word over in my mind. Somehow, I equated a 'boyfriend' with someone like Teddy or even Erik more than I did with Zev. My feelings for Zev were stronger than anything I'd felt before. Maybe 'soulmate' was more appropriate, but I cringed at how vapid the word sounded, like something out of one of those novels, the ones Grandma Bug had always called 'bodice-rippers.' You know, the ones that have pictures of shirtless guys, hair waving in the wind as they chased after women whose proportions only existed in the land of fiction. I searched my mind for another, a better, description of Zev and our relationship.

Do you really need a word?

Sometimes, I could almost hear the amusement in God's voice when He talked to me. I figured that with all of the baggage I'd come with, a bit of humor at my expense was the least I could offer. I walked down the hall, answering as I went. "No, I guess not."

He is yours. Isn't that enough?

I paused, one foot inside my room, the other still in midair. After a moment, I answered. "Yes, it is."

I climbed into bed less than twenty minutes later, brain still scrambling around the surplus of new information I'd gained. With each turn, my thoughts moved slower and, before the last song on my CD ended, I'd fallen asleep.

Despite the restlessness and insanity of my last few days and nights, I woke strangely refreshed. For the first time in almost three months, I'd slept, uninterrupted, through an entire night... well, early morning. I didn't try to delude myself as to why things had changed. Everything about me, from head to toe, soul to skin, knew that my life had been altered in some immutable way.

This is just the beginning, beloved.

***

When I reached the school, Zev was already there, leaning against that car of his and sporting a smile that made me need a few extra seconds to compose myself. Zev and I walked to the school, hand in hand, reluctantly moving apart once we crossed the threshold. Neither one of us wanted to push NHCS's 'hands off' policy and risk a detention we'd actually have to serve.

"Well, aren't you Little Miss Popular."

Even Gretchen's snide comment couldn't darken my day. I ignored her and kept pace alongside Zev, stealing glances up at him as we walked. Only the fear of running into some solid object – or loitering student – kept me from staring at Zev the entire time. Out of the corner of my eye, I noticed Susan fall in step beside Gretchen as the pair followed Zev and I to our lockers. In my glimpse of them, I noticed that both girls were wearing the scarves my mother had given them for the previous Christmas. It was nice to know that their disdain for me hadn't transferred to expensive gifts. The sarcasm in my mental voice was quite impressive.

Zev didn't acknowledge their presence, speaking to me instead. "You never did tell me if you were supposed to work yesterday or not."

I groaned. "I need to call Sylvie during study hall or I'll be lucky to keep my job." Sylvie's call had disappeared from my thoughts as soon as Mom had changed the direction of our conversation last night. As soon as that memory entered my mind, I could feel heat rising to my cheeks and prayed that Zev wouldn't notice. I didn't want to have to explain *that* to him. In fact, I didn't really want to try to explain it to myself. Better to leave that entire subject elsewhere. Preferably an entirely different section of the known universe. Or unknown. Either one would work for me.

Something about my statement had apparently confused Zev, so I focused on that instead of the images of dancing purple and blue tissue boxes that lurked at the edges of my mind.

"I'm not sure I understand."

"Um, if I don't call Sylvie to explain why I didn't show up yesterday, she might fire me."

Zev rolled his eyes and pulled his textbooks from the

bottom of his locker. "I meant that I didn't understand why you have a job."

My locker clanged shut and I snapped the combination lock into place. Sad to say, but theivery wasn't out of the ordinary at NHCS. Things had gotten better though; fewer items vanished over the weekends and on Wednesday nights when youth group was in session. Pastor Grant was better at keeping an eye on his charges than previous youth pastors had been. I started to shift my books from one arm to the other as I answered Zev. "Well, you see, there's this stuff called money and if you want to buy things, you need those green pieces of paper with dead presidents on them."

"Funny, Tex." Zev plucked my books from my hands and added them to the pile in his arms. "I thought your family was pretty well off."

"Family?" Susan snorted from her position to my right. "It's just her mom."

In their usual tag-team manner, Gretchen picked up where Susan had left off. "Daddy Dearest never has been in the picture. Then again, I doubt if Mommy even knows who he is."

If Gretchen or Susan had seen the anger crossing Zev's face, I doubted they'd be so eager to gain his attention. I knew he wasn't mad at me and I still felt like running away, most likely to a bathroom. I put a hand on Zev's arm and spoke in a low voice. "Ignore them." Zev's countenance was so severe that I jerked my hand away before I could stop myself. My movement got through even if my words hadn't and Zev's face softened. I added, "That's a story for another time."

Zev nodded, setting my books on one of the back desks. "Work?" He prompted.

I waited for Zev to sit next to me before answering his original question. "Before I go to college next year, I'd thought about going on a mission trip, maybe to Uganda or someplace like that, and my mom said she'll pay the difference if I saved for it."

"She won't just pay for the whole thing?"

I shook my head. "Mom believes in earning things. Also, she doesn't get the whole Christian thing. She thinks it's a phase and I'll grow out of it with time."

"Speaking of phases," Susan slid into the seat in front of Zev and leaned towards him, dark eyes glowing something I recognized from the Discovery Channel, or maybe Animal Planet. Predator stalking prey. Maybe a hyena... in heat. "Let me know when you're ready to move on to someone a bit more your league."

Zev reached towards me and rested his hand on my forearm, bringing goose bumps to my skin even though it was a warm morning. He gave Susan a perfunctory once-over and turned back to me with such an obvious dismissal that Gretchen said something that would've earned her a detention if a teacher had heard her. Hm. Apparently the hyenas hadn't realized that their desired meal would fight back. Okay, no more educational television for a while.

Zev spoke in a low, clear voice. "*Wees kalme sjaalvrouw. Ga weg.*"

At least, that's what it sounded like. I had no clue what he actually said. Apparently, neither did Gretchen, but the tone made it obvious that whatever the words meant, they weren't complimentary.

"Excuse me?" Gretchen stammered, anger making her voice shake.

"*Riamh, olc cailleach feasa*. Go bother someone else."

A snicker from the other side of the room indicated that our conversation was being eavesdropped on, not exactly an uncommon occurrence in a school as small as NHCS. In fact, keeping a secret in this school was harder than getting Gretchen and Susan to shut up – both feats that Zev had managed quite nicely. I couldn't help the pure pleasure I felt when seeing the fury on Susan's face, but I managed to restrain myself and not make any further comments. Instead, I returned to the previous conversation and let the rest of the day slip by.

The afternoon was hot when Zev and I headed for our cars, but I didn't pay any attention to the temperature, too focused on the few precious moments I had with Zev before I had to leave for work. Sylvie hadn't been happy with me, but she'd taken my impeccable record into account and cautioned me that, while she'd let this instance go, another no-show would have consequences. This meant that, no matter how much I wanted to spend the rest of the day with Zev, I couldn't be late.

We stopped in front of my car and faced each other, squinting against the bright sun. I strengthened my grip on Zev's hand and smiled when he returned the pressure. Just as I was getting ready to say good-bye, he spoke up.

"Are you working this weekend?" Zev shifted from one

foot to the other and I took a second to wonder what was making him nervous.

"Saturday morning and early afternoon. I get off at four o'clock." A part of me suspected what was coming next, but I didn't want to assume. As far as I knew, Zev wasn't familiar with traditional dating methods. Not that I had extensive experience in that area myself.

"I was wondering if you wanted to maybe go out on a real date."

The words came out in such a torrent that I almost couldn't follow them. When I did process what he'd said, I felt a blaze of warmth that had nothing to do with the weather. I stared up at Zev, resisting the impulse to jump up and down like a small child, contenting myself, instead, with swinging our joined hands back and forth. With a start, I realized that Zev was talking again.

"...if you're busy, that's okay. I mean, you don't have to if you don't want to."

What was he talking about? My face must've shown my confusion because he expounded, his grip on my hand loosening.

"You don't have to be worried about telling me that you don't want to go."

Oops! I'd been so excited about the question that I'd forgotten to answer. "Of course I want to go!" I'd never truly understood the meaning of the word 'blurt' before that moment. The pure joy on Zev's face, however, far outweighed any embarrassment I felt about my outburst. I hurried to explain. "I didn't think I needed to answer. I figured it was obvious."

"Apparently, I'm not as smart as I think I am." Zev raised our linked hands and skimmed the back of his against my cheek. "I need constant reminding that you want to be with me."

"I'll wear a sign." I glanced at my watch and then sighed. "I've got to go to work." I turned my attention back to Zev, not that it had been very far from him to begin with. "Call me later with details."

"Details?" Zev raised an eyebrow.

I rolled my eyes. "You're right. You're not as smart as you think you are. Details about that date."

"Right." Zev grinned. "In my defense, you're very," he paused to search for a word, "distracting."

"Is that a good or bad thing?" Was I flirting? I think I was.

"Good. Definitely good." Zev stepped away first, maybe knowing that I wouldn't be able to make the first move. "I'll talk to you later."

I climbed into my car, head tingling. I hadn't realized that five words could make me go loopy. Then again, ordinary didn't apply much when dealing with Zev. When I was with him, all the regular rules seemed to go out the window. And down the street and out of the state.

ZEV

With the exception of hearing Tex's voice in my head repeating "you're *my* Immortal," I didn't really remember the drive home from the library. Fortunately, driving was second nature to me and I pulled into my driveway without incident.

Despite my lack of perception on the road, I still had enough presence of mind to notice the lack of a certain ugly vehicle and I breathed a sigh of relief. Only the porch light was on and, with Ellis not in the house, that meant I could make it to my room without encountering inquisitive family members. If Ellis had been present, lack of light could've meant an ambush just as easily as it meant that everyone had retired for the night. While I wanted my family to know about everything that had happened over the past week, I was too exhausted for a lengthy conversation. Fifteen minutes and a quick shower later, I dropped onto my bed and was asleep almost before my eyes closed.

***

"I was wondering if you wanted to maybe go out on a real date." The words poured out of my mouth, speed set by the racing of my heart. Why was I so edgy? I was holding her hand, wasn't I? As soon as I thought it, Tex began to swing our hands back and forth. But she didn't say anything. *O quam cito transit gloria mundi*. The air rushed out of my lungs as precious seconds passed without her answering. I dragged in a breath and tried to repair the worst of the damage. "Of course, I might be rushing into things. If you're busy, that's okay. I mean, you don't have to if you don't want to." The strength drained from my limbs and my hand went slack in hers. "You don't have to be worried about telling me that you don't want to go."

Tex almost didn't let me finish. "Of course I want to go!"

Maravilloso! I wanted to shout, throw my hands into the air and dance around the parking lot like a child, or possibly, a deranged lunatic. Through thousands of years of self-control, however, I managed to limit my show of elation to grinning like an *imbecil*.

Tex continued and I hung on every word, all the while resisting the urge to start bouncing on the balls of my feet. "I didn't think I needed to answer. I figured it was obvious."

An overwhelming compulsion filled me and I was helpless to resist. The flowery language I'd once mocked made more sense to me with each minute I spent with Tex. I lifted the hand that was holding hers and let the back of mine brush her cheek. Her soft skin set mine singing. I smiled. "Apparently, I'm not as smart as I think I am. I need constant reminding that you want to be with me."

Her eyes shone with humor. "I'll wear a sign."

I saw her eyes dart to her watch and I bit back a groan. I knew what was coming and committed myself to absorbing the image of her face. Each time I closed my eyes, I saw every line, every curve and dip, the glowing shade of her tan, but it still wasn't enough.

Wait, she was saying something. "Call me later with details."

"Details?" What had we been talking about? I raised my eyebrow, trying for debonair and suave. I was pretty sure that I managed neither one.

Tex rolled her eyes. "You're right. You're not as smart as you think you are. Details about that date."

Oops. "Right." I tried another tactic. "In my defense,

you're very..." What did I want to say? *Tu es mon destin*? While that was accurate, it wasn't what I was looking for. I settled for a word far too trite. "Distracting." That was a bit of an understatement, but it'd have to do.

"Is that a good or bad thing?"

The grin on my face widened. "Good. Definitely good." It took all of my willpower to release her hand and step away. If I didn't leave now, she'd never make it to work on time and I didn't want her to get into any more trouble on my account. "I'll talk to you later."

I sat in my car until Tex pulled away, debating about going home. Tex may have told her mother, but I wasn't certain I was ready to share with my family.

It's time, Zev.

Guess that settled it. I sighed. He was right. I needed to come clean with my family. About everything. And that wasn't a conversation I was looking forward to. Nevertheless, I'd shirked my duty long enough. No more. I was going to obey now, even if it meant suffering through what were sure to be numerous lengthy lectures. For the first time since I'd started driving, I purposefully drove under the speed limit, wanting to delay the inevitable more than I cared about following traffic laws.

As I pulled into the driveway, my attention was instantly grabbed by a vexing shade of yellow. I smacked the palm of my hand against the steering wheel and cursed in Arabic, pissed that my brother was already here. I was instantly sorry and muttered an apology followed by a plea. "Father, *El malei Rachamin*, I'm sorry about that. Now, please, give me strength. *Dio, aiutami.*"

The house was quiet when I entered, but that didn't mean anything. Millennia of training in the art of undetectable assassination made silence second nature. Mom always said it was a gift with Ellis. Me? I had to work at it. While I was good enough to do what needed to be done, no one could get in and out of a secure, locked facility like my big brother. Well, except Mom. That had been another reason for Ellis's negative reaction to my 'retirement.' He hadn't just lost me. He'd lost an entire team of assassins when our parents followed me.

"You took her into the library."

I took a second to marvel, with only a hint of sarcasm, at my brother's deduction skills as well as his stealthy approach before turning to face him. "Yes, I did."

Ellis's eyes narrowed and his hands balled up into fists. One would think that after all these years he'd have more control over his emotions. I didn't back away, but took a cautious step to the side, putting a plush recliner between the two of us. When Ellis moved in my direction, I tried to remember if my parents had any particular affection for the forest green furniture in front of me. Collateral damage when two Immortals fought tended to be higher than a normal domestic disturbance.

"You should have consulted us." Ellis's voice was low, dangerous.

"What's going on, boys?" Once again, our mother interrupted what could have escalated into a physical altercation.

Ellis continued to glare at me as I answered. "Tex knows

about us."

"Zev?"

I steeled myself against the onslaught to come and answered. "I love her."

"*Vous l'idiot stupide*." Ellis spat the words from between clenched teeth, but even his vehemence couldn't cover the gasp of surprise from my mother.

"You cannot be serious, Zev." Ever the voice of reason, my father entered the conversation. "You barely know her."

"Mr. Hopeless Romantic probably thinks it's love at first sight, like his precious Elizabeth." Ellis hadn't continued his forward motion, but his body language remained tense. "Is that it, Zev? Did you see her and decide to abandon your family and everything you're supposed to be doing?" He sneered. "Wait, you already did that for love."

"*Haista paska*." I won (barely) the fight against chucking my newly re-found faith aside for the simple pleasure of beating Ellis – well, not to death, but as close as we could get. "This is different."

"Sure it is, because you've fallen harder this time, right?" Ellis turned towards our mother. "I thought you said that he'd come to his senses. That we were going to start hunting together again. As a family."

I was momentarily distracted as my previous suspicions were confirmed. I, too, pivoted in my mother's direction. "That's what this whole move was about, wasn't it? The family business." I said the final three words with as much venom as I could muster. After more than four thousand years, I had a lot.

Mom crossed her arms over her chest and I knew that my guess had been correct. We'd all become skilled at reading each other's body language. "Zev, for the past four and a half centuries, you've been avoiding your responsibilities, helping only when we pressure you. Your father and I feel that this has gone on long enough. If we're ever going to rid the world of the Perpetuum and regain our mortality, we must work together."

Ellis gave a snort of derision. "Mother, you don't honestly believe that, do you?"

"You don't?" Mom appeared startled by Ellis's revelation. I took a moment to marvel at how someone with so much world experience could be so naïve when it came to her eldest child.

Ellis shook his head. "I just want to kill as many of them as possible." I shuddered at how casual his reference to murder was. "Which is what we're supposed to be doing anyway. The reason doesn't matter."

Back to Tex.

I scowled. I didn't want to bring the conversation back to Tex. If Ellis and Mom continued down this particular path, there was a good chance I could get away without any further confrontation regarding the woman I loved.

You said you were going to obey.

The tone was gentle, but the reminder still stung. All right. Message received.

"I don't see what this has to do with Tex."

Ellis brought his attention back to me. "Mom and Dad are ready to return to the mission. This girl just complicates things.

Again."

"It's my choice, Ellis."

"Maybe." He glanced at our mother. "Make sure we're ready to move by tonight. I'll deal with the complication myself." He started towards the door and I reacted. Ellis may have been quieter, but I was quicker. I vaulted over the chair, grabbed Ellis's shoulders and slammed him against the wall, ignoring the crack of plaster and the disapproving exclamation from my mother.

His surprise at my aggression gave me a split second's advantage. I used it to press my forearm against his neck, putting pressure on his windpipe. Granted, none of us could die, but suffocation wasn't a pleasant process, even if we always survived. Due to an unpleasant incident involving an iceberg, a small Inuit child and a stranded seal, I knew this to be true. *El Olam* may have made our bodies heal rapidly enough to prevent death or permanent injury, but He had left us the ability to feel everything, including pain. Many of us had a high tolerance for various forms of distress, but we weren't masochistic.

"You want to take your hands off of me." Ellis used up some of his air on a threat I didn't acknowledge.

"You're not going to touch Tex, you *arrogante pedazo de basura*." I resisted the urge to crush Ellis's throat on principle alone.

"She knows about the library, about who we are."

"Let it be, Ellis." Father's voice had an edge. "You know that she cannot harm us."

"That's not the point." My brother's glare didn't waver

from me. "It's been long enough. Another few decades – if she lives that long – is more than I am willing to wait. Zev's loyalty should be to his family, his duty, not to some *muleirculam...*"

Whatever else Ellis meant to add to the insult was lost as the last of his air escaped. The hand against Ellis's chest tightened into a fist and I ground my teeth together, fighting the desire to show Ellis what it would feel like to have my forearm shove his windpipe into his spine. "*Ves a la merda*, Ellis."

"You never reacted like this about the other girls Zev's been with over the centuries. Even Elizabeth didn't anger you until after." Though Mom spoke to Ellis, she put her hand on my arm. "Why now?"

I answered for my brother, partly because he didn't have enough oxygen to form a coherent word, but mostly because I already knew what he would say. "Ellis knew that those other girls," I winced as the memories surfaced. "None of those girls meant anything to me. Tex does."

My mother's fingers didn't relax their grip on my arm. "Zev, let your brother go. Think about it. While I'm sure Tex is a lovely girl, is she really worth all of this trouble? Enjoy yourself and move on, as you have before. You're infatuated, that is all. You cannot love her; you hardly know her."

I pushed backward, putting enough distance between Ellis and myself that I'd be able to outrun him if he came after me, or if he chose to go after Tex. I kept my eyes locked on my brother as he drew in ragged lungfuls of air, but I addressed my statement to my mother. "Isaac and Rebekah, *Mamaja*."

"What?"

"*El Shaddai* designed love at first sight for some." I shifted in response to a movement on Ellis's part, but he was more interested in massaging his throat than retaliation. "And it might interest you both to know that, thanks to Tex, I've found my faith again. Found it truly for the first time." I risked a quick glance in Mom's direction before glowering at my brother once more. "*Je mourrais pour elle.*"

"Some declaration." I found some satisfaction in the rasping edge to Ellis's voice. "You can't die, Zev. Not for her, not for anyone. Or have you forgotten?"

"I haven't forgotten anything." I took a deep breath and added. "*El Echad* chose Tex for me. She's mine, Ellis. Stay away from her. *Alles versuchen und ich werde ihre kehle*." Judging by the deepening scowl on his face, Ellis knew I'd follow through on my threat if he got anywhere near Tex.

***

I growled in frustration and tossed the shirt onto the growing pile of discarded clothing that sat on my bed. I was supposed to pick Tex up in a half an hour and I was currently standing in the middle of my room wearing only black boxers and socks. And my socks didn't match.

"Problems, Zev?" The door behind me opened and I heard my mother take a couple steps inside. Despite the teasing tone of her voice, I could sense something more serious underneath.

We'd all been existing on a minimal contact basis since my confrontation with Ellis. Actually, when I said 'all,' I meant just my parents and I. Ellis had made himself scarce, but I knew he hadn't gone near Tex. Relying on centuries of experience functioning on little rest, I'd kept vigil outside Tex's house most of the last two nights, catching a few hours of sleep when I knew she was safe at work. Ellis wouldn't want a public scene if he had another option. But now, my issues with Ellis took a back seat.

I turned towards my mother, feeling the corners of my mouth curve downwards into a sad frown. "My socks don't match."

Mom chuckled and came forward. "Here." She put some clothes on my bed and then perched on the edge of my desk.

"What's this?" I lifted each garment separately. Besides wanting to look my best for Tex, the examination allowed me to avoid looking at my mother without seeming rude or evasive.

"A peace offering. I went shopping." Mom smiled. "You should know that Ellis left this morning."

That took my attention from the new pair of charcoal gray jeans I held. "What?"

Mom crossed her arms over her chest. Uh-oh, that usually meant she was annoyed. And since she was in my room that probably meant I was the source. "He received a call from Jael late last night. She's in Europe and has a lead on a Perpetuum in France trying to recruit. Ellis went to help."

I tried not to let my euphoria seep into my voice. "That's good. Jael will be glad to see him."

"I'm not happy with this behavior, Zev." Mom held up a hand as soon as I opened my mouth to argue. "I know that the fault lies in equal parts between you and your brother, but that does not mean I have to like how you two treat each other. Now that your faith has been restored, perhaps you will reconcile."

"I don't –" I started to speak but she cut me off.

"I know that your feelings for this girl are strong, and I am thankful that you have found someone." Mom straightened. "But before Ellis returns, you will need to make a choice. If you have truly returned to *El Olam*, then you must acknowledge what we have been commissioned to do, especially since it appears that the Perpetuum are growing bold again in their recruitment."

I considered the truth of her words, but pushed them away. I didn't want to consider the far-reaching consequences of my recent epiphany, and since I had yet to hear *El Olam*'s opinion on this matter, I stuck with what I wanted. "Not tonight, Mother. Give me a bit of time with Tex, then I'll decide."

My mother's dark eyes searched my face, then locked with my eyes, holding them for almost a full minute. Then, with a nod, she released me. She gave me a faint smile before exiting. "Have fun, Zev."

Once she left, I turned my attention back to the task at hand. Tunics and sandals, layers upon layers of ruffles and silk, powdered wigs – none of those garments had presented a challenge such as this. After several minutes of suffering, I decided to trust my mother's impeccable fashion sense and just pulled on everything she'd given me. It wasn't until I was in my car, halfway to Tex's house, that I realized the one thing I'd neglected to do.

My socks still didn't match.

TEX

I squirmed at the expression on my mother's face. I'd never seen her look so happy, and that worried me.

"I've waited for seventeen years to do this!" Mom fairly squealed as she bounced across the room.

"You've waited seventeen years to teach me how to dress?" I considered the question, and then answered myself. "Never mind. Of course you have."

Almost two hours later, my mother put the final touches on my outfit and turned me towards the mirror. Wow. That was me? I'd told Mom to keep it casual, and she had, but I still had a hard time recognizing the image in front of me. After making me try on everything I owned – including two bathing suits and a yellow tutu – Mom finally settled on the following ensemble: fitted black jeans with matching half-jacket (a gift from some designer who wanted to impress my mother), a scarlet spaghetti-strap top, and dressy black sandals. Around my neck was a black choker with a single teardrop diamond that matched the ones in my ears – my mother's gift to me on my sixteenth birthday. Mom had managed to tame my wild curls, adding some glitter stuff that sparkled in the waning sunlight. My make-up was model-perfect, just the right amount of eyeliner and silver eye shadow, a hint of strawberry-flavored lip-gloss and a dab of mascara. For once in my life, I actually looked my age.

"Beautiful." Mom declared, squeezing my shoulders in a one-armed hug.

“Thank you.” I turned to retrieve my purse, stopping when Mom grabbed my wrist. “Yes?”

“You don’t need to get anything from the purple tissue box.” Mom smiled. “I already put some in your purse.”

“Mom!” I screeched. I grabbed for my bag, intending to empty it onto my bed and remove the offending contents, but was interrupted by the familiar rumble of a certain old Chevy.

“Come on, don’t keep him waiting.” Mom tugged on my arm, pulling me out of my room despite my protests. “He doesn’t have all night.”

I tried to muffle a laugh and ended up coughing. Fortunately, Mom was so obsessed with meeting Zev that she didn’t notice my little fit. She dragged me down the stairs just as Zev knocked on the door. Mom opened the door with one hand and reached for Zev with the other. I waited to die of humiliation as she yanked him into the house. Then I saw him and forgot all about my pending death.

Whoa.

“Nice jeans.” I almost slapped myself. *Nice jeans!* What was I thinking?!

Zev sniggered. Another Grandma Bug word that revealed just how befuddled my brain became when Zev was around. “Thanks.” Then, dropping his voice to a conspiratorial whisper, he added. “My mom picked them out.”

I giggled, a decidedly childish sound that earned a dirty look from my mother. I jerked my head in her direction. “She chose this outfit.”

Zev grinned at me, making my cheeks burn. “Then I guess I have her to thank. You look amazing.”

“Summer Novak.” Mom seized on the opportunity, darting between us and extending her hand. “It’s nice to finally meet you.”

“Zev Avatos.” Ever the perfect gentleman, Zev pressed his lips to the back of my mother’s hand. “The pleasure is all mine.”

“Where are you two kids going tonight?” Mom released Zev’s hand, but didn’t take her eyes off of him. On that point, I couldn’t exactly blame her.

“Well, I figured that Tex wouldn’t want to go to Didyme’s since it’s her night off,” Zev glanced at me. “So, we’re going to pick up dinner from King’s Tavern and Grill, then for a picnic in MacClay Park.”

“How romantic.” I could almost hear the amusement in her voice. “And after that?”

Zev’s eyes darted towards me again and I knew what he was thinking. He answered as truthfully as he could. “We might head to the library. For research.”

“Right, research at the library.” Mom shot me a look that made me turn a shade that almost matched my shirt. “I won’t wait up then.”

I opened my mouth to say something, perhaps rectify the situation, but Zev grabbed my hand and spoke. “All right. It was nice meeting you, Ms. Novak.”

“Summer, please.” Mom’s grin widened.

“Summer, then. Have a pleasant evening.” Zev gave Mom a blinding smile that accomplished the impossible: it shut her up. Before she could regain the power of speech, Zev had pulled me through the door and halfway down the driveway to his car. He didn't release my hand until we reached the passenger's side of the Impala, at which point I silently congratulated myself on not being overwhelmed by the contact. It wasn't that Zev's touch had less of an effect, just that I'd found the ability to control my reaction. Or so I thought until I almost hit my head while climbing into the car.

Zev was still smirking when he slid into the driver's seat, so I glared at him. However, I was unable to muster any real annoyance because every time I looked at him, I got... discombobulated. The car rumbled to life as I studied the man sitting next to me. In addition to the aforementioned very nice jeans, he wore a matching dress jacket and a plain shirt the same shade as his eyes, though on him the shirt looked far from plain. Around his neck was a leather string with a silver gothic cross that was probably older than civilization.

"Say something." Zev sounded nervous.

"Hm?" I pulled my attention away from Zev's ensemble.

"You're not talking. Is something wrong?" Zev's eyes darted back and forth between me and the road, but I could read the worry in those indigo depths.

"Oh." He'd caught me. "I was just admiring your outfit." I attempted to make the statement come out dignified, but it didn't work. I turned away, feeling quite sheepish, and focused instead on the scenery speeding by.

I felt his fingers close on mine and my heart stuttered. My eyes fell to where our hands joined and, for the first time, I noticed a band on his middle finger, a twist of silver and copper in glowing contrast to his dusky skin. I should write that drivel down; then, if I ever needed to induce vomiting, I could just read it.

"Where'd you get that?" I asked, drawing Zev's gaze from my flushed face.

"Oh, it's a family thing." Zev's voice was level, but I could sense some tension to the answer. "When I was growing up, the children of the tribal leaders were given rings: gold to the eldest son, silver to the second son, bronze for the third, copper for the remaining sons and the daughters."

With my free hand, I ran my finger over the metal, cool despite the warmth of his skin. Something about the two colors together triggered a memory and I had to ask, "Sister or younger brother?"

"Sister." Zev's voice was flat, devoid of emotion, but I could tell that he'd trained himself to speak that way, that his real feelings were teeming under the surface.

The memory clicked into place. He'd had the same tone when I'd asked about siblings the first day we'd met. "Zev," I kept my own voice soft, eyes still on our hands. "Will you tell me about her?"

"After dinner, all right?" Zev squeezed my hand, and I looked up at him. "I promise."

I nodded.

"Now," he gave me that same heart-stopping smile that he'd given my mother. If he kept that up, I'd be dead before I turned eighteen. I wondered if there was a scientific name for smile-induced heart attacks. "Tell me about your day."

The rest of the car ride to King's Tavern and Grill, and then over to MacClay Park, was filled with inane, pointless chatter from us both, the detailed sharing of those who are genuinely interested in the smallest points of another's life. By the time we spread the blue and white cotton blanket and set out our meal, the sun had already begun disappearing behind the mountains.

"Tex, I was wondering something." Zev paused, weighing the question.

I studied his face, fascinated by the way the corners of his lips were twitching, as if he was thinking of something amusing. Then, there was that thin white line on his bottom lip, a minute scar marring his otherwise perfect mouth... oh, I'd missed something. I asked him to repeat what he'd said and then took a large gulp of my water, hoping to regain my composure.

Zev's eyes danced with amusement, sparkling in delight. "Why was your mom acting so strangely when I mentioned going to the library?"

I inhaled, forgetting that I had a mouthful of mineral water and coughed as I choked on the combination of air and my drink. Zev's amusement vanished and he was at my side before I had time to process the movement. The hand he placed on my back did nothing to help me, but even in my distress, I didn't care. Warmth radiated from his palm into my skin, and I felt the muscles around my lungs start to relax. Okay, maybe he did help. I straightened, breathing normally once more. Without making eye contact, I answered his question as evasively as possible. "When I got home that night, after you told me about who you were, Mom was waiting for me. I told her that we were at the library, but she didn't believe me. She thought we were..." I let my voice trail off, unable to complete the thought without the risk of one of those death-by-embarrassment scenarios.

"Oh." That one-syllable word spoke volumes. Zev knew exactly what my mother had been thinking. After a brief pause, he asked, "Doesn't she know that you're a Christian?"

I plucked a blade of grass, twisting it between my fingers. "She thinks it's a phase, remember?" I forced myself to add the rest. "And she knows about Teddy, so it makes sense that she'd assume..."

"You're different now." Zev interrupted, voice firm enough to grab my attention. I raised my head, eyes widening at the sight of his flashing eyes, the scowl he wore. "We aren't the same people we were when we made those decisions."

We weren't just talking about me anymore. I wasn't stupid. Five hundred years of being angry with God allowed for quite a bit of sinning. And that didn't include anything that might have happened in the millennia preceding Elizabeth's death. I reached for his hand. "I know that." He turned towards me. "And you know that. No one else's opinion matters."

Almost a full minute passed without either of us moving or speaking. Then, Zev sighed and settled back onto the blanket, keeping his fingers twined in mine. With his free hand, he reached for another piece of fried chicken and took a bite. Around a morsel of meat, he asked, "Do you still want to hear about my sister?"

I nodded, feeling the twitch of his fingers between mine when he spoke. I didn't interrupt, listening with growing horror as he told his tale. My grasp on his hand tightened as his pain became mine and I wanted nothing more than to comfort him.

"The worst part of our curse isn't the boredom that comes with the ages. It's watching those we loved aging and dying, knowing that, unless we received redemption, we would never see them again." Zev paused to take a sip of his energy drink. As he spoke, his accent changed, strengthening as he slipped back into memories almost as antiquated as time itself. "You see, while most of our family and friends became Immortals, there were a few who had escaped the curse, leaving before *El Elyon*'s messenger presented our ultimatum. Among those unscathed was my sister Zila. My twin sister." He must've heard me gasp, but he didn't respond, just continued with his story. "She knew what our uncle was doing and had even confronted our father about it. Rather than deal with the issue, Father arranged a marriage to another tribe, one whose language was still close enough for us to have some communication. Zila was sixteen when she left. I didn't see her again for many years. She'd heard rumors of our curse and had been searching for us since her husband had died." Zev's eyes shone. "Zila stayed with us, and I was with her at the end. Just before she died, she made me vow that I wouldn't give up, that I would find a way to make peace with *El Elyon*." Tears spilled over and rolled down his cheeks. "And I didn't keep my word."

I broke, getting to my knees and wrapping my arms around him. "Yes you did." I whispered against his hair, my voice fierce. "You kept your promise, Zev. You've come back to *El Elyon*." Though unfamiliar, the name struck a chord inside, as if my very soul recognized it.

Zev's arms circled my waist as he buried his face against my neck. I was sure he could feel my pulse pounding there, and I took a deep breath to steady myself. Well, that didn't help. He smelled like linen fresh off the line on a summer day. In punishment for my schmaltziness, I mentally kicked myself.

"Thank you, *Anwylyd*." Zev breathed the words out against my skin, raising goose bumps. "After all these years, I needed reminding."

"Glad I could help." My voice shook a little and I knew I needed to pull away now, while I still had some control. Mustering what strength remained, I released Zev and sat back on the blanket. With a trembling hand, I reached for my water again and was pleased to see that Zev's hand wasn't particularly steady either as he also took a drink. I turned my attention downwards, rummaging through my purse for some gum. Surprising myself, I kept from blushing as I saw the foil squares my mother had dropped into my purse. I popped the cinnamon gum into my mouth, and shoved the packets to the bottom of the bag.

"Tex."

Zev's voice was closer than I'd thought and I started. Raising my head, I found myself staring into the purple depths of Zev's eyes. I'd read and heard an abundance of romantic rubbish about how, when you're with the one you love, everything around you fades, pales in comparison. You know, the basic crap responsible for certain winter holidays that shall remain unnamed. But, in that moment, I experienced a split second of clarity that made me realize what all the fuss was about.

Then, Zev was leaning towards me, and any form of clear thinking vanished. All I could concentrate on, all I could see, was him. His mouth met mine as one of his hands slid around the back of my neck, holding me to him as if I needed incentive to stay. I gripped his jacket with one hand, the other coming to rest on the side of Zev's face, smooth skin with the barest hint of stubble whispering against my palm. His lips were just as soft as I'd imagined, and I'd done my fair share of envisioning this event. What I couldn't have thought up was how right, how perfect, this felt, as if some missing part of me had been found.

While one part of my brain was processing all of this, the other had been reduced to a gibbering idiot. It was this part that took over when Zev and I pulled apart, breathless from the magnitude of emotion as much as from lack of oxygen. Zev rested his forehead against mine and my gaze drifted down towards our feet. And that's when my gibbering side took over. I couldn't help it. I giggled.

"That's not exactly the reaction I was hoping for." Zev's voice was equal parts amusement and dismay.

"I'm sorry." I apologized between giggles. "I'm not laughing at the kiss, please believe me."

"Then what?" Curiosity overrode injury.

I kept snickering as I answered. "Your socks don't match."

The hand on the back of my neck pulled me forward again. I forgot about his socks as well as my laughter.

***

I wandered up the stairs in a daze, every bit of me still tingling. In the back of my mind, I wondered if Zev was feeling the same thing. Another thought pushed itself forward, asking if Zev's take on things might be more mild based solely on the fact that he'd lived for so long. I stopped abruptly, as it hit me. Zev wasn't going to age or die. I'd known he was an Immortal, but I'd managed to block out the implications for our relationship.

"All right, Lord, how's that going to work?" I resumed my journey forward with less enthusiasm than I'd had just a few seconds ago. I tried to keep the edge in my voice, but was unable to stop the quaver. "Zev stays the same age while I grow old? I die, knowing he's still living, heartbroken, and will keep living until You come back?"

Do you trust Me?

"Why?" I tossed my purse on my dresser. These conversations were getting to be quite the regular occurrence.

That's not the question. Do you trust Me?

"Yes." I made myself say the word out loud.

A sudden ringing startled me. I'd been expecting another cryptic message from God, not a phone call. I reached for my cell, heart pounding at the mere idea that it could be Zev. I saw the name and smiled. It wasn't Zev, but the next best thing.

"Elle?" I congratulated myself on my restraint. I'd wanted to jump around the room like a five year-old. I'd missed my friend and I hadn't talked to her since she'd left for college two weeks ago. We'd been friends for a long time but had grown much closer since I'd found God.

"Hey, Tex, how're you doing?"

"Great, but isn't it like two in the morning in Ohio?" I sank into my desk chair and kicked my shoes in the direction of my closet. I missed by about a foot.

"Yeah, but I knew you'd be up."

This time, I could hear the note of seriousness underneath the bubbles that formed her normal way of speaking. "What's wrong, Elle?"

I heard Elle take a deep breath before answering. "There's just some crazy stuff going on and I needed to talk to someone I could trust."

"You're worrying me." I leaned forward.

"Things have gotten creepy over the last couple days, Tex. There's this guy on campus and the stuff he's talking about is scary, like horror movie scary. All about cheating death and living forever. It's like he's recruiting for some kind of cult or something."

I didn't need a verbal confirmation to know that this was what God had been waiting to tell me. God hadn't brought Zev and I together so we could have some angst-ridden romance full of compromises and heartbreak. Zev had come back to God, and now, it was time to return to the mission. With one difference. This time, a mortal would be joining the Immortals in their quest.

ZEV

Maganda! I couldn't stop staring. I'd always thought of Tex as beautiful, but when the door opened, I didn't even see Ms. Novak. My field of vision narrowed to just one image. I hardly felt the hand close on my wrist and pull me through the doorway. I did, however, process Tex's own air of admiration and I made a mental note to thank my mother for the new clothes.

"Nice jeans."

I added a gift to my note. An expensive gift.

I couldn't suppress a chuckle. "Thanks. My mom picked them out." Why did I say that? I sounded like a *blennum*.

Tex laughed softly, but before I could take offense, she motioned to her mother and said, "She chose this outfit."

Well then, that changed things. "Then I guess I have her to thank. You look amazing." Color flooded Tex's cheeks.

"Summer Novak. It's nice to finally meet you." Ms. Novak held out her hand.

"Zev Avatos." I turned on the charm, knowing exactly how to win over Tex's mother. After all, I'd spent thousands of years enticing people to trust me. "The pleasure is all mine."

"Where are you two kids going tonight?" She let go of my hand, but kept staring at me. It was nice to know I still had it.

"Well, I figured that Tex wouldn't want to go to Didyme's since it's her night off," I stole a look at Tex, my gaze irresistibly drawn back to her. "So, we're going to pick up dinner from King's Tavern and Grill, then for a picnic in MacClay Park."

Ms. Novak found her voice. "How romantic. And after that?"

I glanced at Tex again. I knew that she might want to learn more about my history, but I couldn't very well tell Ms. Novak that tidbit of information. I decided to be vague. "We might head to the library. For research."

"Right, research at the library. I won't wait up then."

Something about the statement made Tex turn a shade of red that rivaled her shirt. I reminded myself to ask about that later. "All right. It was nice meeting you, Ms. Novak."

Her smile widened and I had to bite the inside of my cheek to keep from chuckling. "Summer, please."

"Summer, then. Have a pleasant evening." I gave Ms. Novak my most dazzling smile and reached for Tex's hand, pulling her after me. When we reached the car, I opened the passenger's side door, repressing a grin as Tex bumped her head. As I slid into the driver's seat, I realized that I must not have been disguising my amusement as well as I'd thought. Tex was glaring. I turned my attention to the road, expecting Tex to initiate a conversation after her irritation faded, but we drove in silence for several minutes. After the first thirty seconds, I began sneaking glimpses of her from the corner of my eyes. I was surprised to find that her gaze was locked on me, but my astonishment grew as each glance showed that her attention wasn't wavering. A thousand thoughts rushed through my mind. Why was she staring at me? Was she having second thoughts? I needed to know.

"Say something."

"Hm?" Tex looked up at me.

"You're not talking. Is something wrong?" I kept glancing back at the road, but was only paying partial attention to where I was going. I could feel anxiety building.

"Oh." Hm, she was embarrassed. My interest grew. "I was just admiring your outfit." She turned her head towards the window, but I could see her face reflected in the glass. Her admission had embarrassed her. I reached for her hand. As my fingers curled around hers, my eyes traced the planes and contours of her face, almost as familiar as my own. I didn't notice where her gaze had fallen until she spoke.

"Where'd you get that?"

My eyes dropped to our hands and my throat constricted at the sight of my ring. I'd stopped wearing it after Elizabeth died, finding the reminder of my broken vow to Zila to be too much. I pushed my emotions down as I answered. "Oh, it's a family thing. When I was growing up, the children of the tribal leaders were given rings: gold to the eldest son, silver to the second son, bronze for the third, copper for the remaining sons and the daughters."

Her index finger ran over the ring, her flesh warm against mine. "Sister or younger brother?"

I desperately tried not to think of my twin. Not to picture the small child with long, dark braids. The young woman she'd grown into, leaving her family to have one of her own. The much older woman who'd returned to us. The one who'd died in my arms. "Sister."

Tex's words were gentle. "Zev, will you tell me about her?"

I squeezed Tex's hand, bringing her eyes up to my face. "After dinner, all right? I promise."

She nodded and I changed the topic of conversation to something a bit safer. I listened intently as Tex told me about her day. I absorbed each detail, eager to know about every minute we spent apart. From the moment she got up (seven thirty), to what she had for breakfast (omelet, bacon and toast), to her conversations with her coworkers (not much about me, to my disappointment), I was enthralled. Judging by her own inquisitiveness, Tex was equally fascinated with the mundane events of my day. It wasn't until we were well into our meal that I recalled one of the questions I'd wanted to ask her.

"Tex, I was wondering something." I paused, deciding how I wanted to word the question. "Why did your mom act so weird when I mentioned the library?"

After a moment, Tex stammered, "What did you say?" Her cheeks were tinged with pink and I took a second to wonder why. When I'd asked the question, she'd been watching me. Was that it? Had she been staring at me and that's why she didn't hear the question? I found the idea appealing. She reached for her water and took a large drink.

I repeated. "Why was your mom acting so strangely when I mentioned going to the library?"

Oops. Should've waited until she was done drinking. I rushed to her side, placing my hand on her back. I couldn't think, couldn't breathe, could only hear Tex coughing and gasping. Then she drew a shaky breath and I found I could take air into my own lungs as well. She straightened, but I kept my hand on her back, now aware of the heat under my palm. I'd forgotten the fragility of the non-Immortal.

When she could speak again, she answered my question. "When I got home that night, after you told me about who you were, Mom was waiting for me. I told her that we were at the library, but she didn't believe me. She thought we were..."

"Oh." I didn't need Tex to finish the sentence. I knew

exactly what her mother had been thinking. I tried very hard not to let those images into my head and grabbed at another thought. “Doesn’t she know that you’re a Christian?”

Tex leaned forward to pick a blade of grass and I let my hand fall back to my side. She twisted the green shoot between her fingers. “She thinks it’s a phase, remember? And she knows about Teddy, so it makes sense that she’d assume...”

I wasn’t going to let her berate herself for past mistakes. “You’re different now. We aren’t the same people we were when we made those decisions.” The words came out rougher than I’d intended them to be, but I wanted Tex to know that I understood the forgiveness of *El malei Rachamin*. I just prayed that she could look beyond my own history, deeds so much worse than hers had been.

I felt her fingers brush against mine as she spoke. “I know that.” I turned towards her, threading my fingers between hers. She continued. “And you know that. No one else’s opinion matters.”

We sat in companionable silence for a full minute before I settled back onto the blanket. My stomach rumbled and I reached for a drumstick with my free hand. I wasn’t going to let go of her, not even if it meant I’d make a mess by eating one-handed. After a few bites, I knew I had to ask her. “Do you still want to hear about my sister?” Just the idea of Zila brought a stab of pain, but I wanted Tex to understand the reality of our lives when linked with mortals. And I wanted her to know about the only person I’d loved more than myself. Well, until now.

Tex nodded and I took a moment to consider where to

begin. An explanation should come first. "The worst part of our curse isn't the boredom that comes with the ages. It's watching those we loved aging and dying, knowing that, unless we received redemption, we would never see them again." I sipped at my drink, fortifying myself for what was to come. "You see, while most of our family and friends became Immortals, there were a few who had escaped the curse, leaving before *El Elyon*'s messenger presented our ultimatum. Among those unscathed was my sister Zila. My twin sister." I heard Tex's sharp intake of air, but didn't pause. If I stopped now, I'd never finish. "She knew what our uncle was doing and had even confronted our father about it. Rather than deal with the issue, Father arranged a marriage to another tribe, one whose language was still close enough for us to have some communication. Zila was sixteen when she left. I didn't see her again for many years." I could feel the wet burn beneath my eyelids. "She'd heard rumors of our curse and had been searching for us since her husband had died. Zila stayed with us, and I was with her at the end. Just before she died, she made me vow that I wouldn't give up, that I would find a way to make peace with *El Elyon*." I didn't stop the saltwater cascading down my cheeks as I confessed my darkest secret, the worst of all my many betrayals. "And I didn't keep my word." I bent my head, unable to look at Tex, so wrapped up in my own grief that I didn't hear her move. Then, I felt her arms around me, and my heart galloped out of control.

Her voice was low, but forceful. "Yes you did. You kept your promise, Zev. You've come back to *El Elyon*."

I couldn't help myself. I wrapped my arms around Tex's

waist and pulled her closer, pressing my face against the soft skin of her neck. *Sjajan potez*, she smelled good. Gardenias. I could feel the thud of her heart against my cheek and heard her take a deep breath. “Thank you, *Anwylyd.* After all these years, I needed reminding.”

“Glad I could help.” Tex’s voice was uneven and I took a second to wonder if I’d caused it. I was surprised by how much I liked that idea. Then Tex was pulling away and I had to try to steady myself with a gulp of oxygen. It didn’t still the tremor in my hands as I reached for my drink. The sweet taste of passion fruit washed away the remains of my meal, and calmed my nerves enough for me to do what I’d wanted to do for the past week.

“Tex.”

I’d been with, kissed, a lot of girls. I’m not bragging. When you’d lived as long as I had, it was pretty much inevitable. Tall, short, in-between. Single, married, divorced, widowed. I had wide tastes and enjoyed diversity.

None of that compared to the first time my lips touched Tex’s.

Mid-Logue: Carry On Wayward Son and Fall Back Into Me

TEX

Once I'd found Zev and let myself fall in love with him, I knew that my problems had just begun. Love is never easy, and I don't think it's supposed to be. More than the 'star-crossed lovers' of Shakespeare's tragedies, Zev and I had obstacles to overcome. Obstacles more difficult than anything good-old William could've foreseen. We had to fight our way forward, all the while in danger of losing, not just each other, but also the mission we'd set out to complete.

ZEV

Before we were finished, I would have traded almost anything for a problem as simple as a blood feud between families. Neither the Montagues nor the Capulets had faced trials as dangerous as those Tex and I were up against. The odds were more than against us. The odds had an army with nuclear weapons while all Tex and I had were sticks and stones. We'd come through the battleground of our own scarred pasts, but we had so much farther to go. *El Echad* had given a command, and it was our choice whether we would carry on or fall back. *Continuer, mon fils rebelle.*

Chapter Seven: This Time Around, Take My Hand

TEX

I wasn't really sure how to broach this subject with Zev. I'd spent most of the night and morning trying to figure out what to say. How do you tell the love of your life that he needs to train you so that you can help him fight his oldest enemy? I laughed under my breath. My life sounded like some strange soap opera, or just a really good sci-fi. You know, written by one of the greats who combine dark, witty humor and complicated plots with twists in all the right places. And I even had the handsome, brooding male protagonist by my side. On second thought, maybe that wasn't such a good thing. Those usually ended with blood and death.

"Something you'd like to share?" Zev whispered in my ear.

Warmth filled me, half embarrassment at having been caught daydreaming and half due to his nearness. We were in study hall, so subterfuge wasn't entirely necessary, but I didn't mind. The more time we spent together, the closer I wanted to be to him. In the back of my mind, I knew that this might be a problem if – when – we embarked on our little adventure. I sent up a silent prayer for strength before answering Zev.

"I was just thinking about what genre my life is." I skirted the reasoning behind my meditations.

"And what did you decide?" Zev glanced towards the librarian. After ascertaining that Mrs. Evans wasn't looking, Zev ran his finger over the back of my hand, leaving a burning wake across my skin. "Romance?"

"No, that's not true!" An exclamation saved me from

having to answer the question.

"Miss Snow," Mrs. Evans snapped. "You will keep your voice down in my library."

"Mrs. Evans, Jackie and I are working on this history project and she keeps saying that the Allied soldiers killed Hitler and I say that he committed suicide. Who's right?"

While Mrs. Evans began a lengthy explanation behind the discovery of Hitler's body, Zev muttered something I didn't quite catch. "Say again?" I whispered.

"I said," Zev had a wry grin on his face. "Neither one is right." He glanced at my face and expounded with a cryptic, but decodable, statement. "I told you that Ellis was good at his job."

I disguised a surprised snort as a strangled sneeze. Hm, alliteration.

"He always did like uniforms." Zev sighed. "Or, at least, he liked the girls that the uniform attracted."

Inspired by the topic, I saw a way to ease into what I needed to tell him. "How often do you guys need to infiltrate military bases?"

"Not as often as you'd think." Zev leaned back in his chair, and a second later I saw why. Mrs. Evans had sidled up beside our table and was now glaring down at us.

"Something you'd like to share with the rest of the room?" Mrs. Evans was more annoyed than I'd ever seen her.

"No ma'am." Zev gave Mrs. Evans a smile, the one that let him get away with almost anything, particularly with the female gender. "Just talking about school work."

"Well, I don't believe you need to be sitting that close just to do your school work." Mrs. Evans's scowl had softened, but she still didn't look pleased.

Zev slid his chair a few inches further from mine. Mollified, Mrs. Evans returned to her roost at the front of the room and I decided to pursue the previous topic of conversation, just with a bit more discretion.

"Do you guys plan out all of the elements of attack, or wing it?"

If Zev was surprised by my interest, he didn't show it. "We've had times when we've had to improvise, but most of our missions require strategy and finesse. Ellis usually takes care of those."

"Did you all do some type of training or does the hunting thing come naturally?" As my true purpose for the questions grew nearer, my nerves became taut, stretched wires under my skin. I pressed my sweaty palms against my knees, drying them on my jeans, for once thankful of the NHCS policy that kept Zev from holding my hand.

"A little of both." Zev's eyes narrowed in suspicion. "Increased healing means we can push ourselves past normal physical boundaries, giving us a natural advantage. Think about it, we can train ourselves for centuries, building endurance, lung capacity, muscles, all of that. We are stronger, faster, with senses unhampered by decay, injury or pollution. The actual fighting skills come from years of practice."

I paused, knowing I was heading out on some very thin ice. Thin ice over a very deep lake. In the middle of spring thaw. "That means anyone can learn to hunt, right?"

I saw the exact moment when Zev understood where my

inquiry was headed. Shock passed through the dark pools of his eyes and he leaned forward again, heedless of the dirty look Mrs. Evans threw our way. "Don't even think about it."

"Wasn't my idea." I kept my voice calm. "This is what God wants, Zev. He wants you to complete your mission."

Zev scowled. "He didn't tell me."

"Because He knew you wouldn't listen. That you'd make all sorts of excuses." The bell rang and I stood. In a low voice I knew he could hear, I added. "If you don't, you know how this will end. Do you really want to go through that again?" Without waiting for an answer, I walked away. Zev needed some time to process what I'd said without my interference.

We didn't have a chance to talk until lunch and, by then, my stomach was in knots. Zev had maintained a polite, if distant, demeanor. By the time we'd made it to our usual spot at the picnic table, I was sure that I'd ruined everything between Zev and I. Fighting every impulse, I remained outwardly calm and waited for it to be over.

"I've made a decision." Zev traced the wood grain with his thumb, eyes following his motions rather than facing me.

My stomach and heart decided to check out how my feet lived. I clasped my hands together, lunch forgotten. Palms pressed together, nails digging into the backs of my hands, I braced myself for the world to end. A small voice in the back of my head told me to stop being melodramatic. A bigger voice argued that I was doing no such thing.

"I've spent the last two classes praying, something I haven't done much of in the last five hundred years."

My stomach and heart began the slow ascent back to their

rightful places, daring to hope for yet another miracle. When he raised his head so that our eyes could meet, my heart did its usual set of flips and twirls, which felt stranger than normal since the organ in question was now located somewhere around my left knee.

"Tex, I don't want to lose you. Ever. You mean more to me than anyone or anything other than *El Echad*. Every day you mean more to me." Zev tucked a stray curl behind my ear, and my misplaced viscera jumped past where they belonged and lodged in my throat. "*El Yeshuatenu* reminded me that, above all, I belong to Him, and so do you. And the only way that we can be together in eternity is if I do as *El Olam* commanded me."

"And me?" I wanted to lean into his hand but resisted the impulse, knowing that the movement would weaken my resolve. "I need to do what God tells me to do."

"I know." Zev sighed. "I might not like it, but He told me that it's not really up to me. It's your decision, and I can either help or hinder you."

Okay, I didn't possess as much self-control as I'd first thought. I brushed the tips of my fingers across his cheek, the light stubble scratching against my skin. "Will you help me?"

"For you, anything." Zev turned his head and kissed the inside of my wrist.

The heat from his lips traveled up my arm like a flame and I realized that I'd discovered the source of spontaneous combustion. Before my brain could catch fire, Zev turned his attention to his lunch and I was able to semi-compose myself. Enough to eat, anyway. Between chewing, Zev and I planned out a training schedule. Neither one of us approached the topic of how, or when, we were going to leave Fort Prince. We'd come this far and, with God's help, we'd go even further.

***

My hands stung from the last blow, but I refused to let Zev see my discomfort. He was already holding back and I didn't want to give him another excuse to slow down or stop my training. I gritted my teeth and braced myself for another attack, the feel of a broadsword in my hands still foreign.

"Now, you take the offensive." Zev instructed.

I glowered at him. He didn't even sound winded! I sucked in a deep breath, feeling the burn in my lungs as if I was some out-of-shape couch potato rather than an athlete. My indignation brought a faint smile to Zev's face. That smirk! I scowled and used my flagging muscles to pull the sword above my shoulders. Zev blocked my feeble swing with a twist of his wrist, and knocked the sword from my numb fingers. I dropped to the cool stone floor and sprawled out, feeling the rock suck the heat from my exhausted body. I closed my eyes, inhaling the scent of old paper. I sensed more than saw Zev sink down beside me, and I rolled my head in his direction.

"Not bad."

I opened my eyes to glare at him. "That was horrible."

He shook his head, one side of his mouth tipping upwards in a half-grin. "For someone who'd never even held a sword before, that was impressive."

"You disarmed me in fifteen minutes without breaking a

sweat, and I feel like I've never exercised a day in my life." I tried to sound perturbed, but only managed pitiful.

"You lasted longer than I did against Jael my first time." Zev stretched out on his side, propping his head up on one hand.

"Really?"

Zev nodded. "She's the Immortals' most skilled swordsman. Each of us has our own areas of expertise. Mom uses poison, and anything else that allows her to be away when the target dies. Dad likes long-range weapons. Neither of them wants to see their victims. Ellis is the most determined. He's good with anything."

"And you?" I wasn't sure that I wanted to know.

"I tend to prefer knives and hand-to-hand combat." Zev kept his voice matter-of-fact, but I could see how much the words cost him. "They remind me that every life I end is a person, not some nameless entity."

"Hand-to-hand." I grinned, trying to draw him from his moroseness. Was that a real word? Maybe. "That sounds promising."

The corners of Zev's mouth twitched, but I was too distracted by them to ask for an explanation. Hm, they were moving. Pretty. Forming words... wait, he was talking to me. Oh, smile... very pretty.

"What do you think?"

My poor muddled brain scrambled for a way out that didn't involve admitting that I'd been fantasizing about his lips. "Um, okay?"

Zev's smile bloomed and I decided that, whatever I'd just

agreed to, it had been worth it. Almost any sacrifice would be worth seeing the sparkle in those eyes, the dimples creasing his cheeks. Crap! I did it again!

"Ready?" Zev stood and held out a hand.

I eagerly slid my hand into his, warm skin smooth against my cool palms. He pulled me to my feet and I found myself much closer to him than I'd thought I would be, our linked hands coming to rest against his chest. Muscular chest... hm, more distracting than the eyes or mouth? I wasn't sure.

"Tex?" The concerned note in Zev's voice broke through my thoughts. "Are you all right?"

I felt my cheeks color and it took all my courage to raise my eyes to Zev's face. I'd blushed more since meeting Zev than I had the entirety of my life previous to September first. "Fine."

Zev's eyebrows drew together in obvious puzzlement. "Have you heard anything I've said?"

"Well, um," I fumbled around for a second, reluctantly settling on the truth. "Not really. I was kinda lost in my own world." Inwardly, I pled with him to not ask for any further explanation.

"Really?" His lips did that really distracting twitching thing again. "Did I make an appearance in this dream world?"

I scowled, or, at least, made the attempt to do so. My face didn't want to obey my brain at the moment. "Can we get back to the subject at hand?"

"I'll make you a deal." Zev still hadn't let go of my hand. "If you can tell me what we were talking about, I'll drop the other topic."

Crap.

By now, I was sure that my cheeks were some brilliant shade of scarlet, but I was unable to suppress my curiosity. "I give. What were you talking about?"

Zev shook his head, his mouth stretched into a full smile. "You first. What were you thinking about?"

I'd never prayed for a natural disaster before, but found myself pleading with God to send a tornado, an earthquake. I'd even take a swarm of locusts or downpour of frogs if it meant I didn't have to answer Zev's question. Of course, I had no such luck. I realized that I'd probably be less embarrassed if I was further away from him, but even that thought couldn't bring me to pull back. Might as well get it over with. I sighed and confessed. "You. I was thinking about you."

Zev did more than just smile. His entire face lit up and I decided that my humiliation was worth it. I'd gladly suffer through worse to see that particular reaction again. I sighed. Time to move on. "All right, what were you talking about?"

ZEV

"That means anyone can learn to hunt, right?"

She couldn't mean what I thought she meant. Even as the denial crossed my mind, I knew that she did. I leaned forward, ignoring everything in the room except Tex. *Len cez moju mrtvolu.* I wasn't going to let her take part in my curse, especially when it could cost her life. "Don't even think about it."

The intensity of my words didn't faze her. "Wasn't my idea. This is what God wants, Zev. He wants you to complete your mission."

I felt my lips twist into a scowl. "He didn't tell me."

Tex's tone was gentle, but her words hit me like a physical blow. "Because He knew you wouldn't listen. That you'd make all sorts of excuses."

I wanted to protest, but I knew she was right. Even now, my mind was formulating arguments. Dimly, I heard the bell signal the end of class and Tex got to her feet.

She spoke again, her voice doing little to soften the sting of what she said. "If you don't, you know how this will end. Do you really want to go through that again?"

I didn't answer. I couldn't answer. I watched her leave, but didn't immediately follow after her. I was still reeling from yet another wrench in my once-predictable life. As other students filed into the room, I finally left my seat and headed for my next class. I walked in a daze, jumbled phrases and clauses scrambling in my brain for some semblance of organization. One coherent sentence managed to form, and I couldn't stifle the accusation even as I directed my statement towards the Lord. *You can't do that to me.*

I heard only silence as I slid into my seat. Apparently, *El Haggadol* didn't find my comment worth contradicting. I knew the foolishness of the words I'd prayed, but refused to take them back. He had given me Tex, and now was using her to force me back into hunting the Perpetuum.

I'm not forcing you to do anything. You always have a choice.

I grimaced at the reminder. I understood, better than most, *El Gibbor*'s gift of free will. As class began around me, I continued my internal conversation with Him. *Some choice. Tex wants to fight now. You gave her to me, how can I protect her like this?*

You are both Mine, Zev. Though you may also belong to each other, My claim supersedes all others.

I squirmed in my seat, earning puzzled looks from several classmates, including Tex. I ignored them all, even hers.

Besides, do you really think you love her more than I do?

Maybe. Even in my head, my voice was belligerent.

Zev.

I sighed. *I know, I know.* I clung to one part of my argument. *But You can't ask Tex to take this burden.*

That's not your decision to make. Tex will make up her own mind, and you may help or hinder her. Though her journey may be easier with experienced assistance.

I'm not promising anything. I grumbled. I wasn't ready to give in just yet.

The rest of the morning's classes flew by as I attempted to argue my way around what *El Echad* was asking me to do. By the end of Bible class, however, I knew that my pleas were in vain. Throughout history, only a few people had managed to change the mind of *El Hashamayim*. I'd never been one of them, and this time was no different. The lunch bell rang and I resigned myself to the inevitable. I was re-joining my people in their fight. And, this time around, I was taking a mortal with me. I swallowed hard, my heart still balking at the prospect of what was to come. My spirit reminded me that I was in God's will. Not that the knowledge made things easier. I waited until Tex and I had settled into our usual seats before beginning.

I couldn't look at Tex, so I focused on the rough surface of the table, running my thumb over it. "I've made a decision." I took a breath. "I've spent the last two classes praying, something I haven't done much of in the last five hundred years."

Look at her, Zev.

I couldn't refuse the command, and, if I'd been completely honest, I didn't want to. I didn't like not looking at Tex. When our eyes met, my mouth went dry and I had to resist the urge to kiss her. Instead, I contented myself with reaching for a wayward curl as I spoke. "Tex, I don't want to lose you. Ever. You mean more to me than anyone or anything other than *El Echad*. Every day you mean more to me. *El Yeshuatenu* reminded me that, above all, I belong to Him, and so do you. And the only way that we can be together in eternity is if I do as *El Olam* commanded me." My fingers grazed Tex's cheek when I retracted my hand and the affected atoms sang.

"And me? I need to do what God tells me to do."

"I know." I sighed. "I might not like it, but He told that it's not really up to me. It's your decision, and I can either help or hinder you." I started to say more, to warn her of the danger, to beg her to reconsider her decision, but her next action drove those words from my mind. The soft silk of her skin rasped over the shadow of hair on my cheek. I hadn't shaved that morning.

"Will you help me?"

No words existed to express just what I was willing to do for her. Instead, I had to content myself with what my limited vocabulary could produce. *Vorrei morire per voi. Vorrei fare qualcosa per voi.* "For you, anything." Then, before I could check my actions, I pressed my mouth against the inside of Tex's wrist. When I felt her pulse flutter under my lips, my own heart responded. I knew that I'd spoken truly. I would do anything and everything for this girl. No sentimental declaration; I meant every word. And that scared me more than anything else I'd ever experienced.

***

"Hand-to-hand. That sounds promising."

I couldn't help it. The comment had been so innocent, but my mind flooded with images of Tex and myself, hand-in-hand, and things quickly veered into the not-so-innocent territory. *Ik moet wegens dat commentaar zingen.* I spoke, trying very hard to get my mind out of the metaphorical gutter and back onto a cleaner street. "Let's put the weapons aside then and spar so I can see what we need to work on." Her eyes watched my mouth as I spoke and I began to wonder if she'd even heard what I'd said. "What do you think?"

"Um, okay?"

Yeah, she hadn't really been paying attention. I smiled at the thought that I could make her so flustered. I held out a hand, hoping she'd take it. "Ready?"

Her hand moved against mine, her flesh chilled from where it had rested against the stone floor. I pulled her to her feet, adding an extra bit of effort to make sure our hands ended up against my chest. I was sure she could feel the thudding of my heart, and I looked down to try to read her. She hadn't moved, her eyes glazed and unfocused. Had she hit her head? Maybe that was why she'd sounded so funny before. Maybe it wasn't me at all.

"Tex? Are you all right?"

New color mounted her cheeks, and she tipped her face in my direction. "Fine."

All right, something was definitely off here. "Have you heard anything I've said?"

"Well, um," she couldn't seem to find the words. "Not really. I was kinda lost in my own world."

Now things were getting interesting. I teased. "Really? Did I make an appearance in this dream world?"

Her face morphed into what I supposed she intended to be a scowl. I found it more endearing than anything else. She demanded, "Can we get back to the subject at hand?"

I sensed an opportunity and seized it. "I'll make you a deal. If you can tell me what we were talking about, I'll drop the other topic."

Tex's face took on a shade similar to a painful sunburn, minus the blisters or unattractive peeling. "I give. What were you talking about?"

I shook my head, feeling the smile stretch across my face. "You first. What were you thinking about?"

Thirty seconds passed, and I began to think she wasn't going to answer. Just as I was about to give up hope, Tex sighed. "You. I was thinking about you."

Had I thought I was happy before? That my smile couldn't be any brighter? If what I was feeling now could be harnessed, we'd never have an energy crisis.

Back to earth, Zev.

His voice was tinged with wry amusement, and that added to my joy. I hadn't heard that sound in His words in a long time.

Tex's question broke through my reverie. "All right, what were you talking about?"

"Teaching you to fight without the weapons." I repeated, managing to keep the reluctance out of my voice. While the prospect of an excuse for close physical contact made me happy, I wasn't sure I was the best one to train Tex. I couldn't bear the thought of harming her, even by accident. Only the realization that someone else could kill her if I didn't do my part made me ready to do what was necessary. I released her hand and took a step back. "Do you want to take the offensive or the defensive?" At Tex's puzzled look, I clarified. "To spar. Do you want to attack me?" I raised one eyebrow and grinned. This was sounding better and better. "Or do you want to take the easy way out and defend yourself against me? Come on. *Atrevo-me a ti.*"

A new expression crossed Tex's face and it took me a second to place it. Confidence almost bordering on arrogance. Before I could process the reasons behind her emotion, she'd crossed the distance between us. I realized what Tex was going to do a split second before she did it, just enough time for me to sidestep the kick Tex aimed at my leg. To my surprise, my movement didn't throw Tex off for long. As quickly as I reacted to her initial attack, Tex compensated, using her momentum to turn around fast enough to keep me from having the advantage. Tex aimed an elbow at my head and my instincts kicked in. I blocked her blow and tried to sweep her feet out from under her.

It didn't work. She was faster than I'd thought, and I began to suspect that my little lesson wasn't going to go as smoothly as I'd anticipated. Even as the idea crossed my mind, I felt the first pain in my leg, followed quickly by a second. I staggered, but managed to keep my feet. Actually, I managed to get far away enough to catch my breath.

"Surprised?" Tex grinned as she bounced on the balls of her feet.

"Little bit." I hated how winded I sounded. *Ma ei oodanud seda.*

Before I'd recovered, Tex struck again. I saw the right hook and dodged... directly into the punch that wasn't a feint. I felt the jab to my chin next, new pain mingling with that already in my head. Without realizing when or how it had happened, I was on my back with Tex kneeling on my chest. Unwilling to acknowledge defeat, I twisted my hips, intending to throw her off. I had just enough time to see something flash across her eyes as she leaned back. Then crushing pain blocked out everything else.

***

Girls can't understand the incapacitating power of this particular injury, so let me put things in perspective. I once had my right leg amputated by a blunt ax due to a minor misunderstanding with a furious Norseman in regards to his twin daughters. It took five days for my severed limb to fully reattach itself. The initial level of pain when experiencing a blow to the crotch is almost as bad as the second day waiting for my tibia and fibula to grow back together. Far from my most painful injury, the elbow I'd received before blacking out was still high on my list, somewhere under the red-hot iron poker Rasputin had shoved through my left shoulder just before I slit his throat.

"Zev? Zev?" Tex's voice drew me out of the darkness. I caught glimpses of her worried face as my eyelids struggled to stay open. There was still pain, but it wasn't the same pass-out-or-throw-up agony as before. It was, in fact, closer to what I'd felt when a disgruntled ferret had gnawed on my forearm. My fifth attempt at opening my eyes proved successful, and I focused on Tex's lips as they moved, running over with apologies. "I'm so sorry. I just reacted. I took some self-defense classes and that's what they taught us and my instincts just took over and I am so sorry." I wanted to smile at her impossibly long run-on sentence, but couldn't quite manage that yet. "Please forgive me."

I held up a finger, and stared at it, proud of my accomplishment even as it doubled and tripled before settling into a single digit. Then, I impressed myself even more by croaking the words, "I'll be okay." Even as I spoke, I could feel my body healing itself. Pain level comparison: hit in the back with a canoe. Never before had I been so grateful to be an Immortal. I let Tex help me sit up before attempting to speak again. "You might've mentioned the self-defense classes before we started."

"Oops." Tex looked impossibly guilty.

Synapses fired, making connections that had been impossible just seconds before. Plural. "How many classes have you taken?"

"Just two." Tex's gaze fell to her hands and she muttered an addition. "And two years of judo."

"Is that...?" I paused when she peeked up at me. "What else?"

"Um, well, I kinda, maybe, have been taking karate since I was seven."

I rested my forearms on my knees and leaned forward a bit, testing to see if the movement brought nausea with it. My stomach stayed firmly in its place. Pain analysis set my current level at less than my broken nose. "And you didn't think any of this was worth telling me?"

Tex's head snapped up, and I was vaguely amused by the annoyance flashing in her pale eyes. Then I thought of how our match had ended, and amusement turned to alarm.

"Ten years of karate, two years of judo and two self-defense classes?" She sounded miffed. I wasn't sure which was more shocking: her tone or the fact that I'd used the word 'miffed.' She continued. "And how many years of experience do you have fighting, Zev? And with how much more ferocity?"

All right, she had a point.

"So, no, I didn't think my paltry bit of 'training' was worth talking about. Besides, you dared me." One side of her mouth curved upwards at my surprise. "I took two years of Spanish."

I raised both hands, palms out in a gesture of supplication. “Truce, all right? I was just caught off guard.” I didn’t add that the event of me being surprised in a fight was shocking in and of itself. The last time that had happened had been in South Africa in the mid-1430s and I’d been taking a nap. Ellis still enjoyed telling the tale of when the twelve year-old daughter of a Perpetuum pinned me to the ground with a spear through the stomach. That ranked in the top ten on my ‘most painful injuries’ list, somewhere between losing a few toes to an angry polar bear and falling off the Sphinx. The last one wouldn’t have been so bad if I hadn’t landed in a nest of scorpions and then ran into a pissed off camel while trying to escape.

Her anger evaporated, replaced by concern. “But you’re okay?”

I was feeling well enough to give her a lopsided smile. I couldn’t even call what I was feeling pain; it was more like uncomfortableness. Yes, that’s a word. Trust me. “I heal fast, remember? No permanent damage.”

Tex reached for my hands, grazing her lips across my scraped palms, sending electric tingles racing along my nerves. *Sangat baik*, definitely no permanent damage.

Zev, mind out of the gutter.

“Why haven’t your hands healed then?” Tex’s question thankfully brought my mind back from where it had been going.

“Major injuries first. Once those are fixed, the smaller stuff gets taken care of.” Even as Tex and I watched, my skin sealed itself. “We even stop infections before they start.”

“Good thing.” Tex glanced down at the floor and I

followed her gaze.

I must've hit the floor harder than I'd thought. Shreds of skin and blood marked the place where I'd fallen. I sighed and clambered to my feet, much less gracefully than I usually moved. I wasn't hurting anymore, but I still used the tentative movements of someone expecting pain. Some things you never lose, no matter how many years you've lived. I plucked some tissues from a box on the desk and wiped up the floor. As I tossed the garbage into a nearby bin, Tex spoke again.

"How long do you think it'll be until I'm ready to fight?"

I resisted the urge to say what I wanted to say. If it were up to me, she'd never...

It's not up to you.

I reached out a hand and Tex took it, letting me pull her to her feet. "There's no rush." I moved a step nearer to Tex and tapped the end of her nose with my free index finger. "Don't worry."

"That's just it, Zev." Tex sighed and tilted her head back so she could look directly at me. "We do need to hurry." My question must have shown on my face because Tex answered it without me needing to ask. "I have a lead on a Perpetuum recruiting college kids."

"How?" I couldn't quite get the whole question out. It couldn't be true. Not yet. I wasn't ready to start this again.

"A friend of mine in Ohio called me, worried about some crazy guy on her campus. It's them, Zev. And we have to go soon."

"'We'?" My mind latched onto one word over the others. My heartbeat kicked up a notch as I thought of running off with Tex. I shook my head as much to clear it as to negate her statement. "Give me the information and my parents and I, we'll take care of it." I could see the protest forming on Tex's face and I kept talking. "Then we'll come back, and we can finish training. Maybe after graduation..."

"No, Zev." Her words were soft, but I stopped, knowing what was coming. "It's our job. We're supposed to finish it."

"But," I tried to interrupt, but Tex put her hand on my mouth, effectively shutting me up. I had to concentrate to catch what she was saying.

"I haven't been a Christian very long, but I know when God's talking to me. Especially when He's this clear. While the rest of the Immortals may be finishing off some of the Perpetuum other places, it's you and I who are supposed to finish it. Here. Ohio's not the last, but it's supposed to be the first."

Tex moved her hand from my mouth, sliding it to the back of my neck and burying her fingers in my hair. All higher brain function stopped. Then she stood on her tiptoes and brushed her lips across mine. Well, there goes the mid-brain function. All I knew was the scorching blaze raging through my body and I wanted more. I wrapped my arms around Tex's waist and pulled her closer to me. My hands pressed against the small of her back, and I could feel the heat of her skin through the cotton tank top she wore. One hand drifted up, intending to rest on the nape of her neck. But, as I passed her shoulder, my fingers found a raised edge, the scar tissue wide enough to tear my attention from kissing her. Under my curiosity, anger simmered, ready to spill over if her explanation involved intentional injury on another's part.

"Tex," I was surprised by how breathless I sounded. "What happened?" I turned her so that I could see the extent of the damage.

Though Tex's back was to me, I could hear the slight edge to her voice. "I fell while I was hiking."

"Fell? Where? Off a mountain?" I didn't even try to conceal the shock I felt.

"Actually, yeah." With little emotion in her voice, Tex told me the whole story, starting at her mother's habit of going through more boyfriends than shoes.

As Tex continued on to her little trip down the mountainside, I studied her scarred back. Without even knowing I was going to do it, I ran my index finger from the top of Tex's shoulder to where the rough line disappeared beneath her shirt. She shuddered under my touch, and I yanked my hand back.

"Sorry." I muttered.

Tex ducked her head, but I could see the flush on the back of her neck. "It didn't feel bad."

All right, we seriously needed to move on, or we'd be heading into the 'too fast' territory. Even that knowledge, though, couldn't quiet the desire I had for Tex. I muttered, "*Centro d'interesse*, Zev. We should go."

Tex shook her head and my stomach lurched. She stepped away before she turned. Maybe she didn't trust herself that close to me, either. The thought made me smile. Or, maybe she didn't want to be that close to me for other reasons. Before I could react, she spoke.

"We have to get back to work." The hitch in her voice reassured me that her reasoning wasn't to get away from me. "We have a lot to do, and not much time left."

TEX

I almost couldn't finish the story. Zev's fingertips ghosted over my back, running the path of my worst scar. Teddy had refused to look at or touch my back after his first glimpse of my decimated skin, somewhat hidden beneath my bathing suit. He made sure his hands never got near my back again. Zev's caress made me shiver. At my movement, Zev pulled away. I barely heard his apology, but I understood that his withdrawal came from his perception of my reaction rather than his aversion to my scars.

I could feel the heat rise to my face, and I stared at the ground. "It didn't feel bad." I admitted, my concern for him greater than my discomfiture.

Zev muttered something that I didn't catch and then spoke loud enough for me to hear. "We should go."

Well, if Zev's voice was any indication, he'd been as affected by our closeness as I had. That realization alone was enough to make me tingle from head to toe. But, unfortunately, I knew we had to keep going. Our feelings would have to wait. And, judging by the rapid percussion under my ribs, that was probably a good thing. I didn't need divine intervention to tell me that if we didn't divert our attention and energy elsewhere, there would be serious consequences.

I shook my head to clear it, and took a step forward. "We need to get back to work." I heard the quaver in my voice and forced myself to calm down. “We have a lot to do, and not much time left.” Even as I spoke the words, I could hear the ring of truth behind them.

“Let’s try sparring again.” Zev shifted his stance. “Best two out of three. Then we’ll see what else I’ll need to teach you.”

Two-and-a-half aching hours later, I stood under the hot and pulsing spray of my shower, praying that I’d be able to move the next day. I hadn’t been this sore since my first soccer practice after a two-month absence; bouncing off rocks for twenty-five feet tended to limit physical activity for a while. And I hadn’t spent that practice time blocking – for the most part – a multitude of punches and kicks. I sent up a small prayer of thanks for the forecasted cooler weather. I was dreading tomorrow’s revealing of what was sure to be a plethora of bruises. Wearing a sweatshirt would at least eliminate having to explain most of the discoloration.

Before I wanted to, my brain returned to the problem at hand. How was I going to convince my non-believing mother to let me more-or-less drop out of high school so I could join my boyfriend (I couldn’t help but be tickled by the word) in his hunt for an immortality-obsessed tribe that pre-dated civilization. I sighed as I dried off. Impossible.

With Me, nothing is impossible.

“This might be a good time to prove it.” I muttered.

God didn’t answer as I headed back to my room. He didn’t need to. The sight that greeted me made me stop in my tracks. My mother was digging in my purse.

“Mom!” I didn’t try to conceal the shock in my voice.

While often absentminded about personal space, she never intentionally violated my privacy.

"Sorry, Tex." Mom's entire face screamed her guilt. Wait, that wasn't just guilt. She also looked... sheepish. She lifted a hand. "I ran out."

To my horror, I recognized what she held. My mouth opened and closed several times as I attempted to find my voice. Evidently, it had fled the country, taking some brain cells with it. Then, proving that things could indeed get worse, Mom continued talking.

"Things are really going well with Dion and I've already used up..."

"No!" Horror ripped the word from my throat.

"And, Tex," Mom's tone became so severe that I blinked, caught off-guard at the sudden change. "You want to tell me why there's the same number as there was when I put them in your purse?"

"Because I'm not using them." I stammered, hoping the truth would be obvious in my words. "I mean, I don't need to use them." Mom raised her eyebrows and I hastily added, "Zev and I aren't sleeping together."

Mom studied my face for a moment and then nodded once. "By the way, I signed those emancipation papers." She turned to go.

"Wait, what?" My head spun as I tried to follow her change of topic.

"Remember, we talked about this a couple months ago? I told you that I had a job offer in Milan?"

I nodded, still confused.

“Well, they agreed to my terms – three months there, one month here – and I’ll be leaving in two weeks. Since you’re not eighteen, I needed to have these papers drawn up so you can stay here and finish up school like you wanted.” She grinned and sailed out the door. “I’ll be home later. Don’t wait up.”

With me, nothing is impossible.

Mom had just given me my way out.

***

I glanced at my watch again, hurrying through the halls as quickly as I dared. I’d been in the office since eight o’clock wrangling information from Mrs. Alan, the school secretary, all the while skirting the truth as to why I might suddenly need my transcripts or withdrawal papers. Now, thanks to Mrs. Alan’s over-inquisitiveness, I was going to be late meeting Zev in homeroom and he’d wonder where I’d been. While I wouldn’t lie to him, I knew that it wasn’t time to divulge the whole plan just yet.

Fortunately, as soon as I slid into the desk next to his, I knew distraction wasn’t going to be necessary, and I understood that the interrogation from Mrs. Alan had been out of concern rather than nosiness. I’d forgotten about my face. The moment Zev saw it, he winced, guilt and shame flooding his features with color. A wave of duel relief washed over me. Relief, first, that I had enough of a distraction that I wouldn’t need to hide my office visit and, second, that Zev couldn’t see any more of the injuries I’d received last night. The dark smudge under my right eye, barely concealed by make-up, and my cut, still swollen, bottom lip were bad enough. My battered knuckles hid under the too-long sleeves of my bulky sweatshirt and I would keep them there as much as possible. As for my arms and torso, I never intended for Zev to see the multi-colored canvas they'd become. I had to work later that day and my tan would cover my fading contusions by the time Zev and I sparred again. Hopefully.

"I don't know if I can do this." The tip of Zev's index finger traced just under my lower lip, eliminating any pain I'd felt and replacing it with a familiar electric warmth. "I hurt you."

"And how badly would a Perpetuum hurt me if I don't learn?" I kept my voice low though no one was paying attention to us. In a school as small as NHCS, it was easy to keep secrets. Everyone knew everything, sometimes even before things happened, making the concept of 'secret' null and void. At times, my sarcasm impressed even me.

Zev scowled and I knew that my point had been made. Before he could argue, the bell rang and Mrs. Peterson called everyone to order. Once attendance had been taken and devotions finished, we only had a few minutes until first period. As I turned towards him, I worried that Zev might have used the previous ten minutes to come up with a strategy to dissuade me from training. I didn't need to be concerned, however, because as soon as Mrs. Peterson freed us to talk, Gretchen and Susan started in on me.

"Did you have your eyes closed when you got dressed this morning?" Susan eyed my faded jeans and black hoodie, criticism dripping from her voice.

"If I looked like you, I'd shut my eyes every time I passed a mirror." Gretchen sneered. Her sharp gaze caught my injuries and she grinned. "Piss someone off, Tex?"

Zev cut in. "You should see the other guy." He dropped a wink.

Gretchen glared at Zev and I had to work to hold back a smile. "No one asked you."

Apparently, her admiration could only excuse Zev so far. The bell cut off any further insults and Zev followed me to physics. Such was my trepidation that Zev was going to end our training that I actually felt relief when Mrs. Conner called the class to order. As I methodically copied notes from the chalkboard, my brain was busy, planning how best to extract information from Zev without him realizing what I was doing. When God gave us the order to leave, I didn't want anything holding us back.

***

"Again." I managed to say the word while gasping. I looked down at Zev where he lay, panting just as hard as I was. I couldn't stop my grin. I'd finally made him work hard at something.

"Tex, you're going to kill me." Zev groaned, rolling onto his side. At my raised eyebrow, he amended his statement. "All right, you'll make me wish you could kill me."

"Afraid I'm going to beat you?" I retrieved Zev's sword from where my final blow had thrown it. "You know, again."

More than a full week had passed since my first training session, and I was surprised at how quickly I'd picked things up. In hand-to-hand fighting, I'd improved enough to land a few blows of my own and prevent most of Zev's. Since that first encounter, he hadn't been taken by surprise and I'd lost every following match. With knives, I'd shocked both of us by beating Zev in three of four throwing exercises, and then pinning him to the ground in less than thirty seconds when he introduced the blades to one of our sparring sessions. This was the first time, however, I'd managed to disarm him with one of the more traditional weapons. I doubted, however, that broadswords would be the weapon of choice very often. Still, it was nice to know that I could handle it if I needed to.

Before I could challenge Zev again, I heard my cell phone vibrate against the top of the heavy pine desk where I'd placed it two hours ago. I was tempted to ignore it, but I was conditioned enough that the phone was in my hand before I had time to consider not answering it. I flipped it open.

"Saturday. Midnight. Abandoned church. St. Francis. Corner of Tucker and Easthom Avenues. Initiation meeting planned."

All good humor vanished as I read Elle's message. This was it. The signal I'd been waiting for. I snapped the phone shut and turned back towards Zev. My face must've altered with my mood because Zev was on his feet in an instant.

"It's time to go." The tone of my voice didn't betray the countless emotions coursing through me. "We need to be in Ohio by midnight tomorrow."

"What?" Whatever Zev had been expecting, this wasn't it.

"Elle just sent me a text." I shoved my phone into my pocket and reached for my bag so I didn't have to look at Zev's face. "Things are getting serious."

"Tex, just wait a minute." Zev's fingers closed around my upper arm, effectively stopping any forward motion I'd been ready to attempt. "We can't go yet. You're not ready."

Excuse me? My temper flared and my head snapped up. "I'm not ready?" I barely registered the flash of surprise that crossed Zev's face. "Don't put your own insecurities off on me, Zev." I shook my arm free. My friend was involved and I wasn't going to put things off just because Zev was getting cold feet. "I'm going home to pack and I'll be leaving in an hour. With or without you."

ZEV

Time to go? My brain couldn't make those three words sensible. I knew she had to be talking about our training for the night even though she'd expressed a desire to continue. She couldn't mean something more? Could she? "What?"

"Elle just sent me a text. Things are getting serious." Her next words confirmed that the sinking in my stomach had nothing to do with my sudden change of position. She truly intended to go through with this insane notion of fighting at my side.

Zev, remember our conversation.

Sometimes, that whole omniscience thing was annoying.

I reached for Tex's arm to stop her from leaving. "Tex, just wait a minute. We can't go yet. You're not ready."

I heard the fire in her voice before I saw it in her eyes.

"I'm not ready? Don't put your own insecurities off on me, Zev."

Ouch. That comment stung enough for me to allow her to pull her arm away.

"I'm going home to pack and I'll be leaving in an hour. With or without you."

I couldn't move, couldn't speak. I could only watch as my world walked out of the room.

Your world, Zev? What part do I play then?

The statements caught me off-guard, rocking my spirit more than Tex's disappearance had.

Whom do you serve?

I froze. This question held more weight than four words should have. The war inside me was brief and brutal. I didn't cry or scream this time. No, this was different. This answer was not born of emotion or heart. This was a question for the soul.

Peace washed over me as I answered in a rush of pent-up air.

"You, *El Yeshuati. El Chaiyai. El Roi.*"

Now go home and pack. Tex meant it when she said she'd be leaving in an hour.

The reminder that I'd lose Tex if I didn't hurry was enough to thaw my limbs. I extinguished the lights and dashed up the stairs, taking the stone steps two at a time. My mind raced as I drove home, trying to figure out a way to get out of telling my parents what I was planning to do.

Trust Me.

I grimaced. Don't get me wrong, I'd made my decision

and I had the faith that *El Gibbor* could handle anything and everything. I just didn't always like the way He did things.

Good thing I don't need you to like what I do.

Again, I could hear a tinge of dry humor. When I pulled into the driveway, however, I couldn't stop a sigh of relief. No one was home. The lights were out and, since it was too early for my parents to turn in, I could safely assume that they'd gone out for the evening. "Thank You." Though soft, the words were heartfelt.

I saw the note on the table as soon as I entered the kitchen and I skimmed it as I headed for my room. Using some of our considerable resources, Mom and Dad had decided to visit Ellis in Europe where he was still tracking a Perpetuum with Jael. They weren't sure when they'd return and reminded me that Ruby'd be coming by twice a week to clean. I tossed the letter onto my dresser even as I pulled open the top drawer.

The routines of packing for a hunting expedition required a small fraction of my attention, allowing me opportunity to decide how to leave things with my parents. By the rules of every society into which we'd assimilated, I was, for all intents and purposes, an adult. Not to mention that my actual age put me well past any other limitations. I could leave without legal ramifications, but, when you've spent millennia watching people age and die around you, you tended to stick with your own kind. So none of us, not even my *goblok* brother, simply vanished into the night. I'd need to word things carefully though, to prepare my parents for the rumors that were sure to abound when people realized that Tex had disappeared around the same time I did. I could always hope that we'd be back before anyone realized we were gone, but I knew to err on the side of caution.

Time to finish it, Zev.

I knew arguing was futile. I just couldn't help myself. "Tex doesn't intend to stay on the road until we wipe out the Perpetuum."

How do you know?

"Because it doesn't make sense." I shoved a t-shirt into my bag with more force than necessary. Fortunately, the material was strong and it didn't rip. "It's her senior year and she won't want to be away from her mom and her friends."

She knows that following Me means making sacrifices.

"Like not graduating from high school?" I reached under my bed and retrieved my weapons chest. These were the good ones, used only in battle.

It's been taken care of.

I decided to forgo further discussion.

Twenty minutes later, I scribbled the note and left it near where I'd found Mom and Dad's message. If they came home before calling or texting, they'd find it. The odds of my parents not bothering to use their cells were pretty much fifty-fifty. Technological savvy combined with their lengthy lifetimes of experience made for a toss-up as to whether or not they'd remember the newest means of communication. Personally, I was hoping they'd come back to the house first. My note had been honest, but vague. I'd be forced to give more details in a verbal (or textual) conversation and that wasn't something I really wanted. Call me chicken all you want, but you've never seen my mom interrogate someone. Medieval England's highest inquisitors had nothing on my mother. In fact, she'd taught some of them a few new tricks.

I read my note one more time, checking each word for truth as well as abstraction. "Mom and Dad, nothing to worry about, but I'm going to be gone for a while. Consider my decision made. There's a Perpetuum back East causing some trouble. I might track some leads when I'm done, so I'm not sure when I'll be back. I'll call if I need help. Love you both, Z."

Satisfied that I'd done the best I could, I grabbed my last bag, did a quick visual search to make sure I hadn't forgotten anything, and headed for the car. I took a moment to come to terms with the fact that I was actually going through with this. I was voluntarily returning to the mission I'd been given thousands of years ago. And I was taking a mortal with me.

Ready?

I exhaled, put the key in the ignition and listened to the car roar to life. As I pulled out of the driveway, I knew, deep in my soul, that this was the beginning of a whole new chapter. No matter how cliché it sounded, how banal the phrasing, it was an apt description of how I felt as I rounded the bend that would take me to Tex's house.

Chapter Eight: Back on the Road Again to Fight the Good Fight

TEX

I groaned as I sat up. The position in which I'd fallen asleep was hardly conducive to a comfortable waking, but at least I'd managed a few semi-restful hours, which was more than I could say for the young man behind the wheel. Zev had been driving for almost six hours, judging by the sun rising in front of us, and I'd been sleeping for almost half of that time. Zev glanced my way and gave a half-smile.

"Where are we?" I blushed as I heard my voice croak. I grabbed a bottle of water and quickly swallowed some as he answered.

"Kansas."

I nodded, not quite ready for full conversation this early in the morning, especially now that my curiosity had been satisfied. As the morning fog lifted, I recalled the events of the previous night with an odd patchwork clarity.

Driving home with tear-blinded eyes, terrified that Zev would refuse to come.

God's gentle reminder that I'd made my choice.

Finding the house empty, my mother out with her newest paramour.

Trying to choose the right words to say good-bye.

Hearing that car pull into my driveway as I was preparing to leave alone.

"Penny for your thoughts." Zev interrupted my reminiscing.

Not quite ready to admit the depth of relief, eagerness and

a different type of anxiety that I'd felt when I'd seen the familiar Impala shape, I settled for just one of the things that had been going through my mind in the past few moments.

"Just thinking about my mom." I ran a hand through my hair and reached for my purse.

"Do you think she's worried about you?" Zev's concern was evident in every word.

I shook my head as I rummaged through my bag. "She knows I can take care of myself." I winced at the triviality of the phrase, but continued. "I'm just picturing the look on her face when she finds my note." I pushed away the memory of leaving the note in her room, leaning the envelope against the blue tissue box on her beside table. That trip down memory lane lead nowhere good.

"Do you mind if I ask what it said?" With an air of casualness that I was pleased to see through, he reached for my hand.

When his fingers curled around mine, I would've told him every word I'd ever written, and maybe some I'd thought, spoken or signed. As it was, I willingly shared what I'd left for my mother. "I told her that I'd taken her advice and was going to finish school online. I said that I was going to visit Elle first and then decide what I was going to do next."

"Finish school online? You're not withdrawing from NHCS."

The tone of his voice made the words an order and I bristled, now completely awake. "I already did." I clarified. "Well, more or less."

"What does that mean?"

Despite the edge to his words, Zev didn't take his hand away, so I guessed that it was at least semi-safe to continue. "I still need to make a call on Monday morning, but I set things in motion a few days ago."

"What things?" Zev's voice was so quiet that I had to shift in my seat to hear him.

"I have emancipation papers, Zev." His eyes darted from the road to my face for the briefest of moments. "Mom had them drawn up because she's leaving for Milan on Monday. A new job that'll keep her out of the country for at least three months, if not more. That was God's way of showing me that it was time to get ready. I talked to Mrs. Alan, told her that I might be pulling out and asked what I'd need to do to graduate. I'm not going back until this is done."

Zev clenched his jaw, muscles jumping as he reached for the radio, letting music fill the silence between us. I turned my attention to the passing scenery that was so vastly different than anything I'd ever known. Gone were the sharp lines and rolling slopes that I'd been accustomed to seeing against the sky. Instead, I could see for miles, could see the curve of the horizon where green met blue. Yep. Definitely Kansas and no place like my home.

After a while – at least six or seven of Zev's alternative rock songs – he broke the relative silence. "When you call, I'll need to talk to Mrs. Alan, too."

I felt the blood rush to my cheeks and mumbled, "No you don't. I took care of that too." Zev's hand tightening around mine was the only indication that he'd heard my confession. "That was the letter I put in the mailbox last night. It said that your family would be gone on personal matters and you'd contact the school regarding transcripts when things settled down. I used your parents' names, but typed the letter." I was aware that I was venturing away from explaining and into babbling, but I couldn't stop myself. "New Hope is used to things like this. Well, not exactly things like this, of course, but we've had our fair share of people coming in and out with little or no explanation. One of the things you deal with when you're a private school..."

"Tex."

My name, combined with gentle pressure on my fingers, refocused me. Basically, I shut up and looked at Zev. The tenderness in his eyes almost made me start babbling again, so I did the only thing I could. I bit my tongue. Literally and unpleasantly. If this kept up, I faced the possibility of permanent damage. I wondered if insurance covered self-inflicted wounds if I needed the tip of my tongue re-attached.

"Thank you. I would've used school as an excuse to go back when we're done in Wycliffe."

I grinned despite the pain in my mouth. "I know." In a totally unlike me, impulsive move, I leaned over and kissed Zev's cheek. The mood shifted instantly, a palpable reaction to an innocent action. Suddenly, I realized that Zev and I were fully and truly alone. No one in the car with us. No one waiting at home, thus ensuring some protection from temptation. No school or church to serve as reminders of promises made. From the expression on Zev's face, he had surmised the same thing.

Not alone.

The familiar voice brought some semblance of calm. I sank back in my seat.

It won't be easy, but I'll be here.

Well, this was going to be interesting.

***

I heard my knees pop when I finally straightened them, and my back let off a similar snap-crackle as I raised my arms high above my head. I-70 stretched to the horizon on either side of the gas station where we'd finally stopped. A nearby sign announced our entrance to Lawrence, Kansas. In the back of my mind, I knew I'd heard the name before. I just couldn't quite place it.

"You know, this is the furthest east I've ever been." I glanced behind me at Zev who was filling up the car. The sight of the sleek black metal triggered the memory of why I'd recognized the city's name. I grinned, recalling my initial comparison of Zev to a fictional character. Fortunately, Zev didn't see my smile so I didn't need to sidestep an awkward inquiry.

By the time I returned, carrying a few food items, Zev was in the car, waiting. I slid into the passenger's seat, commenting as I went, "Did you re-set your watch? I'd never had to do that before. Probably would've forgotten if I hadn't seen the clock in there."

"I've never really gotten used to that." Zev pulled back on the road again. After a moment, he glanced over at me. "Question: how is it, with a social mother and a lot of money, you're not better traveled?"

"Mom wanted me to be settled. When I was little, Mom would leave me with her mother when she went on trips. By the time Grandma Bug passed on, I was old enough to stay home by myself and preferred it to traveling tutors."

"Grandma Bug?"

I smiled as I pictured the only grandparent I'd ever known. Snow-white hair even though she was barely fifty when I was born. Unique sense of style that somehow always included a white handbag. Said white handbag had been full of the most wonderful things. Candy and gum. A book or two. Sometimes a coloring book or some odd, old-fashioned toy. As I child, I'd believed it to be the equal to the magical bag carried by a singing British nanny, and expected Grandma Bug to pull an entire lamp from it one day. Maybe a few chimney-sweeps or a magical umbrella. Alas, my fantasies were in vain, for the best thing Grandma Bug ever took from her handbag was a brown and white guinea pig that I named Gus.

With a start, I realized that Zev was still waiting for answer. "Apparently, when I was starting to talk, my mom referred to her mom as a 'grammar bug' for some reason or other. My brain picked it up and translated it to 'Grandma Bug.' It stuck."

"Cute."

"Some of my best memories are of the times I spent with Grandma Bug. She was as much a parent to me as Mom." I gave a sad smile. "She passed away on my thirteenth birthday. Cancer."

"I'm so sorry." Zev took one hand off of the steering

wheel to cup the side of my face.

"I'll see her again." I closed my eyes for a brief moment, reveling in the feel of his skin on mine. I opened my eyes and he withdrew his hand. "While not exactly conventional with her faith, Grandma Bug's in heaven."

After almost a full minute of silence, Zev spoke again. "You'd mentioned before that your dad wasn't really in the picture."

I could hear the hesitation in Zev's voice as he approached the subject and decided to ease the burden. "They met when she was modeling in Texas." I blushed. "Killeen, Texas, actually. Dad was a talent scout or agent or something like that. They were only together a couple weeks. Mom contacted Dad after she found out she was pregnant because she thought he should know, but she wasn't expecting anything. Didn't want anything really. Mom's never wanted to get married or anything like that. I guess my dad came to see me a couple times, but I don't remember him. Something happened when I was around two and he never came back. If it wasn't for a picture Grandma Bug had saved from Mom's cleaning frenzy, I wouldn't even know what he looked like."

"I'm sorry." Zev apologized again, stretching his hand towards me without even seeming to realize that he'd done it.

"I came to terms with my lack of a father a few years ago. It doesn't bother me." Trying – and failing – to conceal a smirk, I placed a breakfast bar in Zev's questing hand. His look of surprise was so comical that I couldn't help but laugh, effectively lightening the mood. "You haven't eaten anything since yesterday, am I right?"

Zev nodded, tearing the silver wrapper with his teeth as he drove with one hand. My attention was momentarily captivated by the gleam of white against dusky skin. Then Zev took a bite, and I brought myself back to the real world, entertained by the idea of anywhere near Zev being the real world.

"What about you?" He spoke around a mouthful of granola and almonds. "When was the last time you ate?"

"Right now." I opened my own package after showing it to Zev. "So if we're in Lawrence, how far does that put us from Wycliffe?"

"Around fourteen hours."

I glanced at my newly set watch. "With as few stops as possible, we should get there in time." I looked over at Zev. "I forgot to ask earlier, but do you know where you're going?"

"My family moved to Fort Prince from a town near Wycliffe." When Zev reached out this time, I handed him a bottle of water. It wasn't until he'd taken a drink and given the bottle back that I realized that he hadn't asked for it. I dropped the bottle back into the bag, pleased that we seemed to be so in tune with each other that we didn't necessarily need the verbal communication.

"Really?" I'd forgotten that he'd been in Ohio before coming to Colorado.

"About twenty miles away in fact." Zev tossed his wrapper into the back. He must have caught the admonishment on my face because he gave a child-like smile, one that made the slumbering butterflies in my stomach wake up and begin doing the tango. "I'll clean it up. I promise." He held up one hand in a Boy Scout salute.

I grabbed the aforementioned hand and drew it to my lips, lightly kissing his knuckles before settling our hands between us. “I’ll hold you to that.”

“Right.” Zev’s voice was unsteady.

The butterflies were joined by another set of dancing animals, these slightly larger and less coordinated. Time to change the subject. To anything.

Grasping, I returned to his previous comment. “What school did you go to in Ohio?”

Zev’s mouth flattened into a thin line. I felt a flash of anger towards whatever had prompted the involuntary action. “What happened?”

“I went to a Christian school about fifteen minutes from where we lived.”

“And you wanted to finish out high school there?” I guessed, puzzled. As many times as Zev had been through high school, I found it odd that he’d been particularly attached to any one place.

“A month before school let out, the students were told that it wouldn’t be reopening the next year. That the resources weren’t available to continue.” Zev’s tone was laced with hostility.

“I don’t understand. If the money’s not there, obviously the school can’t stay open.”

“Didn’t you wonder, Tex, why I, if I was so angry with *El Olam*, was at NHCS instead of a public school?” Zev’s voice had lost the bitterness, but none of the edge.

“A superior education.” As soon as I spoke them, I

understood how ludicrous the words were.

Zev's eyebrows disappeared under the dark hair that had fallen across his forehead. "Do you know how many graduate degrees I have?"

"I don't think I want to." I answered truthfully. I felt dumb enough without the extra reasons. I steered the conversation back to the point. "Why did you choose a Christian school?"

"Over the years, my family's returned to a few places, visiting the descendants of people befriended generations before. All discreetly done, of course. The founders of New Hope Christian School were the great-great-great grandchildren of a family who helped my parents and I almost two centuries ago."

"Wow." My brain struggled to reconcile the idea of two hundred years, the portrait of the NHCS founders that hung in the chapel and an unchanged Zev.

Zev continued his story. "Another set of their descendants established the school in Ohio, about thirty years ago." He paused, the muscles in his jaw tightening. "Do you really think my family wouldn't have given them the money they needed?" The bitter was back and it had brought friends. "At the start of the year, the new pastor kept talking about how excited he was about the school, about how much he and the church supported it. But as the year progressed, even the students started noticing that all of the changes, all of the improvements, were being done to the church part of the building. Plenty of money was being spent, just not on the school."

"Oh." I really couldn't say anything else. I'd had my issues with NHCS, but I wouldn't want to see it close. It had been a part of my life since I was five. I couldn't imagine it not existing anymore. And to end with such deception. I could empathize with Zev's anger now and, because I couldn't vocalize it, I squeezed his hand.

We rode in silence for almost an hour. As we approached the border, Zev raised our hands and pressed his lips to the back of my hand. Ah, return of the tangoing butterflies and frogs. I'd decided on amphibians for my second cavorting creatures.

"Let's listen to some music. Your pick."

I rummaged, one-handed, through my bag until I found the CD I wanted. When the first lyrics of classic rock blared from the speakers, Zev gave me a quizzical look. "Seemed appropriate since we're leaving the state."

He laughed, a full, loud laugh that begged for me to join in. I was happy to oblige. Then, to my utter amazement, Zev began to sing along. A moment later, so did I.

ZEV

I couldn't stop myself from stealing glimpses of Tex as she slept, studying the way different forms of light reflected off her skin, revealed the curves and angles of her face, shadowed her features or threw them into sharp relief. Passing under bright streetlights, for example, left only one side of her face visible, hiding the other side in darkness, casting strange patterns on her cheek and forehead when her curls got in the way. The moon, however, softened everything, reminding me just how young this girl was. At these moments, I could only bear to look at her for the briefest of seconds, plagued by doubts as to whether or not I was doing the right thing. Each time, I would hear that Voice, the one that rode the wind rather than the storm, reminding me that I was back in His plan, in His hands, in the safest place I could be.

In the silence – I'd turned off my CD as soon as Tex began to drift off – and without anything other than the flat and virtually empty highway to occupy my racing brain, my thoughts returned again and again to the image I was sure I would keep with me until the end of my very long and unnatural life. Whether I regained my mortality or finally heard that trumpet (some part of my mind insisted on questioning the literality of the instrument; maybe *El Echad* would create some new and unknown horn to announce His return), I knew that I would never forget the sight of Tex coming to her door hours before.

Her tiny frame dwarfed by the bags hanging from each shoulder.

The determined set of her jaw.

The light in her eyes that I first took for anger.

The realization that I'd misread those gray pools and the intensity that shone there was for me.

The black cloud of doubt that descended on me as I wondered how I deserved her.

The reminder that *El malei Rachamin*, fortunately, does not give what is deserved.

Back in the present, I snuck another glance at Tex and swept a few haphazard curls away from her closed eyelids, catching my breath as a now-familiar-but-still-exciting charge raced through my nervous system. How I loved this girl.

"*Nuku hyvin, rakas.*" I whispered.

It was close to five o'clock. Almost time for the sun to rise on a brand-new day.

***

Without thinking about what I was doing, I threw my trash into the back seat. Then I saw the disapproving tilt of the head, the slight raise of the eyebrows, that meant my action had not been appreciated. Even though it was my car, I had to concede that, since Tex was going to be spending equal time in it for a while, keeping it neat should probably be a priority. I grinned. "I'll clean it up. I promise." To assure Tex of my intentions, and trying to get a laugh, I gave the Boy Scout salute.

My lame attempt at humor was banished the moment Tex grabbed my hand. When she kissed it, I renounced everything that didn't gain this response. "I'll hold you to that."

I had to concentrate to keep the car on the road, going the right direction, and so my answer didn't come out quite as cool as I'd wished. "Right." Nice work, Zev. Any worse and your voice would've cracked like a twelve year-old boy.

"What school did you go to?" The question doused the fire in my veins better than ice water would have. A moment later, Tex followed her first inquiry with a second. "What happened?"

Either she was getting better at reading my emotions or I was getting worse at hiding them. I hoped the former was true rather than the latter. "I went to a Christian school about fifteen minutes from where we lived."

"And you wanted to finish out high school there?"

Sharing the story with Tex was easier than I'd thought, soothing the raw wound I still had from that experience. With all I'd endured over my extended lifetime, I'd been surprised by how much this particular betrayal had upset me. Then again, I had been close to the founder's numerous-great's grandfather and the situation would have devastated him. Tex's firm grip on my hand steadied me and, as I finished, I found that the rancor had left me, purged by the telling. I didn't say anything for a while, enjoying the sensation of Tex's fingers woven with mine, the wheels of my car moving us steadily towards our destination, the healing taking place in my heart.

As I saw the sign announcing the approach of Kansas City, I raised Tex's and my hands and pressed my lips against the warm skin there. "Let's listen to some music. Your pick."

I expected her to release my hand and felt my insides warm when she, instead, used only her free hand to retrieve a CD from one of her bags. A smile lurked at the corners of her lips and the moment I heard the first words I knew why.

"Seemed appropriate since we're leaving the state."

The laughter burst out of me and Tex joined in, a melody blending together perfectly, one that continued when we both began to sing. At that moment, with the future stretched out uncertainly ahead, and our mutually murky pasts disappearing behind, I knew I'd made the right decision.

The time passed more quickly than I'd been expecting, bringing mixed emotions. On one hand, I wasn't looking forward to getting back into the fight or bringing Tex into it.

On the flip side of the coin – to mix metaphors – I was relishing every minute of getting to know Tex. Before, we had to worry about classes and work and just general life stuff always interfering. Now, our conversation flowed from one topic to another without any clear relation, occasionally lapsing into silence for a dozen miles or so.

After one of these pauses, Tex asked a question that threw me for a loop, as the saying goes. “Do you need a break from driving?”

“Kinda on a timetable. I’m not sure stopping for a rest is the best idea.”

A tug on my hand drew my eyes from the road to the girl, bringing about a dropping sensation in my stomach. She grinned and my aforementioned internal organ skyrocketed.

“I do have this little plastic card that allows me to...”

“You want to drive my car?”

Something about the way I’d spoken must’ve amused Tex because she smiled as she answered.

“Believe it or not, I do know how to handle an automobile.” Her eyes sparkled and I was momentarily dazzled. “Even one as pretty as this one.”

“Did you just call my car ‘pretty’?” I probably should’ve been offended by her incorrect evaluation of my obviously masculine vehicle, but I was drowning in glittering gray and couldn’t muster enough energy for anything more than keeping myself afloat.

“Something wrong with that?”

I looked away, muttering. “*Il camion delle immondizie.*”

“What did you just say?”

My cheeks burned as the spell broke. “Sorry. I tend to, well, talk in other languages when I’m angry or nervous or my brain just short circuits. Plus, I’m trying to get away from cursing and...”

“You babble when you’re tired.” Tex interrupted. “Explains a lot.”

I tried to scowl, but it didn’t end up as threatening as I wanted, so I jumped back to the original topic.

“No offense, but driving a Sunbird doesn’t really compare...”

“Next rest stop, pull over.” There was iron through each syllable. “We can’t afford to waste time. Just do it.”

Startled, I did as she asked. It took only a few minutes for us to switch places. With a smug, self-satisfied smile, Tex pulled out of the parking lot, handling my baby with a smoothness and grace that surprised me. Okay, definitely a foot-in-mouth moment.

Tex’s grin widened when she saw my chagrin, but she only said, “Get some sleep. I’ll wake you if I get lost.”

“Just stay on this road.” I shifted in my seat, getting more comfortable. Now that I knew Tex wouldn’t wreck my beloved car, I could feel exhaustion eating up my adrenaline-fueled energy. As much as I wanted to stay awake, I knew I’d need to be as rested as possible. I wasn’t risking Tex’s life just because I didn’t want to sleep.

“Get some rest.” Tex reached out one hand, resting her fingertips on mine. For a moment, I fancied that I could see the sparks crossing from her skin to mine.

I nodded, already sinking into slumber. I kept my eyes on

Tex as long as they were open. As they closed, the image of Tex's face stayed with me even as I slipped away. A small portion of my brain mocked me for the sentimentality of my thoughts, but I told it to shut up and let me sleep. Fortunately, it did.

***

It was the lack of motion that woke me. The first thing I noticed was that we'd stopped. The second was that Tex's fingers were curled around mine. Oh, and the sun was setting.

"Welcome back, Sleeping Beauty." Tex's voice drove away the last of my fatigue.

"I thought she was woken by a kiss." I sat up straight, hoping that my voice didn't sound as girly to Tex as it did to my own ears.

Tex raised an eyebrow, then leaned towards me and kissed my cheek. "Better?"

"For now." I turned my head towards the window. The way Tex's eyes were glowing, her cheeks flushed as her fingers constricted around mine... well, let's just say that a kiss on the cheek wasn't what was parading through my head at that moment. With great difficulty, I pushed those thoughts aside. "What's going on?"

"Don't know. We've only been stopped for about five minutes, but there's nothing moving in our direction."

I glanced to one side and then the other. Tex was correct. Each lane on our side of the highway was at a dead stop. "How far away are we?"

“About five hours.”

I glanced at my watch. “That’s cutting it close.”

“I’m sure we’ll be moving again in no time.”

Any confidence Tex’s words might have inspired vanished at the sight of a teenager skateboarding down the middle of I-70, weaving through the cars with a carefree manner that could only be caused by the utter lack of fear that the stationary automobiles would soon resume their forward motion.

“That can’t be good.”

Though subtle, I could hear the tremor in Tex’s voice. “Hey, my turn to drive.” I climbed out of the car and walked around to the driver’s side. As I waited for Tex to move, I peered down the highway, seeing nothing but miles of metal gleaming in the setting sun. Once we’d situated ourselves again, I turned my attention back to Tex. “I’ll get us there.”

“I’m just nervous.”

I was relieved to hear her finally confessing some form of anxiety about what we were going to face. “It’ll be okay. Just follow my lead.”

“Zev, I have to ask,” Tex sounded more uncertain now than I’d heard her sound in the past few days. “When we get there, when we...”

Understanding dawned. I took Tex’s hand and pressed my lips to her palm. “I will do everything in my power, *petit ami*, to keep you from fighting, from taking a life.” I released Tex’s hand to slide my arm around her shoulders. I pulled her close and kissed the top of her head.

“Has any of them, any of the people...” The words faded

away and I supplied what she didn't want to say.

"Any of the people I've killed."

Tex winced, but continued. "Have they ever repented?"

"You have to understand that before the Messiah came, that wasn't an option."

"And after?"

"No." I shook my head, staring out of the window over Tex's dark curls. "To the end, they're defiant."

"What if they did want to change?" Tex raised her head.

I looked down, Tex's face mere centimeters from mine. "They wouldn't. We don't eliminate people who are just interested or curious. These are the dedicated, the most devout of disciples."

"But they could change their mind?"

I shook my head slowly, my gaze locked with Tex's. "You've heard of blasphemy of the Holy Spirit?"

"The one sin the Bible says is unforgivable?"

I could see that Tex was confused and I hurried to explain. "It's one thing they have to do. The final step to being a Perpetuum."

"They know what it means?"

"They do." I read sadness in her eyes and knew that she was thinking of the lost souls. The purity of her spirit amazed me, and fresh love, deeper, stronger than the emotion I'd previously called by the same name, pierced my heart. I kissed her then, wanting to erase the pain I'd seen.

TEX

"They know what it means?" I couldn't believe that

anyone, much less an entire group of people, would deliberately do something that couldn't be forgiven. Then again, I'd always believed that something so absolute and harsh could only be committed with full understanding of the consequences. God was a God of justice, not cruelty.

"They do." Zev's voice was gentle as he bent his head the last few millimeters needed to bring our lips together.

Worry, pain, anxiety all fled. All I could think of was Zev's hand at the back of my head, the other resting on my knee, and his mouth moving against mine. Our surroundings didn't matter. The traffic jam, the impossible task ahead, none of it seemed as important as Zev's kisses. His hand slid up my leg and around my side to press against the small of my back. I didn't need any further encouragement to move closer. I wrapped my arms around his neck, breathing in the scent of laundry soap and sunlight that was uniquely Zev.

It could have been minutes, hours, or days before the blast of a car horn startled us apart. All I knew was that it wasn't long enough. Fortunately, the driver behind us blared his horn again and we realized that the traffic was moving once more. Zev quickly released me and we resumed our journey east. This gave me enough time to regain my composure and send a slightly annoyed prayer heavenward.

All right, Lord, I'm not going to be able to do this on my own. You're really going to have to keep sending interruptions our way; otherwise, we're going to have some issues.

Trust Me.

I sighed and glanced at my watch. My eyes widened in surprise. Twenty minutes had passed since we'd first stopped.

Zev had been right. We were definitely cutting things close.

As we neared, then crossed, the Ohio border, my nerves grew more and more ragged, frayed to the point of tearing. Zev must've been able to feel my tension, but didn't say anything, merely held my hand, his thumb making soothing circles on my skin. We didn't bother trying to fill the car with more than the background noise of the same CD, repeating over and over.

For the first two hours, I looked at my watch so often that Zev started giving me concerned looks out of the corner of his eye. Finally, I took off my watch and tossed it into my bag. I'd drive myself nuts if I spent the rest of the drive checking the time.

After, to me, what seemed like an eternity, Zev spoke. "We need to stop for gas." I heard a strange note in Zev's voice and, as we passed under a light, I saw that his face was grim. Once he pulled up to a gas pump, he turned towards me and his next words explained everything. "We're too late to get there before the meeting begins. It's a quarter past eleven and we have at least an hour to go."

"So what do we do?" I tried not to let my disappointment be too obvious.

"Get there as soon as we can and stop who we can, track those we can't." Zev opened his door. "Call your friend and tell her to stay as far away from that church as possible."

As I flipped open my phone, I noticed a missed call from Elle. Hmm. Must've happened in a dead zone. I pressed the key to retrieve my voicemail, only half-listening to the automated menu because Zev was cleaning the windshield and that required my entire concentration. Then Elle's words registered.

"Tex, I've been waiting, but you're still not here, so I'm heading to the church. I wasn't going to get involved, but my roommate's been getting into this whole thing and telling me some pretty wicked stuff. Something really bad is going to happen tonight. I hope you're here in time. See you later."

"Tex?" Zev was tapping on my window, concern on his face. "What's wrong?"

I rolled down the window and quickly summarized Elle's message, knowing he'd share my unease. What I wasn't expecting was for the color to drain from his face and for him to dash around the car. He was in the driver's seat and racing away before my brain had fully processed what had happened. By the time we'd joined the normal flow of traffic, we were virtually flying. "Zev, slow down!"

"You don't understand." Zev didn't take his eyes from the road as he pushed the car forward. His knuckles were white on the steering wheel. "Your friend is in danger. More than I'd thought."

I could feel fear's cold fingers working their way through my insides. "What do you mean?"

"Her roommate wouldn't have told her anything specific about tonight's meeting unless Elle was involved with the Perpetuum. Believe me, they're very careful at the orientation stage."

"Elle would never..."

Zev shook his head, interrupting. "I don't think your friend is going to join. I think she's going to be the final sacrifice."

He couldn't have meant what I thought. Right? Could he? "Sacrifice?" My voice shook, but I didn't care.

"No matter how many ages pass, the majority of their rituals remain the same. When doing a mass recruitment like this, a number is chosen from those who express interest. Sometimes as many as fifty, usually half that. As the night progresses, more of the process is revealed and the faint of heart slip away, making up excuses and forgetting what they heard. When only a handful remains, the final revelation is given. Who they are. What they do."

"And, Elle?" My friend's face swam in front of my eyes. Light brown hair, hazel eyes, warm smile.

"Remember how I told you that the Perpetuum and Immortals are the truth behind certain myths?" Zev passed three cars before returning to the right-hand lane. "This is one of the reasons why." His voice was bleak, more than I'd ever heard it before. "An innocent, usually known by one of the new recruits, is lured to the orientation. Once there, they become both a sacrifice, and a meal."

I clapped both hands over my mouth, unsure if it was to hold back a scream or to keep me from throwing up. Thanks to the lack of a substantial dinner, I had nothing in my revolting stomach to lose, and my horror was so great that I couldn't make any noise. Zev glanced my way and accelerated.

After about twenty minutes of tense, anticipatory silence, Zev spoke. "We're not going to have time to get weapons from the trunk. In the back, there's a small black bag. It has some emergency weapons."

In any other circumstance, the idea of a bag of emergency

weapons might have inspired a snarky or otherwise witty rejoinder, but my sense of humor had disappeared along with any relief or joy I'd previously felt. I unbuckled my seatbelt, slightly uncomfortable with the rule-breaking – I'd always taken car safety seriously – but I knew that this was more important. I twisted around to begin my search. It took me fifteen minutes and half-climbing over the seat to retrieve it, but I finally managed to pull the bag into the front seat and set it on the floor between my feet.

"Get the guns ready. Check the clips, everything I taught you."

I opened the bag and did as he instructed, letting everything else in my mind just slip away. Before I'd finished, Zev spoke again.

"Wycliffe limits." His eyes blazed and I caught my breath, unsure which warring emotion was stronger: fear or desire. "I want the Desert Eagle and the black Beretta. You take the Colt."

"I'm not sure, Zev." I lifted the matte black weapon from the bag. "I'm more comfortable with..."

"You're not shooting unless you need to. Take the boot knife, but keep it hidden. Don't make yourself a threat. Without time to scout the location and plan an attack, this is our best option." This was a new tone to Zev's voice. One I hadn't heard before. Calculated, almost cold. The voice of killer. Shaken, but refusing to let Zev see, I gripped the handle of 'my' gun and listened as he explained what we were going to do.

I waited until he'd finished, by which time we were

turning onto Easthom Avenue, before I asked my question. "How do we distinguish the Perpetuum from everyone else?"

We skidded to a halt directly in front of a large sign proclaiming 'St. Francis Church of the Heavenly Order.' Zev answered me as he reached for the weapons he'd requested, also slipping a nine-inch boot knife into a leather sheath before strapping it to his calf, over his jeans for quicker retrieval. Fashion tended to take second place to practicality and survival. "The final event of an orientation is an identification ritual. Every member of the Perpetuum has a mark tattooed or branded onto the back of their left hands." Zev opened the door. "Come on. We've got work to do."

ZEV

Mentally running through the list of weapons stored in that particular bag, I made my selections. "I want the Desert Eagle and the black Beretta. You take the Colt."

"I'm not sure, Zev." I saw her lift the gun from the bag. "I'm more comfortable with..."

I cut off whatever she was going to say. "You're not shooting unless you need to." I struggled to keep the emotion out of my voice. I couldn't afford to let my love for Tex cloud my thinking, not now. "Take the boot knife, but keep it hidden. Don't make yourself a threat. Without time to scout the location and plan an attack, this is our best option." Out of the corner of my eye, I saw Tex's hands tighten on the butt of the gun and I fought the urge to turn the car around, to speed her away from danger. Instead, I filled Tex in on the simple strategy that was hopefully going to keep her alive. "I'll take point, go in first. Your main job is to watch my back. Protect me while I go after the Perpetuum. I want you at an angle so that our backs are no more than three feet apart at any given time. Keep your gun ready, your eyes and ears open. Don't get distracted by the chaos that's going to happen. Most importantly, if I say to run, you run. No questions, no looking back."

We turned onto the final road and Tex spoke in a voice much steadier than I'd expected. "How do we distinguish the Perpetuum from everyone else?"

I waited until we'd stopped before answering her question, choosing to arm myself rather than look at Tex while I spoke. If I allowed myself more than a glance, I'd be lost to the desire to protect her, to keep her from harm. "The final event of an orientation is an identification ritual. Every member of the Perpetuum has a mark tattooed or branded onto the back of their left hands." I opened my door and climbed out. "Come on. We've got work to do."

I didn't wait to see if Tex was following me. Instead, I headed directly for the cracked and neglected steps, my eyes locked on the lone figure waiting at the top. As I neared the massive, ornate doors, the man stepped forward, hands out in a gesture meant to placate. "Sorry, I'm not supposed to let anyone..." If he intended to say anything else, I kept him from doing so. One well-placed blow, delivered with millennia of practice, knocked the guard out cold. He dropped to the ground, head hitting the concrete with a crack that drew a wince from Tex. I took a second to flip the young man's left hand rather than following Ellis's protocol of eliminating anyone associated with the Perpetuum. No mark. He was probably just a paid lackey. He would live.

"He'll be fine." I straightened and walked towards the doors. Without looking, I knew that Tex had fallen into step exactly where I'd instructed her to be. I couldn't explain it, couldn't take the time to dwell on it at the moment, but I was as aware of Tex's every step as I was of my own. Then, we were inside, and I allowed instinct and training to take over.

The interior of the building was dark, lit only with candles along the far walls and at the front – a familiar setting that had unwittingly inspired so many Hollywood films. A thick layer of dust covered the stone floor, muffling our footsteps as we inched forward. Only the front right pew held people – my quick count said seven – so our entrance had yet to be noticed. The only person facing the back of the building was focused solely on something in front of him.

Not something. Someone.

The sharp intake of breath to my left confirmed my guess that the blindfolded and bound figure stretched out on the altar was Elle Monroe. I felt a flash of concern that Tex would break from our small formation at the sight of her friend, but she didn't falter. I allowed myself half a second of intermingled pride and love before leveling my weapon at the man standing at the head of the altar.

He was tall, though not quite my height, with rust-colored curls and a cruel smile. Even from my position, still a few yards away, I could see the complex series of lines on the back of his left wrist, black ink in stark contrast to his freckled skin. His other hand reached down below the altar and I knew that my time had run out.

"*Stamus contra malum*!" My voice echoed off of the walls and I saw everyone jump. The figures in the seats turned around and the Perpetuum's head snapped up. I used the moment of surprise to address the others while keeping my eyes on the leader. "I am Zev, son of Enos and Dinah, leader of the Immortals. Repent now, leave, seek immortality no more, and you will live. Stay and die."

Two men rose from their seats and ran, disappearing into the shadows. The leader swore, his paralysis broken. He yanked his hand out from the altar, brandishing a wickedly curved blade. He screamed as he raised the knife. "*Esto perpetua*!"

I absorbed the recoil as the gun bucked in my hand, smoothly shifting the barrel to the right before the first body hit the floor. I squeezed off the next five shots in quick succession. The last person barely had enough time to get to her feet before my bullet pierced her heart. I took a step forward, speaking softly to Tex as I did so. "I'm going to check them. You cut Elle free. Make sure she's okay."

To my surprise, Tex didn't immediately run for her friend. "Not until I know they're dead." Her words were low, emphatic, and broke my heart. Why had I agreed to this?

This was her choice. You are her choice.

"She deserves better." I muttered between clenched teeth, knowing I hadn't spoken loud enough for Tex to hear.

She loves you.

I didn't bother to argue. Instead, I glanced down at the unconscious figure on the altar and noted that she appeared to be unharmed. I passed her, expecting Tex to stop once she saw Elle, and crouched next to the man bleeding in the dust behind the altar. His eyes were open, searching, as he labored for air. His raised arm hadn't allowed for a clean shot, but a quick look told me that his wound was mortal. Dark irises locked on my face. I whispered. "*Stultum est timere quod vitare non potes. Nec mortem effugere quisquam nec amorem potest.*"

"*Esto perpetue.*"

I flinched at his final words. As I rose to my feet, Tex spoke behind me.

"What did that mean? What you said."

"When the hunt first began, it was what we would say over the dead. Now, you would call them proverbs, wise sayings. 'It is foolish to fear that which you cannot avoid.' 'No one is able to flee from death or love.'"

"And what he said."

"'May you last forever.'" I couldn't let her see how the statement had wounded me. I didn't need to bend down to see that each of my other shots had been a kill. I turned after the last body and saw that Tex was only a foot away, staring at me with burning, white-fire eyes. *Moje zvijezde!*

"We're going to end this."

Before I could respond to her statement, she jogged back to the altar, pulled out her knife and began to cut her friend free. I stared after her, unsure what was causing the lump in my throat: Tex's words or the expression on her face.

***

Once revived, Elle insisted that Tex and I stay with her. She'd already had a free bed thanks to a third roommate who'd never shown. Now, due to a bullet in the head, courtesy of yours truly, the top bunk bed was also empty. Both she and Tex worried about the wisdom of remaining in Wycliffe overnight, but I'd told them that we Immortals had developed a knack for knowing when we needed to run. Besides, such a cut-and-dry case like this wouldn't throw suspicion our way.

While Tex had driven Elle back to Whitmore Hall, I'd done the second half of my job: protecting my kind from detection. It wasn't as hard as one might expect, especially with the advancements in technology. The criminal justice system loved their forensics. By the time I'd finished, I could've written the 'drug deal gone bad' reports myself. I knew that I'd eventually need to tell Tex about the small bag of narcotics I kept for occasions such as this, but tonight didn't seem like the right time. I took *El Elohim*'s silence to be agreement on His part.

I jogged to the university before calling Tex for directions. Unlike her, I'd neglected to look at a campus map. Even so, it wasn't difficult to find the freshman dormitory and persuade a flirtatious brunette to open the door. With a roguish wink and a raucous laugh, the upperclassman at the security desk pointed the way to my 'friend' Elle's room. I ignored his inference and hurried away, filled with a sudden need to see Tex, to be certain she'd made it through the skirmish unscathed.

She opened the door before I'd completed the first knock and was in my arms even as the door swung shut behind me. I lifted her feet off the floor as I covered her face with kisses.

Unable to stop myself, I brushed my lips across her cheeks, her forehead, jaw, nose and, finally, her mouth. *Mijn liefde gewacht. Mijn alles. Mijn hart.* A great man could lose himself in her kisses, and I had never been a great man. *El amor de mi vida.*

Tex's fervor was equal to my own. Her arms were locked around my neck, bent at the elbows in what must have been an uncomfortable position, her fingers digging into my hair. One leg hooked around my waist, and I increased my hold on her for a split second before rationality crept in. I tried valiantly to ignore it, wanted to ignore it with every molecule in my body.

Zev.

Sometimes I really didn't like that Voice.

Biting back a groan, I untangled myself from Tex and set her on both of her feet. I felt a smug sense of pride when she swayed, her gaze slightly unfocused.

The door behind me opened and I spun around, in a defensive posture before my brain could register the tall, leggy brunette staring at me. Pale pink pajamas with a unicorn on the front of the shirt. Fuzzy pink pig slippers. I registered her as probably not a threat and then realized who she was. I'd been expecting hysterical weeping or immobilizing shock. For someone who'd been betrayed, kidnapped, almost sacrificed and eaten, rescued, and discovered that her betrayer / roommate had been executed, Elle Monroe was surprisingly composed. Her sparkling eyes darted from me to Tex and back again before she stepped into the room and shut the door.

"I don't know about you two, but I'm beat." She crossed to the single bed in the right corner of the room, dropping her shower things on a dresser and tossing her wet towel into a basket as she went. “Extra towels are in the closet. Women’s showers are down the hall to the left. Men’s are down the hall to the right.”

Chapter Nine: Don't Look Back, Come What May

TEX

Frost coated the windshield in opaque whiteness, but I stared anyway. I'd insisted that Zev take the back seat since he'd been driving the longest, and now I couldn't sleep. I wasn't quite awake enough to drive, but not tired enough to sleep. I hadn't been able to turn my brain completely off since we'd left Ohio almost a month ago. Only after a particularly long day, when I barely had enough energy to shower – and sometimes didn't even have that much – could I fall asleep without hours of constant mental chaos beforehand. I pulled my jacket tighter around me, gritting my teeth together to stop the telltale chattering that was sure to wake Zev. He needed his rest, and I didn't want him to know that I'd covered him with my blanket about twenty minutes ago, unable to tolerate the thought of him being this cold. More to keep my mind off of my numbing extremities and aching jaw than anything else, I thought back over the past few weeks and how far we'd come.

We'd stayed with Elle until Monday morning, giving me time to have some much-needed girl talk while Zev sought out another lead. By the time we left for Bisbee, Arizona, I was feeling more in control of myself around Zev. And Elle had instructed me to call her at any time, day or night, if I thought I might be wavering. So far, I'd only had to use my lifeline a few times. All right, fourteen times. In my defense, they were all preemptive. Both Zev and I had been very careful not to put ourselves in situations where we'd be tempted. Luckily – or, more accurately, divinely – every hotel we'd been to had two available non-adjoining rooms next to each other.

We'd stopped at the archway in St. Louis on our way back West, and made it to Bisbee by the first of October. Unfortunately, the Perpetuum had already moved on to Jericho Creek, California, and we followed suite. After Zev eliminated one Perpetuum there in a staged mugging-gone-wrong scenario, a story in the news took us north to Sappho, Washington. On the drive, Zev explained how much of the job would be like this, chasing a single person from town to town, searching through dozens of false leads until something finally broke. And a lot of time in the car. Good thing we never seemed to run out of things to talk about.

I was riveted by each new landscape, able to watch the Pacific coastline for hours, mesmerized by the beauty of Washington state's First Beach, by the forests as we crossed into Canada. For Zev, the countryside was nothing new. He'd traveled North America in every major stage of its colonization. To my chagrin, he found my fascination entertaining, but made up for his amusement by regaling me with stories of other times he'd been to various parts of the US and Canada. I also found his knowledge helpful as I crammed my online American History class into whatever time I could find. There were times, however, that Zev's version of events didn't always match up with the literature, and I found myself immersed in another story about what really happened at Custer's Last Stand or how many Spanish influenza deaths had actually been caused by a battle between seven Immortals and a congregation of twenty-two Perpetuum, the largest in American history.

From Vancouver, we'd headed to Hibbing, Michigan,

looking for a particularly nasty Perpetuum leaving a trail of bodies across several provinces and states. We probably never would have associated the two if we hadn't gotten a call from Elle. A cousin of hers had been visiting and mentioned a string of unsolved homicides running from his hometown of Three Forks, Montana, to Hibbing. She'd had a hunch that these weren't the work of an average serial killer (odd that I now found that phrase normal) and sent the information my way. Zev and I had made it to Hibbing only to find that the Perpetuum had moved on. A bit of detective work later and we were eastward once more. This time, we were going to Gary, Indiana. We'd left Hibbing about four hours ago after pulling an all-nighter searching for clues as to where our target had gone. And, now, we were attempting to get some sleep before continuing on to Gary. My watch beeped. It was now October twenty-sixth, I had no clue where in the US I was, and I was content. With that last thought reverberating in my head, my exhausted body overpowered my busy-bee brain, and I descended into oblivion.

***

I was ringing.

The thought pulled me from slumber even as my brain registered the sound more accurately. Mom's ringtone. I fumbled in my pocket and had the phone by my ear before my eyes opened.

"Yeah, Mom?" I sat up, blinking blearily at the receding dark. Faint pink and gold had yet to appear on the horizon, but black was turning to gray. “Something wrong?”

“No, silly.” Mom’s voice bounced through the phone and into my still foggy brain. “I just wanted to talk to you. Find out what was going on.”

I glanced at my watch. “Mom, it’s five thirty in the morning.” It was nice to know that some things in my life hadn’t changed.

“Oops.” Mom giggled. “Sorry, sweetie. I completely forgot the time difference. I was on my lunch break and wanted to chat.”

“No problem. I’m awake now.” I snuggled back under my cocoon of warm blankets, ready for a mostly listening conversation.

Hold on. Blankets? And the car was moving. When had that happened? I glanced at Zev even as my mother began to prattle. I raised an eyebrow and gestured towards my coverings.

His tone was an amusing mixture of exasperation and concern. “Your lips were blue.”

I almost made a comment about warming them when I realized that Mom had asked a question. Feeling heat rising to my cheeks, I turned my attention back to my mother. “What was that, Mom? I didn’t catch it.”

“I was just wondering where you were now.”

Mom knew that I’d been traveling and I was fairly certain that she knew that Zev was with me, but she hadn’t mentioned him so neither did I. Sometimes having a free-spirited mother who’d once been a rebellious teenager made things difficult. This wasn’t one of those times. I answered her question.

"Indiana." If it wasn't true yet, it would be soon.

"Why?"

"Just checking some things out." I turned the conversation back to her. "How are things in Milan?"

"Wonderful!" She gushed. "I just met the most fabulous designer." And she was off and running.

ZEV

I sucked air into my burning lungs as I ran for my life. I could hear the creature panting as it gained on me. More terrified than I'd ever been, I risked a glance behind me. There, looming over me like a spectre of death, was the giant alien space bunny Waldo. I knew that he'd eat me if he caught me. In fact, I could hear his teeth chitter-chattering together.

Wait, that couldn't be right.

The sound drew me from my bizarre dream back to where I was curled up in the back of my car, warm under two blankets. How did I get two? My sleep-addled brain worked rather quickly to piece together the noise I still heard with my current state. Sometime after I'd fallen asleep, Tex had covered me with her blanket and now her teeth were chattering. Steeling myself against the nippiness (brain fog allowed for unique word choice, or so I told myself) I knew was coming, I sat up and leaned forward. Sure enough, Tex was shivering under her coat. Even in the faint light, I could see her blue-tinged lips quivering with the cold. I pulled both blankets away me and tucked them around Tex, hoping that they still retained some of my own heat. I pressed my lips against Tex's forehead, inwardly wincing at the chill of her skin. "*Dormir bien, querida.*"

Moving carefully so as not to disturb the young woman in the passenger's seat, I climbed into the driver's seat and started the car, hoping she wouldn't wake. She didn't. I cranked up the heat and pulled back onto the road. Every few minutes, I'd allow myself a peek at Tex. To make sure she was all right, of course. I sighed. Who was I kidding? *Ubi amor, ibi oculus*. I knew myself better than that. I hated having Tex out of my sight, even if she was sitting beside me. The time we spent apart was almost painful for me, like she was a part of me, *'m pawb*. And, there were times when I was more cognizant of where she was and what she was thinking than I was of myself. Not like a mind-reading thing, but an awareness, an insight. This was beyond anything I'd ever experienced before, more extreme, more pure, more... just more. *Mo gach rud.* And I didn't understand where this came from.

Are you really that clueless?

Oh. I guess so.

You two were made for each other. Literally.

I kept my voice low, but spoke out loud. "But she was born thousands of years after I should've died."

I knew you both before the earth was made. I created you for her, and she for you.

An echo of a memory tugged at my mind. Far, far back. Back to the court of the shepherd king. I whispered their essence into the early morning air. "You saw me, knew me, before I was even born. Saw who I was, who I would be. Everything I would do, You already knew." I'd always been in awe of that psalm, but now I saw another meaning, another truth in the words that were almost as old as I.

Yes, Zev. This is the task for which you and Tex were created. A matched pair, chosen and called to finish what was begun all those years ago.

I drove on in silence, still absorbing the enormity of what I'd been told even as I continued to watch her sleep. *Matulog nang mabuti, minamahal. Arhosais filoedd chan blynedd atat, 'm cara, 'm bopeth. Ma armastan sind.* Tex's phone was the first sound to break the quiet and pull me back to reality. I glanced at my watch and repressed a sigh of frustration. Only one person would call Tex this early. My suspicions were confirmed by the first words out of Tex's mouth.

"Yeah, Mom? Something wrong?"

I'd bet every dollar in any of my bank accounts that nothing was wrong. Though nice enough, Summer Novak had proven time and again over the past month that her memory regarding anything not directly concerning her was spotty at best. Judging by the resigned expression on Tex's face, I was right.

"Mom, it's five-thirty in the morning." Tex burrowed deeper under the blankets. "No problem. I'm awake now." She looked towards me, eyebrow raised and motioned to the covers.

Had she seriously expected me to just let her freeze? How could I tell her that seeing her shivering had broken my heart? *Vorrei morire per lei.* That I would have given her the last article of clothing I owned during a subzero blizzard even if it meant my death? The words wouldn't come and I knew that trying to explain myself would be impossible even if she hadn't been on the phone with her mother. Instead, I contented myself with a simple statement of truth. "Your lips were blue."

***

We stayed in the car as people exited the tiny church. I could see Tex out of the corner of my eye, studying the neighborhood with less surprise than she would have just a short time ago. Four corners, three bars and one church. One of the bars most likely served as a brothel as well. Inch-thick bars on every window. Heavy iron gates across every door. This was not the ideal place for a church. And it was exactly where Christ would've planted one.

"Who's that?"

Tex's question drew my attention to a distinctive figure crossing the street, heading directly for the car. Tall, slender and obviously female, she had spiky black hair tipped with brilliant blue and green. Each ear was lined with half a dozen silver and diamond studs. Her dusky skin was accented by heavy blue eyeliner surrounding eyes so dark they were almost black and a silver-studded black leather choker hugged her slender neck. A tatty blue and gray camouflage t-shirt over a skintight hot pink undershirt, and a black leather miniskirt that stopped a good three inches above her knee-high boots didn't seem like a wise choice for autumn in Indiana. The rest of her exposed leg was encased in hot pink tights that matched her shirt. She bent down to my window and raised one well-shaped eyebrow. Light glinted off of the silver hoop on her bottom lip.

"Zev, stop staring and roll down the window." Tex's voice had a hint of exasperation but no jealousy.

I was surprised by how much the lack of jealousy distressed me. Didn't Tex care that I'd been watching this girl? If Tex had seen another guy... I was momentarily distracted by the memory of my anger towards Erik. However, I didn't have the time to dwell on any of this. There was work to be done. I cleared my throat. "Neysa Polyxena?"

"Zev Avatos." She grinned at me. "I never believed Mom and Dad when they said you folks didn't age, but you look exactly like the picture with my grandparents."

"She knows?" I heard an accusatory undercurrent to Tex's words. "I thought you said the Immortals were a secret."

"My family and his go way back." The bar through Neysa's tongue clicked against her teeth as she spoke. "Anyway, the guy you're looking for has been staying at the Sunrise Motel three blocks over. The desk clerk over there is a friend of mine. He'll give you any information you need, but I doubt your guy's hanging around. The word's out that the Immortals are hunting again."

Neysa straightened for a moment and scribbled something on a scrap of paper she fished out of a skirt pocket. Then, she was leaning through the open window, just centimeters from me, and I felt Tex stiffen. Neysa must've seen the movement because she tittered. "Don't worry, sweetie. He's not my type." One semi-gloved hand reached across me, and dropped something into Tex's lap. "But, if you get bored, give me a call." With a final wink thrown in Tex's direction, Neysa was gone, slinking down the sidewalk without a backwards glance.

Stifling the urge to laugh, I risked a glance at Tex. Her face had flooded with color to the roots of her hair, and her mouth was moving as if she was trying to speak but couldn't quite manage it. My voice was tight with the effort it took to repress my amusement. "Well, we'd better get to that motel." I didn't comment or look her way until we reached the Sunrise, by which time, her face had returned to its natural color.

Ten minutes later, we were entering room 108. According to desk clerk Benny, the middle-aged man who'd occupied this room, one Hector Stanwick, had checked out earlier that morning. But, after receiving a call from Neysa Polyxena, Benny had put off sending housekeeping. I considered telling him that his concern was wasted. This Perpetuum was good. He never left anything behind. If it hadn't been for my contacts, I wouldn't have known that Stanwick (if that was his real name) had gone to Gary. As soon as I flipped on the light, I wondered what condiments I should put on the words I was going to eat. The room was a disaster.

"We must have been closer than we thought." I entered first, automatically scanning the room for any sign that its occupant hadn't vacated the premises. Once satisfied that Tex and I were indeed alone, I motioned for her to come inside. "Look for anything that might give us a clue as to where he's headed next." I began to sift through the junk that had been piled on the bed.

"Like this?"

I turned towards Tex. She held up two sheets of paper. "They're confirmation numbers for a hotel in Cleveland and one in New York."

"The city?" I crossed to Tex's side in two strides.

She shook her head. "No, it's some place I've never heard of."

I skimmed the information, peering over Tex's head to do so. I caught a whiff of gardenia-scented lotion and drew in a shaky breath. Sometimes, being around her made it difficult to think. She looked up at me. All right, most of the time I found thinking to be nearly impossible with Tex nearby. I tore my eyes away from her face and turned them back to the paper. "It's about three to four hours from Cleveland." Unable to resist any longer, I slid my arms around her waist and pulled her back against me, resting my cheek on her silky curls. *Geweldig.* I was turning into such a girl.

"So we're heading back to Ohio?" The unsteady tone of Tex's voice made me grin.

"Looks like it." I sighed and reluctantly loosened my grip on Tex. "First, we see if Stanwick left anything else behind that we can use. Then, replenish supplies and head for Ohio." I glanced at my watch. "If we leave by two, we can make it to Cleveland by eight o'clock. There's a chance we could catch him at this hotel."

Tex nodded and I could see her mind settling back into hunting mode. *Dei gratia*, she was made for this!

I believe I already told you that.

Don't let anyone tell you that *El Roi* doesn't say 'I told you so.' I silently acknowledged His comment before heading back to the mess I'd been going through before Tex had called for me. Tex went into the bathroom and we worked in silence for almost twenty minutes. Only after Tex finished in the bathroom and started on the desk did she speak.

"Zev, about Neysa..."

There are times when the filter between my brain and my mouth doesn't work. This was one of them. "Did you want to give her a call?"

Ouch. If I could die, Tex's glare would have killed me on the spot. I held up both hands in a gesture of surrender. Then I remembered our first sparring session and decided that an apology would be wise. "Sorry. Continue."

"I was wondering what she meant about her family and yours going back when she's not an Immortal. How does she know who you are? What you do?"

Hundreds of faces flashed through my mind. Michal. Christophe. Phoebe. Rocco. Sara. For a brief moment, I wondered what they would have thought of Neysa. "About three hundred years or so after we became Immortal, my family rescued a tribe who were about to be sacrificed by the Perpetuum. In return, they promised to aid us whenever we needed it. While they assist any Immortal in need, they are most loyal to my family. Many times through the years, they served as members of our household, servants, if you will. Some provided information, kept an eye out for the signs that Perpetuum were around. They still do."

"And Neysa is part of that family."

As I confirmed Tex's statement, part of me wondered if I'd been mistaken before, if Tex had been upset by my initial reaction to seeing Neysa. "Yes. There are around four hundred of them in North America and close to three hundred in Europe. The remaining hundred or so are scattered through the other continents." I tossed the last of the rubbish aside. "How many of them actually believe the stories, I don't know." I turned towards Tex and changed the conversation. "Have you found anything else?"

TEX

My curiosity got the better of me as I came back into the main room after ascertaining that nothing of value was to be found in the bathroom. "Zev, about Neysa..."

"Did you want to give her a call?"

Eyes narrowed, I scowled at Zev, wishing I possessed the power to turn him into a rat, or maybe a halibut. Apparently, he got the message, because he raised both hands and apologized. "Sorry. Continue."

The internal debate didn't take long. My desire for knowledge outweighed my indignation. "I was wondering what she meant about her family and yours going back when she's not an Immortal. How does she know who you are? What you do?"

Zev continued rummaging through the junk Stanwick had left behind. "About three hundred years or so after we became Immortal, my family rescued a tribe who were about to be sacrificed by the Perpetuum. In return, they promised to aid us whenever we needed it. While they assist any Immortal in need, they are most loyal to my family. Many times through the years, they served as members of our household, servants, if you will. Some provided information, kept an eye out for the signs that Perpetuum were around. They still do."

I didn't need any help putting two and two together. Even

my math skills weren't that poor. "And Neysa is part of that family."

"Yes. There are around four hundred of them in North America and close to three hundred in Europe. The remaining hundred or so are scattered through the other continents. How many of them actually believe the stories, I don't know." Zev faced me, asking. "Have you found anything else?"

I shook my head. "No. If you want to make it to Cleveland by eight, we need to get moving."

"Right." Zev started for the door and I fell in step behind him, my own thoughts already occupied with the lists of things we needed to purchase.

I didn't realize that he'd stopped until my face made contact. Strong arms caught me before I stumbled, wrapping around my waist and pulling me forward. My palms came to rest against Zev's chest, absorbing the pounding of his heart and sending my own blood racing to the same rhythm. I tipped my head up, mouth open to say something. Exactly what, I didn't know, but it would have been eloquent. The capacity for speech, unfortunately, fled from me when my eyes locked with Zev's.

His voice was low, intense. "You know that you have no reason to be jealous of Neysa or any other girl, right? I don't want anyone else."

"I know." I gave myself an internal pat on the back as I managed to put a noun with a verb. Optimistic, I attempted a noun, verb and two modifiers. "I wasn't jealous."

"Oh."

Oh no. He had that 'someone kicked my puppy' look on

his face. I moved my left hand from his chest to his cheek. My other hand remained over his heart. I wasn't quite ready to stop feeling the beating beneath my fingers. My thumb brushed the corner of Zev's mouth and I felt the shock race up my arm. "I mean, I know you love me. I don't doubt you. Never will."

Zev smiled, his eyes igniting into blue fire. As he bent his head towards me, he whispered, "*J'ai attendu milliers d'ans pour vous, mon amour.*"

I fully intended to ask what those words meant... after Zev was done kissing me.

***

I ignored Zev's offer to carry my bag, slinging it over my shoulder as I shut the car door. When he started to protest, I grabbed his free hand, threading my fingers through his, effectively silencing him. I gave his hand a gentle squeeze as we made our way to our rooms. I could sense his frustration and knew that it had nothing to do with my independent streak. We'd made it to Cleveland in good time, but this Hector Stanwick guy was nowhere to be found. At least, nowhere under that name. We both knew that an alias was likely, but had no way of tracking one. It had taken me fifteen minutes to convince Zev that we needed to stop for the night. Get food, get rest, figure out our next step.

Zev and I parted just long enough to drop our bags into our hotel rooms and do a quick security check. As I walked through the room, mentally taking note of each piece of furniture and its position, I was surprised to find that I considered this routine natural rather than something I still needed to get used to. Hm, date to note. October twenty-sixth: the day I felt completely normal analyzing every possible trap, hiding place and exit in a low-rate Ohio hotel.

I opened the door just as Zev was getting ready to knock and took a minute to enjoy his surprise. It didn't happen often. "Pie?"

"Sounds good to me." Zev held out his hand and I took it, the press of his ring cool against my skin. "Want to walk?"

"After being in a car for a good part of the last two days, you need to ask?" I smiled up at Zev, swinging our hands between us as we headed for a restaurant we'd seen on our way in.

The evening breeze was crisp but not unpleasant, and despite the dusk, we were able to enjoy the unique beauty of a northeastern Ohio autumn. As we entered the restaurant, I scanned the room and knew that Zev was doing the same. It was small but well-lit, so we would be able to see anything or anyone out of the ordinary. About half of the booths were empty so privacy wouldn't be an issue. But, it was only after we'd been seated and each ordered a slice of apple pie that Zev brought up our little problem.

"So, no one matching the description Benny gave us checked into the hotel. And, no one using the name Hector Stanwick checked into any hotel in the area." Zev's fingers began drumming a steady pattern against the faux wood tabletop. "Which means he either kept going or left those papers in Indiana for us to find. A false trail."

"Which do you think?" I placed my hand over Zev's to

still the restless movement. “What do your instincts tell you?”

Zev paused, eyes glazing over slightly as he consulted some part of his mind that dealt with this supernatural mission. I’d seen him do this a few times over the last month, finally asking him about it during a long stretch of northern California highway. A bit of prompting from the Lord had led me to mention that perhaps this gift was divine in origin. Zev had been astonished at the suggestion, saying that it was just something he did and never really thought about until I’d brought it up. His family hadn’t thought it worth mentioning and he’d never been close enough to anyone else for them to notice it. A few minutes passed and then his eyes refocused. “He skipped over Cleveland and went straight for Houghton. He wants to put some distance between him and us. He’s getting sloppy, not conniving.”

“Then the question is, will he make it out of New York before we catch up with him?” I watched as my index finger traced the tiny scars that marked the back of Zev’s hand. He’d told me the story behind them a few days ago. Apparently, the distant ancestors of wolverines didn’t particularly approve of seven year-old children trying to pet them.

Zev answered my question. “Only if we can figure out some way to stall him, keep him from leaving the hotel.”

I could feel Zev’s eyes on my roving finger and took a deep breath. I’d had something running through my brain for the past hour or so and this was the time to bring it up. However, I hadn’t really been a part of the planning process since we’d left Fort Prince. Tracking, hunting, this was Zev’s job, not mine. Well, mine by choice. His by birth. But I kept hearing God's voice in my head, telling me that I, too, had been born for this. I decided to give it a shot. "I have an idea about that."

"All right. Let's hear it."

No sarcasm or placating tone. That was good. I continued. "Do the Perpetuum have some way of identifying themselves to each other? Besides the mark on their wrists. Something they'd use if they were talking to each other or sending a letter."

"*In aeternum*. It means 'for eternity.'"

"Could you write that down for me?" I handed Zev a pen and a napkin, aware that he still didn't understand where this was heading. He slid the napkin back to me as I pulled my phone out of one pocket and piece of paper out of another. Zev opened his mouth to speak, but shut it again when I held up a finger, asking him to wait. I dialed the number and waited for someone to answer.

A bubbly voice on the other end greeted me.

"Hi. My name is Killeen," I wrinkled my nose at the use of my given name, but didn't change my tone. Neysa had said that the Perpetuum knew that the Immortal were hunting again and I didn't know if that included knowledge of a girl named Tex. "I need to leave a message for a guest, but I don't have a room number. In fact, he might not even be there yet, but it's really important that I contact him."

"What's the name?"

"Hector Stanwick." I heard the clicking of keys and then the young woman confirmed that Mr. Stanwick's reservation wasn't until tomorrow. "But can you write something down for me, make sure he gets it when he checks in? I don't want him leaving without it."

"Of course, miss. Now, what did you want to say?"

"Just write down, '*In aeternum*,'" I spelled it out and then continued. "'I need to see a friendly face. Please wait for me. If I'm not there by three o'clock, assume that I'm not coming. Thank you.'"

"No problem, miss. I'll see to it that Mr. Stanwick gets the message."

"Thank you. Have a good night." I didn't raise my eyes from the table even after I'd hung up, but I couldn't stay that way for long. The silence was too unnerving.

Zev was staring at me, eyes wide and impressed. "Brilliant. You're absolutely brilliant."

I could feel myself blushing at the praise, but was spared further embarrassment as the waitress returned with our pie. Zev and I spent the remainder of our hour in a disjointed conversation that made little sense to anyone outside of our bubble.

"I used to love peas until, one night at the Globe, I saw the boy who was supposed to be playing Juliet shoving them up his nose. Now, every time I see that play, I have an image of a very ugly woman with smooshed peas coming out of her nostrils."

"What is it with boys putting strange things in their noses? Erik once had a pencil eraser stuck in his nose."

"I never understood that either. Had my nose broken more times than I can count though."

"Yeah, sorry about that."

"I should've been watching where I was going."

"Then again..."

"Very true."

By the time we were ready to go, most of the other patrons had already left. Only a group of twenty-somethings wearing t-shirts that read "Focus!" and an old woman wearing an enormous purple fur coat remained. I briefly wondered what poor creature had been forced to suffer the indignity of plum-colored fur before coming to the conclusion that I needed to sleep. Zev tossed a tip on the table and we both turned to leave.

A hand closed around my arm a split second before a man's voice said my name. "Tex Novak! It is you!"

Blond curls. Dark brown eyes the color of chocolate.

I blinked. I had to be dreaming. There was no way this was real.

Closure, Tex.

What?

"Tex, it's me, Teddy."

Okay, not a dream. Wearing the white apron of a busboy and grinning as if he'd never broken my heart – it was indeed Theodore Sanders.

"Take your hand off her."

The anger in Zev's voice shattered my shock and I yanked my arm away from Teddy before something bad happened. Like Zev ripping off Teddy's arms and beating the younger man to death with said appendages. Hm, maybe that wouldn't necessarily be bad.

Closure, Tex.

"How'd you find me?" Teddy kept leering at me and I considered trying limb removal for myself. I was sure I could find a dull knife somewhere.

"Find you?" I didn't recognize my own voice. "I wasn't looking for you."

"Right." He winked at me and I felt my nails dig into my palms as I refrained from hitting him. "You're not here for seconds?"

"Excuse me?"

I sensed Zev's movement forward and put out a hand to stop him. "Let's go, Zev." I started to turn, pushing Zev in front of me so that I was between Teddy and certain death.

"Come on, babe," Teddy's fingers snagged my back pocket. "It's not like I wasn't the best you ever had."

No jury in the world would've convicted me for what happened next. Zev's training, combined with my previous experience, kicked in and, less than ten seconds later, Teddy was sprawled on the floor, unconscious. A lone tooth shone white against the green tiles. Blood gushed from a broken nose. Two fingers – the ones that had been in my pocket – were bent at a strange angle. And I was pretty sure Teddy wouldn't be anyone's firsts, or seconds, for a while.

Well done. Now, no more looking back. Move forward.

It wasn't until Zev touched my shoulder that I realized that I was the center of attention. Every employee and the remaining diners were staring. The old woman in purple broke the silence. "Nice kick to the crackerjacks, missy." She cackled as she walked by and everyone else burst into laughter. None of them seemed overly concerned with the boy on the floor. In fact, I was pretty sure one of the girls in the "Focus!" t-shirts stepped on Teddy on her way out.

A moment later, a comment from our waitress explained why. "Good for you. Teddy doesn't know how to keep his hands to himself. This should get him fired."

"Tex," Zev whispered in my ear as he slid an arm around my waist. "Come on, *mijn liefde gewacht*. Let's go."

As we crossed into the chilly night air, I asked, "What did you call me?"

Zev smiled down at me. "'My love.'"

My mind was still spinning from what had happened and latched onto a stray thought. "And what did you say to me back at the hotel in Indiana? Right before you kissed me."

"I said," Zev pulled me closer so that my head rested against his side as we walked. "'I have waited thousands of years for you, my love.'"

"Oh." Great, Tex. The most perfect man in the world declared his love in a totally romantic way, and you said 'oh.' I stumbled around for words that could compare and came up empty. "There's nothing I could say that would come close to that."

Zev grinned and pressed his lips against my hair, heating me from headtop to tiptoe. "I don't need you to say a word."

ZEV

"Take your hand off her." I hadn't felt rage this potent towards anyone who wasn't my brother, and I struggled to rein it in. Tex pulled away from Teddy and the boy let her go. Good thing, too, or I might have been forced to remove the entire arm for him.

"How'd you find me?"

The *napakapalalo piraso ng masasamang salita* had the nerve to ignore me and keep ogling Tex. I ground my teeth together, petitioning *El-Kanno* for permission to maim this... I couldn't think of a word in any language that was foul enough for him.

"Find you? I wasn't looking for you." Tex's voice brought me back from the edge of giving in to my anger and unleashing four thousand years worth of fighting on the busboy in front of me.

"Right." He winked and I smothered the urge to shove a butter knife through his eye. It was getting harder to curb my impulses. "You're not here for seconds?"

Conluvio! *Me oportet propter praeceptum te nocere*! "Excuse me?" I took a step forward, fully intending to reduce Teddy Sanders to the bloodiest pulp possible. The sensation of Tex's hand on my arm made me hesitate. I would have pushed past her if I hadn't heard *El-Kanno* speak.

This is Tex's battle.

I barely registered Tex maneuvering herself between the busboy and me. Instead, I argued with *El Tsaddik*. Yes, I know, I'm an idiot. But, I couldn't help myself. I begged *El-Kanno* to let me hurt this boy who'd injured Tex's so badly.

Trust Me.

"Come on, babe. It's not like I wasn't the best you ever had."

I didn't even get the chance to react. Tex's left hand clamped down on Teddy's wrist, holding his hand in place as she turned. I heard the cracking of his bones half a second before Tex's right fist made contact with the boy's jaw. A tooth flew as Tex brought her foot up between Teddy's legs while simultaneously grabbing him by the shoulders. He doubled over in pain and Tex added to his downward mobility by slamming his face against our table. He landed in a bloody mass on the floor. The entire process had taken only seconds.

I wanted to burst into applause, but contented myself with putting a hand on Tex's shoulder. The old woman in purple said something, but I wasn't listening to her. Instead, I concentrated on the sound of Tex's heart as it slowed from its adrenaline-fueled racing to a more normal rate. I caught the end of our waitress's comment. "That should get him fired."

It was time for us to leave. I put my arm around Tex's waist. "Tex, come on, *mijn liefde gewacht*. Let's go."

***

I let Tex sleep while I packed up the car, filled the gas tank and grabbed some breakfast for both of us. Since we always asked for a second key to each room, I was able to get most of her things as well. By midmorning, the only thing not ready to go was the seventeen year-old curled up under the ugliest hotel blanket I'd seen since a cross-country trip in the 1970's. I stood over her, contemplating dozens of ways to wake her before coming to the conclusion that I didn't actually want to. I slipped my worn leather jacket from my shoulders and, using my considerable skills of stealth and grace, scooped Tex from the bed, wrapped her in my coat, and carried her to the car. She was still sound asleep in the back seat when I returned a few minutes later, having grabbed the last of her belongings before checking us both out of the hotel.

Tex woke two hours later, completely mortified at still being in her pajamas. I assured her that I found the dancing monkey flannel pants and matching camisole endearing, but immediately stopped teasing when she threatened to beat me to death with a toaster. After the previous night, I wasn't entirely sure if she was kidding. I no longer doubted her ability to do it. At our next stop, Tex changed her clothes and we both strapped on our weapons. We were only thirty minutes outside of Houghton and wanted to be ready if Stanwick had indeed hung around.

As we approached the town limits, Tex spoke. "Let me go in alone and ask for Stanwick."

I was shaking my head before she'd finished the sentence. "No way. It's too dangerous. He could be waiting for us."

"I'm the one who called. The clerk will be expecting a woman." Tex eyed me and added, "And I don't think you could pass."

More to mask my trepidation about her involvement than anything else, I quipped. "Are you suggesting that I'm not pretty enough?"

Tex smiled, but it didn't quite reach her eyes. "Seriously, Zev, I'll go in, find out if Stanwick is still here and what room he's in. Then you can take point. I'll be a good girl and stay out of your way and everything. All right?"

I parked the car before answering. I turned to Tex and took both of her hands in mine. "Please, please," I implored, "be careful."

Tex leaned forward and kissed the tip of my nose. "I will." Then, before I could recover from a tingling nose, she darted from the car and vanished into the hotel.

I sat, every muscle tensed, one hand on the door, the other on the handle of my throwing knife: a seven inch, double-edged silver blade, custom made for me by Jael some time before Sodom and Gomorrah had burned. This was my oldest and favorite weapon, the one I relied on, the one that had spilled the most Perpetuum blood. It was my very pointy security blanket.

As soon as Tex emerged from the building, I was out of the car and walking towards her. She didn't wait for me to reach her before she started talking. "He's still here. Room one twenty-one. It's around back." She led the way, but as we rounded the corner, I sidestepped in front of her.

"You promised." I spoke before she could complain. "I'll go in first, you..."

"Watch your back. I know." Tex's tone wasn't as annoyed as I'd thought it would be.

With her safely behind me, I surveyed our surroundings, slowing my gait to compensate. A fair number of trees and shrubs hid us from the road and neighboring buildings. That was good. No people in sight. That was better. There had only been four other vehicles in the parking lot when we'd pulled in which made for good odds that the rooms around us would be empty. I stopped just short of the door and spoke over my shoulder to Tex. "When I knock, you call out for him."

"He's going to see you." Tex pointed to the small hole in

the door. “I have a better idea.”

Why did those five words chill me to the bone?

“You stay out of sight. Let me knock; let him see me. When he comes to the door, then you step in.”

“And if he has a weapon?” I put as much ferocity in my whisper as possible.

“Then I hope you’re as good with that thing as you say you are.” Tex motioned to the knife in my hand. “This is the best strategy, and you know it.”

Thing was, I did know it. And I knew that I didn’t have the time to come up with a better plan. I growled and positioned myself a few feet away, out of sight but not out of range. Once confident that Stanwick couldn’t see me, Tex stepped forward and knocked on the door.

“Mr. Stanwick, please, open up!”

Wow. She was a good actress.

“Someone’s after me. Please, I need your help. *In aeternum*!”

Oscar-worthy, really.

There was noise behind the door. The rattle of a chain lock. And then the door opened.

Hector Stanwick was a short, balding man with wire-rimmed glasses and a good forty extra pounds. This was the serial killer leaving a string of bodies across several states? I lifted my blade.

“Show me the mark.” The cold voice didn’t mesh with the physical appearance.

I didn’t wait for him to discover the ruse. Praying that Tex wouldn’t move, I threw my dagger. It flew past Tex’s cheek and buried itself in Stanwick's chest. The momentum toppled him backwards and I dashed towards the open door. As always, Tex waited for me to enter first, then she was closing the door behind us as I pulled Stanwick further into the room. One glance was enough to tell me that the blade had struck true. The Perpetuum had died almost instantly.

After ascertaining that Stanwick had been alone, I retrieved my knife and cleaned it. Tex had already begun straightening the room. As always, the job wasn't finished when the hearts stopped beating. Clean-up and cover-up was part of the life as well. Tex and I had to make sure no one connected us with Stanwick. Now, more than ever, we needed to be careful. A murder arrest for me would mean serious legal difficulties and possible exposure. Tex didn't have the luxury of such small consequences. And, somehow, I doubted anyone would believe the story of immortal assassins from God.

"Zev."

I looked up in time to catch the car keys Tex had tossed my way. Stanwick's room key was in her other hand.

"I'll check him out while you dump his car and the body. The desk clerk hasn't seen you yet, but she did see your car. Call me when you're done and I'll pick you up. We can go through Stanwick's things once we find a place to stop for the night."

Tex must have read something in my expression because she stopped halfway to the door. "What is it?"

"You're getting good at this." I took a step towards Tex.

"That doesn't sound like a compliment."

I crossed the remainder of the distance between us and

took both of her hands in mine. "I'm not sure if it is." I lifted both of her hands and kissed her knuckles. "I don't want blood on your hands. I have enough on mine."

Tex twisted her hands so that she held mine. She raised them, palms up. "They look clean to me."

"I'm not joking, Tex." Part of me wanted to pull away from her, but a stronger part didn't. Guess which one won?

"Neither am I." Tex's voice was soft, but serious. "I was created for this, Zev, and you know it. Now, we need to get moving before someone gets curious."

She kissed the palm of each hand and left before my brain could finish processing. Then my synapses fired and I remembered that I was standing next to a dead body with the cause of death sheathed and tucked into the waistband of my jeans. I got to work.

TEX

I desperately missed real food. You know, something not made to eat on-the-go, not pre-packaged, hand-delivered or made by someone who graduated at the bottom of their culinary class. I knew that Zev would have taken me to some expensive restaurant if I'd asked him to, but I figured, if I wasn't going to make the food myself, it might as well be fast and easy. A small part of my brain recognized a joke in there somewhere, but I ignored it for more important things. I tossed my chopsticks back into the container of sesame chicken and frowned at the laptop in front of me. I'd always been too impatient for this type of work.

"Tex," Zev spoke slowly and I looked up to see him

staring at the computer. “That doesn’t look like your laptop.”

“That’s because it’s not.” Where was he going with this?

“Did you steal Stanwick’s laptop?”

Seriously? “Yes.” I continued as if I were speaking to a two year-old. “We need information. Computer has information. Hence, we need computer.”

“But...” he seemed to be having difficulty finding the words. “You stole it.”

I almost laughed out loud, but managed to keep a straight face while answering his accusation. “Number one: he was a psycho serial killer. Number two: he’s dead. And, number three: you killed him. So, why are we arguing the morality and / or legality of me taking his laptop? It’s not like I’m planning to keep it.”

Zev finally lifted his eyes to my face. “Just surprised me, that’s all.” He reached for the sweet and sour chicken, and gave me a dirty look when he discovered that it was gone.

“I was hungry.” I grinned. “You can have the rest of the pork fried rice. I think there’s some left.”

“For such a tiny person, you consume a lot of calories.” Zev plucked the box from the table and plopped down on the floor next to my bed. “And still manage to stay little.”

“Good genes.” I muttered, turning my attention back to the computer.

“Yes, they are.”

I felt his hand curl around my calf and closed my eyes. The heat of his skin burned through my jeans, effectively scrambling my thoughts... what had I been doing? Right, work. I opened my eyes and playfully swatted at Zev’s hand.

"You're distracting me."

Zev smiled, his eyes dancing. "Good to know I can still do that."

I stuck out my tongue. "You're making it difficult for me to work."

"You want me to go?"

Crap. It was that 'kicked puppy' expression. How could I defend myself against such a lethal weapon? "I thought you were all about finding out what Stanwick was up to."

Zev sighed. "Yeah, well, focusing around you tends to be an issue with me, too."

My internal gymnast decided to try for the Olympics one more time. Then Zev rested his cheek on my knee and the aforementioned gymnast tripped over her own feet, sending everything spiraling out of control. A beep from the computer saved me from needing to make a desperate call to Elle. Again.

"What's that?" Zev turned his attention back to the food.

"E-mail alert." Relief and disappointment mingled when Zev lifted his head. "I'm trying to figure out his password."

"Try variations of 'forever.'" Zev spoke around a mouthful of chicken and I tried to decide if it was cute or gross.

Giving that particular thought up as a lost cause, I followed Zev's suggestion. A few minutes later, I was logged on to Hector Stanwick's e-mail account. I skimmed the subject lines and deleted the junk, including two notices that our deceased Perpetuum had won foreign lotteries and only needed to pay a minimal fee to collect his winnings. I selected the first of the two remaining new messages and read through the contents. Suspecting what I would find in the subsequent e-mail, I moved on, waiting until I reached the end before sharing the information I'd gleaned.

"Stanwick wasn't just on a killing spree, and he wasn't running east to get away from us." I pulled my legs under me and faced Zev, who had finished off the last of the rice while I'd been reading. "He was meeting with at least two other Perpetuum for something big."

"When?" All flirtation had gone out of Zev's voice.

"Four days."

"Samhain."

I nodded.

"Where?"

"I could only find a city and state." I glanced at the computer screen again. "Bangor, Maine."

***

We'd been in the car for two days, so the decision to walk to find a place to eat dinner was a no-brainer. Over the meal, which would most likely be seafood of some sort, we would discuss our next move. The Maine hotel where Hector Stanwick had reserved a room only had him listed for one night. Since this was the twenty-ninth and whatever the Perpetuum had planned wouldn't occur for two more days, we needed to find out where Stanwick had intended to go from here.

While the temperature had been quite a shock for me – I hadn't expected the smell of snow in October – I received a jolt of another kind before we'd gone too far. From somewhere between the buildings came two figures running down the street. A thin blond man. A tall brunette woman. Both completely stark-naked as they streaked past. Both screaming something about giant spiders with clicking pinchers.

I was rooted to the spot, brain misfiring as I attempted to process what I'd just seen. From beside me, I heard Zev chuckle and then felt his hand grip mine. "Come on, *kullake*. It's cold out here." I fell in step beside him as he continued to speak. "If you think that was bad, you should've seen Hollywood in its Golden Age."

Zev's comment brought up a question that had been nagging me for some time. Well, no time like the present. "After all this time, does anything catch you off guard? Is anything ever new?"

Zev looked down at me, formerly twinkling eyes now burning with raw intensity. He stopped and cupped my chin, tilting my head up. Without a word, he captured my mouth in a kiss so scorching that I fully expected to find the city catching fire around us. When he finally released my lips to let us breathe, he spoke, voice ragged. "Every touch, every moment with you, *l'amour de ma vie*, is something I've never experienced before."

"Ok." Good work, Tex, you sound quite erudite. I was unable to form a decent sentence until we'd settled into a booth at the front of a small, pleasant diner, but Zev didn't seem to mind my silence. Instead, he steadily filled the space with more stories, these involving various actors whose names I dimly recalled from conversations with Grandma Bug.

After we'd both ordered, we tackled the problem at hand. Throughout the meal, we batted ideas back and forth, unsure of the best course of action. It wasn't until I saw the lights and heard the sirens that I remembered how numerous fictional characters had dealt with similar situations. As I watched Bangor's finest load the still-ranting, and still-unclothed, streakers into the back of a squad car, I shared my thought with Zev. Once he'd finished berating himself for missing the obvious, we finished our meal, paid the bill, and headed in the direction our helpful waiter pointed.

"Let me try." I knew Zev would hate the suggestion, but it made the most sense.

"Why?"

I carefully laid out my reasons. "One, you're kind-of, well, scary."

"I am not."

Zev was so cute when he was indignant. I mentally smacked myself. Focus, Tex! I continued. "Yes, you are. And, two, if the desk clerk is a woman, I have a story for a sympathetic ear."

"And if it's a man?" Zev raised one eyebrow in that infuriating way that made me want to respond with either violence or a kiss.

I could feel the heat rising to my cheeks and it wasn't all a result of me thinking about kissing Zev. I had to be honest, though, so I told him. "Then I'll flirt with him."

"You mean like you did with Teddy?"

I took a step back, stung. Fighting back tears that were a mixture of anger and mortification, I didn't give Zev a chance to say anything else. I darted around him, bypassing his outstretched hand, and ran into the police station. No matter what I was feeling, I had a job to do. The mission mattered more than anything else. At least, that's what I kept telling myself to keep the hot tears behind my eyelids from spilling down my cheeks.

ZEV

Did she just call me scary? "I am not." For a moment I considered how much I must have changed since charming strangers was part of my repertoire.

"Yes, you are. And, two, if the desk clerk is a woman, I have a story for a sympathetic ear."

All right, maybe she had a point there, but we didn't know who we'd be dealing with once we got inside. I cocked one eyebrow and pointed out the obvious. "And if it's a man?"

I watched the flush creeping up Tex's neck and repressed a smile. She was so cute when she was embarrassed.

"Then I'll flirt with him."

Oltre il mio corpo morto! Just the thought of Tex flirting with another man cut to the bone. I had to say something, anything, to keep her from going through with it. And, as it usually did in such situations, my brain-to-mouth filter turned off. "You mean like you did with Teddy?"

I wanted to call the words back the moment they crossed my lips. Then I saw the hurt on Tex's face and reached for her, apologies and contrition ready to spill out. Tex avoided my grasp and ran into the building, leaving me standing on the sidewalk, hand hovering in mid-air as all of the oxygen rushed from my lungs. *Deus, me ajude.* I implored *El Olam* for help. Why didn't I think before I spoke? My impulsive nature had gotten me into trouble in the past, but all that dimmed by comparison. Tex had done nothing to provoke such a cruel barb.

I finally remembered to drop my hand, but I still couldn't form any thought other than a plea for divine assistance. *Diyos, tulungan ninyo ako.* None seemed to be forthcoming. *Le do thoil, Dia Athair.* The hand squeezing my heart didn't ease up when Tex emerged from the police station. The wet shine in her eyes had disappeared, but in its place was a coldness that had nothing to do with the Maine air. *Bu iyi olamaz.* When she spoke, her voice was clipped, arctic.

"A few families outside of town have been reporting missing pets for the last few days. Police suspect the people renting a group of summer cabins about an hour northeast of here, but haven't been able to get any proof. All of the renters arrived at different times and from different places, but appear to know each other. A few cops have noticed that several of them have identical tattoos on their wrists. The woman who owns the cabins lives on the other side of the city, but I have her phone number." The entire time she spoke, Tex stared at a spot just to the left of my shoulder. "Officer Tyler recommended that we wait until tomorrow to call because Gertrude goes to bed early." Without waiting for me, Tex began walking back towards our hotel.

I let her go a few feet before following, head spinning with this sudden change of events. An hour ago, we'd been standing on the sidewalk, kissing. Now, she was hurrying away from me without so much as a backward glance. Suddenly, the pain of my previously mentioned amputated leg took second place to my shattered heart. What had I done?

Go after her.

I had the vague impression that *El De'ot* had almost added 'you idiot' to the end of his instruction. I didn't stop to argue or contemplate. I ran, managing to catch up to Tex before she reached her room.

"Tex," I grabbed her arm.

"What?"

I pulled back in shock. I'd been expecting hurt, resentment, even rage. What I hadn't foreseen was this flat tone, devoid of emotion. Tex wouldn't look at me. When I raised my hand to touch her face, she took a step back.

"We have a lot of work to do tomorrow." She turned away and unlocked her door. "Good night."

I stood in front of her closed door for an hour, waiting for her to come out. To forgive me. But she didn't come.

Go back to your room.

"You told me to go after her." I set my jaw and didn't take my eyes from the peeling red paint. "*Hva skulle jeg tenker?*"

You weren't thinking. That was the problem.

"I have to talk to her."

Tomorrow.

My whispered voice cracked. "I don't think I can make it until tomorrow." One trembling finger brushed my bottom lip where the memory of her mouth lingered. I could still taste her mint lip balm.

Tomorrow, Zev. For tonight, sleep.

I walked away, knowing that there would be no sleep for me tonight.

When dawn broke, hours later, I was still in the same position I'd taken upon entering the room the night before. Sleep hadn't come, as I'd known it would not. The seconds had slogged by as I stared at the ceiling. Only the gradual lightening of the room told me that time had passed. I was lost in my own torment, reliving my cruelty, the pain on Tex's face, the ice in her gaze, the stiffness in her words.

My cell phone buzzed and I rolled off of the bed in my attempt to remove it from my jeans pocket. I ignored the throbbing in my hip where I'd landed and hungrily retrieved my text message. "Gertrude will meet us in thirty minutes. Meet at the car."

I read the words again and again, searching for some hidden meaning, some hint that all had been forgiven. Then, I realized that I hadn't showered the night before and had an aroma similar to one I'd had after spending two days riding in the back of a meat truck. In July. In Georgia. Without refrigeration. I'd had to burn my clothes.

Twenty minutes later, a freshly-showered and better-smelling me was waiting at the car. I couldn't seem to stand still, shifting my weight from one foot to the other, all the while sending wordless pleas to *El Olam*. The objective of today's trip hovered in the back of my mind, lost to the importance of gaining Tex's favor once more.

So it's not about her, it's about you?

What?

You're more concerned with whether or not she forgives

you, to ease your pain, rather than with righting the wrong.

Ellis's words came back to haunt me again. "You're not selfless enough to put someone else before yourself and, until you do that, you'll never truly be in love."

Was that really what I was doing?

Yes.

Leave it to *El De'ot* to answer a rhetorical question.

Tears pricked at my eyelids as I mumbled, "I get it."

"Ready to go?"

My heart pounded out a complex percussion composition. I sent up a silent prayer for wisdom and took a tentative step towards Tex. Guilt inundated my entire being as I took in her appearance. Jeans and a baggy green sweater that were probably the first things she'd grabbed from her bag. Curls that looked as if they'd been tousled to remove excess water, but still dripped onto wearied shoulders. Dark shadows under guarded eyes. Still the most beautiful woman I'd ever seen. *Olin toivottoman rakastunut.*

I reached for her, closing the distance when she tried to back away. She stiffened when I drew her into my arms, but I didn't stop until her head rested against my chest. "I was a fool. *Ljubomorni mali majmun.*" I quickly translated. "'Jealous little monkey.'" I felt a snort of laughter and the vice around my heart eased the slightest bit. I kept one hand on her back and brought the other up to tangle in her wet hair. I felt the first hot drops slide down my cheeks as I whispered, "Forgive me, *Minamahal. Ikaw ay ang aking mga dahilan para sa pamumuhay.*" Again, I translated. "'You are my reason for living.' I will never behave that way again. Come what may, we are in this together, equal partners. Can you ever forgive me?"

Tex raised a tearstained face. "Of course, *mi amor*." She chuckled at my startled expression. "I do know some Spanish, remember?"

I gently touched my fingertips to her cheek, thumb tracing the small scar under her bottom lip. Tex leaned her head into my palm, closing her eyes. I knew I had to be completely honest. "I couldn't stand the thought of you flirting with someone, even if it was just for information." I added, "A part of me still wants to go back to the police station and let Officer Tyler know that you're spoken for."

Tex opened her eyes and I saw humor dancing in the luminous depths. "I didn't flirt with Mrs. Rebecca Tyler."

"Officer Tyler's a woman."

Tex nodded, mouth stretching into a grin. "I told her that an 'acquaintance' of mine had left town before I could tell him some very important news, and the last I'd heard, he was coming here to meet with some friends. Basically, I kept the story simple and let her draw her own false conclusions."

"Brilliant, *Liebling*." I could resist no longer. I lowered my head the necessary amount to brush my lips against hers. With electricity humming between our skin, I murmured against her mouth, "*Eu te amo, meu anjo*." Then Tex shivered and I remembered that we were standing in a parking lot, in Maine, in late October, and Tex wasn't wearing a coat. I sighed. "We should get to that meeting."

Tex nodded and pulled away. Before she could cross to the other side of the car, I shrugged off my coat and handed it to her. Her mouth opened and I knew she was going to protest, so I beat her to it. "Don't argue. Just wear the coat. Please."

As she pulled the much-too-large coat over her sweater, she gave me a smile that made my knees go weak. Seriously. I felt as if my legs had turned to jelly, or water, or some other less-than-solid substance. I barely made it into the driver's seat without making a fool of myself. Tex settled into the passenger's seat before giving me directions to the small B&B owned by Gertrude Stamhel.

Six hours, two meals and a ten-minute hike later, Tex and I dropped our bags in the main room of the small, one-bedroom cabin we'd rented for the duration of our stay in Maine. We didn't bother with anything more than a cursory perusal before heading back into the brisk autumn air. The space Gertrude had given to the Perpetuum was less than fifteen minutes away, and both Tex and I wanted to check it out before darkness fell. According to Gertrude, five people with tattoos, and three without, had asked for a secluded area over Halloween. More than happy to take the extra cash in the off-season, she'd given them a section where several cabins had been built in the same clearing. The renters had mentioned that more people might be coming, but hadn't given Gertrude an exact number. This had me worried. I was willing to bet that a few of those gathered were intended victims, but the ratio of Perpetuum to Immortal made me more nervous. Even if Tex fought, we were still going to be gravely outnumbered.

Chapter Ten: We Are Toy Soldiers

TEX

I stared in the mirror, trying to decide if I had enough energy to try to hide the purple shadows under my eyes. I knew that going into something as dangerous as what lay ahead would require more than the half hour or so of sleep I'd gotten the night before, but it was a moot point at the moment. I hung my towel over the shower bar and headed for my suitcase. I didn't bother to turn on the light as I pulled on the first pair of jeans I grabbed, and then felt around for something warmer than a t-shirt. The sweater I found was dark, but I couldn't tell what shade, and didn't particularly care. In fact, I wasn't entirely sure if my socks matched and the realization caused a sharp pang of memory. I shoved it aside. I'd spent most of the night praying, asking for answers to Zev's behavior, asking for guidance. And I'd gotten nothing in return. I wasn't sure who I was more angry with at the moment: Zev or God.

You promised to trust Me.

The gentle rebuke brought tears to my eyes and I scrubbed at them with the sleeve of my sweater. "I left everything behind to do what You wanted me to do. Isn't that trust?" I knelt next to my bed and rummaged through my bag.

Do you only trust Me for the things you want?

"I wanted to spend my senior year roaming around the country, sleeping in a new hotel every few days?" I could hear the childishness in my voice but didn't care. My hand closed on the hilt of my Smith & Wesson boot knife and I yanked it from my bag.

You wanted Zev.

I scowled as I slipped my sheathed blade into my hiking boots, adjusting my jeans to make the weapon accessible, but concealed. “And that’s turning out real well.”

One fight and you’re going to give up? You’re better than that.

I closed my eyes, resting my forehead against the hotel bedspread. “I don’t feel better than that.”

It’s not about what you feel, it’s about what you are.

“And what am I?”

Silence.

“That helps.”

Trust Me.

The alarm on my phone sounded. Time to go. I stood and ran a hand through my hair, flicking droplets of water from the tips of my fingers. I didn’t know if I was ready to see Zev again, but it didn’t matter. We had a job to do. I squared my shoulders, took a deep breath, and stepped out into the frosty Maine morning. My brain didn’t register the cold. In fact, it didn’t register anything but the tall figure standing by the car. The misery and enmity I felt didn’t stop my heart from launching into an enthusiastic rhythmic display at the sight of Zev. He hadn’t noticed my approach and, judging by the faint crease in his brow and the frown he wore, he was engaged in some form of interior dialogue. I took the extra moment to compose my face into an impassive mask, and then I spoke. “Ready to go?”

When Zev turned towards me, I was startled to see that he appeared to have had as sleepless a night as I’d had. A spark of hope fluttered inside me, but it couldn't stop the automatic step back I took when Zev moved towards me. To my surprise, he didn't stop, but kept coming until he'd wrapped his arms around me. His embrace was gentle but firm, pulling me towards him until there was no space between us. Unable to look him in eye, but equally powerless to move away, I compromised and leaned my head against him. His heart raced beneath my cheek and my eyes burned. Nothing could stop how I felt about this man and, if the pounding in his chest was any indication, his feelings for me hadn't changed.

"I was a fool. *Ljubomorni mali majmun.* 'Jealous little monkey.'"

Well, there was one I hadn't heard before. Laughter bubbled up. One of the hands on my back slid up, leaving a humming trail across my skin to where it came to rest in my hair. Everything inside me quivered as I heard Zev whisper, "Forgive me, *Minamahal. Ikaw ay ang aking mga dahilan para sa pamumuhay.* 'You are my reason for living.' I will never behave that way again. Come what may, we are in this together, equal partners. Can you ever forgive me?"

"Of course, *mi amor.*" His eyes widened slightly and I grinned. "I do know some Spanish, remember?" Then his hand was on my face and I forgot what was so funny. His thumb ran across the thin white line that marred the skin under my lip and my heart skipped a beat. Seriously, it did. I closed my eyes and pressed my face against his hand, heat flooding me from head to toe, enough that I didn't care about the weather.

"I couldn't stand the thought of you flirting with someone, even if it was just for information. A part of me still wants to go back to the police station and let Officer Tyler know that you're spoken for."

I opened my eyes and confessed. "I didn't flirt with Mrs. Rebecca Tyler."

"Officer Tyler's a woman."

"I told her that an 'acquaintance' of mine had left town before I could tell him some very important news, and the last I'd heard, he was coming here to meet with some friends. Basically, I kept the story simple and let her draw her own false conclusions." I couldn't stop the smile.

"Brilliant, *Liebling*."

Then Zev was closing the distance between our mouths and everything around us faded away, dimming to nothing more than a backdrop. In the recesses of my mind, I imagined that any curious pedestrian could see the sparks between us, silver and indigo electricity flowing from my cells to his. Pulling back enough to let us both breathe, Zev spoke again. "*Eu te amo, meu anjo*."

It was close enough to Spanish for me to understand what he'd said, but before I could tell him that I loved him too, I shivered. I heard Zev sigh and say, "We should get to that meeting."

It wasn't until I pulled away that I felt the bite in the wind and remembered that I'd left my coat in my room. Before I could go back for it, Zev was handing me his coat. I wanted to tell him no, but he raised both eyebrows and said, "Don't argue. Just wear the coat. Please."

As I slipped my arms into the oversized coat, I smiled. The worn leather was still warm from Zev's body. That thought brought goose bumps that had nothing to do with the weather. I climbed into the car, breathing deeply the familiar scents that I associated with Zev: leather, the slight metallic tang of weapons and the clean smell of soap. All things I'd begun to think of as home.

***

As a child, I'd loved Halloween, the chance to be someone, something, I wasn't. It had also been a time that my mother and I could enjoy together since she seized any opportunity to dress me up. Once I was old enough to start picking my own costumes rather than the faerie princesses Mom always seemed to pick out, my preferences became clear. Gone were the fluffy, poufy, glittery dresses of pink and lavender. Instead, I'd wanted to be a superhero, a vampire hunter, anything other than the delicate flower my mother desired or the plain girl I'd become. As I grew older, I continued to dress as strong female characters instead of using Halloween parties, like many of my friends, as an opportunity to show as much skin as possible without negative repercussions.

Now, as I readied myself for – I wanted to name it truly – battle, I felt the strangest sense of deja vu. The final costume party I'd attended, I'd dressed as a spy, complete with prop weapons. It hadn't felt eerily prophetic at the time, but, as I looked in the bathroom mirror, I could see a resemblance to that self-conscious child pretending to be someone full of confidence and strength. A part of me felt that I was merely playacting the soldier, a pretend warrior trying to be real.

I shook my head to clear it and gave myself a once-over. For something this big, one missed detail could mean the difference between life and death. Well, for me anyway. I pushed the thought aside. Zev and I had gone shopping late last night, and then spent today preparing. Aside from a plan of attack, I had needed to be fitted with more specific clothing than Zev had to wear. He didn't need as much protection as I, and had vastly more experience fighting in various forms of dress. As he'd pointed out, once you'd fought in lederhosen and half stockings, you really weren't particular about apparel anymore. My outfit was a bit more fight-friendly. I wore black pants and a matching long-sleeved shirt, both form-fitting but fluid enough not to hinder movement. Over the shirt, I had a vest made of some lightweight material that Zev assured me was a newer form of a flak jacket that his mother had purchased from a government test lab. I didn't ask for more details and he didn't offer. Part of my brain wondered how literal the word 'purchased' was, but I pushed the thought aside after just a few seconds. I had more important things to worry about.

My boot knife was strapped to my calf to allow for easier maneuvering in my hiking boots. For ready access rather than secrecy, a silver combat knife, specially designed for Immortals, was secured in a thigh sheath. Over the past month, at my insistence, Zev had designed a weapons belt for me. It hung around my waist now, snug enough to stay in place, yet loose enough not to hinder movement. From the belt hung four throwing knives, all Immortal-designed silver. Two had five-

and-a-half inch blades; the other pair was a little over half that size. In a shoulder harness, a small crossbow lay across my back. Because of Maine hunting laws, any gunfire after six o'clock would be investigated, so Zev and I had decided stealth and blades would be the best tactical advantage. Though we wouldn't be using guns, tucked into the back of my pants, and held in place with my belt, was my Colt. Zev had insisted I bring it. He'd rather, he said, risk legal trouble for unlawful firearm use than lose me. It was a mark of how much this life had changed me that I found his comment rather romantic.

I sucked in a lungful of air and let it out slowly. "All right, Lord," I kept my voice low enough that Zev wouldn't hear me through the bathroom door, "You said I was supposed to do this. Well, I'm going to need Your strength because tonight, I'm probably going to have to take a life. Don't let me fail Zev, fail You."

I am your strength. I will not let you fall.

I nodded once and then left the bathroom. Zev was lounging on the couch, waiting for me. His eyes widened when I walked into the room.

"What?" I looked down at my attire, worried that I'd forgotten something important. A weapon. Socks.

"*Bello*." He let out a low whistle. "You're hot."

I felt my temperature rising. "No so bad yourself." And, boy, wasn't he! Loose-fitting black pants, more liquid than cloth. A tight black shirt that clung to every contour of his muscular arms and torso. Black leather straps crossed his chest, holding ten silver throwing daggers of varying lengths on the front and, in duel sheaths, two wicked Marine Corps combat knives on his back. He had a blade on either hip and, hidden, a nine-inch boot knife strapped to his calf. Unlike me, he wasn't wearing a gun, but, after training with him, I doubted he'd need it. I allowed myself one more appreciative look and then joined Zev at the table to go over our plan.

After the incident with Stanwick, Zev had acknowledged my superior planning ability and turned that part of our job over to me. Our natural talents complimented each other and, as this particular mission had progressed, I'd begun to see how this life suited me as much as it did Zev. After learning from Gertrude (who seemed to have a soft spot for Zev) that four more tattooed campers had arrived and only Hector Stanwick had yet to appear, Zev filled me in on the usual practices observed before a Samhain sacrifice. I came up with an idea, presented it to Zev and then made changes based on his observations. In just a few hours, we'd had a decent strategy, one that I was certain would probably work. I left off the 'probably' when sharing with Zev because I knew that the slightest hesitation on my part would make him reconsider my involvement. And, there was no way Zev could take all nine Perpetuum out by himself without risking the three sacrifices, even if he used a gun.

By eleven thirty, we stood in a thicket of trees, ready to strike. As Zev had predicted, the clearing was empty save for the four cabins. He'd explained to me that the Perpetuum would have revealed their intentions to their captives about ten minutes ago and then retired to their cabins for further preparations, leaving the sacrifices with just one guard. When

I'd asked how Zev knew there would be only one, he'd said that since Stanwick wasn't coming, the odd one out would have been put on guard duty alone.

Zev motioned to the cabin furthest from us, but I hadn't needed his help on this point. The other three cabins had every light blazing. The far one only had light showing in the main room. I glanced up at the half-hidden moon, unsure if I wanted more or less cloud cover. I felt Zev's hand close over my forearm, and turned back to him. He tapped his watch with his other hand. I nodded to show that I understood. We had only fifteen minutes before the Perpetuum would gather their sacrifices and celebrate the closing of Samhain.

I started to move only to be pulled back, right in to Zev's embrace. One arm caught me around the waist, leaving the other free to run up my arm, shoulder and neck before stopping on my cheek. The left side of my body smoldered under his touch. He rested his forehead against mine, features barely visible in the blackness of the night. "Come back to me, *mi amor. Et necessito.*"

"I need you, too, my love." I whispered back. Time was slipping by, too fast, and we needed to go. I raised myself on my tiptoes and covered Zev's trembling lips with my own. The kiss was too brief for both of us, but we had to move.

I freed myself from Zev's grasp and ran. I didn't hear Zev behind me, but I knew that he'd followed, breaking for the cabin to the right of where I was headed. I darted around the back, locking away thoughts of Zev, distractions that could get me killed. Less than two minutes later, I dropped to the bedroom floor with what I hoped was a quiet thump.

No such luck.

“Did you hear something?” A quavering female voice came from the other side of the door.

“Shut up.” A man replied, sounding more distant than annoyed.

I didn’t wait to see if the woman would press the issue. I crossed to the door, sliding one of the larger throwing daggers from my belt as I moved. I made sure that my grip was perfect before closing my other hand around the cool metal doorknob. *Lord, make my aim true.* Knowing that further hesitation would hinder more than help, I yanked the door open.

Despite the light suddenly flooding my eyes, I saw everything in God-given and adrenaline-induced clarity. Three figures sat on the couch, only their profiles visible until they turned their heads. Two were brunette women in their early thirties, similar enough to be related. The third was a slender male close to my age, dyed blond hair streaked with dark blue glitter. A fourth figure stood in the center of the room, mouth dropped open in surprise. A gun lay, useless, on the table a few feet behind him. I didn’t wait for him to make a move for his weapon. In the smooth motion I’d used every time I’d practiced, I brought my arm forward, releasing the weapon at the correct time.

The man staggered backwards, dark eyes widened as they peered down at the hilt protruding from his chest. I was moving before the blade landed and reached the man just as he sank to his knees. The knife from my thigh sheath was in my hand, ready to silence the Perpetuum if necessary, but he fell to the side without making a sound. I stared down at him, waiting for the horror movie moment when he would bolt upright with an unearthly roar, ready to wreak further vengeance. All right, Tex, fiction versus reality. Focus. I studied the figure on the floor. The tattoo on his wrist was the only such mark on his tanned skin. To my surprise, the face beneath his golden hair was handsome. I'd been expecting a monster. Instead, he'd just been a man. A man I had killed.

ZEV

I waited until Tex was a few yards ahead of me before sprinting out behind her. I tried to ignore the warmth where her lips had touched mine and was successful... after half a minute or so. The window into the bathroom was a tight fit, but I managed. I lowered myself to the floor without a sound and paused in the dark, listening for clues as to where the Perpetuum were lurking. I heard a noise from the right. Okay, maybe 'lurking' wasn't the correct word. I slipped into the hallway and then through the open door.

Less than two minutes later, I left the way I came, pausing only to wipe blood from my knife. As I crossed the space to the next cabin, I glanced towards the one where Tex was even though I knew she wouldn't be foolish enough to do anything that would alert the other Perpetuum that something was different. Just as I'd thought. Nothing had changed. I took comfort in the fact that this meant that Tex had won – or the fight hadn't yet occurred. I didn't dwell on the second option.

The couple in the third cabin were dispatched as quickly and quietly as the previous pair, so absorbed in their depravities that they didn't realize they'd been caught until my blade was at the throat of the second one. My mental tabulation told me that the final cabin would be the biggest risk. Once inside, I took an extra moment to swing my crossbow over my shoulder and load a bolt. Based on the activities in the last two cabins, I had a good chance that I'd be able to use one shot to bring down two targets. Even if it didn't kill both, it would buy me enough time to take care of the rest. What I hadn't counted on was one man's refusal to die.

***

Oddly enough, the first thing I registered was the small, soft hand on my forehead.

Then came the pain. I'd forgotten what a fractured skull felt like.

"Zev, wake up."

Something wet landed on my lips and I tasted salt. Tex was crying? I opened my eyes and pushed myself into a semi-sitting position, stopping when I felt my dinner trying to make a reappearance. "*Ei, vaikeli. Du er skinnende.*"

"Is he drunk?"

An unfamiliar voice made me whip around my head. And then made me wish that I hadn't moved. Or been born in the first place. I was considering placing this injury above the poker through the shoulder when the dark-haired woman spoke again. "Are they all...?"

"Dead." Tex answered the unfinished question and I, slowly this time, turned back to her. "Are you all right, Zev?"

I started to nod, then thought better of it. I doubted Tex's affection would withstand me vomiting all over her. "Give me a couple minutes. Do we need to leave right away?"

Tex shook her head, and this time I saw the shadows in her eyes. She must have seen the question in mine. "The other one's outside."

"It was my husband. My Jacob." The woman who'd spoken before moved into my sightline, followed by a younger brunette and a teenage boy. The resemblance was uncanny. "He brought us up here. My sister, my son, me. Told us it was a vacation." She buried her head in her hands and burst into sobs.

The other woman put her arms around her sister. Her green eyes were razor-sharp as they moved between Tex, myself, the body on the table and the two in the hall behind me. The boy sat next to his mother, staring at his hands. The shock hadn't worn off yet.

"This is the Knight family." Tex had taken her hand from my cheek, but I didn't protest because it was now on my knee as she shifted into a more comfortable position. "Tessa." She motioned to the crying woman. "Stacy." The sister. "And Ben." The son. "They're from Massachusetts."

"Can you get them on the road?" I closed my eyes, feeling the pounding at my temples spike as bits of bone rearranged themselves. Sometimes healing was almost as painful as the injury itself. See previous account about the crazy Norseman who'd mistaken me for my brother.

"Are you sure you're okay?" Tex's fingertips ghosted over my forehead, brushing down the side of my face.

"Better now." I opened my eyes and gave her a smile. "I'll

be fine, *Amato*."

Tex studied my face for a moment, searching, I assumed, for the truth. Then she nodded once and stood. She turned to the trio on the couch and I closed my eyes again, concentrating on my inhalation / exhalation rhythm rather than the specific words she was saying. Just the sound of her voice was soothing. I heard footsteps, the creak of rusty springs, the click of the shutting door. By the time Tex returned, I was back on my feet, with only the dullest ache at the back of my head. I gingerly explored the area, expecting another flash of pain. I was pleased to find a small lump that I could feel reshaping under my fingers. It, too, would vanish. Whatever had caused the blood in my hair, staining my shirt and fingers, had healed already.

"They're heading down to Bangor with a pretty good story." Tex crossed to the kitchen sink and wet a paper towel. "Seems that while on a family vacation, Tessa and Jacob had a fight. Tessa, Stacy and Ben left Jacob at the cabin they'd rented." She crossed to my side and reached for my hand, carefully wiping off the blood. "In a few days, she'll get concerned because she hasn't heard from Jacob. She's just sure that something awful happened to him and the other campers. And she'll be right. Based on the scene, some type of wild animal attacked them."

"That'll work." I was having difficulty following the details, all too aware of Tex's gentle touch. "What made you think of that story?"

"I didn't." Tex released my hand. "The kid, Ben, thought of it."

"Really?" I kept my eyes on Tex as she threw the paper towel into the fireplace. *Meget godt.* She'd remembered that we couldn't leave evidence of our presence. That in mind, I set about mopping up the blood I'd left on the floor.

"He said he's been reading up on wildlife attacks in the area. I didn't ask for more information." Tex tossed a bloody piece of wood into the flames. In answer to my unspoken question, she said, "I'm guessing that's what Jacob hit you with."

"I can clean up on my own."

Tex shook her head. "There's a lot to do."

I looked her way, concerned by the matter-of-fact tone. "*Nobiyo*, are you all right?"

She hesitated, a good sign. If she'd answered to readily, I would have doubted the truth of her statement. "Enough for this. I'll deal with the rest later. When we're done."

I opened my mouth to argue, to convince her to return to our cabin and leave this gruesome necessity to me.

Let her be.

I was too tired to argue. October night passed into November morning as we worked. We didn't stop until we were certain we'd done all that needed to be done. By then, the sun was almost directly overhead, though virtually invisible through dark clouds. I was glad for the weather. Tex didn't need to know the horror of blood and flesh as it ripened in a warmer environment, the stark tragedy of blood in the daylight. We made our return trip in silence, drained of almost all energy. As it was, I feared Tex would fall asleep in the shower. I waited until she'd dropped onto the bed, asleep before she'd crawled under the covers, and then cleaned the gore from my aching body. After tucking her in, I collapsed onto the couch and gratefully sank into a deep, dreamless sleep.

When I woke, the first thing I saw was Tex, standing by the window, a halo of morning light casting a warm glow... *vidunderlig*. I was rambling. I sat up, stretching the stiffness out of my muscles and joints. As I swung my legs off of the couch, my previous observation caught up to me. Morning? I grabbed my cell phone off of the nearby table and checked it. Sure enough, I'd slept the whole night through. It was Sunday morning. I stood, my feet bare against the cold wooden floor. I crossed to where Tex was still standing. "Good morning." Judging by her lack of surprise, she'd known I was up.

"Morning."

I slid my arms around Tex's waist and she sighed, leaning back against me. I rested my chin on her head and joined her in staring out of the window. The light was so bright that it took my eyes a moment to adjust, to figure out why.

"Good thing Gertrude kept this cabin stocked with non-perishables." Tex's voice was surprisingly nonchalant. "I don't think we'll be getting out of here any time soon."

Taking in the white blanket covering the forest around us and the still-falling flakes, I had to agree. While we'd slept, the first day of November had brought with it at least three feet of snow.

***

Tex and I enjoyed a quiet Sunday, spending most of it on the couch, curled together, each reading a book. The stone fireplace provided cozy warmth that was accented by the hand-knitted afghans Tex had found at the top of the bedroom closet. We each kept one wrapped around our shoulders as we moved about, refilling mugs of hot cocoa or finding something to eat. Neither of us had the energy to make a full meal, but it didn't seem to matter. The whole day held a surreal quality that deepened as the sun disappeared behind the trees. Soon, only the fire lit the cabin, making it difficult to read, even for me. Though Tex and I both set our books aside, neither one of us made a move to turn on the overhead light or even one of the lamps.

"Zev," Tex continued to stare into the fire, but I could feel tension stiffen her body. "Do you ever get used to it?"

I didn't need clarification. I secured my arms around her waist as I answered. "No, not really."

"Do you think about them?"

"All the time, *Elskan*." I shifted, moving Tex so that her back rested against my chest.

I heard the hitch in her voice as she asked her next question. "How do you deal with it?"

"I remind myself that they had a choice, just like me. That *El Tsaddik* is the judge and He hands down the sentence. My job is to obey."

"Does that help?"

I considered lying, telling her that it did. That the taking of a life didn't bother me because I knew that I was carrying out *El Tsaddik*'s edict.

Tell her the truth.

I tried to match *El Rachum*'s gentle tone. "Sometimes."

Tex took a shuddering breath, her pain piercing me more deeply than any weapon ever had. "I'm afraid to sleep. Afraid that I'm going to see them when I close my eyes. That they'll be in my dreams. That I'll wake and they'll be here."

My own tears streamed down my face and my voice was a cracked whisper. "Then I'll stay awake; hold you all night. And if you think anything bad is going to happen, just feel my arms around you, and remember that I'm here. That you're safe."

"You'll do that?" Tex twisted around so that her cheek rested against my chest.

"*Chiudete gli occh, amore mio.*" I pressed my lips to the top of her head. "Close your eyes and rest. *Caea 'ch chreuau.*" I felt her breathing slow and continued murmuring reassurances against her hair. "I'm not going anywhere, *Mahal*. Sleep, *l'amor de la meva vida. Et estimar per sempre.* I won't leave you. *Voi nu te pierd. Sunteti mea putere.*"

Half-asleep, Tex mumbled, "you're babbling."

I smiled and continued babbling until I was sure she'd fallen asleep.

TEX

I could hear him, that liquid-gold voice that never failed to flood my body with warmth, but I couldn't understand half of what he was saying. My sleep-deprived brain put two and two together and managed to get three and-a-half. I needed to say something very important before I succumbed to the dim temptation of sleep. Summoning the last of my willpower, I spoke. “You’re babbling.” Then I let myself go.

If I dreamed that night, I didn’t remember the next morning. Zev’s finger brushing back some hair drew me from my slumber, and I opened my eyes to find that Zev had been true to his word. He hadn’t moved. My question came out with a puff of visible air. The fire had died some time in the night. “Did you sleep at all?”

Zev shook his head, combing his fingers through my sure-to-be-wild curls. “I can function on only a few hours and I got a lot yesterday.” His hand moved down to my cheek and I felt the familiar searing heat of his skin on mine.

My stomach growled, breaking the mood. I let out a breath I hadn’t realized I’d been holding as Zev twisted around so that he could get to his feet. With a shaking hand, I dug into my hoodie pocket for my phone. I needed to call Elle. Immediately. I could hear Zev rummaging through the cabinets as I flipped open my phone.

No service. This was so not good. Not a single bar. I hadn’t even thought to check reception when we’d first arrived and now it was too late. I stumbled to the window, desperately hoping that the snow had melted. My insides twisted into strange and foreign shapes as I saw a new layer blanketing the old, and more flakes falling from an overcast sky. We weren’t getting out of here any time soon. I glanced back at Zev and my heart decided to do jumping jacks on the newly distorted platform of my stomach. He was whistling an unidentifiable tune as he arranged plates and silverware on the table. I’d never seen anything so beautiful.

Crap.

I was in for a very long couple of days.

***

Try twelve very long days. By the tenth of November, the snow had stopped, but what was on the ground didn't start melting until the twelfth. Even then, with it as deep as it was, we couldn't hope to get to the car, much less to the nearest town. We had enough food to last to the end of the month, but I wasn't sure my self-control would make it that far. On the afternoon of November fourteenth, I made Zev promise that we would try to leave the next morning. Each night, I found it more and more difficult to leave Zev on the couch and return to the bedroom alone. Part of the problem was lack of distraction. No television, internet or phone. Only a few board games and the books we'd brought with us. By the fifth night, I was thinking longingly of the bag of books I'd left in the car. As for the games, well, there's only so many times you can play Yahtzee without succumbing to the temptation to stick a fork in an electrical outlet, just to keep things interesting.

After Zev and I had packed up most of our possessions, we settled in front of the fire to read, and I tried to concentrate on a book I was rereading for the second time in two weeks. After the third attempt to get through a particularly difficult sentence regarding a fight against ultimate evil, I gave up and tossed *Tru Shepard* onto the table. I glanced over at Zev and was annoyed to find him immersed in what appeared to be a leather-bound journal. Curious and bored, I tapped the cover.

"What are you reading?"

"*Romeo and Juliet.*" Zev held the volume out to me.

I took it, flipping through the pages at random. It was handwritten, not typed, but I wasn't curious enough to study it at first. I'd barely gotten through this particular classic the first time in Mr. Specktor's eighth grade reading class. My eyes caught something odd, and I looked down for clarification. '*Dydy 'm arglwyddes O, dydy 'm cara!*' That's funny; I didn't remember Romeo speaking in tongues.

"It's Welsh." Zev grinned.

"You have a Welsh version of *Romeo and Juliet*?"

"And a couple other of Shakespeare's works."

"I didn't realize you liked his plays."

Zev's smile widened. "He was a nice guy."

"What?" I knew my voice had risen in surprise, but I couldn't seem to stop it.

"Remember I told you about the boy who played Juliet shoving peas up his nose?"

I nodded. That was a mental image I wasn't likely to forget anytime soon.

"I wasn't attending that performance. I was in it."

"In it?" Another rise in pitch.

The smile vanished. "The guy who played Mercutio was a Perpetuum. He was always surrounded by people, making getting to him very difficult. I got the part of Tybalt. A slow-acting poison on my sword, a slip during our fight scene." Zev dropped his gaze to his hands, as if imagining them stained crimson. "No one connected the small scratch I'd given him with his illness later that night."

"Why you?" I tried to draw him out of his gloom. "I thought you'd given up hunting Perpetuum by the time Shakespeare came around."

"It was a special favor to Ellis. He needed me." The corner of his mouth twitched up once more. "While my brother may have a proclivity towards the dramatic, he's a lousy actor."

I smiled. "So you were feeling nostalgic?"

Even in the dim firelight, I could see the flush stain Zev's cheeks. "I tend to read Shakespeare when I'm bored... or need distracting."

"Really?" It was nice to know I wasn't the only one struggling.

Zev started to say something, hesitated, and began again. "I was translating it to Italian in my head."

"You were translating Shakespeare?"

"Where do you think that copy came from?" Zev shrugged. "I have two tragedies and three comedies in six different languages each. French, German, Hungarian, Estonian..." Off of my look, he added, "I got bored."

"When?" Of all the questions, that's the one I asked?

"The 1920's." He paused. "Through the 1940's."

"Right." I looked down at the book in my hands, this time recognizing the handwriting. "And you're reading it in Welsh, but changing it to Italian? Why? Does it sound better in Italian?"

"'*Forse il mio cuore l'amore fino ad ora? Giuro che, vista! Per non ho mai visto la vera bellezza fino a questa notte.*'" Zev reached for his book, his eyes locking with mine.

I forced words past numb lips. "Which part is that?"

"When Romeo first sees Juliet." Zev dropped his book next to *Tru Shepard* without taking his gaze from me. The temperature in the room skyrocketed. Or maybe that was just me.

"Oh."

"And from the balcony scene: '*O, ancora parlare, angelo luminoso!*'" Zev leaned towards me. "What do you think? Does it sound better in Italian?"

I wanted to tell him that a grocery list would've sounded good if he was reading it, but my brain wasn't quite functioning well enough to manage more than the simplest of words. "Mh-hm." All right, not even words.

Nothing had ever contained more heat and energy than the purple-blue eyes absorbing mine. "Song of Solomon: '*Lawer ddyfroedd all mo ddiffodd cara, na all 'r boddfeydd bawdd 'i.. 'm anwylyd ydy chloddia, a dwi eiddo... Chusaned 'm ag 'r chusanau chan eiddo cega...*'" His lips brushed against my no-longer-numb ones. "*Fi angen 'ch.*"

Not Italian. My short-circuiting brain tried to make sense of the words Zev spoke against my mouth. I told it to shut up and pulled Zev towards me. He tasted like cinnamon and chocolate, a combination of gum and hot cocoa. I released the front of his shirt and wrapped my arms around him, digging my fingers into the hair I'd trimmed just a few days before.

Zev made a noise low in his throat. "*Seni istiyorum. Sana ihtiyacum var.*" He whispered as his lips traced my jaw. I didn't need to know the words to understand the meaning. He paused at my ear. "*Mawarku. Saya semua.*" He kissed the spot just under my earlobe. "*Cara 'ch.* I love you. *Addola 'ch.* I adore you."

It seemed so unfair that I had only one language with which to return his sentiments. I put a hand on his cheek and turned his face towards mine, hoping to convey in tenor what I lacked in fluency. "I love you." I repeated his words back to him. "I adore you." My free hand skimmed the expanse of skin where his shirt had shifted up in the back.

Before I could register the movement, Zev's shirt had joined our books on the table and he was pulling me towards him again. His hands scalded, seared, as they slid from my waist, under the hem of my shirt, to the small of my back, the molten lava of skin on skin. My hands had a mind of their own as they traced the defined muscles of Zev's back and shoulders, running down his arms and up again. Dusky silk over steel cords.

I hooked one leg around his waist and Zev gasped against my lips. "*Akarlak, szerelmem.*"

My mouth opened under Zev's, his teeth scraping over my bottom lip. I made a sound I'd never made before.

Wait.

Some part of me – definitely not my hormonally-loaded brain – screamed at me. How it was loud enough to be heard over my desire for Zev, I could only chalk up to divine intervention. My hands gripped Zev's shoulders and pushed him back with a strength I knew I didn't possess.

"Wait." I dragged air into my aching lungs and said the most impossible thing. "We're not going to do this."

***

Snowdrifts threw off the sunrise like diamonds, blinding me as I watched the landscape slowly changing around us. We managed to get to the car and on the road by six o'clock, neither of us wanting to risk a repeat of the night before. As we crossed the southern border into the lower New England states, Zev interrupted whatever CD had been providing us with background music. "About last night. Tex, I'm..."

"If you apologize one more time, I'm going to make our previous sparring sessions feel like a day at the spa." I tried to keep the edge from my voice, but wasn't sure that I'd succeeded. "Now, where are we going?"

"South." Zev grinned at me and I knew we were okay. "As far from the snow as we can get."

Shortly after we passed through Boston, we stopped for lunch. I never thought I'd be so glad for fast food, but two weeks of canned and freeze-dried fare made French fries smell gourmet. As we waited for our food, Zev's phone rang.

"Your parents?" I asked as he took his cell from his pocket. When I'd expressed surprise that neither of his parents had contacted him since we'd left Ohio, he reminded me that, after living for four millennia, a few months didn't seem very long. He glanced down at the number and shook his head.

"Hello?" Zev stepped out of line. He paused, heading for the doors. "Yes, I know who you are." The rest of his conversation faded as he slipped outside.

By the time I'd taken our food to an empty booth, Zev was on his way back. He slid into the seat across from me and took my hand. Before I could ask about the phone call, he bowed his head and uttered a quick prayer over our food. Then, as he reached for a fry, he spoke. "We're going to Virginia."

"What's in Virginia?" I savored the tang of salt and grease as I waited for an answer. I'd gladly suffer high-cholesterol if it meant never eating from a can again.

"*Enverto venator*." Zev took a gulp of his cola before offering further explanation. "The call was from one of the contacts my family has in the US."

"Like Neysa?" I hoped my mention didn't result in more teasing.

Aside from a quirk of the mouth, Zev didn't acknowledge the Indiana incident. "Yes. Any time something odd happens, something out of the ordinary, they give us a call."

"And there's something strange in Virginia?"

"No. Jesse says that there are reports of a flesh-eating goat in Arkansas."

"A what?" I almost dropped my sandwich.

"A flesh-eating goat." Zev repeated the phrase with the same sincerity he'd used the first time.

"How does that connect to the Perpetuum?" It was a testament to how strange my life had become that my first legitimate question had nothing to do with the validity of such a claim.

"It doesn't." Zev started on his second hamburger, punctuating his statements with quick bites. "But, there are others who deal with the supernatural. I'll give you the history lesson later. For now, we need to get in touch with one of them, and to do that, we need to get to Roanoke."

"Wait, I know that name." Pieces of history cropped up in the back of my mind. Something about a mysterious word on a tree.

Zev smiled. "I'm sure you do. First, we eat. Then, when we're on the road, I'll tell you the story."

ZEV

"What's in Virginia?"

"*Enverto venator*." The phrase brought back vague memories scattered through the years. Different places, faces, races... syrupy-sweet carbonation stopped my absurd rhyming, and I continued. "The call was from one of the contacts my family has in the US."

"Like Neysa?"

I fought the urge to make a clever reply, and won. "Yes. Any time something odd happens, something out of the ordinary, they give us a call."

Thirty minutes later, Tex and I were back on the road. As we pulled onto the highway, I began to give her the short version of the story. "While we exist to eliminate the Perpetuum, they aren't the only dangers to have survived through the years. All sorts of demons and creatures roam the earth and most people don't even know. Some time after the ascension, *El Olam* chose a group of believers to be *enverto venator*. Demon hunters, though they technically hunt animals and only take the occasional cases of demonic possession." I paused to change lanes. "There are others who hunt demons themselves, but not much is know about the *Astrum Veho*, the Star Riders, other than the fact that they have extraordinary abilities. The *enverto venator*, however, were ordinary people, not like the Immortal, but they fought the evil side of the supernatural. Naturally, our paths crossed not too long after their calling. They're scattered all over the world, most growing up as *EV*, some choosing the life for other reasons. If we hear of a non-Perpetuum related incident, we make contact with the local *EV*. Likewise, if they discover information about our mission, they send it to us."

"Why Roanoke?"

Tex never failed to impress me with how well she dealt with the otherworldly aspect of my life. I corrected myself. Our lives. I reached for her hand and continued. "The *EV* spread out, covering the known and unknown world. The ones that came to America assimilated into the native tribes hundreds of years before the first Europeans landed. By 1587, only a few *EV* still remembered their calling. A family of these was part of a tribe in Virginia. A tribe located near the English settlement at Roanoke."

"The Lost Colony." Tex had turned halfway in her seat, our linked hands resting on her bent leg. "Is that what happened? Something supernatural killed the settlers?"

I nodded. "Most of them anyway. The rest joined the tribe that had saved them. Some of the *EV* took in a child who had survived the attack. A little girl named Virginia Dare. Her descendants became the protectors of North America. Because there are so few *enverto venator* left, they do occasionally go outside of their primary area, but they always return."

"And the *EV* for North America live in Roanoke?"

I shook my head. "It's just a contact point. There's a very

small church run by a family who knows about the Immortal and the *EV*. One of Neysa's distant relatives, actually. Last I'd heard, it was a woman named Krystal Gregory. We give her the information, she passes it to the *enverto venator* and we go on our way."

"Who are they?"

"Don't really know." I shrugged. "It's pretty much down to one family and a handful of loners."

"When we're done with this, could we, maybe, help them?"

"*Saya tidak mengharapkan itu.*"

"What?"

"Sorry." I glanced at Tex, enjoying the way the sight of her always made my pulse race. "I just wasn't expecting that." I took a few minutes to consider her question. "Let's win this battle before we start on another."

After a moment, Tex nodded. "All right." She squeezed my hand and I thought my heart would explode. Vaguely I wondered how long it would take me to heal from that particular injury. Tex's voice brought me back, which was a good thing since I was driving and a wreck would not be a pleasant thing. "Tell me about some of these other supernatural creatures. Start with the flesh-eating goats."

***

The next ten days passed in a blur. After meeting Krystal, who turned out to be less colorful, but just as helpful, as her distant cousin Neysa, and giving her the tip concerning what may or may not have been a flesh-eating goat, she had one for us. A Perpetuum named Antoinette Badeau had passed through two weeks ago while moving to Florida. After restocking supplies, Tex and I headed for Deltona. Probably the easiest hunt we'd had, we arrived on Monday and found Antoinette on Tuesday. In her mid-thirties, Ms. Badeau was a paralegal at a law firm specializing in clearing Perpetuum of ritual-based charges. Because her firm often defended unscrupulous clients (including, but not limited to, Perpetuum), it was easy to stage a botched break-in by a disgruntled former client. Tex searched the house while I'll left vague but incriminating evidence. In Antoinette's diary – a place I never would have considered looking – Tex found correspondence with a Perpetuum in Ypsilanti, Michigan, and we went north the next morning.

We were around the Jefferson National Forest when Tex remembered that the next day was Thanksgiving. On the twenty-seventh, Tex and I enjoyed a completely nontraditional Thanksgiving dinner, complete with pepperoni pizza, grapes and chocolate-covered pretzels. After the meal, Tex and I swapped holiday stories. She told me about her day-after-Thanksgiving tradition of decorating her entire house for Christmas, and I described the meal my family had shared with the president who'd just declared the national holiday. Tex shared about the time she decided to invite an entire orphanage over for dinner. In turn, I related the problems with turkey hunting in the Wild West, the least of which was finding an actual turkey. Both of us had plenty to be thankful for.

On Friday, we joined hundreds, if not thousands, of other

Americans on the roads. We didn't need much research once we were in Michigan since we had an address. But, because there was a link between the recently-deceased Antoinette Badeau and the soon-to-be-deceased Misha Clayton, this death needed to look like an accident. Tex and I made it work: a missing battery and some faulty wiring leading to carbon-monoxide poisoning. Our vandalizing B&E session also gave us a tip towards Louisiana. We stayed in Bowling Green, Kentucky, the first night, and made it to Venice just before midnight on the eighth of December. We spent the next few days searching for clues as to who our next target would be. As December tenth turned into the eleventh, Tex and I stumbled onto an online article regarding the sudden relocation of local doctor Jared West, his wife Kate, son Nathan, and the wife's half-brother Oliver Robinson. I didn't pay much attention until Tex pointed at the smudge on the wrist of the teenage son. An hour later, we'd discovered the new location: Jasper, Texas. Driving through the early morning, we reached Jasper around ten A.M. Finding a Mercedes with Louisiana license plates wasn't difficult, and that's how Tex and I found ourselves between an empty baseball field and a thickly wooded area, facing off with four Perpetuum.

Tex was driving, so I didn't wait for the car to come to a complete stop before throwing open my door. I heard Tex call my name, but I didn't take my attention from my target: the largest of the four figures who was wielding what could only be described as a machete. I saw a sneer forming on Oliver Robinson's face before I collided with him, sinking all seven inches of my knife into his chest. We grappled for a few chaotic seconds until Robinson realized that he was dead and dropped to the ground. At some point in that struggle, I'd felt a sharp pain in my left hand and now saw that I was missing a good chunk of that hand, as well as my last two fingers. *Dritt.* That was going to take some time to grow back.

"Look out!" Tex's warning came from behind me, but I'd already caught movement in my peripheral vision. I spun that way, letting instinct guide me as I threw my bloodied blade. It caught Dr. West in the throat, releasing a spray that turned the ground a strange shade of red. I could feel the throbbing in my hand that meant the bleeding had stopped and I turned to help Tex. She was leaning over Kate West, retrieving her knife, when she staggered back, the crack coming less than a second later.

I didn't remember grabbing Robinson's machete from the ground and throwing it towards the shooter, but I must have, because Nathan West flew back five feet, his uncle's weapon lodged in his nearly severed neck. All I knew, all I saw, was the slow-motion stagger and fall of the only person who mattered.

TEX

The kid was in my sights first, but I couldn't bring myself to kill him. According to the article we'd read, Nathan was only sixteen. Younger than me. I couldn't do it, so I went for his mother. As the blade slid between Kate West's ribs and into her heart, I saw the husband running towards Zev. I yelled out a warning as Kate fell to the ground, taking my knife with her. I reached for the hilt, ready to assist Zev if he needed it. I felt a thump against my shoulder, and didn't realize what had happened until I heard the shot. Then came the pain.

The world around me shimmered, glittered, shone. Shapes and sounds merged as I went first to my knees. I heard Zev scream my name and wanted to go to him, to stop the anguish in his voice, to comfort him. It wasn't that bad. Okay, it hurt, but falling off the mountain still held the number one spot for me. Then Zev was at my side, doing his multi-language babbling thing as he reached for me. Something was wrong with one of his hands and I tried to reach for it, but couldn't seem to lift my arms. They were so heavy. So I just listened to Zev's voice, even though I could only understand half of what he was saying.

"Tex, *cara chan 'm buchedd.* Please, *ljubljeni.*" Some of Zev's tears fell on my cheeks. "*Reste avec moi, amoureux.* Don't leave me. *Je t'aime. Moje srce pripada vama. El Rachum*, please, don't take her from me. *El malei Rachamin. Te rog, Dumnezeu Tata. El Shaddai. Deus, succurro mihi.*"

I felt one arm slide behind my knees and the other move under my neck. Even the agony of being moved couldn't completely obliterate the way his touch made my skin sing. I still had the presence of mind to want to hit myself for such romantic rubbish, but I settled for knowing that a gunshot to the shoulder was enough punishment.

"Where are we going?" My words were slurred, but Zev understood my question.

"A hospital, *ijubavnik.* Where do you think?"

How Zev managed to get the door open, I don't know, but I suddenly found myself in the familiar passenger's seat of the

Impala. I was going to stain the upholstery. His words registered and I shook my head. At least, I tried to shake my head. It was more like a feeble bobble, but I didn't care. "No hospital. They have to report gunshots. It'll be traced to the bodies." Concern for Zev made my voice stronger.

"*Ach 'n feddw*? You've been shot!"

"Yeah, got that memo." I could feel the darkness trying to steal me away and fought against it. "I'm sure you've patched up worse."

The car roared to life, but Zev turned to me rather than driving away. He put his hand on my cheek and the agony on his face pierced me more deeply than the bullet had. His eyes were wide, normally dark skin paled until it was lighter than mine. Though some might have been from blood loss (my mind wanted me to find out what had happened to his hand), I knew that most was because of me. "*Ma ei kaota sind.* Tex, *saya akan melakukan apapun untuk Anda*. Don't ask me to risk your life." He swallowed hard. "I can't lose you, *kochanie, moje powodu*."

I put the last of my strength into what I had to say. "You won't. Get me to a hotel. Fix me. God'll take care of me."

"Tex, *'m asgre*, please."

"Trust Him, Zev." Grayness came, taking Zev's stricken countenance from my sight. I could still feel the heat of his hand though and I clung to that. "Please, my love, *mi amor*. Please."

Only when I heard Zev whisper, "I will," did I release my tenuous grasp on the world and sank, gratefully, into painless oblivion.

***

I slipped in and out of consciousness over the next thirty-six hours while my body dealt with the trauma and shock of being shot. I'm not sure why my body was shocked. My mind had been prepared for this scenario for a while. As I drifted, I was occasionally aware of Zev at my side, alternating prayers with endearments, only part of which I could understand. My dreams were no less confusing. Vampires and werewolves and cowboys, oh my. It seemed that every book I'd ever read decided to unload itself into my already overloaded brain, resulting in a convoluted twirly soup of unreality.

It was from one of these surrealistic dreams that Zev's voice drew me.

"*Aros gyda mi, cariad.*" His fingers curved around mine, pulling me closer to waking. "Don't you dare leave me."

"Hadn't planned on it." My voice crackled. I blinked away some of the fog.

"*Szia kicsim.*"

I tried to swallow and winced at the burn. "Water."

"Here." Zev was standing over me, his hand no longer in mine. Instead, it held a cup of tepid water. "Tex, *miele*, you scared me." The fingers that brushed my cheek trembled. He set the empty cup aside.

"Sorry." My voice sounded a bit better. I struggled to sit up and Zev immediately moved to help me. It was then I saw the bandage and recalled a hazy memory of blood that wasn't mine. "Zev, what happened?" I cradled the misshapen hand in both of mine.

"Nothing, *szivem*." His free hand rested on my cheek.

"Zev," I surprised myself with the severity I managed.

"I lost a couple fingers, but they'll grow back."

"Lost a couple... yeah, no big deal." Had I thought my dreams were surreal? For me, real life was no less so.

"Look." Zev unwrapped the bandage. "I just keep it covered because seeing flesh in stages of re-growth can freak people out."

I saw what he meant. The fingers had reformed up to the first knuckle and it looked like some of his actual hand had regrown. Though not quite fast enough for the human eye, I knew that there would be a noticeable change by the end of the day. I watched him rewrap his bandage with practiced ease. "The Perpetuum?"

"Taken care of." Zev's dismissive tone made me raise my head. "I called in a favor."

"A favor?" I raised Zev's hand and lightly kissed the tips of his remaining fingers. I couldn't help but smile when his next words came out shaky.

"An FBI agent owed me one for a kidnapping I helped her father solve back in the sixties."

I nodded and shifted, wincing as my wound made itself known. Zev was on his feet in an instant, something close to panic on his face. I tugged on his wrist and he sat on the edge of the bed again. "I was shot, Zev, it's going to hurt." I sighed. "Now, give me the facts."

"About?"

"What day is it? Where are we? And, how bad is my

shoulder?"

My matter-of-fact approach seemed to calm him. "It's Friday night. We're at a hotel in Jasper. And you were very, very lucky. The bullet went straight through. Missed everything but the muscle."

"Not lucky." I shook my head. "Blessed."

"I'll agree with that." Zev gave half a smile and lifted my right hand to press his mouth against my palm.

Even a hole in my shoulder couldn't stop my insides from doing their usual set of antics as his dry lips brushed my skin. "How long until I can fight again?"

Chapter Eleven: I Will Believe, Whatever It Takes

ZEV

By the time I'd wrapped my hand, I could barely keep myself from descending into total panic. Tex hadn't regained consciousness and her blood had soaked into the seat of the car. I knew that shoulder wounds were tricky. If the bullet had nicked an artery, I didn't have much time, but I couldn't bring myself to break my promise to Tex about not going to a hospital. As I hurried into the hotel lobby, I could only pray "*Por favor, Deus Pai*, save her," over and over in every language I knew. If the desk clerk noticed anything out of the ordinary about my behavior or the blood on my black clothes, she didn't say anything, just handed over the key and continued texting.

Trust Me.

Two words cut through my panic and calmed my nerves. Well, enough that I was able to get Tex into our room and examine her shoulder with a clinical eye. The shot had been clean and, with minimal invasion, I could see that there'd been no artery or bone damage. In fact, the bleeding was already slowing. Despite my relief, I knew that I wouldn't rest easy until I saw her wake and heard her speak. I couldn't do anything but sit at her side and alternate between praying and talking to her. Then, when she finally did wake up, after a few minutes of conversation, she asked the one question I'd been dreading. The one I knew she was going to ask because she just couldn't quit.

"How long until I can fight again?"

"*Mitte kunagi*!" I hadn't meant to shout, and seeing Tex

flinch tore at me, but I couldn't bear the thought of going through this again. I resorted to begging. "Tex, *mesi*, no more. Please. *Ewyllysia mo choll 'ch*. You could have died."

"Zev," Tex's voice was steadier than mine. She cupped my cheek and I leaned into her hand. "We're not having this discussion again."

"You didn't almost die before." I pointed out.

"I could almost die anywhere, anytime. Riding in a car. Sitting in a classroom." Her voice was soft and I knew that the argument was taking its toll on her.

"You need to eat." I held up a hand to stop the protest I knew she was considering. "Food now, discussion later." I handed her a package of crackers.

"It's not up for debate."

I ignored her and went to get her more water. I wouldn't press the issue, but there was no way I'd be giving in without a battle. For the next four days, I managed to avoid the topic entirely, focusing on replacing my bloodied upholstery and monitoring Tex's recovery, both of which went considerably quicker once my fingers were done growing. She was healing faster than I'd thought possible, but, as I reminded myself, it had been a while since I'd paid attention to how mortals healed. By the time we left Jasper on the seventeenth, she could move her arm without too much pain, though lifting or strenuous activity was still beyond her. She hadn't mentioned fighting again, but I knew it hadn't completely left her thoughts.

It was the call from Ellis that did it, that got me to move Tex before I'd been fully satisfied that she was ready to go. I'd been in the shower when he'd called and Tex had been sleeping. She didn't like taking pain pills, but sometimes did at night so she could get some rest. She'd been deep enough that the ringing hadn't woken her, so Ellis had left a voicemail.

"Mom and Dad said you're out and about. They seem to think you're hunting again, but I doubt it. You always were a *sauhuta huono tekosyy* for an Immortal and a *broer*. But, on the off chance that they're right, I figured I'd pass along the information I got out of my last kill before he, um, expired. There's a couple in Hill City, South Dakota, by the name of Holmes. Do your job for once, *vigliacco*, and take care of them."

Leave it to Ellis to use my penchant for languages to insult me. As always, my brother's eloquence won me over. Tex and I headed north, tracking Gorden and Tamara Holmes. By the nineteenth, we were in South Dakota. By noon on the twentieth, we'd found the Holmes residence. I didn't give Tex the chance to argue her way into a fight. Instead, I came up with a plan that kept both of us more or less out of harm's way. Unfortunately, it involved burning down a three-story, ten-bedroom, multi-million dollar house. Fortunately, fire pretty.

After making sure the Holmes' home – I made no attempt to say that five times fast – had serious electrical shorts in their Christmas lights, I wreaked some mean-spirited, Puck-like havoc with their alarm system and then returned to the hotel to discuss the next move with Tex. I anticipated a long, drawn-out debate over whether or not she should keep fighting. What I hadn't expected was to find Tex gone. I panicked for about two minutes before remembering that Tex had her cell phone. That's the problem with four thousand years of living: you don't always remember the newest forms of communication when you're flustered. I almost fumbled my phone as I dialed.

"Where are you?" The cheery sounds on the other end calmed my nerves, but didn't satiate my curiosity. Tex didn't make me wait long.

"Shopping."

What? Had she hit her head at some point? "For what?"

"Christmas. You know, that holiday that started about two thousand years ago."

"Yeah, I remember." I was so dazed that I just agreed. She was Christmas shopping? The sheer joy in her voice affected me. I couldn't stop a bubble of laughter... make that a manly guffaw. "Guess that means I have a few things to purchase." After a pause, I asked, "Do you want to head home for the holidays? We've got time."

Though still happy, Tex's mood seemed tempered by what she had to say. "I'm not even considering going back to Colorado until this thing is done."

"It could take years." I had to speak around a lump in my throat. "More than you have."

"I guess you're stuck with me then." I could hear a bit of weight behind Tex's quip.

"Promise?" Our conversation had suddenly become heavy.

"Only if you want me."

"*Fi beunydd angen 'ch.*" I could almost feel the heat of Tex's blush over the phone even though she couldn't have known what I'd said. "*Zauvek.*" I repeated the last bit in English. "Forever."

***

"Tex, what are you doing?" I let Tex lead me into her room, guided only by my hand on her uninjured shoulder.

"It's a surprise." Because she was too short to cover my eyes with her hands when we were both standing, Tex had blindfolded me with something. When we had reached what I was pretty sure was the center of the room, I felt Tex circle behind me and tug at the knot of the floral-scented cloth covering my eyes.

Dazzling colors filled my vision and it took me a moment to see what she'd done. When I did, it took my breath away. *Cantik.* The entire room was lined with Christmas lights, slowly alternating between reds and greens, clears and blues. In the center of the room, draped with silver garland and tiny glass bulbs was what appeared to be a plastic fichus. Or maybe it was fern. Due to the massive amount of decorations, I couldn't quite make it out well enough to tell. Under the makeshift tree was a shiny red bag. *Niesamowity.* A pair of socks hung next to the mirror, Tex's name written in silver glitter, mine in blue. The small table was covered with food. Cinnamon rolls that, judging by the smell and the thick icing oozing down their sides, had been taken from the microwave just minutes before. Christmas cookies in the shapes of angels and stars, covered with sprinkles. Chocolate chip meringue bars sat next to buckeyes on a red paper plate featuring cavorting reindeer. And, of course, two steaming mugs of hot cocoa, steaming under whipped cream. *Maravilloso*.

"Zev," Tex's timid voice came from behind me. "Say something, please."

I turned towards her, opening my mouth to tell her how amazing, how beautiful, everything was, but nothing came out. I tried again. She must have seen what I couldn't say because the anxiety on her face faded away and she smiled. *Vera enn minn hjarta*.

"I don't believe it." She chuckled. "You're speechless."

I considered the irony for about one-sixteenth of a second. Then I had one arm around her waist and my other hand at the back of her neck, crushing her against me as I kissed her breathless. I'm not bragging. We were literally gasping when we parted. I released her, taking a step back to refocus, to regain control. *Noriu*. I sucked air into my burning lungs. *Deus, me axude*. My erratic heartbeat began to slow. After a minute, I stretched out my hand, the one with two new fingers, and smiled.

We sat on the floor, leaning against the foot of the bed and watching the lights reflect off of the ornaments on our Christmas fichus / fern. At some point that Christmas Eve, we watched a few specials, mostly keeping them in the background as we chatted, stopping long enough to see our favorite scenes. Tex and I ate sweets and sipped from our mugs, occasionally crossing to the window to watch fat, white flakes drift to the ground, covering it in clean, pure snow. The previous tension had bled away, leaving us with comfortable contact: my arm around her shoulders, her head resting on my chest, our hands clasped together. Temptation stayed far away and, as evening transitioned to late night, Tex shared favorite Christmas memories, of sleigh rides and caroling with Grandma Bug. Then, I told Tex about the first Christmas I remembered. The first one ever. How it had been just Mom and I, unable to sleep that spring night, who had seen the sky blaze with light, had heard the angels, had watched the sheep while the shepherds left to find the King.

"Didn't you want to go?"

"We saw Him later." I brushed back the stray curl that never wanted to stay in its place. "We weren't supposed to be the first to greet Him. We had to stay unseen, for the most part."

Silence settled for a while after my story. When our phones alerted us to the change from Christmas Eve to Christmas Day, Tex straightened. She leaned forward, catching her breath as the movement pulled at her shoulder. I didn't say anything, but it took most of my self-control not to. Then Tex was sitting back again, the small red bag gone from under the tree, now in her hand. She held it out to me. "Merry Christmas."

"I have something for you too." I started to reach into my jeans pocket, but Tex touched my wrist.

"Open mine first."

How could I deny those eyes? That face? I took the bag from Tex and reached inside. It was a silver chain, too delicate to be gaudy but too thick to be feminine. On the end of the chain hung a simple ring of matching silver. I let the ring fall into my palm and lifted it for closer inspection. Inscribed inside were two words: *My Immortal.*

"I thought you could put your other ring on the chain, too." Tex's voice was soft, tinged with a bit of dark humor as she added, "Since you seem more inclined to lose a few digits rather than a necklace, I thought it'd be safer."

For the second time in hours, and only the fourth time in my entire life, I could find no words to express what I was feeling. I settled for the advice 'show, don't tell' and pulled the ring from my finger. Copper and silver sparkled as I slide the ring into place next to the one Tex had given me. After dropping the chain around my neck, I found my voice. "*Salamat, kendi.*"

"You're welcome."

Since when did she speak Filipino?

Tex grinned at my look of surprise. "I guessed."

"Good guess." I dug into my pocket for Tex's gift.

TEX

"You're speechless." I meant to laugh. Really, I did. But then everything exploded around me, through me. It was light and heat and fire. And burning. I definitely felt a burning sensation in my chest. Wait. Oxygen. Yeah, kinda need that. My shoulder throbbed from Zev holding me so tightly, but it was nothing compared to the pain in my lungs as I drew in great gulps of air. My head was whirling, twirling, swirling... and apparently rhyming. Zev hadn't kissed me like that since the night at the cabin and I needed time to regain my composure.

Things quieted to a smolder after that, a pleasant and safe

warmth that permeated the room. Sitting on the floor, eating sprinkled cookies while watching old classics on TV, Zev's arm around my shoulders – it was the best Christmas ever. As soon as it was Christmas, I snagged the bag containing Zev's present and turned towards him. "Merry Christmas."

"I have something for you too."

I touched Zev's wrist. "Open mine first."

Zev took the bag and reached inside. I held my breath. What if he didn't like it? I'd actually only known him for four months. It seemed ludicrous, really, to think... then I saw his eyes darken as he read the inscription in the ring. Before things could get too heated again, I spoke. "I thought you could put your other ring on the chain, too. Since you seem more inclined to lose a few digits rather than a necklace, I thought it'd be safer."

Zev didn't respond, but since he was taking his family ring from his finger and putting it onto the chain, I knew the lack of words wasn't from displeasure. "*Salamat, kendi*."

While the extent of my spoken foreign languages stretched to two years of high school Spanish and a few random words in Italian and French, I caught the gist of what he was trying to say. "You're welcome." Based on the startled expression Zev threw my way, I'd been correct. "I guessed."

"Good guess." Zev muttered as he stuck his hand into his pocket.

He was wearing the same charcoal gray jeans he'd worn on our first date. I really liked them. He held his hand out and I forgot about the pants. I cupped my hands under his fist and into it dropped a small box. I willed my fingers to still as I reached for the lid, but I couldn't make them completely stop. Somehow, I managed to open the box despite my hand-quivering impediment. There, centered on black velvet, was a ring very similar to the one currently resting at the base of Zev's throat.

"Great minds think alike."

I could hear the smile, but didn't see it. I couldn't take my eyes off of the simple band. Finally, I lifted it and read the words carved into the metal: *'na, awron, beynydd, 'm Cara.*

Zev's voice was barely a whisper. "'Then, now, always, my Love.'"

I could feel my eyes welling up but made no move to stop the hot saltwater that spilled down my cheeks. Suddenly, Zev was kneeling in front of me, wiping my cheeks with his sleeve. "*Amore mio*, what's wrong?"

"Nothing." I sniffled. "Happy tears." I could see Zev's smile now.

He plucked the ring from between my fingers and reached for my right hand. As he slid it onto my ring finger, he said, "Someday, I'll put this on the other hand." He lightly kissed the cool metal and then pressed his lips against the empty finger on my left hand. He then stood and pulled me to my feet. "Time to get some sleep."

I sighed. As much as I wanted him to stay, I knew that tonight was just a reprieve. Once Christmas was over, the mission continued. I stood on my tiptoes and gave Zev a brief kiss, sweetened with the mint-flavored cocoa we'd been drinking. "Good night, *mi amor*. And, merry Christmas."

Zev returned my smile. "*Da nos a 'n arab Nadolig.*

Chwsg bydew, anwylyd." At the door, he paused and turned back. "'Good night and merry Christmas. Sleep well, beloved.'"

My shower was warm, the sheets cool as I slipped between them thirty minutes after Zev had returned to his room. I was asleep less than five minutes later. I didn't stir until a familiar song cut through my pleasant dream starring a gigantic mountain of dark chocolate and a pickax. I hadn't even opened my eyes as I flipped open my phone. "Morning, Mom." I mumbled.

"Merry Christmas!"

I wondered if morning perkiness could be grounds for justifiable matricide.

"Where are you, sweetie?"

"South Dakota, Mom." I rolled onto my back, but stayed under the covers. "Are you still in Milan?"

"Of course! In fact, they asked me to stay on a bit longer."

"What does Dion think of that?"

"Who?"

I waited, giving her time to remember.

"Oh, Dion, right. Honey, we broke up ages ago. I've met the most wonderful man over here. Horatio Perceval Macmillian III. Isn't that just the most marvelous name?"

***

Everything had been packed up the night before so I had only to stuff my pajamas into the bag that had held the jeans and dark gray sweater I now wore. I didn't bother putting on my coat for the few feet I had to cross to get to the car Zev had so considerately warmed. We were heading south, so there was a good chance I wouldn't need more than my sweater by the time we finally stopped. We'd spent Christmas Day watching parades and specials while searching for our next clue. Then, we spent the next day doing the same thing, substituting random movies for the previous fare. The break had come just as we contemplated reheating some sweet and sour chicken for dinner. Perpetuum and agent to the stars Thomas Nansan had just opened an office in Las Vegas.

We left Hill City at eight thirty on the morning of December twenty-seventh and stopped that night in Utah. By ten o'clock, we were back on the road and had reached Las Vegas in time for dinner. With neither one of us favoring the party scene, we splurged and ordered room service, eating in Zev's part of the suite we'd rented while we discussed what to do next. According the voicemail account at Nansan's business, he wouldn't be at the office until after New Year's and we hadn't been able to find a home address through any legal means. We spent the twenty-ninth scouting Nansan's office and asking about him in various casinos, hotels and clubs. Either we were really bad at this job or Nansan knew how to cover his tracks. Both Zev and I were inclined to believe the latter. On the thirtieth, we returned to Nansan's office with the intention to commandeer information using not-so-legal ways.

"The weakest point is the bathroom window." Zev pointed. "It's high enough that it's not easy to get to and small enough that it'll be a tight fit."

"Not for me." I held up a hand to silence the forthcoming protest. "It's been closed for days and we didn't see anyone coming in or out yesterday. If Nansan has security, they live in the office."

Zev scowled as he nodded. "Fine. I'll disable the alarm and you'll go inside."

I tried not to let my excitement show, but I couldn't stop a smile. Zev's scowl deepened, but he merely continued giving instructions. "All we need is the address. Don't leave fingerprints or take anything. Nothing that could physically link us to Nansan. And if something goes wrong, you get out. Forget everything else, just get out." His voice dropped, as if the next words had broken him. "Just come back to me, *ukochany*. *Wracaj*."

"I will." I raised myself as high as I could and brushed my lips against Zev's cheek. "Now, let's get to work."

A few minutes later, I pulled myself through the bathroom window and dropped to the floor with barely a sound. Much better than my first felony entrance and barely a twinge in my shoulder. The office was deserted and small enough for me to find Nansan's desk without difficulty. I rummaged through his drawers, careful to return everything to its original position once I'd finished. The penlight gripped between my teeth offered little light, but I finally spotted what I'd come for. I read the address five times and made myself check it twice before I was satisfied that I'd remember. As I returned the business card to where I'd found it, my light passed over a few picture frames. One caught my eye. Nansan, looking about twenty years younger, had his arm around another man who also sported the Perpetuum tattoo on his wrist. Sensing another target, I started to reach for the picture. Before I could reach it, however, I heard the signal Zev had arranged if anyone was coming near the building. A loud and seemingly drunk rendition of some Christmas carol.

I squirmed back out of the window and landed next to Zev just as he rounded the corner back into the alley. "What took you so long?" He hissed. If I hadn't known that it was concern making him sound so obnoxious, I might have slapped him. I hadn't yet ruled it out when he hugged me. "I was worried that something had happened to you again. *Du er min grund til at leve*."

"I'm fine." I reluctantly extracted myself from his grip. "Come on, we've got a location to scout."

"You got the address?"

I rolled my eyes. "Of course." The memory of the picture niggled – a Grandma Bug word from my early years – at the back of my mind. I let it go. If it was important, it'd come to me. I followed Zev to the car and by the time we'd reached Nansan's house at the edge of the city, I had refocused on the job at hand.

Thomas Nansan had done well for himself, but as someone who'd grown up on the outskirts of the celebrity world, I could see why he'd stayed in Las Vegas instead of moving to New York or Los Angeles. There was a lot to be said for being a big fish in a little pond. Well, comparatively little. Though by all accounts a lifelong bachelor, Nansan had a sprawling one-story, obviously custom-built house. I wondered how many rooms were dedicated to his 'lifestyle' and then realized that I probably didn't want to know the answer to that.

After several hours of meticulous surveillance, Zev and I returned to our hotel. Tomorrow night, while Nansan would certainly be out at a New Year's Eve party, we'd break into his house and wait for him to return. We'd have the element of surprise and be able to stage a robbery-gone-bad cover-up. Though Zev tried to argue that he could handle one Perpetuum by himself, I convinced him that my involvement was necessary. Besides, as I pointed out, I could always show up anyway. I couldn't quite explain why I needed in on this particular task. I only knew that something in my spirit kept insisting that I be there. When I tried questioning God about it, He remained silent.

The remainder of our waking hours was spent in preparation. Guns were cleaned and oiled. Knives sharpened. Belts and holsters checked for any tear or snag that might impede a quick draw. At Zev's insistence, I once again donned my black outfit, complete with vest and knife belt. I did, however, refuse to wear the thigh sheath or take the crossbow. There is such a thing as overkill. Zev didn't comment on my word choice, but also returned his crossbow to the Impala's trunk.

We reached Nansan's place around eleven o'clock. Like the majority of houses on this road, the one in front of us was dark. Far down the street, dozens of cars were parked in front of the only well-lit home around. Judging by the sounds echoing around us and the lack of police cars, the entire neighborhood was either at the party or deaf. Ten minutes later, Zev and I made our way into the darkened kitchen, our path illuminated only by the faint yellow of the streetlights.

I didn't hear footsteps or creaking hinges. The first hint I had that Zev and I weren't alone in the house was the hand over my mouth, dragging me back and down.

ZEV

I didn't want Tex there. Her shoulder wasn't healed, at least not well enough for her to be fighting. But when she'd threatened to come on her own, I had agreed. Better that I keep an eye on her than run the risk of her impulsiveness getting her hurt. I took a moment to appreciate the irony of me being annoyed at someone else for one of my primary character traits. Besides, ambushing one man who would probably be so wasted from partying all night that he'd be seeing frolicking faeries, nixies and pixies, didn't sound like the most dangerous of jobs. And I continued to think that until the dark figure yanked Tex through the door and down the stairs.

I choked back the scream coming up my throat and ran for the door. Trusting instinct, I raced down barely visible stairs without hesitation, skidding to a stop only when light flooded the room. I blinked rapidly to clear my vision and saw, less than six feet away, a man I knew to be Thomas Nansan. He was taller than he'd appeared in the picture I'd seen online, but shorter than me. The top of Tex's head was even with his shoulder. He held her in front of him, but her tiny figure couldn't cover his bulk. Nansan was easily twice Tex's width, making him appear even larger than he was by comparison. His salt-and-pepper hair was thinning, but not quite gone; his face still held a bit of the handsome features he must have had in his youth. His dark eyes burned with the madness I'd only seen in the Perpetuum. I saw all of this in an instant, gauging distance and space as well as Nansan's proximity to weapons and his ability to harm Tex before I could rescue her.

"You're the one who's been killing my people." Nansan's voice was surprisingly gentle for such a large man.

I didn't answer. What was the point? Pleading or bargaining for Tex's life would be pointless. Based on what I could see of the room with just my peripheral vision, Nansan was a murderer several times over. And judging by the variety of instruments hanging on the wall behind him, Nansan liked to play with his food before he ate it.

"Maybe then I should kill one of yours." Nansan drew a deep breath and smirked. "Does she taste as good as she smells?" Without taking his eyes from me, Nansan bent towards Tex and flicked his tongue out, licking Tex's temple. "Delicious."

I felt a deep desire to find out how slowly I could peel the skin from his body. My fingers twitched, imperceptible to anyone but me or another Immortal. I knew, though, that I had to wait for the right moment. I allowed myself a moment of pride that Tex hadn't even flinched. Then I let my anger begin its slow burn, ready to explode as soon as I needed to call on it.

Nansan glanced down at Tex, started visibly and took a longer look. I saw recognition dawn in his eyes, but didn't know what it meant. I didn't care either, the moment was enough for me to act.

The overhead lights threw diamonds off of the silver blade as it flew through the air. I saw Tex move and Nansan jerk a split second before my knife sunk into his temple as neatly as Jael's tent peg had impaled Sisera. It wasn't until Nansan fell back that I saw the second knife hilt jutting out from between his ribs. He'd most likely been dead before my knife had reached its target. Part of me wanted to praise Tex for a brilliant and gutsy move. Another part wanted to yell at her for taking such an insane risk.

I compromised by running to her and lifting her in my arms without a word. I rested my forehead against hers, staring into those endless pools of gray. We might have stood there for hours if I hadn't heard a discrete cough behind me. One I hadn't heard in a very, very long time, and had never expected to hear again. I set Tex on her feet and turned.

"Zev, son of Enos and Dinah." He was average, nondescript in every way but one. No matter the form, one characteristic always remained the same. Blazing blue eyes that promised a swift and painful death to anyone who dared defy them. "You have not changed."

"Viator." I stepped forward, myriad emotions rushing through me.

"Zev?" I felt Tex's fingers brush my back.

"I am a messenger, Killeen Texas Novak." Viator's visage never altered.

"A messan... oh."

"Why are you here, Viator?" I squashed the hope that kept wanting to surface.

Those ice blue eyes shifted to the body on the floor and then back to me. I shivered. "Thomas Nansan was the next to last Perpetuum. Only one remains who bears the mark."

One? After all these years, just one? Suddenly, what had once seemed an impossible task raced towards completion. “Who is it?” I expected a frown, a shake of the head. The angels had intervened once and only because Sodom and Gomorrah had been corrupted not just by Perpetuum, but by enough other influences that the cities themselves had to be eradicated.

“Little over fifteen years ago, a Perpetuum visited his child. Like Samuel, before birth this child had been dedicated to the life of the parent. While alone with his child, the Perpetuum branded the mark onto the shoulder of his daughter.”

I really didn’t like where this was headed.

“That child is now past the age of accountability.”

My hands curled into fists, but I made myself ask the question again. “Who is it?”

The answer came from behind me. “It’s me.”

TEX

This is what an angel looked like? Plain features. Sandy brown hair. Average height and weight. Then I saw his eyes and suddenly understood why the angels in the Bible always told people not to be afraid. If I’d thought Zev had a scary expression that made me want to run and hide, it was nothing compared to the firepower in the eyes of this man – that wasn’t the right word, but it was the best I could do. And I finally understood the origin of the word ‘firepower’ because that’s exactly what I saw in those eyes.

“Thomas Nansan was the next to last Perpetuum. Only

one remains who bears the mark."

So soon? I felt a flash of joy.

"Who is it?"

I couldn't tell what Zev was thinking from just those three words. I wanted to step up beside him, but the angel's story stopped me cold. "Little over fifteen years ago, a Perpetuum visited his child. Like Samuel, before birth this child had been dedicated to the life of the parent. While alone with his child, the Perpetuum branded the mark onto the shoulder of his daughter."

I felt a flash of pain on my shoulder, under the scar that ran from one side of my back to the other, and I knew.

"That child is now past the age of accountability."

"Who is it?"

I closed my eyes and spoke the truth. "It's me." I took a step forward without opening my eyes. When I felt Zev's hands on mine, I continued. "In Nansan's office, there was a picture. I didn't see it clearly, but I realize now what it was. Or, more accurately, who it was." I opened my eyes and forced myself to meet Zev's gaze. "My mother met my father in Killeen, Texas, where she was modeling. He was a talent scout and I think Thomas Nansan was his partner, or at least his friend. I've only seen one picture of my dad and I'm pretty sure the man standing next to Nansan in the photo on his desk was Abraham Thompson, my father."

Viator interjected. "Another Immortal dispatched Thompson eight months ago."

Zev didn't acknowledge the announcement. "But you don't have..."

I interrupted, dismissing the news of the death of the father I'd never known. My true Father was all that mattered. "I fell, remember? I told you about it, but I didn't tell you a small detail. It seemed small at the time. Just some strange scar from an accident I was too young to remember, and Mom never talked about. She wanted me to have plastic surgery to remove it, but I kept putting it off. Never liked doctors very much. Then, when I fell, cut up my back, new scars covered the old, and I forgot about it."

"But that's not your fault." Zev's eyes burned brighter than I'd ever seen them. He looked towards the angel, beseeching in a broken voice. "She didn't choose it."

I tugged one hand free and reached down, pulling my boot knife from its sheath. "Zev." He turned back to me. I carefully gripped the blade as I extended my hand, the black hilt pointed towards him. "It's okay."

"No!" Zev yanked his other hand free and jumped back, horror etched on every feature. "I won't."

"You have to." I stepped towards him, still holding out the knife. "I'm not going to let you suffer any more." I reached for his hand and he let me take it, staring down at me as all color drained from his face. I placed his hand on the handle and moved so that the tip of the knife rested just over my heart. My eyes locked with his, that indigo color that made my knees weak, my insides melt, that made earth's most potent beauty pale. "It's all right, *mi amor*. I love you, my Immortal. End this. Send me home."

Zev took a deep shuddering breath and moved. For a moment, I didn't realize what he'd done until he turned towards the angel, my knife dropping to the floor. “No.” He was talking more to the angel than to me. “I won’t.”

“You have to.” I protested.

Zev didn’t take his eyes from the stoic figure on the other side of the room. “Viator, I serve *El Echad* and He would not ask this. *El Tsaddik* does not require another sacrifice. That price was paid. I was there.”

“As was I.” The angel’s voice held no emotion, but neither did it seem indifferent. “But *El Echad* commanded that those who bore the mark be destroyed.”

“He also gave us free will.” Zev’s jaw was set and his color had returned. “She did not choose this for herself. She chose Him. And if He wants her life, then He must take it. It is not my place. And if He requires a final life, then He may take mine.”

“No!” I meant to scream the word, but it came out a whisper. Neither the Immortal nor the angel acknowledged the sound.

Then, inexplicably, the angel smiled. “It seems, Zev, son of Enos and Dinah, that you have learned to love someone above yourself. That your own life is no longer the most important thing to you.”

“It’s not.” Zev’s tone had softened.

The angel nodded once. “Then you have fulfilled the charge given to your people. Your curse is lifted.”

I started to cheer, but the sound died in my throat as Zev dropped to his knees. For a second, I thought it was from relief, then I saw his entire body convulse and fall to the floor. I was at his side, accusing even as I moved. “What did you do?"

"He is mortal, and no mortal is allowed to live this long." The smile had left the angel's face, and he was impassive once more.

"He's dying?" I laid Zev's head against my knees and pressed my hands to his cheeks.

"They all are. The Immortal are no more."

My tears splashed down onto Zev's face and his eyes fluttered open. "Tex, *amor de mina*."

"You can't go." No pain could compare to what I felt now. My heart, my soul, my entire being was being ripped to shreds.

"*No lo lamento*. It'll be all right." Zev covered my hand with his and moved it so that his lips rested against my palm. "*Aion odottaa, rakas*." I felt the words as much as heard them. "I will be waiting, beloved."

His eyes closed and the warm air against my hand ceased. "Zev?" I whispered his name, but knew that it was useless. I held him in my arms. Ran my fingertips over his cheeks, his nose, his lips. Buried my fingers in his soft hair. Felt his skin cooling under my touch.

After an eternity of agony, I looked up and saw, through the water-shimmer in my eyes, that the angel still stood, watching. "What do you want?" I heard the anger in my voice and was startled to find that I didn't care that I was speaking to an angel.

"I'm waiting."

"For what?" I wiped a hand across my eyes.

"For you to ask."

"Ask? What am I supposed to ask? Ask why?" I glared at the angel. "God doesn't tell why." I inhaled, then exhaled slowly, feeling some of what I'd felt only a few times before. Supernatural peace permeating the grief, making it manageable, bearable.

"No, not why." There was a new emotion in those scary-blue eyes, one it took me a moment to place. Intrigue. "I'm waiting for you to ask what any other human would ask in your place."

"And what's that?" Fatigue was settling into my bones.

"To bring him back."

For one wild moment, I considered it. I saw it all in my head. A life with Zev. Marriage. A family. Growing old together. A new shard of pain went through me. I shook my head. "No."

"What?"

Hm, hadn't known that angels could be surprised. I repeated myself and then explained. "No. He's home. He's where he's supposed to be, and if I asked for him to come back, it'd just be selfish. So, no. I won't ask."

To my complete and utter astonishment – and anger – Viator began to smile once more. Then I heard a gasp and forgot about the angel.

"Tex."

Everything went gray and the next thing I knew, I was the one being held and Zev was doing the holding. I grabbed at his shirt as my eyes focused, pressing my hand against his chest and feeling the strong beat of his heart, as familiar as my own. I started to run my other hand over his face, but he bent towards me and I knew I wasn't imagining or dreaming. The electricity running from his cells to mine where our mouths met, where his hands rested against my waist and neck, where my hands lay against his chest and cheek… my imagination wasn't that vivid. When we pulled apart, I directed my words to the angel without taking my eyes from Zev. Part of me was afraid that if I looked away, he'd disappear forever.

"I didn't ask."

For the first time, I heard emotion in the angel's voice. "You didn't. He did."

ZEV

Black and then brilliance beyond description. I stood in the one place I'd never dared to dream I'd stand. And, as I fell to my knees in front of my Creator, I heard the two words I'd wanted to hear more than I'd wanted anything in my long life.

"Well done."

I was home. After four thousand years, I'd made it. I'd done what was asked of me, fulfilled my calling. And yet, something was... off. I couldn't place it. Nothing could be wrong here, but I knew that there was more. Then He spoke again.

"Tex has shown great love for you, more than you know. She was asked if she wanted you to return and, despite her personal desire, she said no. She would rather live in pain without you than cause you the pain of leaving here to return to the earth."

Tex. Her face appeared in my mind and I felt a flood of love, more pure and wonderful than anything I'd ever felt on earth. And I knew what I was supposed to do. “May I return? Live out a mortal life with her?”

I heard and felt my Father’s smile. “Yes, my son. Well done.”

Air rushed into my lungs and I was in darkness once more. I opened my eyes and saw her face. “Tex.”

She swayed, starting to crumple to the floor. I reacted, catching her before she could land. Even with that movement, I could feel the difference in my body. I was immortal no longer. Then Tex’s eyes opened and I didn’t care about anything other than pulling her to me and kissing her. In fact, I hadn’t even noticed Viator until Tex and I broke apart and she spoke to him.

“I didn’t ask.”

“You didn’t. He did.” Viator addressed me. “Now, leave this place. Your work here is finished.” He paused and then added. “I will see you both again.” I heard the familiar crack as air filled a space where an angel had been.

“You asked?” Tex let me help her to her feet.

I smiled down at her as we started to walk up the stairs. “Of course, *liefde van mijn*. I waited four thousand years to find someone worth being here for.” I slid my arm around her waist as we exited the house. The winter air filled with cheers as a new year began.

“So we celebrate the new year now?” Tex leaned her head against my shoulder.

“One more thing first.”

***

Tex pulled her hand free long enough to hand her phone to the twins we'd asked to accompany us. "My mother will never forgive me if I don't get pictures."

The girl gave a wry smile as she took Tex's cell. The blond boy next to her muttered something under his breath and she elbowed him in the ribs hard enough to make him wince. "Shut up, Aidan." The girl gave her brother another dirty look and then turned her attention back to Tex and I. "Well, get on with it."

Tex slid her hand back into mine. "I love you."

"*Ti amo, l'amore della mia vita*." I nodded at the minister. "Go ahead."

He looked from Tex to me and continued. "By the power vested in me by the state of Nevada, I now pronounce you husband and wife. You may kiss the bride."

I didn't really need the prompting. As Tex's and my lips met in our first kiss as husband and wife, I was vaguely aware of whistling from at least one of our witnesses, but, above that, I could've sworn I heard another voice. The voice of *El Hanne-eman*, the faithful God.

Well done, beloveds. Well done indeed.

Epilogue: An End Has a Start In Me

TEX and ZEV

So that's how the love story that was our lives ended... and how it began. We found each other, found our purpose and found out what love really meant. And our job's not done.

We still have work to do.

Foreign Languages Used

Disclaimer: These were translated using Google Translate.
I apologize for any errors in translation and ask that
you chalk it up to Zev using a slightly different dialect. ;)

- *Kvenkyn.* – Feminine. – Icelandic
- *'m cara* – My love - Welsh
- *Ad vitam aeternam* - for all time – Latin
- *Kamangha-mangha.* - Wonderful – Filipino
- *Potes curreve sed te occulere non potes* - you can run but you can't hide – Latin
- *het casgen ,'n ddiwerth adwr* – butt hat, worthless coward – Welsh
- *'n wenwynig anifail* – poisonous beast – Welsh
- *Buais mo yn disgwyl a.* - I was not expecting that. – Welsh
- *Besmislica.* – Crap – Serbian
- *Stebinantis.* – Amazing – Lithuanian
- *'n anhyddysg llyffant* - ignorant toad – Welsh
- *Hrokafullur stykki af skitur* - arrogant piece of filth – Icelandic
- *Berlendir musang* - slimy weasel – Malay
- *Iontach.* – Wonderful. – Irish
- *Thirrje admirimi!* – Wow! – Albanian
- *Beteken-soek* – mean-looking – Afrikaans
- *nzuri*, ya *kushangaza.* – beautiful, wonderful – Swahili
- *Kamwe*! – Never! – Swahili
- *Pleh.* – Crap. – Albanian
- *Io sono uno stupido idiota.* – I am a stupid idiot. – Italian
- *Crnomanjast kurva* – dark-haired whore / prostitute – Croatian
- *Meiga* – witch – Galician
- *Mal de brujas* – evil witch – Spanish
- *Tudatlan varangy* – ignorant toad – Hungarian
- *Udskud af jordens* – scum of the earth – Danish
- *Feitur svin* – fat pig – Icelandic
- *Hajvan* – moron – Albanian

- *nevjerojatno.* – amazing – Croatian
- *Ik voel je om me heen.* – I can feel you all around me. – Dutch
- *Zagnjurivanje stakla krtica* – ducking glass mole – Croatian
- *Ja sam utapanje u vama.* – I am drowning in you. – Croatian
- *Ya kupendeza.* – pretty – Swahili
- *Se segueix el meu cor.* – Be still my heart. – Catalan
- *Eu estarei esperando.* – I will be waiting. – Portuguese
- *Uau*! – Wow! – Galician
- *Yn gostwng pen gwydr dwrch daear* – ducking glass mole – Welsh
- *Ddisglair* – glittering – Welsh
- *Fermoso* - beautiful – Galician
- *Frater, ave atque vale* - brother, hello and good-bye – Latin
- *Frater* – brother – Latin
- *Purra minua.* – Bite me. – Finnish –
- *Git kendini vida.* – Go screw yourself. – Turkish
- *Ninyi ni kama miaka mitano tarehe ufa.* – You are like a five year-old on crack. – Swahili
- *Uimitor.* – Amazing – Romanian
- *Diamlah hatiku.* - Be still my heart. – Malay
- *Jama. Mul oli muutunud lalisemine loll.* – Crap. I had turned into a babbling fool. – Estonian
- *Jdu pro tebe.* – I am coming for you. – Czech
- *Ielasmeita* – whore / prostitute – Latvian
- *Ti si moja usoda. Za vedno.* – You are my destiny. Forever – Slovenian
- *Da mihi basilia mille* - kiss me with a thousand kisses – Latin
- *Nunc scio quid sitamor* - now I know what love is – Latin
- *Merci.* – Thank you. – French
- *Aldrei.* – Never – Icelandic
- *Dashuria e minave* – love of mine – Albanian

- *I bukur* – beautiful – Albanian
- *Inima mea* – my heart – Romanian
- *Ara naqra*! – Wow! – Maltese
- *Dashuria ime, arsyeja e mia, zemra ime.* – My love, my reason, my heart. - Albanian
- *Il mio angelo, il mio tutto* – My angel, my all. – Italian
- *Sorprendente.* – Amazing. – Italian
- *Domus dulcis domus.* – Home sweet home. – Latin
- *Vacker* - beautiful – Swedish
- *As vitam Paramus. Adversus solem ne loquitor* – We are preparing for life. Don't speak against the sun (don't waste your time arguing the obvious) – Latin
- *Fratello* – brother – Italian
- *Lillebror* – little brother – Danish
- *Dieu, aide-moi.* - God, help me. – French
- *Ewyllysia erioed faddau 'ch* – I will never forgive you. – Welsh
- *Rwy'n gadael.* – I am leaving – Welsh
- *Laissez-moi tranquille.* – Leave me alone. – French
- *Lasciate ogni speranza voi che entrate* – Abandon hope all who enter here – Italian
- *Nebudu ztratit.* – I will not lose you. – Czech
- *Inutile* – worthless – Maltese
- *Frikacak* – coward – Albanian
- *Gunoi de pe pamant* – scum of the earth – Romanian
- *Moja zvezda* – my star – Slovenian
- *Ero perdutamente innamorato.* – I was hopelessly in love – Italian
- *Fan liom.* – Stay with me. – Irish
- *Dwi yn boddi ynoch.* – I am drowning in you. – Welsh
- *Limane nirk* – slimy weasel – Estonian
- *Otrovnim zvijer* – poisonous beast – Croatian
- *Eu podia sentir-lhe tudo ao meu redor.* – I could feel her all around me – Portuguese
- *Moj razlog, moja ljubav* – My reason, my love. – Croatian
- *Co jsem myslela?* – What was I thinking? – Czech

- *Je suis noyade en vous.* – I am drowning in you. – French

- *Drwg Rhywbeth hon y ffordd hon.* – "Something wicked this way comes." [*MacBeth*] – Welsh

- *Noli me tangere* - don't touch me – Latin

- *Ek aanbid jy.* – I adore you. - Afrikaans

- *Ei koskaan.* – Never – Finnish

- *goeie Christelike meisies* – good Christian girls – Afrikaans

- *Je veux que vous.* – I want you. – French

- *Amicule, deliciae, num is sum qui mentiar tibi?* - Baby, sweetheart, would I lie to you? – Latin

- *Salach francach* – dirty rat – Irish

- *zadek klobouk* – butt hatt – Czech

- *Selama-lamanya. Selalu.* – Forever. Always. – Indonesian

- *Dduw, chyfnertha 'm.* - God, help me. – Welsh

- *Froncer en haut, bucko. Il ne travaillera pas.* – Pucker up, bucko. It ain't gonna work. – French

- *Lavdi Zotit!* – Praise God! – Albanian

- *In exordium , Deus partum polus quod orbis terrarum.* - "In the beginning, God created the heavens and the earth." [Genesis] – Latin

- *Erinomainen.* – Excellent – Finnish

- *Certum est, quia impossibile* - it is certain, because it is impossible – Latin

- *Ang aking puso-aari sa iyo, magpakailanman. aking anghel.* – My heart belongs to you, forever, my angel. – Filipino

- *Ylistys Jumalalle! Jumalan kiitos!* - Praise be to God! Thanks be to God! – Finnish

- *Alabado sea Dios!* – Praise God! – Spanish

- *Hala kalbim ol.* - Be still my heart. – Turkish

- *Ich bin kein Eimerkapf.* – I am not a bucket head. – German

- *chipiron en un chaco* – baby squid in a puddle – Spanish

- *Cintaku* – My love – Indonesian

- *Eleganti* – Elegant – Maltese
- *Agraciado* – Graceful – Spanish
- *Amor est vitae essentia* - love is the essence of life – Latin
- *Jeg vil elske deg for alltid.* – I will love you forever. – Norwegian
- *Wees kalme sjaalvrouw. Ga weg.* – Be quiet scarf woman. Go away. – Dutch
- *Riamh, olc cailleach feasa* – Never, evil witch – Irish
- *Maravilloso*! – Wonderful! – Spanish
- *O quam cito transit gloria mundi* - oh how quickly passes the glory of the world – Latin
- *Imbecil* – moron / jerk – Romanian
- *Tu es mon destin.* – French
- *Dio, aiutami.* - God, help me. – Italian
- *Vous l'idiot stupide* – You stupid idiot. – French
- *Haista paska.* – Screw you. – Finnish
- *Ves a la merda.* – Piss off. – Catalan
- *muleirculam!* - bimbo! – Latin
- *Arrogante pedazo de basura* - arrogant piece of filth – Spanish
- *Je mourrais pour elle.* – I would die for her. – French
- *Alles versuchen und ich werde ihre kehle.* – Try anything and I will slit your throat. – German
- *Mamaja* – mother – Albanian
- *Anwylyd* – Beloved – Welsh
- *Maganda* - beautiful – Filipino
- *blennum!* - doofus! – Latin
- *Sjajan potez,* – Wow – Croatian
- *Continuer, mon fils rebelle.* – Carry on, my wayward son. – French
- *Len cez moju mrtvolu.* – Over my dead body – Slovak
- *Vorrei morire per voi. Vorrei fare qualcosa per voi.* – I would die for you. I would do anything for you. – Italian
- *Ik moet wegens dat commentaar zingen.* – I need to sing because of that comment. – Dutch
- *Atrevo-me a ti.* – I dare you. – Galician

- *Ma ei oodanud seda.* – I was not expecting that. – Estonian

- *Sangat baik.* – Very good. – Indonesian

- *Centro d'interesse*! – Focus! – Italian

- *Goblok* – moron – Malay

- *Nuku hyvin, rakas.* – Sleep well, beloved. – Finnish

- *Oh, il camion delle immondizie* – Oh, garbage truck – Italian

- *Petit ami* – Sweetie – French

- *Stamus contra malum* - we stand against evil – Latin

- *Esto perpetua* - let us / it be forever – Latin

- *Esto perpetue* - may you last forever – Latin

- *Stultum est timere quod vitare non potes. Nec mortem effugere quisquam nec amorem potest* - No one is able to flee from death or love. It is foolish to fear that which you cannot avoid. – Latin

- *Moje zvijezde!* – My star! – Croatian

- *Mijn liefde gewacht. Mijn alles. Mijn hart.* – My love. My everything. My heart - Dutch

- *El amor de mi vida* – love of my life – Spanish

- *Dormir bien, querida.* – Sleep well, beloved. – Spanish

- *Ubi amor, ibi oculus* - where love is, there is insight – Latin

- *'m pawb* – My all. – Welsh

- *Mo gach rud.* – My everything – Irish

- *Matulog nang mabuti, minamahal.* – Sleep well, beloved – Filipino

- *Arhosais filoedd chan blynedd atat, 'm cara, 'm bopeth.* – I have waited thousands of years for you, my love, my everything. - Welsh

- *Ma armastan sind.* – I love you - Estonian

- *Vorrei morire per lei.* – I would die for her. – Italian

- *Dei gratia* - by the grace of God – Latin

- *Geweldig.* - Wonderful – Dutch

- *J'ai attendu milliers d'ans pour vous, mon amour.* – I have waited thousands of years for you, my love. - French

- *In aeternum* - for eternity – Latin

- *Napakapalalo piraso ng masasamang salita* – arrogant piece of filth – Filipino

- *Conluvio*! *Me oportet propter praeceptum te nocere* – Scum! I'm going to have to hurt you on principle – Latin

- *Kullake* – Sweetie – Estonian

- *L'amour de ma vie* – love of my life – French

- *Bu iyi olamaz.* – That cannot be good. – Turkish

- *Le do thoil, Dia Athair* - Please, Father God – Irish

- *Diyos, tulungan ninyo ako.* – God, help me. – Filipino

- *Deus, me ajude.* - God, help me. – Portuguese

- *Oltre il mio corpo morto.* – Over my dead body – Italian

- *Hva skulle jeg tenker?* – What was I thinking? – Norwegian

- *Olin toivottoman rakastunut.* – I was hopelessly in love - Finnish

- *Minamahal. Ikaw ay ang aking mga dahilan para sa pamumuhay.* – Beloved. You are my reason for living. – Filipino

- *Ljubomoran malen majmun* – Jealous little monkey – Serbian

- *Mi amor* – My love – Spanish

- *Liebling* – darling – German

- *Eu te amo, meu anjo.* – I love you, my angel - Portuguese

- *Bello* - beautiful – Catalan

- *Et necessito.* – I need you. – Catalan

- *Ei, vaikeli.* – Hey, baby. – Lithuanian

- *Du er skinnende.* – You are shiny – Danish

- *Amato* - beloved – Italian

- *Nobiyo* – Sweetheart – Filipino

- *Meget godt.* – Very good. – Danish

- *Vidunderlig.* – Wonderful – Danish

- *Elskan* – darling – Icelandic

- *Chiudete gli occhi, amore mio.* – Close your eyes, my love. – Italian

- *Caea 'ch chreuau.* – Close your eyes. – Welsh

- *Mahal* - love / darling - Filipino

- *Amore mio* – love of mine – Italian

- *L'amor de la meva vida. Et estimar per sempre.* – Love of my life. I will love you forever. - Catalan

- *Voi nu te pierd. Sunteti mea putere.* – I will not lose you. You are my strength. - Romanian

- *Dydy 'm arglwyddes O, dydy 'm cara!* – "It is my lady, O, it is my love!" [*Romeo and Juliet*] – Welsh

- *Forse il mio cuore l'amore fino ad ora? Giuro che, vista! Per non ho mai visto la vera bellezza fino a questa notte* – "Did my heart love till now? Swear it, sight! For I never saw true beauty till this night." [*Romeo and Juliet*] – Italian

- *O, ancora parlare, angelo luminoso!* – "O, speak again, bright angel!" [*Romeo and Juliet*] – Italian

- *Lawer ddyfroedd all mo ddiffodd cara, na all 'r boddfeydd bawdd 'i… 'm anwylyd ydy chloddia, a Dwi eiddo… Chusaned 'm ag 'r chusanau chan eiddo cega* - "Many waters cannot quench love, neither can the floods drown it… My beloved is mine, and I am his… Let him kiss me with the kisses of his mouth." [Song of Solomon] – Welsh

- *Fi angen 'ch.* – I want you. – Welsh

- *Seni istiyorum. Sana ihtiyac?m var.* – I want you. I need you. - Turkish

- *Mawarku. Saya semua.* – My rose. My all. – Indonesian

- *Cara 'ch.* – I love you - Welsh

- *Addola 'ch.* – I adore you. – Welsh

- *Akarlak, szerelmem.* – I want you, my love. – Hungarian

- *Dritt.* – Crap. – Norwegian

- *Saya tidak mengharapkan itu.* - I was not expecting that. – Indonesian

- *Ljubljeni* – Beloved – Slovenian

- *Cara chan 'm buchedd* – love of mine – Welsh

- *Reste avec moi, amoureux.* – Stay with me, sweetheart. – French

- *Je t'aime.* – I love you - French

- *Moje srce pripada vama.* – My heart belongs to you. – Croatian

- *Te rog, Dumnezeu Tatal* – Please, Father God –

Romanian

- *Deus, succurro mihi.* – God, help me. – Latin
- *Ijubavnik* – Lover. – Serbian
- *Ach 'n feddw?* – Are you drunk? – Welsh
- *Ma ei kaota sind.* – I will not lose you. – Estonian
- *Saya akan melakukan apapun untuk Anda.* – I would do anything for you. – Indonesian
- *kochanie, moje powodu* – my love, my reason – Polish
- *'m asgre* – my heart – Welsh
- *Aros gyda mi, cariad.* – Stay with me, sweetheart – Welsh
- *Szia kicsim.* – Hey, baby. – Hungarian
- *Miele* - Sweetie / Honey / Darling – Italian
- *Szivem* – my heart – Hungarian
- *Por favor, Deus Pai* – Please, Father God – Galician
- *Mesi* – honey – Estonian
- *Ewyllysia mo choll 'ch.* – I will not lose you. Welsh
- *Mitte kunagi.* – Never – Estonian
- *Sauhuta huono tekosyy* – Piss poor excuse. – Finnish
- *Broer* – brother – Dutch
- *Vigliacco* – coward – Italian
- *Fi beunydd angen 'ch.* – I always want you. – Welsh
- *Zauvek.* – Forever. – Serbian
- *Niesamowity.* – Amazing – Polish
- *Cantik* - beautiful – Indonesian
- *Noriu.* – I want you. – Lithuanian
- *Vera enn minn hjarta.* - Be still my heart. – Icelandic
- *Deus, me axude.* - God, help me. – Galician
- *Salamat, kendi* – Thank you, honey. – Filipino
- *'na, awron, beynydd, 'm Cara.* – Then, now, always, my Love.
- *Da nos a 'n arab Nadolig. Chwsg bydew, anwylyd.* – Good night and Merry Christmas. Sleep well, beloved. – Welsh
- *ukochany. Wracaj.* – beloved. Come back. – Polish
- *Du er min grund til at leve.* – You are my reason for living. – Danish

- *No lo lamento*. – I have no regrets. - Spanish
- *Aion odottaa, rakas.* – I will be waiting, beloved – Finnish
- *Amor de mina* – love of mine – Galician
- *Liefde van mijn* – love of mine – Dutch
- *Ti amo, l'amore della mia vita* – I love you, love of my life – Italian